Going Home

By Richard S. Wheeler
from Tom Doherty Associates

SAM FLINT
Flint's Gift
Flint's Truth
Flint's Honor

SKYE'S WEST
Sun River
Bannack
The Far Tribes
Yellowstone
Bitterroot
Sundance
Wind River
Santa Fe
Rendezvous
Dark Passage
Going Home

Aftershocks
Badlands
The Buffalo Commons
Cashbox
Fool's Coach
Goldfield
Masterson
Montana Hitch
Second Lives
Sierra
Sun Mountain
Where the River Runs

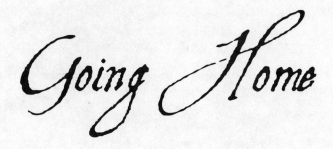

Going Home

A BARNABY SKYE NOVEL

RICHARD S. WHEELER

A TOM DOHERTY ASSOCIATES BOOK / NEW YORK

GOING HOME

Copyright © 2000 by Richard S. Wheeler

This book is printed on acid-free paper.

A Forge Book
Published by Tom Doherty Associates, LLC
175 Fifth Avenue
New York, NY 10010

www.tor.com

Forge® is a registered trademark of Tom Doherty Associates, LLC.

Library of Congress Cataloging-in-Publication Data

Wheeler, Richard S.
    Going home : a Barnaby Skye novel / Richard S. Wheeler.—1st ed.
      p. cm.
    "A Tom Doherty Associates book."
    ISBN 0-312-87310-7 (alk. paper)
    1. Skye, Barnaby (Fictitious character)—Fiction. 2. Trappers—Fiction. 3. Baja California (Mexico : State)—Fiction. I. Title.

    PS3573.H4345 G6 2000
    813'.54—dc21

                                               00-031525

First Edition: December 2000

Printed in the United States of America

0 9 8 7 6 5 4 3 2 1

Dedicated to the memory of Barbara Puechner,
my beloved friend and literary agent who
was there at the beginning.

Going Home

One

arnaby Skye did not have a care in the world, except perhaps for those big doings yonder in the shade of a brush arbor. He took his ease on a buffalo robe before his small lodge, watching puffball clouds spin out of the mountains and the gents in the brush arbor divide up the world. The wild times, when every trapper in the beaver country quenched a mighty, yearlong drought, had died, and now in the somnolent mid-July heat, rough trappers played cutthroat games, spun yarns, snored, or flirted with enterprising red hoydens.

His Crow wife, Victoria, had abandoned him to his trapping cronies and gone to drink spirits and tell bawdy jokes with the Flatheads, allies of her people, who were present in force to trade at the Rocky Mountain Fur Company store and sponge up the bacchanal. She had female friends and even distant relatives among the Salish.

The Flatheads and other tribes had swarmed to the great 1832 summer fair, this time in Pierre's Hole, the navel in Mother Earth just west of the Great Breasts, or Grand Totons, which Barnaby Skye thought was plumb center, the best of all places for the great annual gathering of trappers.

Pierre's Hole offered a mild climate, vast stretches of lush grazing ground for all the ponies, icy creeks tumbling from the mountains, abundant firewood, plentiful game—though not any buffalo—and saucy breezes eddying out of the Tetons to freshen the spirit as well as body. What better place to bake the year's aches out of the body, swill the Sublettes' firewater with new and old rivals, and engage in nefarious sins that ruined body and soul?

This year, the frosty waters of the Tetons had been mixed with pure grain spirits carried in great casks from St. Louis, and seasoned with some ancient plugs of tobacco and cayenne pepper to produce trade whiskey, the alchemist's potion that set trappers and redskins to baying at the moon and marking trees. Skye had finally had his fill of that, and of the nausea that dogged each binge, and had sunk into a summer of indolence, his mind meandering and untethered and his keen eye observing the daily passage of dusky and predatory females.

These were some doings, all right. For the first time, the American Fur Company had shown up, a big brigade of trappers led by William H. Vanderburgh and Andrew Drips, and they planned to set up a store of their own just as soon as Lucien Fontenelle arrived with that company's trade goods, which were being shipped up the Missouri and then carried by packhorse to the rendezvous. That was the big doings. They were late, which gave the Rocky Mountain Fur Company an edge for the moment. But from a longer perspective, the well-funded opposition probably signaled the end of the outfit.

Nor was that all of it. This year an American army officer named Bonneville, fat with East Coast capital, had ventured west with his own expedition. And an odd Bostonian ice merchant named Nathaniel Wyeth had marched out with a whole troop of idiot *mangeurs du lard* in uniforms. And in addition to that, there was a big party of free trappers in camp, all of them ruthless rivals of the men Skye had allied with for years: Bridger, Fraeb, Gervais, Fitzpatrick, and Sublette.

The new competition troubled Skye. The mountains were

his mother and father. He wasn't a Yank, but a pressed seaman who had jumped his Royal Navy frigate at Fort Vancouver in 1826 and ended up in the Rocky Mountains, a man
without a country. He had never eyed the settled United
States, and had no great wish to.

England was a closed chapter in his young life. He had
Victoria, and if he belonged to anything other than the Trappers Nation now, it was the Crow Nation, into which he had
married. He could scarcely imagine his slim Crow consort
padding the lanes of London in her moccasins. But sometimes,
in the still of the night, he wondered how his family fared, and
how the streets of his own city would appeal to him now. And
he missed those things.

Of his family he knew little. He had been a merchant's son,
destined to take over the family export business, when a press
gang snatched him from the cobbled streets hard by the London Dock at East End. He never saw his family again. They
surely did not know his whereabouts or even whether he was
alive. And would never know.

Black Harris folded his lengthy frame beside Skye.

"What's the word?" he asked, nodding in the general
direction of that willow-covered brush arbor where the
brigade leaders from several outfits dickered with each other.

Skye squinted through the heat, and shrugged. "They'll
make my fate, or I'll make my fate," he said.

"Nothing'll change. American Fur will gouge us just as
mighty as our outfit for possibles. We'll still fork out mountain
prices for every blanket and trap and jug of lightning, and
they'll still offer mountain prices for every plew, take it or
leave it," Harris said. "Everything changes except prices."

"It reminds me of my first rendezvous, when I walked in
from the sea. That's when Ashley sold out to Smith, Jackson,
and Sublette. Now we're seeing big doings again."

Rendezvous was the time to reoutfit, buy some white
men's marvels such as calico, knives, ribbons, copper kettles,
and thick blankets for his Crow woman. And of course, take

the edge off his thirst. Each spring his thirst built up in his parched body like a plugged volcano. And the day the supply caravan rolled in, Barnaby Skye could be found near the head of the line leading toward the kettles of mountain whiskey, ready to pickle his brains for a week.

The Skyes had done well with the old firm.

But Barnaby Skye wasn't sure about the future. Which of these outfits, wrestling with each other under that brush arbor, would survive and which would go under? How would things line up? Suddenly life in the mountains wasn't a sure bet. Maybe he'd be out of salaried work as a camp tender or brigade leader or hunter, his occupations these several years. It nagged him. He didn't like trapping. Trappers lived hard and dangerous lives, wading in icy streams, always in danger of freezing, drowning, starving, and from arrows and scalp knives.

He was the stray dog without a country. A man ought to have a home, a nation, a people, but all his allegiances were nothing more than transitory alliances formed at summer rendezvous like this one. He knew he was set apart in their minds. He spoke the polite English he was born with, and not the bizarre vernacular of the Yanks.

"I think I'm about to become a free trapper again, Black."

"No man'd do better at it. You know which way the stick floats."

"I never much cared for it. But I could make a warm camp and keep men healthy. I can hunt, make meat."

"That's plumb center, Skye."

"*Mister* Skye, mate."

Harris was grinning.

For six years, they had called him Skye and for six years he had told them to preface it with a *mister*. That's what the Royal Navy did to him, all those gentlemen officers calling each other mister, but addressing enlisted men by their last names.

It was the joke of the camps. Call Barnaby Skye anything but mister and watch the response. Trappers would send greenhorns, *mangeurs du lard*, or "pork-eaters," as they were called, over to Skye just to watch him fume at the way they addressed him. That was all right with Skye.

Barnaby Skye had filled out in the mountains until he became a barrel of a man. He still walked with a rolling sailor's gait, as if the mountains were the pitching decks of men-o'-war. He squinted out at the wilderness from deep-set blue eyes, set apart by a formidable ridge his friends swore was the king of all noses, long, thick, mountainous, dominant, and overmastering the rest of his jowly red face.

They made sport of his nose, betting that no one at any rendezvous would ever match it, and he let them. His nose was the fleshly evidence of a thousand sailor brawls, a nose that had been erected by fistic abuse into the lord and viceroy of all mortal noses. The mountaineers treasured his nose even more than they treasured Skye.

His other hallmark was his splendid beaver top hat, black and silky, climbing up from his skull like a cannon's barrel. It was the hat gentlemen habitually wore, and that is why he wore it. In England, and in the Royal Navy, he could not be a true gentleman. In this, the New World, he could be what he chose. And so they called him Mister Skye, and he wore his top hat, much battered now and bearing evidence of the uninvited passage of two arrows, and the whole of this, the royal nose, the top hat, and the way he required others to address him, they saw as crown and scepter and purple and ermine.

"Skye, I'd pass the jug with you tonight, but your nose would get in the way," Harris said. "It wouldn't be fair to the rest. You can snort a whole snifter of firewater and hold it in your nostrils."

"It is a rare English talent, Black," said Skye. "I accept. I will drink your party dry."

Black Harris yawned and headed to his robes for a nap.

Skye thought he'd sleep to dusk, carve some meat off the hanging elk haunch, and then buy another jug of mountain whiskey. The supply had declined alarmingly, and Skye wanted one last celebration before the casks went dry, or the firm began watering the last of its stock, reducing woeful trappers to sniffing a cork and sighing.

Thus passed a July afternoon, while the adventurers who ran the business, took the risks, carted supplies a thousand miles from St. Louis and a fortune in furs back to that gateway of the West, haggled through the day.

Skye snored, until late in the day when a shadow darkened his leisure. In any place other than rendezvous, that shadow would have evoked a lifesaving bolt upward and twist to one side. But here, the one place in the wilderness where it was safe, he contented himself merely to open his eyes and squint upward, past the ridgeback of his nose, to the young man above.

Ogden.

Skye blinked.

"Mister Skye," said Ogden.

"You're the only gent in six years who's addressed me as I wish. For that I am tentatively in your debt."

Skye sat up. Ogden was grinning. They had not seen each other for six years. When Skye was fleeing pell-mell from the Royal Navy, he ran smack into Peter Skene Ogden and his brigade of Hudson's Bay trappers in the Oregon country. He expected to be captured and hauled back to Fort Vancouver and sent in chains to London and a life in durance vile. But this Canadian was no ordinary man, and actually listened to Skye's story rather than scoffing and threatening. In the end, he helped a desperate and hungry seaman escape into the wilderness of North America.

And here was his benefactor, wanting to talk. Ogden was seven hundred miles away from Vancouver. Barnaby Skye sensed that there was portent in all this.

two

Ogden. Barnaby Skye knew he was in the presence of one of the most impressive men in the mountains. He was flattered that this brilliant brigade leader of the Hudson's Bay Company was pausing to say hello. Peter Skene Ogden was a match, maybe more than a match, for any Yank in the wilderness.

Ogden settled himself on the buffalo robe. "Have you a moment, Mister Skye? I should like to talk privately. Your choice. Here or somewhere up the river."

That was no choice. "Here, Mr. Ogden. I don't go sneaking about, and if there's business to be done, let it take place before my mates in the Yank company."

"Here, then." Ogden grinned, obviously liking the decision. Skye saw a man as powerful as himself, stocky and clean-limbed, as lithe as a mountain cat, and as skillful as any in dealing with men, women, animals, weapons, and war. But Ogden had more: he was a thoroughly educated man who kept a journal, knew his way through English literature, and was, above all, a Loyalist. His family had been obdurate Loyalists during the American revolution, and had moved to Canada to remain within the circle of British power. Ogden was bred to those beliefs, and worked through Hudson's Bay to extend British dominion over the North American continent.

"You've come a long way," Skye ventured.

"I came all the way to see you and only you. We always observe these Yank festivals, of course, and the scoundrels make us welcome even if we're rivals, but that's not what brought me here. You did."

"I can't go home and I can't work for Hudson's Bay," Skye said bluntly.

"I know all about that, Mister Skye. You told me your story on the banks of the Columbia long ago, and I found myself believing it entirely." He smiled. "Some others, you may recall, didn't credit you with an ounce of truth."

How well Skye remembered. He had barely escaped with his life from one HBC post, Fort Nez Perce, more commonly called Fort Walla Walla.

"You've risen from a greenhorn to a brigade leader, and one of the top men in the mountains. Smith, Jackson, and Sublette put great store in you. So have their successors."

Skye grunted, his gaze resting a moment on that brush arbor where the fate of his company and his employment rested.

"Watching me, mate? To snatch me back to England and a dungeon?"

Ogden shook his head. "John McLoughlin took an interest in you once he heard my report about you. Cursed the Royal Navy for misleading him."

"An interest, yes. His men chased me five hundred miles and almost killed me."

"He no longer thinks that way. He sees a gifted Englishman who can't go home, a man who'd be a great asset to HBC, an experienced mountaineer with a proven ability to lead, stay out of trouble, deal with fractious men, and bring back the pelts at a profit."

"This is an employment offer? Sorry, mate. I'm beholden here, and these Yanks have treated me honestly and generously."

"Hear me out, Mister Skye. Let's talk as one Englishman to another."

"I'm a man without a country."

"Because the Royal Navy wants you? That has been looked after."

Now, finally, Skye paused. "Looked after?"

"Yes. Let me tell you the rest. John McLoughlin, a most formidable man known through the West as the White Eagle, a Canadian doctor and indomitable force in the Northwest, took it upon himself to make certain inquiries about you in London. It took some while to get responses. His letters found their way to York Factory, carried by our voyageurs, and were carried in our barks to England, and in London they were slowly acted upon because of the disinterest of the lord directors. But at last Dr. McLoughlin, these three years later, has his reply. Would you like to know what this was about?"

"If it's about working for HBC, or returning to the Crown, no, I don't."

Ogden continued, undaunted. "Well, it's about exactly that. One of his letters asked the directors to make inquiry about your family."

Skye's body stiffened. He wasn't sure he wanted to hear this.

"Everything was as you told me and the others. Your father's in the import and export business, and you vanished from their bosom suddenly and mysteriously. They haven't heard a word about you since."

Skye choked, his throat clamped upon the feelings he had swallowed back all the brutal years in the Royal Navy and all the years of his exile in the American wilderness.

"My father lives?" he said, hoarsely.

"He does, but he's ill and not long for this world, so we hear. Your mother . . . is gone. She went to her grave not knowing whatever became of her son. Your older sister lives and is happily married. Your younger one, a maiden, is with your father."

"And do they, did you . . . ?"

"Yes, the lord directors delegated the Reverend Father Hargreaves, our company chaplain, to visit your father. He told Edward Barnaby Skye you were alive, and what had happened, and gave him to understand where you are."

Skye stood and turned his back, not wanting Ogden to see what was written on his face or the tears welling in his eyes.

"Your father rejoiced at the news, Mister Skye, but was saddened as well. A deserter from the Royal Navy, a blot upon his honorable name. He does not wholly grasp your circumstances."

Skye turned again to Ogden. "What took my mother?"

"Bilious fever. If she had lived six more weeks, Mister Skye, she would have known that her son lives."

Beatrice Marlowe Skye, from whose womb he was torn, gone. "Is there any more bad news?"

"I should think it would be good news, a father restored."

"I am a shame to him."

"No, the company doesn't see it that way. Our Honorable Mr. Leeds took it upon himself to visit the king's privy chancellor about the matter, describing the way a merchant's son was rudely abducted and ill treated, denied the rights of Englishmen or any recourse in the navy, reduced to abject servitude for seven years, which is two years longer than the usual enlistment. It was the failure of the Royal Navy, sir. Desperate men in unjust circumstances shall do what they will, and without blame."

"And what did your company man find out?"

"The pardon is assured, but the navy is objecting and refuses to believe a word of the story. Frankly, it's covering its abuses, hiding them from the Crown."

"So no pardon is assured."

"Not assured, no. But should you present yourself to the king's court of equity, matters will go in your favor. The HBC has been assured of that. You can go home. You can see your father before he passes. You can see your sisters. You can go to London, get redress, and walk away from London entirely a free subject of the Crown. And you will not have to wait, either. HBC has that assurance."

Skye felt torn to pieces. "Mr. Ogden, I'm not a subject. I'm not a piece of baggage to be shuttled about by merchants and bureaucrats. This is the New World, and I am a sovereign man."

Peter Ogden measured his words. "You have the rights of all Englishmen, Mister Skye. Those Magna Carta and common law rights may have been abused, but they exist and your case is now well known and the Crown will make amends. We want you to go to London and then return to the Northwest. HBC wishes to make you a senior man with responsibilities equal to my own. You are a born and bred Englishman, sir. And unless I misunderstand you, a man whose allegiance is unshaken, even by the brutal treatment afforded you by officers who should have known better."

"You know me all too well, sir."

"Dr. McLoughlin sent me on this long passage to lay these matters before you, Mister Skye. We consider it a matter of utmost gravity. You may trust the honor of Hudson's Bay, and we are sworn to do you no wrong. There is no trickery in this. There is not the slightest thought of capturing you and shipping you in chains to England and your fate. Dr. McLoughlin sees only a wronged man and a great talent he wishes to employ.

"You, more than any other Englishman, know the Yanks, their ways, their attitudes, their genius, their failings. Your knowledge would be invaluable to HBC. Your knowledge could help England control the whole of Oregon, now jointly claimed. Your expert knowledge would help England possess the Pacific coast of North America, from the arctic down to Mexican California, from the continental divide here in the Rockies down to the northern most boundaries of Mexico.

Your employment by HBC would keep the United States from ever becoming a transcontinental power."

"You have not spoken of my wife, Mr. Ogden."

"We have thought of her. Dr. McLoughlin has a half-Cree wife, understands your sensitivities, and is adamant about protecting your union. If you wish to take her to London, HBC would undertake her passage. When you return, wherever we post you, she would be your helpmeet and be free to visit her people."

"She doesn't think much of HBC, mate. Your company arms the Blackfeet, her people's enemies."

Ogden shrugged. "We cannot deal with all the facets of this. We can only propose. Now, Mister Skye, think on it, but think quickly. It's already too late to go with our voyageurs to York Factory and embark there for England. Nor would we want you to. Our governor, Mr. George Simpson, who resides there, is not persuaded of the soundness of any of this, and might cause trouble."

"So there's trouble, after all."

"Dr. McLoughlin and I prefer another option. Fort Vancouver, you know, is resupplied by sea. Each year a schooner, usually the *Cadboro*, leaves Portsmouth, sails clear around Cape Horn, and works its way up the Pacific Coast to the mouth of the Columbia, there to disgorge the year's supply of trade goods and necessaries, and take on the peltries our voyageurs are unable to canoe and portage and haul across the Canadian wilds. We want you to be on that vessel when it leaves about the middle of September.

"Come at least to interview the man who has done so much on your behalf, and caused you to receive news of your family."

"I will think on it," said Skye.

three

Victoria Skye, named among her Absaroka people as Many Quill Woman, loved the high sweet days of summer most of all. And especially the trappers' rendezvous, when everything new and exciting in the world gathered together to insult the past.

This year she would not see her Kicked-in-the-Belly band, or her chief, Rotten Belly, or her father, Walks Alone, or her second mother, Digs the Roots, or her Otter Clan brother and sisters. They lived far away in the land of the Yellowstone, not here where the Salish and Shoshones hunted and fished. Here the waters drained into the Snake River, and emptied in the western sea somewhere beyond imagining. There, in the land of her people, the waters ran east into the great seas beyond the sunrise.

No woman worked much at the trappers' fairs, so women could be as evil as they chose. She loved being evil. Somehow there was always food aplenty, elk and deer hanging from limbs high above the yapping dogs, and stew boiling in every kettle.

So it was a time for scandalous gossip, jokes, laziness, and sipping firewater while visiting the lodges of the tribes that had come to trade with the white-eyes. The finger-talk sufficed. She did not need to know the Snake people's words to have a merry afternoon with them. She spent one whole day learning new white men's oaths from cheerful trappers who delighted to demonstrate them to her. She marveled that they had so many curses, and wanted to perfect her use of them, so she had them repeat their mighty oaths over and over.

Already, though the rendezvous was young, she had bought yellow ribbons, jingle bells, Venetian glass beads, thread, a new awl and knife, a copper kettle, and a real pair of five-point, thick, warm, Hudson's Bay blankets, gray with red bands at either end. Before she left she would add flannel to her purchases. That is, if Skye didn't squander everything on his whiskey.

She corrected herself. Their whiskey. She enjoyed a good jug just as much as he did, but she didn't indulge herself the way he did. Someone had to look out for him when he visited the other world, so she did. The elders did not approve, but she was young and reckless and willing to try anything. There on the great grassy flats, mountain men and tribesmen alike flouted the wisdom of their fathers, and relished doing it. Later, she would pray to the Above Ones and ask them to come back to her.

She had borne no children, and neither she nor Skye could understand it. But that was what the First Maker had decreed, and she bore this with patience and resignation. It had freed her to help her man during the hard trapping seasons when they sometimes ventured into the lands patrolled by the Siksika, the dangerous Blackfeet. If she could not be a mother of Skye's children, she could be one more warrior and the medicine woman who could divine the future and nurse the ill and steer the grimy, awkward, and buffalo-witted pale men out of trouble.

She had often pondered the greatest of all mysteries: where were the white women? This alone consumed most of the gossip of the Shoshone and Salish women. Where did they hide? Why did white men not bring their women out to this beautiful land? No one could answer it. No one had ever seen a white woman.

Perhaps such women were frail and disease-ridden, or so ugly the men hid them in lodges beyond the sunrise and enjoyed lusty moments with the more beautiful and healthy brown-skinned women of the tribes. She smiled. Skye had enough lust for ten women. She wished he would get another two or three wives so they could all share his manhood.

Once she asked Skye about white women, and he said they were kept away in towns with big houses in them, and they did not like to come to savage places.

That puzzled her. Was this sweet plain beneath the great breasts the trappers called the Tetons a savage place? No woman of the tribes had ever received an answer. But it was rumored that some Lakota, or Sioux, had once traveled far, far east and had seen the cities of the white men, and their women, all pale and so dressed in clothing that only their faces and hands were exposed to view. Something clearly was wrong with white women.

This white men's year of 1832 was different, and she sensed that it boded ill for her man. For all the years they had been together, there had been only one band of mountain men, but now there were several bands, fiercely opposed to one another, and each determined to wreck the prospects of the other. Yet they were all present at this rendezvous, drinking, sporting, bragging, lying, and getting girls pregnant.

This soft evening she padded across the flats, past knots of horses, some of them guarded by Shoshone boys. The new jingle bells on her moccasins delighted her. The yellow ribbons bobbing on her black braids pleased her. She was pretty, though too thin. She wished she could put on some good weight, and be full and round like her mother and sister. She found Skye alone, silent, and lifting a jug, all of which were bad signs. She knew trouble when she saw it, and now Skye exuded trouble.

"You hungry?" she asked.

He stared at the blue band in the west, and nodded.

"I'll make some goddam stew. You gonna get drunk alone?"

He nodded.

"What's wrong?"

"Nothing, Victoria. Got me a job offer from Hudson's Bay."

"An offer? We should not go to them. They put many guns in the hands of the Siksika."

Any friend of the Blackfeet was an enemy of the Absarokas.

"I will tell him no."

"Who?"

"Peter Ogden."

"Him? He is a great chief."

"The best they've got. And he came seven hundred miles to say they want me."

"It is a bad thing. They will catch you and turn you over to the water men looking for you."

"He says it's not so."

A chill ran through her. There was more to this.

"Give me that jug, dammit. I will drink with you."

She sat beside him, took the jug, and poured the firewater into her throat. It burned like a river of lava as it went down.

"Aaaie!" she cried.

"I got news today. Ogden told me about my family."

This was big doings. Skye had word from this place called London, the many-houses place near the great sea, this place she could not even imagine. This news had traveled far, for many moons, maybe many winters, and found its way to this summer festival.

Slowly, measuring his words, he described Ogden's visit. His mother was dead. His father still lived but was frail. His older sister was fine, married, and had a family. His younger one remained at home. The Hudson's Bay Company had verified everything that Skye had told Ogden long ago, during his flight from the Royal Navy. They had approached the elders, the ones who advised the great chief, the one called king, to see if Skye could be welcomed back to England. They were proposing that Skye return to London, receive his pardon and visit his family, and then work for HBC . . .

With sudden insight, Victoria saw her life with the trapper coming to its end. He would return to his own people. He would resume a life she had heard of but could not imagine, working in big houses, working where there were thousands of people, more people in one big village than in her entire tribe, at home again, happy to be with his own.

"You're going away."

"I haven't decided yet."

"I'll go back to Absaroka. It is a good land. I will find someone. You go back."

"Victoria!"

Some animal feeling seemed to erupt from him, rumbling up his windpipe into a great roar. He had bear medicine, and now the grizzly in him roared. He stood, wobbled, roared at the quiet camp, and roared at the sunset, and roared at the Great Breasts.

"Give me the jug," she said. She took it from him and downed another fierce swallow of firewater. It was eating her belly and stealing through her limbs.

"Go to your people," she said, her soul leaden.

He stared at her, hurt in his eyes. "Is that what you want?"

"No, dammit. But you must do this now."

He settled heavily onto the robe.

"Maybe I have to," he said. "Maybe there's things a man has to do whether he wants to or not."

"I will go to my people."

"I don't want you to go home. You are my wife."

"That was the past. Now your people call you."

"I'm a free man here. I bloody well make my own choices."

"Skye," she said and clasped his hand. "No one is always free."

He nodded. "If I go, it's because of duty. My father's old. He got word of me. He's expecting me. Home, that's what it is. I don't even know what home means any more."

"Home is where your people are."

"This tears me up."

"Wait, then. There is no need to hurry."

"Yes, there is. They want me to meet the factor at Fort Vancouver—that's not far from the western sea—soon. Before their supply ship leaves for England in two moons. They want me on it."

She knew what was tearing at him, and she knew darkly that his decision was beyond her. She could only stand apart and watch and wait, not knowing her own fate. After six winters, was this how her life with the white man would end?

"Skye, we must talk to this Chief Ogden some more. It is dangerous. We must find out everything."

He nodded. "If this goes awry, they'll just pitch me into the gaol," he said. "Hard labor, maybe send me to Australia."

"What is Australia?"

"Another land across the western sea, where England sends it criminals."

"We send bad men to other bands. Your people do this, too."

"I have to go," he said. "And I don't want to. I can't afford to take you. Maybe I'll be back. Maybe not. Maybe I'll never see you again. Maybe you'll be standing on the hillside, waiting for me to ride in some dusk, waiting with the lodgefire lit, waiting for a man who has vanished across the seas. Waiting for your husband who had to do what duty required of him."

She didn't grasp all of that, but she understood all too much.

four

Skye detected a heaviness in the spirit of his Victoria
that night. Sometimes she stared solemnly at him.
Sometimes she plunged into a leaden silence. He well
understood her feelings. She was uncertain of her fate, and
likely to see their union come to a painful end.

The fate of "mountain wives," as the Indian spouses of the
trappers and traders were called, was well known. Whenever
a mountain man wished to return to the States, he abandoned
his dusky lady and all his children with untroubled con-
science, and they never saw him again. This was not a scandal
among the tribes. These things were understood and dealt
with. But often a woman who had enjoyed years of happy
companionship with a white man suddenly found herself
alone, with children and no support.

So Victoria imprisoned within her whatever she was feeling, and only the dour turn of her mouth suggested that this
was a painful moment in her life. She had loved, and maybe
now would lose.

Skye felt himself being torn to bits, tugged this way and
that, unable to reach any shore. He knew that this opportunity
cut to his very heart. Through the good offices of the Hudson's
Bay Company, he could become an Englishman again,
restored to his birthright, his family, his people, his home, his

traditions. He could abandon this rough life if he chose. He could keep or abandon Victoria if he chose.

But there was a dark prospect. He knew that she would find only torment in London, the object of vicious curiosity, made fun of behind her back, and regarded as a savage, far below the most brutish of the English. He doubted it would ever change—that the European assumptions about other peoples would ever evolve into anything kinder. It could be a terrible thing to take her with him if he should choose to return to England.

But did he really want to go?

He spent a troubled night, she beside him as always, but somehow separated by an invisible wall. He fathomed only that these things were momentous and could radically change both of their lives. He crawled out of his lodge in the depths of a moonless night, and found solace in the stars, which were always there like faithful friends. The North Star gave direction unless the world was clouded. The fragrance of woodsmoke drifted by. The great encampment slept. Not even the diehard gamblers and drinkers remained awake. Herders guarded the horses against theft, but he did not hear them or the horses. The air stood still, and the breezes told him nothing at all. He wanted decision to come on a breeze, but the air brought nothing upon it. He felt stupid and bewildered.

This encampment lay in a sunny plain in the warmest season of the year, but the mountains were mostly cold and cruel and tortured his flesh. Soon cold would numb his fingers and toes again, and a small buffaloskin lodge would be his sole protection against vicious storm and arctic cold. There would be no refuge from all of nature's onslaught, or the onslaught of hostile tribesmen, or even the wiles of malicious Fate.

In London there would be.

But of course, if he accepted HBC's offer, he would be bound to serve the English company for a time. He would become a top man in the fur trade, but a man with a country, a people, a tradition, a common language.

He didn't have to decide for a day or two. He would see how Victoria felt at dawn, when vision and sun came together, pale and then bright. And he would again talk to Ogden.

He crawled back into his tent, and settled on his robe, upon the hard ground he had never quite gotten used to. Her small brown hand found his and pressed it.

That was all. She always seemed to know where he was, what he was thinking, and what he needed. The still night air, the stars, had schooled him in nothing, and he would await the day.

The next morning he found Ogden touring the great encampment. HBC men usually showed up at the Yank rendezvous and were welcomed heartily, with much joking and raffish humor, for they were all white men in wilderness, even if they all competed ruthlessly. That Ogden was collecting information, counting trappers, counting bales of plews, examining prices in the canvas-sheltered RMFC store, and perhaps trying to entice a few free trappers to take their trade elsewhere, didn't really matter. Bourgeois and trapper alike gabbed with the Englishmen or their Creole employees, and made friends. In the wilds, a friend could be the most precious of all assets.

Ogden, it turned out, had made his own camp with two French Canadians, settling rather closer to the American Fur Company outfit than to the Rocky Mountain partners and their brigades. Now, with the sun lapping up the slopes, breezes danced the breakfast smoke up and away, and filled the camp with that heady scent of pine forest, wilderness, meat, and coffee. It was a fine, hearty smell that stirred something in Barnaby Skye.

Ogden turned to him. "How are you faring this fine morning, Mister Skye?"

Skye grunted a noncommital response.

"Is there anything you wish to know, or which I can do?"

Ogden lifted a blue-enameled pot and poured tea into a tin cup and handed it to Skye, who sipped it gingerly. Skye had rarely had tea since his abduction from England. He wasn't sure he liked it after years of coffee.

"Mr. Ogden, there's a heap of things to think about."

Ogden nodded, but remained silent. Ogden was a realist who knew how easily he could drive Skye away.

"Suppose I go to London, get my name cleared, see my family, and ship back to York Factory, and out here. How long would HBC require me to stay in its employ?"

"Some considerable while, Mister Skye. The company would go to great expense to clear you, and would expect a quid pro quo."

"Suppose I don't go to England."

"We would be pleased to employ you in any case, but as a trapper at one of our outposts."

"Is there danger in that?"

"Considerable. Governor George Simpson, for one, sits on his throne, wondering how to clap you in irons and turn you over to the next royal frigate that makes port. And we are visited frequently, both in Hudson's Bay and at Vancouver, by the Royal Navy. And there probably would be those in the company eager to betray you. The navy's ten-pound reward for your capture still stands."

That was forthright. Peter Skene Ogden didn't waffle or conceal.

"I am a married man, Mr. Ogden. Victoria isn't merely a mountain wife, but my chosen mate."

"John McLoughlin feels exactly as you do, Mister Skye. Marguerite, his part-Indian wife, is his mate and helpmeet, and she's devoted herself to his comforts. She's not particularly distinguishable from white women after many years as the mistress of his hearth."

"Victoria does not wish to be a white woman. She thinks white women are hopeless. Far from trying to become a white woman, she teaches me Absaroka ways and expects me to become her own white Crow."

Ogden smiled. "The company respects such arrangements. Or, again, McLoughlin does. I can't say the same for George Simpson, or for the Anglican clerics they ship out here to enlighten us. That is something you'd have to deal with."

"Would the company finance Victoria's passage to and from England?"

Ogden paused. "Yes, I imagine, if there is genuine commitment on your part. Hudson's Bay is not a charitable society, and wishes to make a profit from its arrangements."

"Five years?"

"Seven. Five is not enough for the investment in you."

"And if matters don't work out, then what?"

"You would be bound for your indentured term."

"With no possibility of buying myself out?"

"I won't ask where you'd find the means."

"Victoria, mate. She works furiously and produces the finest tanned skins and trapper clothes anyone could ask for."

Ogden studied Skye's rabbit-trimmed shirt, leggings, and moccasins. "It's often said that Skye is the best-turned-out man in the mountains. Well, talk to McLoughlin. I imagine he would permit a buyout provision in your contract."

"I don't know, I don't know," Skye muttered.

"Talk with John McLoughlin. It's a long trip, but well worth it. You don't need to commit. From the looks of things here, everything is unstable. More Yank outfits, free trappers, Bonneville, Wyeth, American Fur Company. This might be your moment to go for the highest bidder. HBC's going to bid high, Mister Skye, not only with a good salary but with your freedom, your honor, your good name, and a future in England. You're an Englishman. You're an Anglican."

"I'm a drunk."

Ogden laughed. "So are we all, at rendezvous, until the jugs run dry."

"I'll think on it, mate," said Skye.

Skye left the brigade leader and wandered through the

vast encampment, feeling at home on these grassy flats beneath the Tetons. This was his ground, his people, his weather. This was near the land of his wife.

He discovered that the American Fur packtrain had arrived from the Missouri River, and that AFC men were swiftly setting up shop. He wandered through Nat Wyeth's camp, set up on a military model, everything as rectangular and right-angled as the orderly New England mind could make it. Its contrast to the anarchy of the rest of the camp amused him. Wyeth's bivouac had been the talk of the tribes.

He headed back to his lodge, where Victoria was patiently mending Gabe Bridger's moccasins while he squatted beside her and told crazy stories.

It was morning, but Skye was wandering through the dark.

five

Skye had never felt so torn. Through the mists he saw his father beckoning him urgently, and his sister reaching out. Not since he had been a pressed seaman had the urge to go home risen so strong in him. Something stirred within: he was an Englishman, born to the Island Kingdom, his soul a part of the bone and sinew and soul of his people. He could clear his name, reunite with his family, rejoice to be among his proud people.

But his friends were here, and this land beneath his boots was his, and his woman belonged on this soil, not across the salt sea. He could take her there, but her tears would flood their union.

He knew himself to be one of the most daring breed of men ever born. These mountaineers about him were masters of the wilds, and he admired each of them. They included him among them but he felt like a poor imitation of the likes of Bridger and Meek and Fitzpatrick and the Sublettes. There was, in these awesome fastnesses, a brotherhood forged from danger and joy.

These men were so isolated that most of the world's news never reached their ears. They could survive, even if the fragile supply lines back to civilization were snapped in two. They could endure, even when all the furies of nature were unloosed on them. And they had made him one of them, given him his diploma, magna cum laude. He lived in a small male society where greenhorns approached him with respect and begged advice from him, where veterans slapped him on the back and welcomed him to their campfires. They had saved his life more times than he could remember, and he had rescued so many of them that the bonds they had forged would last as long as they lived.

It hadn't all been pleasant. This extreme life had drawn the misfits and scoundrels, the ones who could not endure ordinary society, the mad, and angry, the desolate, the wounded.

He'd had his fill of trappers who ragged him about the condition of the camps, challenged him to absurd contests, mocked his Englishness, hated him just because he existed, or because he didn't cuss, or because he spoke the true tongue of the English. The mountain men were a vicious breed, and he hoped no one back in the States would ever romanticize them or their squalid, desperate lives.

But on a summer's eve, when the woodsmoke tinted the air with joy, and the tall tales began, and a generous jug found its way around the circle, he knew these men were his brothers, and he was their brother, and this hardy band was his one and only nation.

Thus did he pass a morning in anguish, his glance occasionally falling upon the great men gathered under that brush arbor beneath the wilting cottonwood leaves that shadowed them. This rendezvous was different. Three companies in the field, plus a large and organized band of independent trappers. And they were talking to one another. Who would Wyeth ally himself with? How would they carve up the mountains? What would Hudson's Bay do? What would happen with the muscular American Fur Company in the field, competing for every beaver pelt? It had been hard enough for one Yank company and one British company to survive; how would things go now?

The answer came that very afternoon, when the powwows

in the arbor broke up. Skye watched Tom Fitzpatrick, still frail after a harrowing ordeal just before the rendezvous, hobble toward him, leaning heavily on his staff.

"Afternoon, Mister Skye," he said. "Mind if I light a moment?"

Skye waved him to the robe.

Fitzpatrick eased himself slowly to the ground, still sick and weak, pain around his eyes. Just before the rendezvous, the partners sent him out to look for Sublette's packtrain with the resupply, to tell him to hurry up because of the competition from American Fur. Tom Fitzpatrick delivered the message and was hurrying back to Pierre's Hole when he ran into Blackfeet, not once but twice, narrowly escaping both times. He lost everything, including his rifle, and survived only because of his magnificent skills as a mountaineer. By the time he was discovered by two friendly Iroquois hunters he was in rags, his moccasins were used up, and he was starved down to nothing.

But here he was, and a hundred hardy men like him.

"Mister Skye," he said without preamble, "the long and short of it is, we're facing stiff competition and we're cutting back. The only salaries we'll be paying is to the partners and a few top men. We'll not be able to afford camp tenders. The trappers will do that themselves. We're counting on you to stay on as a free trapper. You join one of our brigades, but it'll be mostly the same."

The news stung Skye.

"A trapper's plews, even in a good campaign, won't come close to what I made as a camp tender, will they, Tom?"

"No, I reckon they won't. But we've no choice. We're not alone any more."

"What's Wyeth going to do?"

"He's going west. Wants to talk to HBC, start a fishery on the Columbia, ship preserved salmon east, and trade for a few furs as a sideline. He's going to trade directly with the tribes if he can. His New Englanders don't know the nose of a beaver from the tail, but they can run a store." Fitzpatrick paused. "And he might succeed, and if he does, that's all the more plews we'll never see."

"And Vanderburgh and Drips?"

"Eyeball to eyeball with us at every beaver ground in the Rockies, Mister Skye. And they've got support. The Chouteaus of St. Louis and all their Frenchy cousins are in. And experience. Those people were in the fur business before we were tadpoles."

"It's bad, then."

"We'll give 'em a run for it. It's not the end, but we're going to stay lean. We're going deep in hock just to pay for next year's outfit."

"Who are you keeping on salary?"

"Black Harris, two or three others."

"All Yanks."

"That wasn't considered. You're as good a man as any in the mountains."

"And not a Yank. You're sticking with your own. I'm as good as any, but not one of your countrymen."

"You'll be a free trapper."

"Maybe I won't." Skye's temper boiled upward. "Maybe I'll start my own opposition. I could take ten men with me."

Fitzpatrick stared. "Don't do anything foolish."

"I don't like being cashiered. I was a loyal man."

The RMC man's affability vanished. "Cool down, Mister Skye. We'll talk some more about this. Forget going into opposition. We'll crush all opposition. We have the means and the skills. Don't be dumb."

Tom Fitzpatrick stood slowly, recovered his staff, and hobbled into the sun. Skye watched him go, his mind roiling with bitterness.

Skye felt something hard and cold and ruthless down in his gut. Suddenly he knew he had no flag to follow, and no allegiance to offer. Just when life seemed good, Fate knocked him two rungs down the ladder.

Well, change was in the wind.

He stood and stretched, feeling the power in his limbs, feeling their constancy and obedience to his will. The somnolent camp seemed changed. He could not fathom it. He wandered willy-nilly, going nowhere. He visited with Wyeth's men, clearly more educated and cultivated than the rest of those in the mountains, and yet not one he wanted to befriend. He meandered through the AFC digs, good men, many of them Creoles from St. Louis, brilliant in the mountains, wild in drink, crazy among women, and the best travelers on earth.

He hunted for Peter Skene Ogden and finally found him in earnest conversation with the Sublettes. They waved him off. Company business.

The earth under his feet was no longer his. He no longer owned the sun, or possessed this warm flat nested in the mountain shadows. He could not put a name to this change that had slid quietly into the place. He thought it was something like leaving an inn, where he had visited with friends and had a grand time, and enjoyed fine feasts, and then stepping into a world that no one owned.

The only things that hadn't changed were the buffalohide lodges of the Shoshones and Flatheads. But even those portable lodges would be dismantled in a few days and carried away on travois. The various tribes were always at home and had no perception of wilderness.

He thought about going into opposition with a dozen free trappers, cleaning out beaver before the Yank company even got to the trapping grounds. But he didn't want to devote his life to a small, mean ambition like that. No man worthy of respect could devote himself to revenge.

Skye let his anger drain away. There was no point in nursing it along.

Then at last a decision did gel in him: he would go to Fort Vancouver, discover what the White Eagle really thought and wanted, and make his decision about Hudson's Bay, a trip over the seas to England, and a new life as an HBC brigade leader.

He would read the correspondence about his family, understand what was wanted, assess the man who had set HBC's blood-hounds after him six years before, decide if this legendary prince of the company would be a good man to work for, a man he could trust. He had come to trust and admire his Yank friends—Bridger, Fitzpatrick, Jackson, Smith, the Sublettes—men who now were rejecting him. He would need to be more careful in the future, and take a hard, cold look at the chief factor.

Thus was his decision made, but he was uneasy with it. What would it mean to Victoria, and indeed, to his marriage? She was off among the Shoshones again, so he wandered in that direction until he came upon the gaudily dyed buffalo-hide lodges of that tribe, and paced among them, enjoying the smiles of the old men and women, the parade of pretty girls flaunting their newly won jingle bells, ribbons, combs, beads, and calico, and their bold flirtations.

It was not hard to find Victoria: she lounged under a majestic cottonwood tree, along with three other matrons, each doing beadwork as they gossiped.

She rose at once upon seeing him. He never came here or interrupted her day, and he beheld worry in her thin, sharp face.

"Yes, what?" she asked.

He touched her arm. "I'm wanting to go to Fort Vancouver and talk with the White Eagle, and I'm wanting you to come with me. If not, I'm wanting you to wait for me because I'll be back, sometime, some way, even if a winter or two winters pass."

"From this place across the sea?"

"Maybe."

"Would you like me to come to this place of your birth?"

"I'm thinking it, if it doesn't scare you. Maybe there's a way."

She laughed. "I'll go. I will see with my own eyes what place this is and what strange people live there, and then we will be closer, eh? Goddam, Skye, do you think an Absaroka woman is afraid? What a big place the world is!"

He squeezed her and rejoiced.

six

kye found Peter Skene Ogden at dusk enjoying something he poured from a silver flask, along with half a dozen HBC men, all French Canadians.

"Ah, Mister Skye, have a drink. What I have here is single-malt scotch, the likes of which you'll never see again at a Yank rendezvous."

"Can't say as I've ever sampled it."

"Let me pour you one. It's all the smoke and heather of the Highlands in one distilled essence. Have you come to a decision?"

Skye settled himself on the ground and took the proffered tin cup. "A sort of one, Mr. Ogden, a sort of one. We'll go to Vancouver and talk with Dr. McLoughlin, and see."

"Good! See how he stands."

"I'm not entirely persuaded, Mr. Ogden. If I come over to HBC, you'll get a gifted woman, too. She's my mate, and she'll go wherever I go. Will you pay her?"

"Ah, Skye, when I heard you'd named her Victoria, after the royal princess, I knew you belonged with us and I urged it upon McLoughlin. I think, within reason, you can propose terms of employment we'd accept, eh?"

"I have little love of the royal family, mate. Her family's among the finest of the Crows. She's a Crow princess."

Skye sipped the Scottish whiskey, intrigued by its smoky flavor and silkiness. But what did he know? The only whiskey he'd ever sampled in his constricted life had been the outlaw variety manufactured for wild Indians and wilder trappers.

"If you're choosing this course, then it's necessary for you to be off at once, at dawn, so you can sail on the *Cadboro*. You'll be going alone. I can't go with you."

Skye sipped. The scotch was seducing him.

"Why aren't you coming with me?" he asked.

"Because I'm still negotiating some territorial agreements with the Yanks. So far, it's gone badly. We offered to stay out of the country east of the divide if they'd stay out of the west slope. But they have us there. Oregon country's contested, and we can't keep the Yanks out. We're at a disadvantage. HBC won't spill a drop of spirits to acquire a pelt from a savage. There are now two or three Yank companies competing with us, and some freelancers, too. What are we to do? Make alliances. I'm going to talk with Wyeth. He's newest and easiest to deal with."

"Nothing'll come of it, mate. The Yanks go where they please and do what they please, and they don't take kindly to HBC. They know you've been stirring up the Blackfeet against them, and arming them, too."

"Well, that's our trump. We could cut off the Blackfeet—if we get something in return."

"Mr. Ogden, I wonder if you know the Yanks at all. They're spoiling for fights, half of them."

"So it seems," Ogden said.

Doubts and details nagged at Skye. He needed an outfit. He was in debt to the Yank company. Who would supply him and Victoria with suitable attire for London?

He and Ogden dealt with these and other details, and within the space of an hour they had hammered things out. Skye would proceed down the Snake and Columbia rivers with saddle- and packhorses. HBC, in exchange for a term of service, would outfit the Skyes.

Then it was done. He rose stiffly, discovering that night had embraced them. A mountain breeze eddied cold air through the camp, bringing woodsmoke on its wings. Men were crawling into their robes. This rendezvous was growing long of tooth and most of the trappers had squandered a year's income on wild times, whooping it up, outfitting themselves, and now they had little to do at night except play euchre or monte or spin tales.

In a week or so it would all be over, and then the lonelies would crawl into the belly of each man, and the mountaineers would silently pack up and leave. Now the lonelies struck Skye hard. He would be ditching all this, maybe forever.

He made his way past campfires, most of them little more than glowing coals, looking for a certain one. He found the fire he wanted, and spotted Tom Fitzpatrick, Bill Sublette, Davy Jackson, Jed Smith, Gabe Bridger, and others, talking quietly among themselves, no doubt planning the year's campaign. He approached cautiously, top hat in hand, but old Broken Hand Fitzpatrick waved him in.

This was going to be hard.

"I guess I've come to say goodbye, gents," he said.

"You goin' somewheres?" Bridger asked.

"Probably home to England for a spell," he said. "I've a chance to clear my name. I never figured jumping ship was wrong, not when I was pressed in and kept a slave, but the lords in the admiralty feel otherwise."

Briefly, he described the news he had received from Ogden, and finally said that he might be working for HBC. They sat silently. HBC was the enemy, the supplier of the Blackfeet.

"Guess you want to see your family, Mister Skye," said Jackson. "Now, out here, most of us coons, we don't ever want to see our famblies."

The laughter went thin. He could have announced his move to American Fur and they would have cheered him. But not HBC.

"I owe the store one hundred fifty-four dollars and some cents," he said. "I've come to offer you a good packhorse, worth over a hundred, and my nine-pole lodge. Not many a man gets to stay in a tent with a fire inside it on a January night. It's worth a piece. I figure the package, a good Crow-trained travois and packhorse, and the lodge, well, it comes to my debt."

"Don't know what the company'd do with a lodge," Sublette said.

"Sell it," Fitzpatrick said. "All right, Skye, I'll go for it if the rest will."

Skye saw the nods, lit by flickering flame.

"Done, then." He saw the Yanks distancing themselves from him. "You're good men. Took in a starving limey and let me make my way. Maybe, when I come back, I'll see you. Maybe not. But as long as I live, I'll remember you."

These were great-hearted men and they put aside their differences, just as Skye had set aside his anger.

"You go tell that pa of yourn, and them proper sisters of yourn, how it be in the mountains, and fill 'em full of tall tales," Bridger said.

"Don't need to, mate. The real tales are more than anyone in London'll believe."

"You taking Victoria?"

"Yes."

"Well, that's some. But not the first time. I heard tell, long time gone, some Iroquois shipped over there to France and half them Frenchies went mad just to get a look at 'em. You go run old Victoria down that Piccadilly Circus, and watch the dogs come sniffing!"

Skye didn't like the vector of this. "She's got courage. Imagine her pulling up from her village and coming with me. She's never even seen a Yank village, much less a city. And the biggest boat she's seen is a canoe. How do you think it'll be to see a three-master?"

"She's some, she is," said Milt Sublette.

Fitzpatrick spoke for them all. "Sorry we couldn't keep you on salary, Mister Skye. Thought you'd be happy enough as a free trapper, you and the missus. But you go on across the sea now, and get your name cleared. And watch out. There's those in HBC that'd sooner skin you alive than call you an Englishman. Stuffy outfit. They won't be calling you mister, like we do." He laughed. "At least like we try to do.

"There'll be those as have long knives out, those naval officers you told us about. And there'll be those who'll think you're a rough man unfit for London. The mountains turn us all rough, and it won't get you into tea parties. But seeing your father who thought ye dead and gone. Ah, there'll be tears aplenty. And seeing the sisters, there'll be tears of joy. You've got your chance, and you're taking it, and there's been no finer man in the mountains."

One by one they stood to pump his hand, give him a bear hug, thump him on the back, and then the shyness came over them, and he wound his way back to his small lodge where Victoria lay in the robes awaiting his news.

"It's all set," he said. "We'll be riding at dawn with just a packhorse. They'll take the other nag and the lodge to clear my debts."

"It's a good lodge," she said. "It has kept us warm and safe. It was given to us by the People."

"They made us a fine lodge, but we made it a safe home," he said. "Now we'll walk into danger. You're a brave woman, Victoria."

"I am not afraid, dammit. I'm Skye's woman, and you honor me by taking me to your people."

Skye stared out the smoke hole at the bright stars, one of which was lying beside him.

seven

S kye and Victoria left the rendezvous at first light, following the Teton River northwest. At the edge of the
great, somnolent encampment, Skye reined up, lifted
his top hat, and settled it over his long hair. That was his
farewell to the men of the mountains who had taken him in
and made him part of their wild nation. His life with the
Yanks was over. Their images came to him: Fitzpatrick,
Bridger, Sublette, Smith, Jackson . . . Goodbye, goodbye, to
them all.

"We're hell and damn right all alone," Victoria said. Skye
nodded and touched heels to his thin, tough mustang, gotten
from Victoria's people. They were alone, and shifting from the
protection of the rendezvous to danger. From now on they
were prey.

It was his fate to be alone, without allegiances. But he was
going home and that thought reached so deep into his heart that
it lifted his sagging spirits. He was going home, but Victoria
was traveling farther then ever from her home family. That's
how their marriage was, one outbound, one inbound, she
never quite happy in the white men's company, he never quite
at home among her Crow people. He saw no help for it. And
yet they had grown close to each other, a tiny nation of two,
separate from the whole world.

She rode beside him along the icy river that deposited the snows of the Tetons into Henry's Fork of the Snake, and ultimately into the Pacific Ocean some short distance beyond Fort Vancouver. It would be a long ride, but not so desperate as his odyssey six years earlier, as a seaman escaping the long arm of the navy.

Home to see his father, home to see his sisters and children he had never met. And his cousins, too. Home to the small vistas and towering majesty of the Island Kingdom. Home to the friends who would have been his classmates at Cambridge, men who would be shocked by him now. No doubt he would repel them, just as he most likely would repel his father and sister and all of his relatives. And if his roughness offended them, Victoria's ways would appall them. But it had to be done.

A good name counted for much, and he wanted his good name and his citizenship back. Then he would be what he had been set upon the earth to be, a free and honorable Englishman.

As the sky lightened behind the eastern mountains, he and Victoria wound their way along grassy parks dotted with mottes of aspen or cottonwood, past long slopes of lodgepole pine, the grades gentle and easy on their horses and the surly packhorse behind them. That beast was not heavily laden. The Skyes could travel light, and on this trip they chose to: at Fort Vancouver, they would shed everything they owned for a very different sort of attire.

Skye paused repeatedly to examine the world behind him.

That was an ironclad rule in the mountains: know what lay before, and what lay behind. He squinted sharply into the dull light, the sun still canceled by the blue mountains, and discovered motion, something yellow and low, probably a coyote.

He nodded to Victoria and pointed. But the movement had ceased, and whatever creature lay a hundred yards back would not reveal itself. He reined the mustang around and headed downstream again, leading the packhorse while Victoria kept to the rear.

Over the next miles they spotted the animal trailing behind, and knew it was either a stalking coyote or a dog. Then, mid-morning, when they paused at streambank to water the horses and rest, they beheld a yellow dog on its haunches watching them; some mutt from one of the tribal encampments.

"I hope he goes back," Skye said. "I don't want a dog."

"The sonofabitch isn't gonna get close, anyway," she said.

When Skye concluded, from a ridge, that the land was open and level enough, he cut west, straight for Henry's Fork, abandoning the north-trending Teton River. They rode through lodgepole forests and open grassy parks, across a vast country in which a man couldn't see far because of the trees. But they were far off any trails and didn't expect to run into any trouble except perhaps for a bear.

The yellow dog followed, now approaching to within fifty yards.

"I'll shoot it," Skye growled.

"Dammit, Skye, just leave it."

A few mountaineers put much store in dogs, arguing that they warned their masters of approaching enemies. But most of them found, to their sorrow, that it was the other way around. A barking mutt led stalkers straight into camp, and the dog-lovers lost their scalps and their lives and their mutts.

All that quiet day the cur crawled along behind them, sitting, watching, squirming, hiding in grasses, running through concealing shadows. Skye watched warily, looking for a clear shot.

Victoria disapproved. There were usually dogs in Indian camps, and they were useful, cleaning up offal and guarding against horse raids. For some of the peoples, they were also a handy source of food.

"Maybe he is a goddam spirit-dog," she said. "Medicine dog, come to help us."

"He's just looking for some vittles," Skye replied. He would not let his woman soften his decision. Dogs were dangerous and a burden to feed. A he-dog got into scraps and had to be doctored.

A she-dog caused more trouble, stirring up all sorts of headaches, whelping and confronting its owner with pups.

"Horseapples," she said.

Victoria had picked up the trappers' rough lingo in the brigades, year after year, and had no idea that there was such a thing as polite society and that such words were simply unacceptable to them. Skye wondered how he could prepare her for London, for European ways, and knew he couldn't. This was her version of English, and that was how it would be, whether in a Mayfair drawing room or in the camps of the mountain men. But at least he would tell her what words to avoid.

They reached Henry's Fork late in the day and camped in a leafy bower well back from the trails tracing its banks. This was a sweet land, with stretching vistas and snowcapped mountains poking through the distant haze. The yellow dog made itself at home just one rifleshot away. Skye didn't much care. The mutt wasn't slinking in, and disappeared for long periods, no doubt hunting.

He was more concerned about Indians. This was savannah country, with plenty of cover for stalking war parties. It was best to dodge them all, even the friendly ones. The loss of one horse would plunge them into trouble. He had ridden over rock and hard ground, walked down rivulets and creeks, hidden their passage to all but the most observant eye. But it was never enough, and luck usually decided who went under and who lived. This was Bannock country, or so he had heard, traversed by Flatheads and Shoshones and Nez Perce. But it was not unknown to the adventuresome Blackfeet, either, and it wouldn't help him an iota to be in the company of a Crow woman.

Henry's Fork teemed with trout, but Victoria wouldn't

touch them. Demons from under the waters she called them
and always watched dourly when white men caught and
cooked them. It surprised her that they didn't die on the spot.
But she always said that they sickened after eating underwater
things; she could see it.

They hadn't hunted this day and now Victoria pulled
parched corn from the packstores, built a tiny fire against a
low bank, and boiled the corn into mush in her kettle. They
would eat simply.

"It is lonely, Skye," she said, after scouring the pot and
dousing the tiny fire. "One day we are with friends. The next
day we are two and a dog."

"Just two. I'm thinking to run that dog off."

"Let us see. It is a spirit-dog."

"It's a mutt."

Skye rose, restlessly, and looked to the horses. He had
picketed them close to camp on good grass. Later, when he
was ready for the robes, he would bring them in and tie them
to the aspen a few feet from his bed.

Some coyotes gossiped somewhere over the horizon and
Skye waited for the damned mutt to howl, but it didn't. It lay
there, out in the darkness, silent and full of its own purposes.

He had never owned a dog, didn't know whether he
wanted one.

The mountaineers argued dogs in camp, often with such
heat that men got into brawls. Some claimed that a man and
dog made a family, if not an entire nation. Others cursed dogs
and said the redskins should eat the whole dog nation for the
sake of the world. Skye didn't much care.

After he'd had his pipe of the precious leaf, he knocked
out the dottle, tied the horses close, and drew his robes around
him against the high country chill. The ground was always
hard and his head never enjoyed a pillow and he had never
gotten used to the privation.

She joined him. She had always come to him in the night, if
only to be held or to hold her man. She held him now, and no

word passed between them. He felt the wash of tenderness again, knowing that this union was more important than going home to England. Much would depend on what McLoughlin had to say. But whatever his fate, it would be Victoria's fate as well. He didn't know why that was so. They hadn't spoken of it or pledged it to each other. Perhaps she was his only nation, his only people, and the two of them, molded by danger and hardship into one heart.

He awakened at first light and everything was all right. He could always tell. Some intuitive understanding, honed from years of danger in strange places, told him when things were amiss at the first gray coloration of the eastern sky. His hip was bruised where he had slept on a rock, but that was all.

She slept. He wondered why they had bred no children, but neither of them knew. Something in her slender form, or maybe within him, made her barren. He didn't know whether to regret it. The wilderness was not a place to rear a family. She would disagree with him. She never understood the white men's idea of wilderness, a place apart from civilization. The whole land was her home and the home of her people, so why not an infant in a cradleboard?

The horses stood stock-still, dozing. All was well.

The outfit snugged beside him, untouched. His Hawken lay in its quilled and fringed sheath within reach, covered with dew. His flint and striker lay beside him, his powder horn next to the rest. Moisture lay thick over everything, including his blankets.

The dog lay ten yards distant, staring directly at him. Ugly yellow thing, big scar over one eye, half an ear off, distrustful and ready to bolt. Skye hunted for a rock to pitch, but the dog crawled back and waited.

"Skye, dammit, let it be," she said. "I got feelings about that dog. It's a he-dog, and he's watching us."

"Put an arrow through him," Skye said.

She stared, stonily. He knew she would not reach for her bow and quiver.

Going Home

The dog stood, stretched, front legs first, and then rear, and waited.

"Well, don't feed him," he said, not yet surrendering.

"He'll quit us if we don't."

But his instincts told him that wasn't true.

eight

They spotted game all the next day: an antelope, mallards bobbing on an estuary, a mule deer, beaver, but Skye would not make meat, and he stayed Victoria every time she strung her bow. She complied, but sullenly.

He was not going to surrender to that yellow dog. There would be no offal, no bones, no scraps, no hide for that hideous creature to gnaw on and thus lay claim upon the House of Skye.

No! But the starved and ribby beast never quit, sulking along behind, and then to one flank or the other, sometimes disappearing. They passed an ancient deer carcass, nothing but bone and hide, and the mutt lingered. Skye hoped that foul pile would poison the beast and they would never see him again.

But an hour later, as they rode along Henry's Fork of the Snake, the hellish creature trotted along, just beyond rifle shot. The dog knew full well how Skye felt: time after time, Skye dismounted, gathered a handful of pebbles, and threw them. The dog gauged Skye's accuracy and ignored the missiles. Skye was feeling defeat and climbed into himself.

Victoria turned stony. "It is spirit-dog. You make trouble for us," she said. "He has come to protect us."

He ignored her. He was not going to endanger her, him-

self, or his property by accepting the company of some dis-
ease-shot yellow parasite that would howl at the first sign of
trouble. If there was one lesson he had squeezed out of his six
years in the wilds, it was to hide from danger. Hide from passing villages, hide from angry bears, hide from unknown bands
of horsemen, hide from solitary warriors, hide from storms
and wind and cold. If he welcomed that miserable excuse for a
dog, he could hide no more.

The bright day invited a sunny heart, but his spirits darkened. Victoria refused to speak to him, her frown beclouding
an otherwise perfect summer day spent upon a sweeping
grassland surrounded by hazy mountains.

That dawn, when he had discovered the dog lying on the
very edge of his camp, he threw off his robes with a roar and
plunged barefoot after the cur, his bear-rumblings driving the
animal far afield. Two minutes later the dog sat on its
haunches laughing at Skye.

Then, midday, the mutt circled around the right side of
Skye's small caravan, trotted out ahead, paused occasionally,
sniffed, and trotted even farther forward. Skye, always the
wary man, unsheathed his Hawken and checked the load. A
fresh cap covered the nipple. He preferred the percussion lock
version of the Hawken brothers' mountain rifle to the flintlock, even though there was always the danger of running out
of caps in a place so far from a resupply. But the caplock
Hawkens fired when you wanted them to, and rarely failed in
damp weather.

The man meandering through a sunlit meadow ahead
clearly was no Indian. He wore a high-collared white muslin
shirt, a proper tweed jacket with elbow patches, and laced
hightop boots. He carried a rucksack. A panama, tilted at a
jaunty angle, covered his head. Skye tugged his reins, the sight
of the lone traveler straining credulity.

"Goddam!" muttered Victoria, pulling up beside him.

The yellow cur had frozen ahead, nose and tail pointing,
as the man studied the earth and occasionally plucked some-

thing from it as if he were hunting for lost gold. Close to him walked a nondescript gray dog carrying a small pack of some sort. It turned toward the yellow dog but did not attack.

"Hello," yelled Skye.

The gentleman straightened up.

"Ah! Company! Come see this. It's a sport variety of the death camas. Look at this. The raceme is really a panicle."

He waved a limp stem at them. The man behind that weed seemed to consider Skye and Victoria old friends.

"Where's your party, sir?" Skye asked.

"Party? Why, I don't believe I know. Back at the camp, I suppose. Wyeth, of course. He'll be along sometime."

"I'm Mister Skye, and this is my wife Victoria."

"Oh, forgive me. When I'm out in the field I forget my manners. Nutmeg here, Alistair Nutmeg, on a small sabbatical."

"You are an herbalist? A doctor?"

"Ah, no, sir, a naturalist. Here we have a whole virgin continent filled with species never collected or recorded, and that's what I'm doing . . . now hold on, Dolly dear, don't growl at our visitors."

He caught the collar of his gray dog and smiled. "Do come down off those steeds and we shall have some Darjeeling, eh? What a jolly coincidence!"

Skye scarcely knew what to make of it. "You came with Wyeth?"

"Yes, a fine little jaunt. He's got twenty of his New Englanders with him, pleasant chaps but timid sorts, and half of them are out of temper and going home. The rest'll come along to the coast. He's got a trading ship going there, you know, the brig, *Sultana*, and I'll return to Boston on it. Visionary fellow. I'm a lecturer at Harvard but actually an Englishman. I didn't get this far last time; that was with the trapper Manuel Lisa in 'aught-ten. But I got a fine bag from it. Hundreds of new species. Wrote it all up. And it's only the beginning."

An Englishman.

"Well, sir, so am I an Englishman. London born. And you?"

"Leicester, sir. I came over here in 'aught-eight, apprenticed as a printer in Philadelphia, but that was a mistake, eh? This is what I was born to do, born, born, born. This pup here, Dolly, carries some good, watertight panniers where I keep my notes and sketches and dried samples."

"You aren't armed?"

"Why should I be, Skye?"

"It's Mister Skye, sir."

"Yes, of course. Professor, here. Professor Nutmeg." He discovered a moth floating by. "Now look at that white beauty. I wish I had my net. But I can only do one thing at a time. We'll leave the bugs and get the herbs. Of course, when a species lands in my lap, I record it. Do you know how many cottonwoods I've found? Three. All unknown to the world. I propose to name one *Populus nutmega*. Vanity, you know."

The professor lifted his panama, and Skye discovered that it had shaded a high-domed pink forehead and receding hairline. The man peered up at Skye with boyish blue eyes, innocence in his countenance. His was the face of a man who'd never heard of evil, a man born before Adam.

The man was a fool.

"When's Wyeth coming?"

"Oh, whenever the rendezvous breaks up, I suppose. He'll find me."

"He knows you're here?"

"He'll catch up with me."

"You're saying you got ahead of him? And he doesn't know it?"

Furrows plowed across Nutmeg's brow. "I suppose I should have notified him."

Skye was aghast. "Don't you suppose he's looking for you? Sending out searchers? Combing the country for a body? Expecting to find a corpse with a scalped head, maybe?"

Nutmeg reddened but held his peace.

"What was the arrangement? Did you tell him you'd be wandering wherever your fancy took you?"

"Why, sir, I scarcely thought of it."

"Did he ask you to stay close?"

The professor nodded.

"There's a rule in this wilderness, Professor. Men stick together always. Lives depend on it. If a man's missing, the whole outfit stops and searches and camps at that place until the missing man is found. Are you aware of that?"

"Oh, yes, they were always talking about it coming out from St. Louis."

"Have you seen any Indians?"

"Well, I believe one sits astride her steed beside you, Mister Skye. Nice specimen, properly dried and pressed she'd last forever. Get into the British Museum. What species?"

"Goddam Absaroka."

"Ah," he said, amusement crinkling the corners of those innocent eyes as he gazed upon her. "She speaks the king's tongue with great vigor."

Skye liked him and laughed in spite of his indignation. "Where do you sleep? What do you eat?"

"Why, this is July, Mister Skye, and this whole continent bursts with wild strawberries, grapes, cherries, huckleberries, blueberries, wild onions, nuts, chokecherries, various tubers that resemble carrots . . ."

"And how do you feed your dog?"

"I don't. She's on her own. She has to use her little dog brain. Sometimes the Indians give me meat. Very pleasant people, these North American Indians. Some fine chaps in black-dyed moccasins dropped by just yesterday and left me some venison for the pooch. But Dolly is quite adept at hunting. Is that your fine canine there, the yellow one?"

"Professor, he's yours. He's loyal to a fault, totally disobedient, and without honor."

Nutmeg sighed. "If I had a pack rig for him, I would, but you see—"

"I'll rig something. He's all yours."

"Why, how extraordinarily kind."

The Skyes and Nutmeg repaired to a grove of noble cottonwoods sheltering the bank of Henry's Fork. There the professor and Victoria ignited a small fire, boiled water, and produced tea, while Skye restlessly watched horizons. He didn't like the news of Blackfeet in the area.

"Professor, how many Blackfeet in that party?"

"Blackfeet were they? Oh, perhaps twenty. Young men, all painted up like a bunch of Zulus."

"On horse?"

"Yes, everyone, and most had a spare."

"What did they do?"

"Jolly fellows. I invited them to step down and see my collection. I pulled out my sketches and pressed flowers and notes, and they had a fine time. I made a sketch of one fellow, and he laughed."

"You damn lucky to have your hair," Victoria grumbled.

"Oh, they were perfectly cordial." He touched his breast. "They have good hearts."

"Painted up means they were going to war, Professor," Skye said. "You should learn that."

"We shouldn't be fussbudgets, Mister Skye. Worry, worry, worry, and all that."

Skye listened dourly. He didn't tell Nutmeg that most Indians leave crazy people alone and some even honor them. He and Victoria exchanged glances.

"Here, try this Darjeeling. I've nursed my little canister of it. A fine brew, I'd say."

It did taste good to Skye, even in a tin cup. "Professor, which direction did they go?"

Nutmeg pointed downstream. The Blackfeet were ahead, then, and that was the answer Skye least wanted to hear.

The professor's gray dog settled in the shade, panting slowly. The damned yellow cur sulked just beyond a stone's throw. Skye didn't know how he would catch the thing and fit a harness to it.

"Professor, your dog's starved, and you're surviving on a few berries that won't be here long. Then what?"

"Yes, poor Dolly's having a time of it. Old carcasses, that sort of thing."

"Where are you heading?"

"Vancouver, of course, and on to the coast. Atlantic to Pacific, gathering botanical specimens. I'll sail home. There's Wyeth's brig to go back on, with Captain Lambert, but also Hudson's Bay runs a supply ship out there each year and back to Liverpool."

Skye pondered that. The man would never make it alive to Vancouver unless Wyeth caught up with him.

"I think, mate, that we'd better have a talk," Skye said. It would be irresponsible to leave this man-child here. He would start Nutmeg toward the rendezvous and hope the man survived.

nine

The strange Englishman's dog was starving. Victoria wondered whether the man was even aware of it. It lay miserably at the man's feet, its ribs poking out, its flanks caved in and skeletal. It was in worse shape than the yellow dog, which had some ability to fend for itself.

Victoria itched to put an arrow through the mallards or the Canada geese she saw everywhere and feed the meat to the hungry dogs. But she held her peace. She was Skye's woman and Skye did not want her to feed the dogs.

He obviously didn't want to feed the Englishman, either.

"Professor," said Skye, "I think you'd better bloody well turn around. Go back to the rendezvous and find Wyeth. You owe that to him. He's no doubt worried aplenty about you, and it's your responsibility to inform him of your whereabouts just as fast as you can. You've probably delayed him for several days. You just can't do this to a captain of a brigade."

"Well, I'm sorry, but my work engrosses me. I'll just wander along, then. Don't you worry about old Nutmeg."

Skye visibly pushed back the anger percolating through him. "This isn't safe country. You're unarmed and unable to defend yourself even against an animal. I'll give you some parched corn, and any other necessaries you might need, and I insist you turn back and relieve Nat Wyeth of his worries."

"But Mister Skye. That's the wrong direction. I'm heading for the Pacific coast. Wyeth will catch up."

Skye lifted his black top hat and resettled it. "Professor, you have no idea what lies ahead. I do. Here you're in an Eden. But when you reach the Snake, the country'll turn harsh, dry, volcanic, and there won't be fruits and berries hanging from every tree. Then you'll need to cross the Blue Mountains, and there's nothing much in them but pines and dry meadows. Then it gets worse. You'll pass through desert . . ."

"Your dog, it ain't gonna last two days," Victoria added.

Nutmeg gazed mildly at her through his oval gold-rimmed spectacles. "She does all right, don't you think?"

"Look at her," Victoria snapped.

"Yes, yes, but that yellow dog of yours looks just the same."

"It's not ours, mate. It's a stray."

"Well, I see. But I'm traveling west. Suppose I go with you?" He smiled. "Consider me a stray. The world's full of stray dogs."

Skye shook his head. "We're mounted and we're in a hurry. We've business at Fort Vancouver. Sorry, mate."

"But I can keep up."

"Show me your boots."

The Englishman reluctantly pushed his feet forward. Both soles were worn and the uppers were separating from the soles. This man would be barefoot in a little while. Skye shook his head.

"That's one more reason we can't take you. Sorry."

Victoria didn't like this. Why was Skye treating a man from his own nation this way? She arose, angrily. There were moments when Skye angered her, and this was one.

The yellow mutt watched her.

Nutmeg bowed slightly. "Well, I'll just putter along, then. Much to do. This day I've found two subspecies of grass unknown to botany. I plan to publish, you know. Complete notes, dried specimens to take East, sketches . . ."

"Goddam," she snapped, and hiked away from the men. She could not understand white men, and especially Englishmen. She poked along the banks of the placid river until she reached a widening where cattails thickened and the waters scarcely eddied. There she strung her bow, plucked an arrow, and drove it through a Canada goose, which flapped once and lay still in the water. She waded out, retrieved it, freed her arrow with her skinning knife, and shot another goose just as it lifted into flight. This day the starving dogs would get some meat and she would make sure the two Englishmen didn't get a morsel.

Happy at last, she gathered the geese by their necks and trudged back. Skye would glare at her like a thundercloud, but she didn't care. The two men were fussing with their kits. The professor was settling his little canister of tea in his ruck-sack, while Skye was adjusting the pack on the horse.

They paused, watching her enter the shady bower bearing her big geese. Both dogs stood, alert, aquiver.

"Dammit, this is for the dogs. They deserve meat more than you do," she snapped.

"Why, you have given Dolly a little treat," said Nutmeg. "How pleasant. Thank you."

Skye said nothing, his face a mask.

"The Englishman has thanked me," she said to Skye.

The dogs quivered and crawled, but neither pounced. Angrily she plucked feathers by the fistful and singed away the residue in the dying fire, choking on the foul smoke, turning the birds until the coals had reduced them to naked flesh, while the dogs whined. Then she gave one big bird to each mutt. They each nipped at it, tore gently, whined, and finally clamped their paws over the booty and worked flesh loose with their teeth.

Skye's gaze radiated his anger, but she didn't care.

"You have done Dolly a great service, madam. I am in your debt. I shall name a new species after you."

"Sonofabitch."

"I don't know of any such species, but I'll manage the Latin version."

Skye laughed. Something suddenly eased in her big man, and she saw the merriment in his face.

"Professor, if you're going to tag along I can't stop you. But you'll walk along right smartly and not go chasing daisies. Maybe Victoria and I can see you out to Fort Vancouver and maybe we can put some meat in Dolly's paws now and then. But we're going to leave messages for Wyeth. Lots of them. Starting right here."

That was one of those many moments when Victoria loved her man more than she had words to describe. Something passed between them and she knew that everything had been made true and good again.

"Now, there'll be some rules to follow," Skye said. "We've a Blackfoot war party ahead of us and we'll be traveling as silently as we can. I think Victoria can make meat with her arrows. She's a good and quiet hunter. But we're no match for a dozen Blackfeet and our only refuge is to flee, to hide, to make ourselves invisible."

"Oh, Mister Skye, they're fine fellows. You oughtn't worry a bit."

Skye didn't respond. She could see him swallowing back everything that he wanted to say to Nutmeg. Indeed, she would have pitched in with a few words of warning about the Siksika, ancient enemies of her people, but she didn't. There was something in Nutmeg's innocent eyes that showed them how it went with him.

"Before your boots fall off your feet, you let us know. We can patch. Victoria has an awl and plenty of thong and thread. But above all, we can't delay. That's the one thing I must impress upon you." The storms in his eyes passed. "Here we are, a pair of limeys in paradise."

"I say, you have a humor of your own," Nutmeg said.

"You lead the packhorse, Professor, and I'll have Victoria work ahead of us. She'll be our advance scout."

Skye asked the professor for some paper, wrote a note, wrapped it in a patch of greased buckskin, built a low rock cairn smack in the trail, and placed the note under the top rocks.

"We're going to leave more notes for Wyeth," he said. "I still prefer that you go back, but you won't, and I don't have time to argue. Now let's go."

And so they started. The dogs were still gnawing at their feasts, but would catch up soon enough. Victoria urged her pony forward, solemn and alert, watching the way birds flew, listening for unusual silences, studying the air ahead for dust. She saw and heard nothing unusual, but that didn't mean much. A number of unshod ponies had gone by, leaving faint prints in dusty ground, and these she studied as she rode.

From time to time she paused on a slight rise, examining the great basin they were piercing. She knew Skye was suffering. Nutmeg was zigzagging along, veering from tree to plant to brush, pausing to snatch a leaf or a root or a bloom. Whenever Nutmeg fell too far behind, Skye stopped and waited, his body rigid. She could see him admonishing the professor all that afternoon, but little good it did. The naturalist meandered wherever the breezes took him and the wandering was costing time. She knew they would make barely half of their usual distance on this day.

By late afternoon Skye slouched grimly in his saddle, ignoring the professor, his glare restless. She knew he was worried. Nutmeg would slow them so much that they would never reach Vancouver in time. He rode angrily behind her, glaring at the dogs, at the professor, and trying to stay alert to that war party. If they ran into the Siksika they would be in trouble and it would come so swiftly that there would be little they could do. It was not a land where one could hole up and hide.

They were traveling directly over the tracks of the war party, which worried her more and more as the sunny afternoon dragged by. Evening found them at the confluence of Henry's Fork and the Snake, in a broad basin surrounded by distant benches and bluffs. The tracks of the Blackfoot party headed relentlessly down the Snake.

She paused there, waiting for Skye.

He studied the place and nodded. She and Skye and Nutmeg would camp in this area. A cutbank near the river would permit them to build an unseen fire and cook something.

Nutmeg trudged in, his countenance radiating good cheer.

"We're going to stay here tonight," Skye said.

"Capital. I could use a bit of a break and some tea," the professor said. "Are those rascals still ahead of us?"

"Yes," Victoria said. "We're going to scout after sundown and look for a fire. Then we know."

"We could invite the chaps over," the professor said.

Skye looked as if he was about to lecture the man but held his peace. Swiftly he unloaded the panniers and packframe from the packhorse and put the animals on picket lines. The dogs showed up, looking ready for another feast, but Victoria had nothing to offer them.

She built a small cookfire well concealed from view under arching brush that would dissipate the smoke, and boiled more parched corn. They would not risk a shot on meat, so close to a war party that would love nothing more than to torture them all before killing and scalping them.

Skye urged the professor not to talk. There would be time ahead when they could get acquainted.

Nutmeg nodded. He was accepting Skye's direction, which Victoria thought was a good sign.

She had never seen Skye so miserable and she knew every way in which he was suffering.

And then Nutmeg's dog, Dolly, barked.

ten

Skye dipped into deep shadow, cursing the dog. Artfully, Victoria doused the small fire, which hissed and spat its defiance and then faded in a cloud of acrid steam.

"Professor, lie quiet and don't talk," Skye whispered in a voice so low it scarcely traveled ten feet. "Hold that dog. Try to keep her from barking."

"The mosquitos are a bit thick," he said.

He was right. A maddening swarm of them whined around them, poking and probing, lancing Skye's neck. It had been a terrible choice for a campsite.

When his eyes had adjusted to the starlight, he studied the surrounding country but spotted nothing. He knew that Victoria, who had better night vision than he, was padding through the area in search of trouble. She was good at this; something in her Absaroka blood had given her the gift.

She slid down beside him a few minutes later.

"Nothing, Skye. The horses aren't interested, either. They ain't making noises. They aren't even staring the same direction."

"His dog's going to get us into grief," he whispered. "Where's the yellow mutt?"

"Keeping silent, Skye. He's a smart one."

"I should shoot the pair of them."

They hugged the ground for another ten minutes, and then Skye rose quietly.

"These mosquitos. We're moving."

"I'm covered with bites, the bloody devils," Nutmeg said.

Mosquitos had been the ruin of many a man trying to hide. He slapped gently at the whining devils that hovered about his ears. The horses were restless, and when Skye ran a hand over them he knew why. He brushed scores of blood-filled mosquitos off their backs. He had chosen the worst possible place to camp and now they were all paying the price.

He was in a black mood he couldn't shake.

He headed for the open and arid benches, hoping to escape the maddening mosquitos. Twenty minutes later, and several hundred feet higher, they were high above the valley.

On the distant western horizon, at a distance hard to calculate, a campfire flickered.

"There," Skye said.

"Sonofabitch Siksika," Victoria growled.

"I hope those chaps don't suffer the way we did," Nutmeg said.

Victoria grunted.

They walked the bench country through thin grasses, lit only by a new moon and starlight, until they found a sheltered bank, a cleft in rock, actually, and paused there. No mosquitos troubled them. Skye picketed the horses on thin grass, hoping they would crop enough of it to fill their bellies, and they unrolled their robes on stony ground.

Dolly panted beside her master. The yellow mutt was nowhere in sight and Skye devoutly hoped that mosquitos had carried him off to dog Valhalla.

This wasn't so bad. No mosquitos. Absolutely barren approaches in every direction. He knew where the war party had settled for the night. He was hungry, and so were the rest, but they wouldn't cook this night. A night without food would darken his mood even more.

Angrily, he dug out some jerky, one of few pieces he had collected at rendezvous. Jerky never satisfied hunger and usually made it worse.

"Professor," Skye said, "I'm going to give you a piece of jerky. Keep it in your pocket. When Dolly looks ready to bark, stuff jerky in her face. We'd be in trouble now if those Blackfeet were crowding us."

"Why, certainly, but she gave us a warning, didn't she?"

"A false one, and she gave us away."

Slowly, he relaxed. They were safe enough here. The animals were watered. A clean breeze filtered through his buckskins and cooled his bitten flesh. His mood lifted a bit; it always did sooner or later.

Victoria quietly scraped out the cookpot, whose contents had doused the fire, while the professor settled himself against the rock. He dug for his briar pipe, but Skye stayed him. "No, not a match, not a flame," he said.

"It is my one small pleasure," Nutmeg said, desolately.

"Friends of mine have gotten themselves killed for less."

"I should like to be a noncombatant in these wars," the professor said. "Is there no signal I can give them, or sign or banner, that will tell these people I mean them not the slightest harm?"

"No. The best bet is a gift of tobacco. We always carry a few plugs. It's a peace offering."

"I wish to enlist them in a great enterprise," the professor said. "They could all be valuable to me. Would you help?"

Skye peered into the night, listening intently to soft sounds on the wind. "Maybe I can, Professor."

"Well, you see, sir, here's an entire continent whose flora and fauna are almost unknown. Imagine it: a land larger than western Europe, and science knows very little. Back in Philadelphia, my former colleague, Professor Barton, showed me an armadillo. What an amazing creature. I'd never seen or heard of such a thing. I knew instantly what my life work would be.

"Now, imagine it. I couldn't cover this continent in ten lifetimes, and yet I'm committed to a project so grand that I must find the means. I'm not alone, of course. Our fellow Englishman John Bradbury has taken up the work, too, a most admirable and intrepid soul, who lets nothing, neither disease nor storm nor hostile natives nor disaster stay him. He's sent hundreds of species to the Liverpool Botanical Gardens, you know. I only hope, sir, that I may in some pale way emulate so great a soul."

Skye marveled that a man's passion could lead him into such dangerous corners of the world and render him almost oblivious to that danger.

"Some tribes might help, Professor. Not all."

"Well, sir, the Indians could be my salvation. Tell them that I want at least one of everything that grows, small enough for me to sketch, and to dry between papers. Tell them that I need to know the exact habitat, high or low, moist or dry . . ."

Skye was skeptical. "Unless you know their tongue, you won't get what you want."

"But surely there are translators?"

"Very few. Some French Canadians know Indian tongues, and have intermarried with them."

"Then I must find some!"

"And would you employ them?"

"Oh, I haven't a pence with me. But once they see the importance of this work, the majesty of it, surely they'll bend the oar . . ."

Skye was reluctant to say what he thought. He was still bleak of mind, worried about the delays this man would cause him, worried about shepherding a fool another five hundred miles. This man's passion and dreams towered higher than those of ordinary mortals, and no practical matters would curb his mania. He didn't want to help this impossible man, but he had to.

Things puzzled Skye. "Professor, where's the rest of your collection?"

"Why, sir, back with Wyeth. He'll bring it along. I've a packmule with him, and I'm already running out of room. We'll find another mule, eh? Maybe I could buy yours. I'd like to stay right here. Hardly scratched the surface. We'll meet in Fort Vancouver or some place. Wyeth's going to ship every-thing."

Skye wondered if the professor had absorbed anything Skye tried to teach him.

"Have you a family, Professor? A wife? Children?"

Nutmeg sighed, happily. "Yes, the old dear. But this is my whole life, Mister Skye, my contribution to human knowledge. I hope to organize and publish in between expeditions. And you, sir. Have you an enterprise?"

"No, nothing except surviving."

"A pity. A good man like you could serve king and country most admirably."

"My dreams are small, Professor. Once they were large, before the Royal Navy robbed me of a life. But yes, I do have a passion. A chance to go home. We're going to see about it. Hudson's Bay is clearing the way for me. My father lives. I yearn to see him while I can; see the old man who remembers only the boy, the pale student. He won't recognize me, sir. Not at all.

"I'll walk into his parlor and he'll think me a tradesman or some such, and I'll tell him who I am, and we'll not say much, not at first, but I know just how it'll be. He'll stare. And I'll be ill-at-ease there, with my wife beside me, and it'll be like a gla-cier thawing, but then the water's going to flow, Professor."

"That's your goal, then?"

"I didn't know how much England meant to me until I was offered it once again."

"But that's not a goal. You must join me. You and your savage, you come help me. I'll arrange a few dollars if I can from the American Philosophical Society, and then we three'll go on a little field trip across the continent. I want to do a southern trip next, and especially a trip to those deserts of

Mexico. Frightful succulents there, you know. Simply frightful. I must dig them up and send them East. I need a strong
man built like an ox. This is a work of such importance, such
magnitude, such seriousness, that I must have all the help I
can manage."

Skye shook his head. "My goals are smaller, Professor. I
would give all I possess just to see my family, even for one
hour."

Mister Skye turned away from the conversation, his mood
so low he couldn't stand another word.

eleven

The Skyes visibly relaxed when the hoofprints of the Blackfoot war party veered into a ford of the Snake River and death went with it. Just to make sure, Skye forded the river himself, swimming his saddlehorse a few yards to cross a channel, but otherwise walking through shallows. The party, he reported, had headed south toward the Bear River.

"That's how it goes, Professor," he explained. "Most of the time you never see them but you know they're nearby."

"Well, those chaps didn't harm me," Nutmeg said. He privately believed the Skyes' caution was exaggerated and he was growing impatient with them.

They hiked along the Snake, entering a volcanic and arid land. Nutmeg devoted himself to new species he was finding everywhere: a new prickly pear, a new shortgrass, two new sagebrush variations. One of these, which he named *Artemisia tridentata*, he found on the river benches. The new prickly pear he called *Opuntia fragilis* because its lobes fell off so easily. All these he sketched, regretting that he lacked the space to send whole samples back to the American Philosophical Society in Philadelphia.

The Skyes kept pressing him to hurry, but they simply

didn't understand. What he was doing was timeless. Why couldn't they accommodate him?

He felt he was scarcely touching the surface: he ought to be capturing every bug and snake and bird, too, but the Skyes were always pressuring him to hasten. He always agreed to, but then he would discover new things and lose track of time. He roved far from the riverbank trail and his collection bag swelled with divers species, and he sketched furiously, ignoring the dark looks emanating from his trail companions.

This was a harsh land, but it lured him into its wastes with the promise of discovery. Finding something new! He was treading where no naturalist had gone! Was ever there a more joyous occupation? How could he resist when every leaf was a bonanza? Every creek and trail leading out of it seemed to head for cool mountains, forested slopes, and lush meadows, and a dozen new species.

Twice he had strayed far away from the riverbank trail, and Skye had come after him, finding him miles from the river. His guide rebuked him gently, stressing the importance of staying together and never losing sight of one another. And each time, Nutmeg earnestly agreed to be more considerate of his companions. But the whole business, which kept repeating itself, was demeaning. Must he always apologize?

Skye was having trouble subsisting his entourage, and things worsened when game vanished. Nutmeg saw not an antelope, deer, bear, or any other creature larger than a marmot. His dog starved again even though the Skyes did their best, occasionally downing a mud hen or killing a snake. The yellow mutt trailed behind distrustfully, in perpetual sorrow for intruding where he wasn't wanted, and Nutmeg wondered why it was still following the Skyes.

Nutmeg was not a young man, but he brimmed with vigor and the joy of his quest. Behind him, in Boston, his American wife Hattie lived quite alone, though she didn't lack the companionship of faculty wives at Harvard College. She had gotten used to his wanderings, good old sport was she, and resigned herself to a life less domestic than she had hoped for. He occasionally felt a bit guilty about that, but not very. His great North American botanical catalog was the important thing. She understood perfectly, but so far he had not been able to bring the Skyes to the same frame of mind.

The evenings were better. He had come to cherish those campfire times when Skye and Victoria relaxed a bit and even allowed themselves a conversation. Victoria fascinated him: he had never met a woman of such contrasts: fierce, warm, suspicious, generous, loving, savage in her feelings toward other tribes. He learned swiftly to avoid the slightest condescension toward her or Skye, because she responded explosively.

Skye proved to be reticent at first, but Nutmeg drew the man's story out of him. The wretch had been caught by a press gang on the East End, near the London Dock at Wapping, within hailing distance of his father's brick warehouse. His father, it seemed, was an importer of tea, coffee, and spices and an exporter of finished cottons, linen, and Wedgwood. The East End whelped hooligans, and press gangs commonly roved the crowded, crabbed alleys snatching up young billies for service in the Royal Navy. But when they caught Skye, they nabbed a youth who was destined for Cambridge and eventually a vocation in a large merchant firm.

"After that, Professor, it was war. I tried to get word out to my family, fought everyone and everything, got a reputation so bad they wouldn't let me on deck in port because they knew they'd never see me again. I stopped just short of mutiny. That would have been the end of me. They had a way of dealing with a rebel, you know. Tie him in the rigging under the bowsprit and give him a knife to cut himself loose when he can't stand it any more."

Skye told him about his escape after seven years of perdition, and his desperate flight up the Columbia, hounded by the Royal Navy and Hudson's Bay.

"And now you're going straight back? To Fort Vancouver?"

"That's right. It's a risk, but a chance to clear my name and see my family and rejoin the country of my birth. To England I was born, and to England I must return."

Thus did Nutmeg acquire a good grasp of the young man's life, and the more he heard, the more he marveled at Skye.

"I'm going home, sir, but not for long. I'll soon enough have my fill of Fishmonger's Hall and Westminster, and the swans on the Thames, and then I'll sail back and work for the company I once hated so much I spent my hours plotting its ruin in North America. This is all the doing of John McLoughlin, sir. He's a mountain of a man, both physically and mentally, and he took an interest in me."

"So I've heard. But why do you trust him?"

"By his reputation, sir. He is known in the mountains, and there's not a Yank at the rendezvous who doesn't admire him."

"Then you've put your trust in a good man. We must trust; not to trust, not to have faith, is the doom of many a good soul."

Some evenings Nutmeg deliberately focused on Victoria, but she was shy as a field mouse around him and regarded him as some sort of rival, taking Skye into realms of science and white men's learning of which she hadn't the faintest comprehension. But his patience eventually prevailed, and she warmed to him.

She had taken over the task of feeding Dolly and that strange yellow mutt, and that was no easy burden in a land increasingly harsh and volcanic. Yet, by day's end, she usually had speared or shot some sort of vile meat: snakes, fowl, lizards, hares, chucks, once a kit fox, once a wounded coyote, and these morsels she divided between the dogs.

Skye had stopped trying to chase off the yellow dog even though he ritually warned Victoria that the miserable beast would get them into trouble.

"He's a spirit-dog," was all she ever said, and that shut him up properly.

"When we get to Fort Vancouver, that's the end of him,"

he grumbled. "He does nothing but exploit you. At least Dolly, there, carries a pack for the professor. But that ribby devil's nothing more than a parasite, taking what it can and giving nothing. I've met a few men in the mountains like that and usually they don't last long or win any friends. I've seen trapping brigades drive such men out."

"He's looking out for us," she insisted.

"He'll betray us," he retorted.

Then one day the yellow dog went hunting and returned dragging a three-month-old antelope it had killed up on a bench somewhere above the Snake. This he laid at Victoria's feet, circling wide around Skye, who watched hard-eyed and cold.

The ugly, battle-scarred mutt had not ripped one bite out of the antelope but presented it whole to the Crow woman.

She lifted her arms skyward and sang a warbling song of thanksgiving and praise, her back arched, her fingertips touching the sky, and Nutmeg knew she was blessing the yellow cur and thanking her gods.

Then she reached out to touch the mutt, but it crabbed back violently and watched her with unblinking brown eyes.

They were camping in a wash draining out of the north, with a few scrub cottonwoods in it and she hung the baby antelope from a limb and butchered it. Nutmeg doubted that there was more than ten pounds of usable meat in it. Victoria first fed the yellow dog, cutting prime flank meat for him, and then gave Dolly a good feed, and finally cooked the last of it for the three mortals present at that campfire.

That night the mutt wiggled closer to the camp than it had ever done before. Dolly drifted over for a sniff and the two didn't fight, so Nutmeg let them make their rapprochement. The Skyes had, willy-nilly, acquired a dog. That amused the professor. Skye was a force of nature, but he proved to be the loser of this contest.

As the August days and weeks rolled by uneventfully except for an odd storm that boiled out of the north, an idea began to take form in Professor Nutmeg's mind. The more he shaped it and tested it and argued it, the better he liked it.

"Mister Skye," he said. "I've been observing you almost as closely as I've been observing the flora and fauna here. I hope you don't mind. What I see is just the sort of man and woman I need as assistants. You are naturalists without even knowing it. I have a great enterprise before me, and need help. I think I can arrange some funds from the estate of my friend Smithson. What I propose, sir, is that you become my guides and assistants. Together, sir, we shall advance science."

Skye stared at him, and then at unseen shores.

twelve

Skye did not say no, although that was what he was thinking.

All that remained of the fire was a circle of embers and an occasional sniff of acrid cottonwood smoke. Below, trapped in a dark deep canyon, the Snake was sawing through volcanic rock. It was like the river of his own life, trapped between walls of black rock. He did not like this country. He didn't much care for the west slope of the Rockies, or the arid lands stretching to the coastal ranges.

The yellow mutt was out patrolling, sniffing the night winds, and Skye grudgingly admitted to himself that maybe the thing was performing a service after all.

"You're a man of exceptional ability," Nutmeg said. "I saw that at once. Your American friends saw it, too, and promoted you. Hudson's Bay Company sees it, and wants you. It's gone to great lengths to get you.

"You have intelligence and will and courage. There's nothing to stop you if you wish to make something of your life. The Royal Navy only delayed the bloom. I suppose what I'm doing here is lifting your sights a bit. Showing you what lies beyond your horizons.

"I have a grand passion, the botanical cataloging of this continent. I lecture at Harvard as a means to stay here, take time off now and then to plunge in again. But as hard as I might struggle, I'll achieve in my lifetime only a fraction of what needs doing. I've been looking for a man to follow me; a man I can train in the field, an intelligent man, able and strong. A man to continue when I no longer can. I've been watching you, Mister Skye, and I think you're the chap."

"I'm not educated."

"Oh, yes you are. You're a man acquainted with books, comfortable with ideas, but practical. You'll take over from me some day, sir, and there'll be some royal recognition: Order of the Garter, maybe knighthood. You have all that in you, and all it takes is a nudge from someone to awaken you to it."

Skye eyed Victoria, her face lit by the last orange glow of the coals, caught in a darkness of knowledge. She sat cross-legged beside him, listening to things of which she had no grasp. There were chasms between her world and the world Nutmeg was opening to them around a faltering fire this nippy August night. He wondered whether she could bridge that chasm. Whether she would be miserable in England and pine away until she died. For now, she was keeping silent. Sometime soon she would pepper questions at him, but he knew he couldn't really explain much to a woman who had never seen a white man's city and could not grasp what lay within a library.

"All that's fine, Professor," he said. "But not bloody likely."

He deliberately used the vulgarity to emphasize the gulf that lay between them. Professor Nutmeg seemed to ignore it, but Skye knew he had drawn the linguistic line between the professor's gentility and whatever it was that Skye had become.

Nutmeg shifted to another tack. "You know, my friend, I need someone to keep me out of trouble. Botany is my passion, and I sometimes forget all else and ignore the dangers of the wilds, and the tribesmen, and the weather. That's why I need you. It's a blindness in me. You're an experienced man in this unsettled land, but at the same time you've a keen intelligence and a grasp of what I'm about.

"I think I can get some funds. My old friend James Smithson died a few years ago, and gave his considerable fortune to his nephew. But he also gave me a letter urging the nephew, Henry Hungerford, to fund any worthwhile project. Quite a man, Smithson. Oxford, best chemist and mineralogist in Europe. A passion for science."

Skye did not share that passion, nor did he intend to work for any man without wilderness sense. He would make a poor botanist, anyway. He was not a sorter by nature, nor a collector, nor organizer. The things that awakened his interests were more spiritual and even aesthetic. There had been sunrises, quiet and still and sublime, that he would never forget, craggy mountain prospects that were etched in his soul, moments when he sensed he was not alone and not abandoned, and seemed to hike effortlessly a foot above the earth. He hadn't a single file drawer in his mind, but sometimes he had a yen to paint. Could he ever capture the ephemera of the wilds on canvas?

"I appreciate your interest, mate," he rumbled. "I've other plans. Visit my family, then come back here and work for a fur company. That's what I want to do."

Nutmeg absorbed that for a moment. "If you should change your mind . . ."

"Time to crawl between my robes," Skye said.

They began their evening ritual. Nutmeg always unrolled blankets at some distance from the Skyes—too far, Skye thought, but it was a sensitive gesture. This man was not so naive after all. Skye and Victoria were given the privacy they sometimes needed. Dolly had taken to shuttling from one bed to the other, and sometimes Skye found himself pinned in, or the dog lying on his ever-ready Hawken beside him. The yellow cur never came close.

There was no such thing as safety in the wilds, and Skye

slept lightly, a part of his mind sorting out the faint night-whispers.

Victoria said nothing. Tomorrow, when Nutmeg drifted out of earshot in hot pursuit of a burning bush or the Ten Commandments graven on a petal, she would approach Skye crossly, wrestling with the pain of her ignorance and afraid of losing him if he drifted back to his own world. And then he would reassure her that he had no plan to do that.

Nutmeg's proposition intrigued him. There was an income in it; a sense of building something enduring. But he would probably commit to Hudson's Bay Company. He tossed in his blankets, knowing that the matter would not be settled until he had a long talk with the most formidable man in the Northwest, Dr. McLoughlin.

"You gonna do this?" Victoria whispered.

"I'm thinking on it."

"I don't know what the hell he's talking about."

"You'd pick it up fast in London."

"You do what you want. White man things. Maybe I'll go visit my family."

Maybe she should. Maybe this would tear them apart. Their union might work in the wilderness, but would it survive in London? She would be treated as a great curiosity. She might have trouble finding friends there. On the other hand, maybe she would take London by storm. The trappers loved her; why not Englishmen? After he had completed his service to Hudson's Bay, would she enjoy life in London, his home but not hers?

The more he wrestled with it all, the more perplexed he became. Go back to the world he knew, and work as a trapper? Victoria would be happiest if he did that. Work for Hudson's Bay? He could do that. She wouldn't like it much. Work for Nutmeg? She would soon find herself excluded no matter how hard Skye tried to draw her into the botany.

He had no answers and no wisdom to help him along. He'd never had an employment opportunity before; years of slavery aboard ships of war, then working in a trapping brigade, glad to find some way to feed and shelter himself. Now he felt bewildered.

"You gonna flop around like a fish on the grass or let me sleep?"

"Stuff on my mind."

"You want what I think?"

"Yes."

She didn't answer, but instead pulled herself close to him, and he felt her arms draw him tight, and then he felt her cheek and it was wet.

"You go home," she said. "You're a man with no people. I got people, everyone else got people. You got to go back to the people who make you."

She was offering herself, and their love, as a sacrifice to him. He had no response except to hug her back. What she said was true. He needed his people. He desperately wanted to see his father. He was curious about that. What was his father like now? He remembered a demanding man who didn't have enough time for a boy; a man sometimes testy and usually kinder to his sisters than to him. He remembered being anxious to please his father, and a little afraid, and often feeling he never could win the man's esteem.

But he also remembered his father's confidence in him, and the paternal gaze that rested upon him with pride. His father had not been a harsh man, but not given to much affection, either. Now Skye was a man, inured to hardship, independent, bruised by a painful life. He would be a man visiting a man, not a dutiful son visiting a father . . .

"You're right," he said. "A man needs a country."

He felt the hotness of her tears on his stubbled cheek and knew her anguish. She felt out of place in his world, the world of the English, the people across the Great Waters to the east. She understood the gulf and was immolating herself and her love so that he might return to his home.

"Come with me and see my country," he said. "They'll not

be friendly, but your people weren't very friendly to me. That's how the world works. Remember how it was for me in Rotten Belly's village?"

"Yes," she said. Skye had been scorned by most, and derided by the young warriors. Only an old shaman granted him any honor.

"It'll be like that for you."

"I'll go to this England if you want me to," she whispered.

The mutt had crept close, watching in the murky darkness, irritating Skye. Then it growled, so low that Skye could barely hear its throaty menace.

"Sonofabitch," Victoria said, throwing off the four-point blanket.

"What?" said Skye, irked at the dog for wrecking this moment.

Victoria grabbed her bow and strung it with one swift flex. Then she snatched an arrow from her quiver.

The mutt growled again.

"Goddammit, get up, Skye!"

He wallowed around, finding his sheathed Hawken, and extracted it. Damned yellow dog, starting a ruckus.

He heard a swift confusion of sound, a low voice, the snort of nervous horses, and then the sharp clatter of hooves. Skye sprang up, checked the load on his Hawken, peered into a thick gloom looking for a target.

The rattle of hooves diminished. The horses were running straight back from the river and into the arid benches to the north.

He ran after them, seeing nothing but smelling the dust driven into the air by the hooves.

Some damned Indians had stolen the horses. He had watered them and then picketed them on some good bunch grass not ten yards from their camp. He found the place and found the butts of the picket ropes, which had been cut.

"What was all that, eh?" asked Nutmeg.

"Horses gone," Skye said.

"Stolen?"

"They didn't walk off by themselves."

"Long walk to Fort Vancouver," Nutmeg said.

"I'll get our horses back," Skye said. He had done it before and he would do it again. And maybe in ways that would shock the genteel professor.

thirteen

Skye plucked up the Hawken. The sooner he started after the thieves, the better.

"Who were they?" Nutmeg asked.

"Any damned one," Skye replied. "This is Shoshone country. But this river, it could be anyone. Who knows?"

Angrily he scanned the skies, seeing a quarter moon dodging silver-edged clouds. It wasn't the blackest of nights, but there wasn't enough moonlight to help him. It would be too gloomy to see hoofprints, moccasin prints, or much of anything else. He would have to track the thieves mostly by intuition and smell. Horses left an acrid odor and manure behind them.

He reckoned it was still three hours to dawn.

"I'll go with you," Nutmeg volunteered.

"Professor, this is war. Stealing horses is a way of fighting enemies. You'd better let me handle it."

"How can one man deal with a war party?"

"I'll never know until I see what I'm up against."

"If you can't recover the nags, you'll not get to Fort Vancouver in time."

"Not before that ship sails," Skye said.

He watched Victoria tug the pack and gear under the lip of the ledge behind their camp. She would stay and take care of

Nutmeg and guard their gear. She would know how to hide herself and Nutmeg if she had to.

She turned to Skye, saying nothing, and touched his hand. That was her goodbye and blessing. They had long since come to the point where they didn't need to say much to each other. He couldn't tell her when he would be back. The thieves were only a few minutes ahead, but on horse, and minutes could be an eternity.

"Professor, if Victoria asks you to do something, you do it. She'll try to keep you safe."

"Oh, I'll just be collecting samples."

Skye's response was sharp. "If she says you can, mate."

There was no answer. He hiked into the gloom, across arid benchland on the right bank of the Snake, directed more by intuition than sign. He would heed the old tracker's wisdom: if there was no sign to guide you, think about where your quarry is going and head that way. Distant in the moonlight was a vague notch. He would go there.

A mile out, he discovered the yellow mutt dragging along behind. A rage built in him and he hunted for rocks to throw, but he knew there was nothing he could do. The hound would simply follow just out of range of his arm. He knew he ought to be grateful: the damned dog had furtively awakened him, growling in his ear instead of barking, and that had given Skye the warning he should have heeded. But he couldn't bring himself to thank the miserable cur.

It would be tough without horses. He'd walked before and would walk again. But being put afoot by some damned savages in some damned wilderness, and being forced to abandon the gear needed to survive—that was hell.

He trudged quietly through the pillowed darkness while the pale moon swung lower in the sky, and vanished behind the drifting night-clouds now and then, plunging him into utter gloom. Still he persevered, fueled by his own fury.

After an hour he struck lava country and knew that unless he was careful, the knife-edged stone would slice his moccasins to bits. But he was hiking along a dry watercourse that had butchered its way through the black rock that tumbled upward on both sides of him, the jumbled volcanic debris spearing the black sky.

This was ambush country, and Skye began to sweat. One warrior with a bow and arrow could wipe out pursuit. He wondered whether he would die suddenly in this remote place, his body never to be found by his wife or anyone else.

But he abolished the thought from mind. He was frightened, yes, but he harnessed his fear to good purpose, studying the jumble of rock, his senses so whetted that he could almost peer around the next bend. He would not be a coward, dying a thousand times before his death.

The cur stayed ten yards ahead. Skye raged at the mutt. The yellow dog would find something, bark, and give Skye away. Once in a while the dog paused, sniffed, and slowly slinked forward. He wasn't a proper dog, slinking like some back-alley thug. He was a sneaking, rotten dog, ugly and scarred, with no manners. Skye knew he could probably kill the stalking animal with one good toss of his Bowie knife, but he didn't do that, either.

He was on the right trail; that's all he knew. The acrid smell that hung in that watercourse, and the occasional manure, told him that.

The eastern skies began to stitch threads of light, and Skye reckoned he had walked five miles. It would be a long hike home if he didn't recover his nags. He was sorry to see daylight, which dashed his hope of sneaking into the Indian camp, finding his ponies and sneaking out with them under the cover of darkness. He persevered, wanting a drink and a rest, but knowing that his quarry might be fleeing even faster than he was chasing.

The yellow mutt paused, sniffed, sprinted ahead, turned to watch Skye, and vanished from sight. Skye found him ahead, low on the ground, his tail slathering across clay, his nose pointed. This time the mutt didn't bound forward. Skye took that for a caution, and peered around a black rock, discovering a sort of grassy park of several acres where the lava flows had parted. He spotted the dull forms of perhaps twenty horses. His would be among them.

Smart dog.

At first he saw no one, but then, on closer study as the light quickened, he saw several bedrolls and two men sitting up, staring at nothing. Cautiously Skye examined the scene. The men were gathered around a vegetated hollow, probably with a spring supplying water. The dim bulks of the horses ghosted over the grass. He could not tell his from the others.

The mutt whined, but so quietly Skye knew the sound did not carry. Maybe that verminous creature had some sense after all. Skye hunted for an upstream exit. If this was a widening in a watercourse, there would be a gulch stretching toward the distant mountains. He did not see it at first, which worried him. Under siege, these warriors would flee upslope, pushing their ponies before them.

Then things were taken out of his hands. The mutt slithered into the park, heading toward the ponies. Skye wished he could shoot the damned thing. The critter was going to stir up the horses, which Skye didn't want at all. Yet he was powerless to stop what a small canine brain had set in motion. Skye did slip into the park, and drifted to one side of the gulch leading back to the Snake. If the mutt was going to stir trouble, maybe the milling horses would head for the river if he didn't block the way.

It occurred to him that maybe he could turn all this to his advantage, but he hated like the devil to admit it. The slithering dog caught the eye of a horse, which stared at it. The dog bounded a few paces and halted. The mutt was not headed into the horses, but past them, to the upper end of the park. Could it be that this dog was a natural herder, getting around behind the animals?

Skye marveled.

Then one of the savages shouted.

"El coyote! Cuidado!"

Men bounded up, grabbing their rifles. The horses stirred. These were not savages, but Mexicans, and they were about to shoot the yellow mutt.

"Alto ahi!" Skye bellowed. They turned and stared. Some swung their rifles toward him.

The trouble was, he didn't know more than a dozen Spanish words, and now he was in a jackpot. He ran straight toward them, his big Hawken leveled, and began yelling.

"I'm getting my horses back, and I'll kill the first man that moves," he roared, not knowing or caring whether they understood him. One lifted his rifle but found himself facing the huge bore of the Hawken, and lowered it.

"You stole my nags. Go ahead and try to kill me; one of you'll die and maybe more before you get me," he rumbled.

They spread, making themselves less a target. The yellow dog was cutting through the dancing horses now, nipping at the flanks of one of them, dodging the kicks.

"Drop your rifles and raise your hands," he roared, swinging toward one Mexican whose hands were busy.

They didn't.

Skye didn't stop moving, but circled closer to them, proddy and dangerous. He had caught them in a sleepy moment, but they were gathering their wits.

"I'm getting my horses, and whoever stops me is a goner," he roared.

Keep talking, keep them from doing anything.

One older man raised an arm. "Senor, I talk."

"Tell them I'm taking my ponies. If they try to stop me, they're dead."

He had, for the moment, the upper hand. He faced four Mexicans.

He risked a glance at the yellow mutt, which had cut out two of Skye's horses and started them south. But the rest milled. He marveled at the dog.

There was no need to shout any more and addressed the

one who knew a little English. "Go get my other one. If you do, no one gets hurt."

"That is a dog of many wonders, Mister Skye."

Skye turned sharply. "How do you know my name?"

The man shrugged. "Everyone knows the man in the black hat. Mister Skye is the greatest of names." He turned to the others. "Senor Skye," he said. "Senor Skye." Then back to Skye. "We did not know it was you, friend. Come sit with us and we will talk, eh? We are *hermanos*, brothers, from Taos, Nuevo Méjico, and we have come to make our fortune, eh? Gold, silver, beaver, horses, who knows? You do us honor with a visit."

"How do you know me?"

"In the winters, the Yankee trappers stay with us in Taos and you are spoken of."

Skye watched the yellow mutt cut the last of Skye's horses and start it south.

He lowered the Hawken.

fourteen

So they knew him. Skye glowed. His fame as a mountaineer had traveled even to Mexico. He had worked long and hard for the fur company, done well, and now he was known as a good man.

But then his glow vanished.

They were laughing, the bores of their big dragoon revolvers pointing at him, their eyes lit with glee.

"Ah, Senor Skye, it is so, you are a great hombre. And now we will honor you. Ah, it is pleasure to honor so great an hombre. In all the world, under heaven above, there is not so great a man as *Meester* Skye. This we hear from Christopher Carson and other Yanqui *hombres grandes* who live among us."

Skye debated swinging his Hawken upward and shooting the man. But not for long. Three big pistols and a venerable fowling piece would make a swift end of him. His skin crawled. Rarely had he looked into the black muzzle of a loaded firearm, and the sight of four such bores pointing at his chest catapulted his pulse and squeezed his throat.

"You will do us the honor of dropping your Hawken, very very carefully, to the groun', si?"

Skye did as he was told. At least they weren't shooting at him. He trembled so much he could not control the spasms in his hands.

"Now, the powder horn, si?"

Skye lifted the horn and deposited it on the grass. It was a beauty, with an ornate box that held his caps.

"Ah, muchas gracias, Senor Skye. This is to pay for your horses. You have bought them back from us, did you know that? A fair trade. One fine rifle for tres caballos. Our papa, he says, there is wealth everywhere. Go get the riches and bring them to me. Make us *ricos grandes*. So, my brothers, we go get the riches. He is right. They are everywhere. Now we will be the envy of Taos, si?"

"You letting me go?"

"It is an honor to meet the mountaineer. Shall we kill you? Only if you are foolish, amigo. Go. You have your horses, we have a fine Hawken, made in St. Louis, the rifle that puts a ball right in the center. Ah, half of Nuevo Méjico would sell their souls to el Diablo for that rifle."

Skye scarcely dared to turn his back, knowing these brigands might have one final surprise for him. But it mattered little whether they shot him from front or rear, so he retreated.

They were silent.

He rounded the bend and smelled the dust raised by his horses.

Shame swept over him. He had succumbed to his own vanity. All they had to do was flatter him, crudely and grossly, and he had lowered his guard. Sugared words. He had heard few of those in his life; not once in the navy had anyone praised him. And his father had not been one to commend him. Only among the Yank trappers had he heard a word about his worth.

He vowed that, if he lived, he would never be tricked again, and the flattery of others would never be of consequence to him for as long as he survived. Rarely did anyone have a second chance in the famous college of the Rocky Mountains, as his trapper friends called it. He counted this as a lesson learned, and a lesson he would never forget.

He rounded a bend in the black rock and breathed easier. They had had their fun, humiliated a gringo, and let him go. But he was unarmed and facing hundreds of miles of travel.

He walked quietly, knowing the horses were ahead, herded by the yellow cur. He owed that mutt his loyalty. The mutt was more dog than he had supposed.

He focused on the good things. He had the horses. They could ride and pack. Victoria was a gifted hunter, and she had a dozen deadly arrows in her quiver. They would be traveling among friendly tribes and could barter for food.

The August heat rose, and he was parched, but there would be no water anywhere on that long dry gulch. But by the time the sun reached its zenith he would be back in camp, explaining to Victoria his humiliation. He resolved not to hide it. There had never been anything hidden between them, including his defeats.

He walked another mile, abraded by the reproach of his soul, and then came upon the horses, which stood somnolently while the panting dog lay in the dry gulch. The mutt did not rise at his approach. He wondered if he could catch a horse and ride it barebacked. The horses were haltered, but he had nothing with which to make some reins. He could not control his saddler, but it had no place to go but forward, hemmed on both sides by jagged volcanic rock.

He owed the dog something.

"You're better than I allowed," he said. "Like Victoria says, you're looking after me."

The dog stared but made no move toward him. And he feared he'd be bitten hard if he tried to pet the dog. It lay there, sinister, yellow, scarred, vicious, slackjawed, and stupid, except that it wasn't stupid. It had its own approach to life, its ways, and they had kept it alive.

He wondered if his big spotted horse would let him get on, and eased slowly toward it, watching the beasts sidle away from him. But he talked quietly, finally grabbed the halter and tugged the horse toward some rock that would help him mount. The horse obliged him.

It stood quietly while he clambered up the jagged rock and then slid a leg over its hot back. Moments later he was seated, nervous because he had little control. But the yellow dog was on his feet again.

Skye tapped his moccasin heels into the side of the horse, and it walked forward. The dog didn't need to herd the others; they followed naturally.

And so he rode back to camp, relieved not to walk, feeling better because he had gotten his horses.

As he approached the sunken river, which slashed this land into north and south, he found Victoria and Professor Nutmeg nestled under an overhanging slab of rock back from the well-used trail along the north bank. She watched him come in, her gaze surveying the horses and then watching the yellow hound.

Skye slid off, landing awkwardly, while Victoria bridled the horses.

Nutmeg handed him a water flask, and Skye drank greedily.

"They took my rifle," he said.

"Who?" Victoria asked.

"Mexicans from Taos."

"But you got the horses."

"The dog did."

Her eyes lit. "It is as I said."

"You'll have to make meat."

"The dog will feed us."

"I've got to tell you something. I let the Mexicans trick me, Victoria. They told me I was a great man and invited me to sit and visit."

She eyed him solemnly. "I will not condemn you. You are a great one among the trappers. You have not heard this with your own ears. But it is said of you everywhere. The Absaroka know it. My people respect you. The white men I talk to, they know it. So now the stories about you have flown to Taos, in Mexico. That is not bad. It is good. I am proud to be your woman."

He peered at her, amazed.

She busied herself with the horses again. "We are three now. You, me, and the dog."

He peered at the beast, which lay panting again.

"Let's go down to the river, fella," he said.

This time the dog followed him as he descended a steep and treacherous path that took him to the swift-flowing Snake. The mutt lapped the water and then waded into the current. Skye knelt, drank again, sloshed water over his stubbled face, and drank once more.

The dog swam to the bank, clambered up the muck slope, and shook himself.

A bond had been forged. Skye settled himself quietly beside the river and the dog wiggled toward him in short bursts, ever ready to bolt. Skye dared not reach out and kept his big, blunt-fingered hands to himself.

"I owe you," Skye said.

This earned him the first, tentative switch of the dog's scruffy tail.

The dog wiggled closer and Skye knew that this was a long delayed but important moment in the lives of each of them. He eased his hand outward, palm up. The dog squirmed closer and sniffed it. Then, tentatively, the dog licked Skye's hand. The tongue rasped over his flesh and Skye made himself hold still.

"I guess I have a dog in my family," he said.

The dog edged closer and sniffed Skye's moccasins, buck-skins, back, and shirt. Skye glanced behind him and discovered Victoria watching from the bank high above.

Then her face vanished. She was leaving this rapprochement to Skye and the dog.

Skye studied the mutt. Its ears had been chewed on. Its

face bore scars, so many they formed almost a hatchwork of ridged flesh. One eyelid drooped. There were patches of hair missing, bare gray hide poking through its abused torso.

He scarcely dared move his hand for fear the ugly thing would bite it off. But tentatively he did, slowly, letting the dog see every move in advance. Once the dog went rigid and Skye retreated, but after a moment Skye's hand was running down the dog's neck and over his back.

The cur growled and Skye retreated. That was enough for one day. His hand was still intact.

They clambered up the steep slope together.

"What you gonna name the damned dog?" Victoria asked.

"What do you think?"

"I don't know. He's your dog. You name him." She sounded testy.

"You've domesticated the dog?" Nutmeg asked. "Ah, he and Dolly are a match. You need a name for him."

"I don't have a name," Skye said, irked. "He's just a bloody ugly dog."

"He will tell you his name," Victoria said. "He is a spirit-dog, and his name is secret. But you will get it in a dream. Or maybe a vision quest."

Skye grunted. He didn't put much stock in all that.

"Let's move. We've an appointment at Vancouver," he said.

fifteen

They toiled through blistering August heat, sometimes making little visible progress. The Snake River sulked in a black canyon on their left day after day; the hazy benches and mountains brooding on their right never changed. It seemed to Professor Nutmeg that they were on a treadmill, doing each day's progress over again.

He would have been more assiduous in his botanical collecting, but sheer hunger had enervated him, and so he roamed less far from the trail, conserving his energy. Finding places where they could descend to the river and water their horses became a problem. Few streams entered from the north.

But the overarching worry was hunger. They had only Victoria's bow and arrows, but not even Skye's rifle would have helped much in this arid land. They saw no large animals; only an occasional hare. The dogs stalked gophers and various other small beasts, hunting at night. But they starved, too.

Skye had fallen into silence, his eyes peering from slits in his swollen face, his gaze ceaselessly raking the world for something to eat: antelope, deer, sheep, even a stray horse. But neither he nor Victoria, who rode off now and then to try her luck away from the trail, succeeded. Even the fowl had deserted this stretch of the gloomy river.

The parched corn vanished and then the pemmican and the jerky. They devoured the small hoard of sugar and molasses the Skyes had kept in their gear. They boiled the last of the tea. Victoria showed Nutmeg which berries were edible and after that the professor haunted the river bottoms, hunting for the occasional bitter chokecherry or wild grape. He found little in that arid land, and the hole in his belly was not filled.

Only the horses flourished. Bunchgrass, unending, fed them, along with lush green shoots in the river bottom. Nutmeg, who was forced to walk for the want of another horse, trudged wearily onward, thinning down each day and aching for any sort of food. He fantasized food, dreamed of sausage and milk and cheese and butter and fresh bread.

Then the river seemed to rise in the canyon, or rather the land and the river reached much the same elevation once again, and the malevolent Snake rolled by, offering them nothing but wetness for their parched bodies and grass for their beasts. Somehow the dogs did better than the humans, but Nutmeg didn't know how they survived. Once he found them carrying chunks of an ancient carcass, which they chewed upon whenever the party rested.

Dolly roved so much he feared he would lose his precious samples and drawings that she bore in a waterproof harness on her skinny back. He didn't have much to add to his collection these days, and regretted that he lacked the strength to roam.

He began to wonder whether he would survive. Then one day Skye stepped down from his mount.

"You're done in, mate. You and I'll share. Victoria needs a fast horse to chase game, but we'll make do. You ever ridden before?"

"Very little."

Gratefully, Nutmeg clambered into the saddle.

"I'll take the reins and lead for a while. You just relax and if you see a specimen, we'll stop and get it. Who knows, maybe it'll be something to eat."

Those were gentle words and arrived unaccustomed.

And so the professor found himself periodically sitting on Skye's horse, conserving his energy. From that high vantage point he saw occasional flora he would have missed, and Skye always obliged him while he plucked up something or other and made some notes and a swift sketch.

Nutmeg had come to admire Skye. The man never complained, never relaxed his vigilance, looked constantly for hiding places now that they were virtually defenseless, and most importantly, tried to accommodate the professor's every botanical need. The more Nutmeg talked to Skye, the more he discovered an emerald waiting for a good cutting and polishing. This was no ordinary wilderness ruffian but a man who might yet serve the Crown and bring glory to himself and to his native England.

Nothing more had been said about Nutmeg's proposal, but Nutmeg knew that Skye was weighing it as an option if the Hudson's Bay arrangement fell through. Nutmeg began to see his guide as a junior partner, a man who, with a few books and some field observation, might make a first-rate naturalist.

Whenever the well-worn trail departed from the river, Victoria patrolled close to the water where game might be. But she found nothing. She tried her luck on a hare, but it fled too fast for her arrows, and she made no meat that day. That bad day she lost two arrows.

They were in serious trouble and weakening daily. Were it not for the strong horses they might have no hope at all.

Then one morning they discovered Victoria sitting her horse dead ahead, waiting for them. When they reached her she pointed.

A mile or so ahead they saw the faintest plume of smoke. It apparently rose from the south bank but they could not say for sure. Maybe succor, maybe trouble.

"I will go look," she said. "You come a little way and wait."

She rode ahead, gaining ground on them while they

walked slowly behind. Nutmeg was on foot, although he no longer had the strength to walk much at all. Skye had let him put his backpack on the packhorse, perched on a mound of equipment, but he preferred that the professor hike if at all possible.

Skye settled them in thick reeds close to the river and waited.

"Sorry, mate. I'm unarmed and all we can do is hide," he said. "That's the first rule anyway. Never confront if you can hide."

Dolly sat down beside him, panting and gaunt. Skye's yellow cur settled a yard from Skye and stared. The cur had an odd quality about him: he rarely took his gaze away from Skye, but seemed to focus on the man constantly. So far, no one had named him, and Skye simply called him the mutt.

Victoria materialized from the riverbank.

"It is a fishing village," she said. "Across the river. A stream comes in there from the south. They saw me and some are coming now. We go meet them, yes?"

There would be food if all went well.

Skye brightened visibly. He mounted slowly, while the professor collected his walking stick. They started down the trail once again. Before them, half a mile off, a party of the Shoshones awaited them. Water dripped from their ponies, and that suggested a ford, probably just upstream from the village and the confluence.

A dozen honey-fleshed men on horseback watched them. They were nearly naked, wearing only breechclouts. But they bristled with bows and arrows, lances, war clubs, hatchets, and one of them had a musket and powder horn.

Skye lifted his hand and they lifted theirs. He rode right up to them, and then his fingers began to work. Nutmeg wondered how a few signs could convey much, but apparently they did. One of the Shoshones addressed Victoria, and she responded in her own tongue. Skye dismounted, went back to his packhorse, dug out a twist of tobacco and some jingle bells, and handed the twist to the headman and a jingle bell to each of the others. They smiled and escorted the Skyes and Nutmeg to the village. They crossed a shallow ford at a wide point, and then splashed across the small tributary, and walked in. One of the Indians gave Nutmeg a lift over both fords and deposited him on the far banks where a great crowd of silent Shoshones had congregated. The camp was located in a ravine where a river debouched into the Snake.

"I told 'em we're hungry and would trade some good things. They have plenty of salmon. Told 'em we're all going to Fort Vancouver. Told 'em you're a great wise man among the whites and a healer with herbs. They'll want to see your samples. Probably bring you some."

"But Mister Skye, I'm not a healer."

"It's the closest thing I could think of to say about you, mate."

"They'll want me to heal them!"

"No, you tell 'em you want to learn their secrets."

Nutmeg thought Skye had pushed truth beyond its limits but remained silent about that. What would these people know of academics and naturalists and science?

Their escorts led them through a large village, mostly consisting of buffalohide lodges, but there were other lodges of thatched reeds as well. These were people of medium build and height, many of the women dressed in traders' cloth.

"I'd guess these are the Malad River Snakes—one of two bands south of the Snake River," Skye said. "And I'd guess this is the Bruneau, up from the south. It cuts through some canyons to get here."

For once Nutmeg didn't much care.

"I need food," he muttered.

"We'll get it. Some ceremony first. They'll welcome us and after that I'll dicker."

The Snakes weren't strong on ceremony. A headman spoke to the assembled villagers. At one point their gazes all rested on Nutmeg, and he wondered what was being said about them.

Victoria responded in her Absaroka tongue, which was translated to the Snake tongue.

"Crows and Snakes are mostly old friends," Skye explained. "Some Crow women live here. It's hard to describe Snakes. They're always shifting around, switching bands. Some are like Plains Indians, living on buffalo, some not. These are mostly fishing people."

The sight of thousands of salmon drying on makeshift racks, and the smell of salmon stew in dozens of kettles dizzied the professor.

"Food, Mister Skye, before I faint."

"They'll feed us in their own good time, mate. I told 'em you're looking for herbs that heal, and I imagine you'll be hearing from plenty of 'em."

"Food, Mister Skye."

Dolly and the yellow cur stole fish from the racks, but the Snakes just laughed.

"You tell them what a fine people they are and how you want to learn from them," Skye said.

Nutmeg did, while Victoria and others transformed his thoughts into things the Snakes would understand.

Then the guests were led to a salmon feast and Nutmeg abandoned spiritual pleasures for the sensual.

sixteen

Skye, Victoria, and Professor Nutmeg tarried for two days in the Snake village. The Skyes had endured starving times in the mountains during the terrible winters, but Nutmeg hadn't, and now he could scarcely stop wolfing any food at hand.

Their hosts fed them bountifully, and with each meal Skye reciprocated with gifts from his trading supplies, mercifully plentiful in the wake of the rendezvous. He had knives, awls, fire steels and flints, vermilion and foofaraw for the women. With each exchange, the potlatch grew more lavish: Skye's larder swelled to include pine nuts traded from the Paiutes to the south, a fish-type pemmican, mounds of sun-dried salmon shredded and sealed in gut; yucca fruit, wild onions, jerky from the meat of mountain sheep, antelope fat rendered and packed in gut, and all sorts of desiccated roots and berries, the half of which he didn't know, all of which lifted Victoria's spirits.

Skye loaded these gustatory treasures into his panniers knowing how fast they would vanish. His burdens had expanded to include two mutts and a pilgrim, five mouths in all. He ached for a beaver trap, just one, knowing that it could be used to catch all sorts of cur cuisine and stewpot meat while he slept, but he could not talk any of the Snake men out of theirs. So he faced six hundred miles of travel with mouths to feed and no way, save for Victoria's arrows, to make meat.

But Skye was not the cynosure of the village. From the time Professor Nutmeg greeted the day by scraping away his blond beard to the time he rolled into his stained blankets, the Snakes crowded about him as if he had descended from Valhalla. They came to behold his leaf collection and his sketches, and he patiently turned one page after another, showing them well-wrought drawings of plants they instantly recognized. He showed them his samples, carefully pressed between absorbent pages, and they marveled at this amazing and novel sight.

Then undreamed-of fortune fell to him. Shyly at first, the Snake women and children presented various species to him. Many were items he could but little use, having been torn from the earth in pieces and without any caring about their location or the neighboring species. But then a matron presented him with a whole yucca that was new to him, and showed him how they made soap from its roots. With Victoria's help he managed to learn where it grew. He sketched it while the Snakes watched diligently, seeing the graphite pencil miraculously reproduce the yucca on paper. Then he measured the plant, took notes, and pressed one of its spiky leaves between his papers to preserve it, but with little success.

Whatever he lacked by way of knowledge of the Snakes, he made up for with innate courtesy and good cheer, so that much of the daily life of the village slowed and people gathered about him.

That suited Skye fine. It was time for a rest. The horses cropped good grass with the Snake herd. The dogs gorged themselves and snoozed. The yellow cur stole fish, ate until bloat set in, and then rolled onto his back, four paws aimed toward the four winds of heaven. But whenever the cur awakened, it followed Skye as if it were heaven-sent to guard him, his new benefactor.

Skye scarcely knew what to make of that. Dogs were new

to him. His London family had none. The Royal Navy had
none that he knew of, though an occasional admiral might
own one. And his entire experience with dogs was confined to
those wretches that lived off the bands of Plains tribes, gorging offal during hunting times and starving the rest.

There were fat dogs running with the Snakes and maybe
some of them ended up in the cooking kettles, though he
wasn't sure of it. Some tribes were dog-eaters; many weren't,
and these despised the ones that did break the neck of a puppy
now and then and drop it into the stew.

But Skye knew time was flying and he had to hurry west
for his appointment with destiny.

"Professor," he said after a day of feasting and trading and
gift-giving, "you know, this is paradise for you and Dolly.
Wyeth should be along in a week or two, and you could rest
here, fatten up, collect new species, entertain these people, and
then rejoin Wyeth's party."

"But, Skye, don't you want me to accompany you?" Nutmeg looked dismayed.

"Of course I do. But I'm always thinking ahead. We have
food for a couple of weeks, but we're still six weeks from Fort
Vancouver and bloody likely to starve again. With Wyeth you
wouldn't have to worry about your meals or Dolly's. And I
would have fewer mouths to feed. This has nothing to do with
you personally. It's simply a matter of survival. If you choose
to stay, I'll give you a few trading items to bargain for food."

"I see," he said. He looked crestfallen and Skye felt as if he
were the spoiler of good times. "But what if Wyeth doesn't
make it?"

"These are friendly people. You could make a temporary
home with them."

Nutmeg sighed. "This is the end, eh? You're rejecting me?"

"Mate, I've got business to attend."

"Very well, then."

Nutmeg turned desolately to his papers, and Skye felt bad.
But the wilderness was a hard master and it wasn't as if Skye

were abandoning the man to his fate. The village was fat. And Wyeth would be along in a week or two.

That soft August evening, a delegation of the Snakes came to Skye, along with Victoria.

"They gonna talk," she said. "This is Pokotel, Yan Maow . . . that's Big Nose, Tisidimit, and Taihi. These are all headmen, but there ain't no big chiefs among these people. They say they gonna go to Fort Walla Walla, that's some Hudson's Bay fort long way away, over the mountains even, and trade. We go with them."

Skye was surprised. "Escort us?"

"Yeah, go on big trip, see the world, go visit friends, all that."

Skye couldn't quite imagine why, but Victoria clarified that at once. "Professor Nutmeg. They think him big medicine. They gonna go with him, show him new plants he never seen. They gonna teach him Snake mysteries, tell him Snake stories, and maybe he make pictures for them."

A trip to Fort Walla Walla, at the confluence of the Walla Walla River and the Columbia. Skye remembered the place bitterly. He had barely escaped with his life from there, long ago, when he had struggled into the interior after escaping the Royal Navy.

He had learned, since, that he had gone out of his way that first trip. The Umatilla River would have taken him eastward faster. But what was a witless limey to know?

The Snake leaders were waiting for a reply, gathered about him. They were a formidable bunch, stocky, rawboned, long-haired, and well-armed.

"What do you think, Victoria?" he asked.

"Dammit, Skye, you are slower than a turtle."

"I just told Nutmeg I'd rather he wait here for Wyeth."

She squinted at him, reading his face. They were all reading his face. Even the yellow mutt was staring up at him. He lifted his top hat and ran weathered fingers through his matted hair.

"I guess I can back up. I know when I'm whipped. But they got to do something for me."

Victoria turned solemn. "Skye, dammit."

"They got to name this yellow mutt."

Victoria cackled and began a monologue at once in her Absaroka tongue, which Pokotel slowly translated. Then they were all grinning.

"Tisidimit says, tonight they name the spirit-dog. Big meeting, big medicine."

They left it to Skye to find the professor. The man was, as usual, surrounded by Snakes, this time mostly shy children who peered at his drawings and squealed happily. They all had wilted leaves and stems to offer this strange white man, and he took each one, examined it, and usually flipped to a sketch of the plant.

"Professor, you can come with us if you want."

"No, Mister Skye, I've learned to take life as it comes and I'll be quite content among these delightful people."

Skye grinned. "A big party's going to escort us to the Columbia just for a lark. It's in your honor, you see. They think you're some."

"Some? Some what?"

"Something special. That's Yank trapper talk. You're some, all right, mate."

"They barbarize the mother tongue, eh?"

"Well, so do the tars in the Royal Navy."

Nutmeg relaxed. "I'll be ready, Mister Skye. I take it that this changes your plans with respect to me?"

"Most likely. That's a mighty bunch of warriors and hunters, and they'll keep us from starving. We're having a little ceremony tonight at dusk. Whole band's saying goodbye and doing a little favor for me."

"A favor?"

"I told them they could escort us if they bestow a name on this yellow mutt of mine. I've been half crazy trying to think of a name. Nothing works. He's a sneaky, snaky dog creeping around, so I won't call him King or Duke or Prince. He's ugly as the devil, so I can't call him Marmaduke. I was thinking of calling him Nutmeg, but you'd be insulted."

"I'd be honored, Mister Skye."

"I suppose it beats naming half a dozen reeds and grasses after yourself in Latin. No, Professor, I won't name this beast. Tonight the Snakes'll do it."

seventeen

The Snakes escorted Skye to an elder, one Tixitl. Skye beheld an ancient man with a piercing stare and seamed countenance. He seemed fragile and half out of his body and into some other world.

He handed the old man a plug of tobacco.

"Grandfather, I have come to ask you to name my dog."

They translated this for the old shaman, who nodded. He spoke briefly to one of the Snake headmen.

"Tixitl wants to see the dog, Mister Skye."

"I don't know where he is."

The old man seemed to understand even without the translating. Then he spoke again.

Victoria translated. "He says you have a dog that knows no laws. He will ask the winds for a name and tonight at dusk he will speak."

"Thank the grandfather for me." Skye said.

That evening they feasted again on a stew made of the flesh of the salmon, with many roots and nuts and stalks in it. He and Victoria packed their kit and prepared for an early departure at dawn. Nutmeg strapped his little leather harness over Dolly, and slid his notes and samples into a waterproof oilcloth satchel.

At the appointed time, Skye ventured to the reed hut of

the shaman and discovered most of the Snake village waiting raptly for him to appear. Even fragile grandmothers and new-borns had been carried to the place, and laid gently down upon soft robes. The yellow cur had vanished, which annoyed Skye. The miserable mutt refused to show up for his own christening.

The Snakes waited eagerly. Skye realized a naming was an important event for them. A name established many things: kinship, natures, expectations, failings, dangers, virtues. So it was with all the tribes Skye knew of. It had overtones of reli-gion, though the Shoshones cared less about such things than most tribes.

The shaman took his time inside that dark hut, and the crowd waited patiently, knowing that the Mysteries could not be hurried, and that revealed knowledge would come in its own time and season. Maybe he was waiting for portents: comets, falling stars, a thunderclap in a cloudless heaven, the howl of a dragon.

Skye settled on the clay before the silent hovel, and then moved a few feet when he found his legs teeming with black ants. The first stars poked through as the light narrowed to a band of blue in the northwest. And still Tixitl tarried. Skye grew restless. He had the white man's itch for swift decisions in him, but Victoria had sunk into age-old watchfulness.

The crowd had fallen into a holy vigil.

Maybe they were waiting for the yellow cur to walk on stage, but it lingered beyond the camp, making its own way, perhaps an ally in life's adventures but no friend of any living thing.

At last the old man emerged from his hut, stood, stretched, and surveyed the great assemblage. Skye thought that the entire village had come for this event and now the Snakes stood in a great arc, the men in the first ranks, the women and children behind them.

A signal from Tixitl drew the translators and Skye to him.

"I have asked the winds for the name. I have asked the

heavens, and the creatures under the earth. I have asked the creatures in the water, and the four-foots that walk. I have asked the before-people, and my own spirit-counselor, whose name is a mystery."

Skye waited patiently, wishing his yellow dog would show up. But the dog stayed well hidden.

"They have given me no name for this dog," Tixitl said. "The heavens give no name. And the winds give no name. And all the spirits give me no name. This dog must not be named. Hairy man, do not give this dog a name. As long as he has no name, his power will watch over you. If you name this dog, you will break him in two, like a twig snapping. Therefore he is No Name. The spirits have spoken to me, and I have spoken to you."

With that, the old man stood silent, letting these words sink into the assemblage, while the translators droned.

"Thank you, grandfather," said Skye, brushing off ants.

He had a nameless dog who would not answer to his call, and yet watched over Skye.

If the Snakes were disappointed they did not show it. Indeed, he walked through faces wreathed in smiles. Forbidding a name was as good as a naming, and maybe all the more medicine because it was so mysterious.

Skye did not see the yellow dog that night and supposed that the cur had found a home among the village mutts and would stay on. At dawn Skye studied the quiet village, still searching for the dog, and missing it badly. His feeling surprised him. But he would be better off without the dog. He would probably have to leave it at Fort Vancouver anyway if he shipped to England. He had no idea whether a wild dog would be welcome on a merchant ship, but he doubted it. So it all was a blessing. He had surrendered a dog and gained a thousand ants in his britches.

Nutmeg was dressed and ready, with his knapsack over his back and fat Dolly beside him, carrying her small pack.

Skye yawned, pulled on his thick-soled moccasins, and hiked out to the horse herd under the watchful eyes of the boys who guarded it. His horses were skittish, liking the easy living and the gossipy society of the Snake brethren. He tried to catch the packhorse, but it sidled away from him. He did better with Victoria's little spotted horse, sliding a hackamore over its nose and leading it back to camp.

It took him until sunrise to catch his own wily horse, which dodged through the herd, stirring trouble. It angered him. He vowed he would spend more time with his willful horses and work with them until they were absolutely reliable. When he finally returned with his nags, the travelers were all awaiting him. The escort party of eleven warriors all had their mounts in hand, ready to go. Victoria was ready; the pack-horse stood ready.

Skye had had no breakfast but decided to forgo it. He had delayed his own departure.

"All right," he said.

Most of the village was up, and people silently watched the party leave camp, riding beside the broad, purling Snake, carrying its burden of mountain snows to the far Pacific. It was a silent departure. Skye hunted for the no-name yellow cur and saw no canine other than Dolly, and was relieved that the mutt had made his home with this band where it could live to fat old age gorging on salmon and buffalo and the offal of a dozen other animals.

This had been a good stop. In all of his years as a moun-taineer, he had found hospitality and succor among friendly tribes.

He turned to the professor, waiting beside Skye's pony. "You rested, Mr. Nutmeg?"

"Entirely, and ready for the next lap. And chock-full of ideas. I can put the Indians to work, Mister Skye! Those people brought me half a dozen items that were new to me; some simple variations, but two were wax-leaf desert shrubs I'd never seen. I hadn't realized I can trade manufactured goods for these things. My work would go twice as fast. I wish I'd thought to stock up at the rendezvous."

Skye nodded. Professor Nutmeg's mind ran one direction.

Their Snake escort set a slow pace, pausing frequently to observe the wonders of their world: the diving eagle, the geese bobbing in estuaries, the track of a mountain lion, the flight of crows, and the ripples in the river that spoke to them of things Skye would never fathom.

The pace at least was more comfortable for Nutmeg, who had time to meander, forgetful of safety and direction as his quest for knowledge took him from plant to plant. But Pokotel and Tisidimit kept an eye on him, sometimes walking their spotted mounts, the famous dappled palouses of the Nez Perce, as outriders well back from the river.

Victoria had slipped into rare melancholia, her dark visions plain upon her sharp face.

"You're gonna find some Englishwoman when we get there, and then I'm no good for you anymore," she said, after reining her pony beside his. "She gonna be like you, big and white, and blue-eyes, and she gonna talk your tongue, not like old Victoria. I don't say things good. I listen to Nutmeg, him big wise man among you, and I know I talk no good, and he thinks you could be big wise man of the English, and then you send me back to the Kicked-in-the-Bellies and you take a young, pretty white woman for wife and make many children. I no damn good at making a baby, so you get none from me. You say so and I will turn around and go back to my people."

He had never heard her talk like that. Always, she had been adventuresome, ready for whatever life brought, fierce and determined. But now he heard despair in her voice.

Skye protested but could not stop this outpouring of worry. There were a few grains of truth in it. He could not himself say how he would feel about her in England. Maybe the woman he loved so much in this great North American wilderness would strike him as alien in crowded London, and maybe he would regret trying to prolong the union.

Skye had the sense that no matter how much he might vow to stick with her, giant forces, such as his cultural memories, probable condescension in London, future trouble within Hudson's Bay Company, might conspire to tear his sweet, fragile mountain marriage to bits.

He was a strong man, and yet he felt helpless.

He reached over to touch her arm. She saw his big blunt fingers on the sleeve of her tradecloth blouse, and he saw a wetness in her brown eyes.

eighteen

The quickening light stirred Skye out of a dream-tormented sleep. He had won no rest that night. He pulled aside his robes and beheld the no-name dog, lying three feet away, gazing intently at him.

He did not welcome the dog. He marveled that the dog would leave the paradise of the Snake village and follow him to this place, two days distant. He would have to betray the dog at Fort Vancouver, have McLoughlin lock up the mutt when Skye boarded that ship . . . if indeed that was to be his fate.

He didn't want any kin just then. Not Victoria, who would suffer in England, not the dog. Not his friends in the mountains. If he stepped aboard that bark, he would betray them all, exchange his mountain family for his English one.

Last night he had decided, while tossing in his blankets, that Victoria was right: he had to choose. He could have England and his family . . . or her. But not both. There lay an ocean and a continent between them, and not just sea and land, but an ocean that divided white people, English people, from these tribes. As usual, she saw the things he didn't see, the things he wallpapered over and tried not to see. She hadn't seen England, but she knew she would wither there and pine for her free, sunlit prairies, shining mountains, and her people, who lived without fences and hedgerows, who went where they pleased and did whatever came to them.

For her, even a one-year visit would be an eternity that would end in a grave in some dank English burial field outside the yard of any church, for they would not bury her in sacred ground. She had vision; he didn't. And he could see no way out. He could abandon England and citizenship and his father and sisters, and keep her. And the no-name dog.

With daylight he banished the dreads that had bored through his soul all night, and now, in dawn's light, things weren't so bad. She could wait for him. He'd be gone perhaps a year and a half—if all went well. If the bark he sailed on didn't founder at sea, if he didn't sicken and die in London, if the Crown truly restored his name, if Hudson's Bay kept its word, if the returning bark to York Factory in Canada didn't founder, if he didn't sicken and die canoeing and portaging from Hudson's Bay over half a continent to Fort Vancouver.

Would Victoria and the no-name dog wait?

He and the dog were the only ones in camp who were awake.

He arose, stretched, and found the mutt pressing its muzzle against his leg, an act of proprietary interest if not ownership. Gingerly he lowered his big hand and stroked the dog's head. The dog let him.

He didn't know what in bloody hell he would do with the dog, and that made him irritable.

They progressed along the Snake River, and he marveled at the fishing skills of his comrades. They could spear a salmon even though the water tricked the eye into thinking the fish was not where it really was. They had small throw-nets that settled over the fat fish.

He also wondered about their utter lack of caution. They traveled without vedettes, scarcely paying attention to danger. If they had done this on the plains, they would be in mortal danger. But it was as if they had no enemies, and perhaps they didn't, at least when they were getting along with the Nez Perce, which they usually did.

They sang and sometimes danced to the thump of a small drum in the evenings, simply as a way to make the evenings pass. He gradually acquired some grasp of their ways. They had little public religion, other than a belief in a spirit-guardian from the animal world. That was a private matter: some of the Snakes had medicine, others never even sought spirit helpers and counselors. Skye thought they were not as handsome as some tribes, such as the Lakota, but he admired their honeyed flesh and cleanness of limb.

When he sought to find out why they had come along on this journey, Victoria's response was simply that they wanted to; it was adventure, and they loved adventure. They loved to honor the great white wise man who was making pictures of all plants on earth. They were celebrating such a wonder, and also honoring Skye, the greatest of the white fur men, and his fine Absaroka woman.

And that was all the reason they needed.

They came one evening to a point near a great bend of the Snake, and there the headman, Tisidimit, conveyed to Skye, by sign, that here they would leave the river and head westward along various valleys, and finally over the Blue Mountains beyond the horizon.

Now they would hunt rather than fish. This was a land of fine hares, and the Snake people treasured the pelts of rabbits almost as much as the hides of buffalo.

So they turned away from the Snake River and started overland through an arid land that gradually greened as it rose. Skye saw at once that this land would yield its wild grapes and berries, its small game, rich and verdant grasses for the horses, springs and creeks, firewood aplenty, yews and willows and cottonwoods for shade. But now, as they pierced into a wetter country, the mosquitos tormented them all, and Skye began dreading the nights when no robe or smudge fire would protect his vulnerable flesh from a thousand blood-sucking insects.

The yellow dog didn't mind. The horses did, and their tails lashed at the vicious clouds of insects. Victoria's face puffed up with the bites she bore stoically, but they all endured, uncomplaining. For some reason the mosquitos barely bothered the Snakes, and Skye wondered what mysterious potions they used upon themselves.

They made good progress. The Snakes did all the hunting and rarely did they make camp without fresh meat. The yellow dog ate and fattened and studied Skye with opaque eyes that hid the mystery of its origins. When was this ugly thing born, and what had it suffered to be so scarred, and how did it learn to hunt and fight and survive? And always, Skye came back to the great question: why had this miserable beast attached itself to him?

Victoria knew the answer, and Skye stopped laughing at her notions.

He did not know where the Snakes were taking him: only that they would go as far as they wanted, and then turn back, having made a lark of a summer's moon. Maybe they would take the dog with them. The test would soon come at Fort Vancouver, and then Victoria would see whether the no-name mutt was Skye's spirit-dog, or just a beast looking for a handout.

They ascended the Blue mountains, traveling through open pine forest dotted with parks, rather more arid above than in the foothill country. Nutmeg found little to interest him; the vegetation was uniform, limited, and dull. He and Dolly roved wide from the plain and well-worn trail, and had nothing to report except an encounter with a black bear that was berrying under a bluff.

"What are your plans now, Professor?" Skye asked one evening.

"Why, wait for Nat Wyeth, I suppose. When his party arrives at Vancouver, I'll go to the coast with them and board their bark, the *Sultana*, at the mouth of the Columbia, and head back to Boston via Cape Horn. If all goes well, I'll land only a few miles from Harvard Yard. I'm sure there'd be passage for you, Mister Skye, if you wish it."

"I'll see what Dr. McLoughlin has in mind, mate. This whole business is bloody mysterious."

"Why doesn't HBC just make you an offer straight out?"

"Because they know I'd never accept. They're tied to the Crown, administer Crown lands, operate the criminal justice system in their territory, and unless I'm cleared and restored to my rights as an Englishman, they'll never put me officially on their rolls."

They descended into a rich foothill country, and then a grassy plain. This was the Columbia basin, and Skye felt a change. The last of the Rockies were behind him, and this land looked westward to the coastal ranges and the great Pacific. Suddenly he felt wary. The Rockies had been his home for six years. The Yanks had been his friends and offered him the means to survive. Now, suddenly, this country, brooding in the sun, seemed alien, and his future loomed as a large question mark. The West was always the future; the East the past.

They reached a large tributary of the Columbia, whose name Skye did not know, and there the Snakes went their own way. They wished to go up to Fort Walla Walla, the Hudson's Bay post built to trade with the Nez Perce.

Pokotel and Tisidimit clasped their white friends, sang songs, laughed, and started north across a great flat that showed signs of the presence of wild horses. The possibility of capturing some of the cayuses excited them.

Just follow the river, they explained to Victoria, who translated.

And then the Snakes departed in a long line, winding their way over the undulating grasses, leaving Skye, Victoria, Nutmeg, and their critters suddenly alone.

Skye felt naked. He had no weapon. Only Victoria's bow

and quiver protected them. They had, at least, the food they had traded for weeks earlier, but it would not last them to Fort Vancouver, which lay a great distance to the west. Skye was struck, once again, by the vastness of this North America, its size unfathomable.

"We're almost unarmed, and we'll be careful, mate," he said to Nutmeg.

They started down a pleasant stream, abounding with game along its banks.

Now, suddenly, the professor found himself in a new botanical zone, and he worked furiously to harvest the treasures of this intermountain land.

Skye rode ahead, scouting a safe passage, and soon spotted a fishing village. He could only hope its people were friendly. It would probably be Umatilla, Wallawalla, or Cayuse, but without a guide he doubted he could tell which.

He rode straight for the village, hoping for the best.

nineteen

sea of heavy-boned friendly faces greeted them as they entered the camp. Skye spotted some small, wiry horses picketed close, and thought these were Cayuse Indians, who caught just such ponies on the vast arid plains of the area. He also guessed that they were fishing the Umatilla River. He wished he had a guide to help him put names to places and people.

They wore little clothing this summery day. They were a people of golden flesh, notably bad teeth, but silky straight hair which the women let hang loose over their breasts. Although a great fishery had been erected of poles out of the nearby mountains, including a framework above the river where spearmen could harvest salmon, no one seemed to be working much. Perhaps they didn't need to.

The place stank of fish offal, dung, and kitchen trash. Whirling clouds of green-bellied flies swarmed over everything and everyone, along with bigger and blacker horseflies. Sulky curs circled as Skye and his party rode in, and sniffed Dolly, who stayed beside the professor. Skye saw no lodges, but only a jumble of shacks and arbors thrown together from river brush and a few poles, not enough to slow the wind but enough to provide a little shade. These people might be fine fishermen, but they did not impress Skye, who preferred the rich culture and hauteur of the Plains Indians.

Skye wondered what the ritual might be: did these far-west people follow the protocols of the Plains tribes? He dismounted, extracted a plug of tobacco from his pack and waited for a headman or chief. But none came and there was no official welcoming. Several old men held out their hands, plainly wanting the tobacco, but Skye tarried.

Victoria took matters into her own hands: her fingers danced. But again, these people stared. It was dawning on Skye that even the universal sign language, which he had thought was known to tribes everywhere, wasn't much used here. One young man stood aside, and from his bearing and an elaborate conch-shell necklace dangling from his neck, Skye thought him to be a leader of some sort, so he doffed his top hat, approached, and attempted by sign language to seek the welcome of the village.

The young man nodded but did not otherwise reply.

Skye remembered the jingle bells. He dug out several and handed them about, first to the young man, and then to the nearest of these people.

Dogs sniffed, growled at Dolly, and Skye wondered where his dog had gone. Maybe the beast was so cowardly that he would not enter a village and was lurking around at the periphery, waiting for his friend—Skye knew better than to suppose he was the mutt's master—to escape this foul place.

But Victoria was busily finding someone she could talk to, and eventually found a Nez Perce woman, a wife of one of the young fishers, who was acquainted with the sign language.

Skye held Victoria's pony while the women sign-talked. Yes, these were Cayuse people. Fishing now, then catching horses in the fall and training them through the winter.

But it was Nutmeg who found a welcome. Children flocked to him, fascinated by the canvas packs carried on Dolly's back. The naturalist sat down, pulled out one of his thick folders filled with pressed leaves and stems and flowers, each between a sheet of soft paper, and his penciled drawings of various species. Sitting crosslegged, he showed these to the children, and then the women who came to see what strange thing the white man possessed, and finally to a throng of Cayuse people, who marveled at each rendering of each plant.

"There, you see?" Nutmeg said. "I collect one of each species and write them up, eh?" He showed them his bulky notes, which they could not in the slightest comprehend. It was the sketches that fascinated the Cayuse people. With each likeness they exclaimed and talked among themselves.

"I have more in my knapsack," he said. He pulled the straps off his shoulders and pulled off the heavy bag. He rummaged in it and pulled out two more folders of pressed plants and sketches.

"See here," he said. "I collect these. I've six notebooks filled with all this."

The village women crowded close so they too could see these amazing drawings.

"No, it's not magic, and I'm a poor hand at drawing, but I have to get things right. Everything perfect and exact, and showing the species to best advantage, eh?"

They listened solemnly, saying nothing. It dawned on Skye that maybe they knew some English but weren't admitting it. They traded, after all, at Fort Walla Walla, and had no doubt spent plenty of time among Englishmen.

"Does anyone speak English?" Skye asked.

A powerful warrior, middle-aged, graying at the temples, his eyes as opaque as basalt, nodded.

"I make trade," he said.

That was good. Skye and Victoria had been trying every way but the obvious to talk to these people.

"I am Skye. We are going to Fort Vancouver," he said.

The man nodded. Then pointed at himself. "Waapita," he said.

"We come in peace."

"You trade?"

"No."

"What people is the woman?"

"Absaroka. Far east, over the mountains. She is my woman."

"You Yank?"

"No, English." He pointed at Professor Nutmeg. "He's English."

"You Hudson Bayee?"

Skye pondered that a moment. "No."

The big man didn't reply and Skye felt him withdrawing. These people were bonded to the great trading company.

"I am going to talk to the White Eagle. Then maybe I am Hudson's Bay."

"White Eagle. Ahhh. You want to trade horse?"

Skye did not like the look of the Cayuse ponies, which were ugly, small, ribby, and deformed. His Plains horses were better stock.

"No," he said. "But maybe buy one?"

He was thinking of a pony for Nutmeg, whose slow passage on foot, in bad boots and on sore feet, was slowing them down to a crawl.

"Trade," said Waapita. "I like you horse."

"No, no trade. But I will give two knives and one awl for a gentle horse with good feet and legs."

"No," said his host, whose gaze flicked to Skye's equipment, and then to the knife at Skye's waist.

Skye suddenly sensed that this was not good. He turned to Victoria. "Get out," he said.

She glanced swiftly at him, and instantly clambered onto her pony.

He walked to the crowd being entertained by Nutmeg.

"We're leaving, Professor."

"But Mister Skye, these people are enjoying my little picture show—"

"Now."

"Oh, pshaw, Skye, don't be in such a dither."

"Gather your things."

Then it happened.

Skye watched some playful urchins unbuckle Dolly's harness and furtively slide Nutmeg's two packs chock-full of his collections and notes into the dense crowd.

"Professor!" he barked. "Your notes!"

"I say, Mister Skye!"

Then Nutmeg's knapsack vanished, and two of the three notebooks vanished, while Skye watched, horrified.

He plunged into the crowd, pushing carefully, fighting his way toward the fleeing children, who dodged, rounded corners, reappeared, and ran free, into the maze of shacks and fish-drying racks and middens of refuse. Astonishingly, the yellow cur followed the boys, a yellow flag for Skye to follow.

Skye sprang after them, a lithe force, and yet he made no headway. The boys separated, one carrying the knapsack going one way, another vanishing into a longhouse, and another bearing Dolly's packs and harness starting for the river. Another boy joyously carried one of the notebooks Nutmeg had exhibited, his laughter a cataract of childish delight. Skye chased that one until suddenly a dark wall of men with leveled fishing spears loomed before him. Skye stood, paralyzed, knowing he was one breath away from death from a dozen iron-pointed lances.

He sat swiftly, knowing that a sitting unarmed man facing warriors is safer than a standing one.

The boys had disappeared.

Skye heard Nutmeg's strangulated bellowing. He sat panting, sensing that he and Nutmeg and Victoria might not leave this village alive.

He gauged the temper of these young fisher-hunter-warriors, and stood slowly, gathering his courage. He elaborately ignored them, turned his back to them, feeling his flesh prickle, and walked wearily across the entire village, in what seemed an eternity, to the silent crowd surrounding the naturalist.

He found the professor slumping at the same place, Dolly at his feet, clutching one remaining folio of species, notes, and sketches. He looked a lot calmer than Skye felt, but Skye knew it wasn't calm. The professor stared, vacant-eyed, into space. Victoria had climbed to her saddle and had grabbed the halter rope of the packhorse.

"You'll get them back, of course, Skye," Nutmeg said in a dreamy whisper. "Five are gone."

"I'll try, Professor."

The crowd had quieted. Skye walked slowly to the one who knew a little English, who stood apart. The man shifted slightly as Skye stopped before him.

Skye lifted his hat and settled it. "Him wise man. Spent many months collecting all plants, for the wisdom of the world. Now you must bring everything back to him, every thing the boys took, or Hudson's Bay very angry."

The big man shrugged.

"I will give you gifts. Everything on my packhorse. You give us everything the boys took."

"They my boys," the man said. "Go away now."

Skye studied the man and knew he meant it. He wondered what he would tell Professor Nutmeg and what faith the naturalist would profess after that.

twenty

The sun scorched the whole world white, and for a moment Alistair Nutmeg was blinded. He closed his eyes against the pain of the sun, but the whiteness persisted. He heard the yelping dogs, listened to the excited Cayuse people, heard running and shouts. When he opened his eyes again, the crowd had pulled back from him. He clutched one folio. Dolly rubbed his leg, the hair of her neck bristling.

He sensed that he would never see the five stolen folios again, but waited tautly until Skye would return with news. He was a born and bred Englishman, and punctilious about displaying emotion. To all the world he seemed collected and in control of his fate. But in fact, his mind tumbled through loss: months of collecting gone unless Skye worked a miracle. He wished he might sit down on the grass and weep, but that would be unthinkable and a ghastly sign of weakness. An Englishman was he, an Englishman, an Englishman . . .

So he stared numbly, his thoughts frozen by grief. It was all he could do to pay attention, and not drift off somewhere in the clouds, to a meeting of the Royal Academy of Science to honor his great achievements in North America, or his lectern at Harvard, educating eager acned boys about hitherto unknown flora of this vast continent.

He smiled at the savages, holding everything in like a draught of air in his lungs, and pausing only to exhale and inhale again, smiling at these brutes who had observed nature closely but had made no systematic note of what they knew. No one would ever accuse Alistair Nutmeg, lecturer at Harvard, adventuresome naturalist, of losing his composure in a bitter moment.

These were friendly people; the urchins were only doing what daring boys do. But as he stood there, awaiting direction from Skye, he grasped how foolish he had been and how valid were the cautions of his wilderness guides. Nat Wyeth and his men had constantly admonished him to be careful. Skye had warned him so often that Nutmeg had privately raged at the man.

But it wasn't war or death or murderous intent that had caused this loss: it was the gulf that lay between him and these people. They did not know the value of his collection or its purpose. They had yet to encounter science or the arts. They had yet to invent the wheel or an alphabet or mine and refine metal or put their own language on paper. They were Stone Age men.

They could not know what this fateful moment meant to a naturalist who had devoted months simply to planning and financing this expedition, and then months in the actual and difficult work of examining flora, categorizing them, checking them against known botanical specimens, drawing them accurately, describing their habitat in detail, and noting any practical purpose for the plant, whether as medicine or dye or food or fiber.

He stood stoically, with a stiff upper lip, an Englishman to the core, weeping at his fate within, a mask to this raw world.

Skye approached. "We've got to leave at once, mate. No telling what'll happen if we stay."

"The folios?"

"Scattered in the camps, hidden by boys, prizes of war . . . I am sorry."

Richard S. Wheeler

"Is there the slightest chance?"

"Always a chance, mate. Hudson's Bay is a powerful force. All they have to do is threaten to close the trading window."

"But this won't happen soon. And the specimens may not survive . . ."

Skye led the professor away from the silent Cayuse people, and Dolly followed. Nutmeg, his movements jerky and stiff, like a windup tin soldier, walked away from the rank-smelling camp, walking alongside Skye, feeling as bereft as if he had lost his entire family, his good name, his reputation, and all that he had ever written into the Book of Life.

Skye leaned over the mane of his horse.

"You all right, mate?"

"Never better," Nutmeg replied.

"How much did you lose?"

"Five of six folios. All my notes and sketches. Almost everything. There are a couple folios with Wyeth, but I will have to start over."

"A year lost?"

"Two, actually."

"That is a great loss," Skye said. "You could change your plans, Professor. Head east overland, next spring, after wintering at Fort Vancouver, collecting all the way. Undo the loss, from west to east."

Nutmeg sighed. "I'm afraid it won't succeed, sir. Collecting requires large amounts of soft absorbent paper. I dry my leaves and stems and flowers between the sheets. I should need reams of that, and reams of writing paper for notes, and reams of paper for sketches, you see. And some waterproof folders to store them. I don't suppose I'd find such a trove of paper at Fort Vancouver."

"Likely not," Skye said. "But if you sailed down the coast to Monterey, capital of Mexican California, you might acquire these things, and a guide to take you east."

"With what, sir?"

Something in Nutmeg's voice gave him away, and Skye

128

turned silent. Nutmeg knew he was barely controlling the festering anger within him. He was doubly angry: at himself for ignoring the warnings of experienced wilderness men, and at Skye, whose very concern now rankled him. One more kind inquiry from Skye and Nutmeg would decant a magnum of bitterness.

But Skye had sensed his rage, and pulled ahead of him.

Victoria rode silently beside them, sharing all this without comment. Then, ahead, they beheld the yellow dog lying in the worn riverside path.

Dolly bounded ahead to sniff No Name. She looked happy without the pack she had carted for so many hundreds of miles. The Cayuse boys had liberated her, and she had instantly become less dutiful. And that festered in Nutmeg, too. Everything in his existence was needling and jabbing him, and most of all Skye and his squaw.

He composed himself once again. It would not do to let himself be discovered in a tantrum like some schoolboy, and be laughed at or condescended to by the likes of that ruffian Skye, who may have started as a cultivated London youth, but now was coarse and brutal . . .

Petulantly he forced his mind from that sort of disdain.

Mostly, he felt despair. He had lost scores of genus and subgenus possibilities, several new species. He had lost numerous new pteropsida: ferns, conifers, firs. He had lost several new dicots: elms, peaches, blackberries, mustards, nightshades, and ragweeds. He had lost a rich assortment of new monocots, including endless varieties of grasses, sedges, lilies, and yuccas. He had lost several new mosses, or bryophyta, several mycophyta, or fungi, mushrooms, and toadstools. He knew he could never recover samples of the rare ones. He would always be in the wrong place, or in the wrong season. Some appeared to be so local that he doubted he would ever find them again.

Worse, he had lost a dozen or so specimens of plant life he could not classify: he was not sure of the order or genus or subgenus of any of them. He lacked the taxonomic skills to place them in the botanic universe. Some were tiny. Some were water-borne. One flourished deep in a limestone cave he had explored. And these were the most exciting of all. They might lead anywhere: even to a new order. Losing those was comparable to losing his health, or the crown jewels, or his mind. All gone, gone, gone.

His surviving portfolio contained some fine new peas and sages, as well as a fine collection of lichen. But he no longer cared. He wished the Cayuse boys had taken it, too.

He stumbled forward amid a quietness that radiated more from the Skyes than from nature. They were leaving him alone to come to grips with his loss.

Then he discovered Skye standing just ahead.

"Would you like to ride, Professor? I need to walk."

Nutmeg felt weary but shook his head. "I am not in need of charity," he said.

Skye turned aside, addressing the empty world. "When I was at sea, and the rails of the ship were the bars of my prison, I didn't know why I was set upon this earth," he said quietly. "I lived a futile life, without purpose, serving masters who wanted only the use of my muscle, men who saw me as no more than a problem in the ship's company."

"What are you getting at?" Nutmeg asked, too sharply, and then regretted the tone that erupted from him.

"We are here on earth for some reason," Skye said, "even though we may not understand it at the time."

"I suppose I was put here so that I might lose my life's work? And therefore learn a bit of humility?"

Skye laughed. The rumble began within him, like the prelude to an earthquake, and then erupted like a volcano, cascading joy and humor over his world.

Nutmeg didn't want to laugh, and loathed himself for starting to laugh, but then he laughed, too, disliking the eruption.

No Name peered at them, sunk its tail between its legs, turned soulfully, and bayed.

"Now you have something to tell your colleagues at Harvard," Skye said, at last.

Victoria was puzzled. She obviously understood very little of this. Whenever the white men's way proved too much for her, she seemed to pull into herself, which was what she was doing now. Nutmeg approached her pony and peered up at her from those wise and guileless eyes.

"What I have lost is very large, and cannot be replaced entirely. But on this trip I have found good things. From you I have learned about the Absaroka, and listened to your wisdom and admired your skills, your beauty, your kindness, and all your fine qualities. These are things that any people, anywhere, from any nation, would admire.

"So all is not lost. You and Mister Skye have been my traveling companions for several weeks, and you have taught me many things I did not know. I was an innocent, wandering a dangerous world without knowing it. Now I have some of your wisdom, and look forward to learning more if you wish to teach me. Maybe, some day, when I am wise in your ways, Victoria of the Crow people, I might successfully prosecute my own work."

She stared down at him softly, smiled, and touched his lips with her slim fingers.

twenty-one

S kye found himself admiring Professor Nutmeg, who soldiered on without further complaint. But never more so than one evening at dusk, when he confessed remorse.

"I imagine Wyeth thinks I'm dead," he said. "I shouldn't have done that to him. He must have spent days searching for me, sending men out and about, tracking me. Worse, you tried to get me to wait but I didn't. I insisted on tagging along. No, Mister Skye, I would now have everything safe and secure if I had abided by your counsel."

Skye found himself liking that. The professor was a decent sort, with all the noble qualities of the English. And maybe some of the eccentricities and weaknesses, too.

"That's the past, Professor. We'll look to the future now. Count it a lesson."

"It's that all right," Nutmeg said. "When I see Wyeth at Vancouver, I'll try to make amends."

They had made good time down the Umatilla River, reached its confluence with the mighty Columbia, and headed along the left bank through an arid and depressing land. Skye and Nutmeg traded seats on the horse, while Victoria ranged ahead hunting and scouting. No Name had taken to scouting with her and had proven to be a valuable bird dog, retrieving an occasional goose or duck she pierced with her dwindling supply of arrows. The meat helped extend the shrinking supply of dried salmon.

There was not enough to feed them to the Hudson's Bay post, but there would be fishing villages en route, and Skye still had a handful of trade goods from the cache he had acquired at rendezvous. Somehow they would make it.

They discovered a fishing camp of a people they could not identify, snugged into a wooded ravine that debouched on the river. As was the custom of the northwest tribes, this people welcomed the visitors and fed them. Skye noticed the large river canoes beached along the bank, and for a while played with the idea of trading his three horses for a ride to Fort Vancouver. It was certainly a temptation, letting the current of the great river, and the strength of the oarsmen, take them swiftly to their destination.

And yet he hesitated, and as he thought about it, he realized why he would not do that: nothing was certain. He might not like McLoughlin's proposal. And if he rejected it, he and Victoria would need those horses to return to the interior. Without those horses he would have nothing. He could even trade the packhorse for a rifle and supplies and still have a pair of them to ride. No, as seductive as the idea was of floating to the post, he would resist.

This time, No Name didn't vanish as he had during other visits. He stuck close to Skye, as if finally attaching himself to his new comrade. Skye knew the dog would never accept a master, but welcomed a friend. The thought of abandoning the mutt at Vancouver disturbed him, but there would be no help for it if they wouldn't let him ship the dog to England.

He remembered that fateful moment when the Cayuse boys had merrily divested Nutmeg of his botanical materials and scattered through the complex village. The dog had appeared out of nowhere and traced the passage of the boys through longhouses and huts and drying racks, his yellow coat a flag enabling Skye to keep track of the scampering boys—until he faced a wall of spears. How had the dog known to do that? What intuition did it possess? It was an intelligent creature that had survived on its own for some indeterminate time, avoiding fights, disappearing, and yet willing to war if war was thrust upon it, and eager to serve Skye for reasons that no mortal could ever know.

Now, in the failing light, he surveyed the dog. He could not even guess its age. Its ears had been cut and shredded by a hard life. One bent forward unnaturally. Its face was seamed with scars. But those brown eyes, which seemed to anticipate Skye's every thought, were what touched Skye. He swore the dog seemed to be following his very train of thought. Somehow No Name knew that this evening, more than any that had passed before, Barnaby Skye had accepted the friendship, nay, love, of the hound and had marveled at the dog's uncanny wisdom.

The dog squirmed closer until it could press its muzzle into Skye's lap as he sat cross-legged before the coals. Skye gingerly stroked its head, still fearful of a sudden, snarling explosion of snapping teeth. But that did not happen.

Victoria watched closely, her face a mask. She had long since made her peace with the dog and formed a hunting alliance with him.

They reached the Dalles of the Columbia a few days later, and headed around the rapids and looming cliffs. Tribesmen fished and loitered through the whole area, ready to portage canoes and boats, or demand tribute for passage past the great obstacle in the river. Skye, unarmed, knew he was at great disadvantage and tried to bluff his way past the alert and treacherous Indians. The bandits wanted a horse and everything in the pack for safe passage. Skye countered with a handful of awls and knives. He would not surrender the packhorse. The impasse lasted until a headman found himself staring at Victoria's drawn bow and realized that this small party was not without weapons after all. That gave Skye the moment he needed to draw his Arkansas toothpick. They ended up traversing the well-worn paths around the narrows without harassment. But it had been a close thing.

Victoria finally returned her arrow to its quiver and unstrung her beautifully crafted double-reflex bow, which compounded the force of her arrows. She rode ahead again, through an arid grassland, scouting and hunting, often with No Name rooting out small game for her.

On the western horizon, like a black wall barring them from a future, lay the Cascades, gloomy and forested. And rising into the misty heavens was the forbidding cone of Mount Hood, aloof, frosty, and arrogant. It did not comfort Skye that the volcano had been named for a British admiral, Lord Hood, some four decades earlier. He knew of Lord Hood, and knowing of him was enough to darken his day. The imperious and frigid mountain reminded him of all he wished to forget about England, and every time his gaze was drawn to it, he felt a renewed dread. Was he doing the sensible thing or merely throwing his life away?

They progressed gradually into the Cascade foothills, and now the mighty river ran between gloomy slopes heavily forested and forlorn. They came to the Hood River and found no way across except to swim the horses in the icy water. Skye hewed a small raft for the pack goods, and put Professor Nutmeg on the pack-horse, and hoped for the best. They made the west bank, but only after being chilled to the bone. Increasingly, Skye wondered how he would cross the vast Columbia, running a quarter-mile wide and cruelly cold. He wished he had tackled the river far upstream, where its breadth wasn't so formidable and it seemed friendlier. He had little choice now but to ride opposite Fort Vancouver and try to summon help.

The September nights turned starkly cold in the dripping Cascade Mountains, and suddenly the trip was no longer a summer's lark. Often the trail catapulted upward, negotiated cliffs and promontories, ran hard against the riverbank, and was hemmed by dense, dark forest. In the rare clearings, the travelers often found fishing sites where one or another of the river tribes harvested the salmon that was their food and wealth.

When they reached the west slope it rained continuously, making fires impossible and drenching them to the skin until they were so chilled that Skye feared they would sicken. They holed up under a rock ledge for an entire day trying to avoid the pelting rain, which still found its way to them whenever a breeze whipped the droplets under the ledge. The shelter had been much-used, and not a stick of firewood lay anywhere nearby. But at least they could huddle up. He was increasingly worried about Nutmeg, who shivered unceasingly and looked ashen. The man's few duds had vanished along with his knapsack in the Cayuse camp and not even his stiff English resolve could conceal the blueness of his face, or his suffering. Victoria, unused to such deluges on the plains, was suffering almost as much.

Skye realized that his stores of goods had dwindled almost to nothing and that he could turn a canvas pack-cloth into ponchos for Nutmeg and Victoria, so he set to work with his knife, sawing the canvas into two rectangles and cutting head holes in it. Both of them donned their ponchos, and both soon stopped their shaking. Once Nutmeg had warmed he was able to repair his sodden boots, which were falling apart again.

They were out of most staples and hadn't come to a village in many leagues, and Skye worried about how to feed three mortals and two dogs the remaining distance. Vancouver was not far, but if the bad weather persisted, it could as well be five hundred miles as one hundred.

Brutally, he pushed westward even though the drizzle had not yet halted, and they splashed along the dreary bankside trail, sometimes making only a few miles a day. Shelter was hard to find, and the mist or rain rarely let up. Skye could not remember any time he was so cold, not even on the North Sea, up in the rigging of a warship during a blow.

Sometimes Victoria magically found dry wood and they

could make a fire; more often, there was nothing dry enough to burn. Skye cut them back to half-rations and they all fought the gnawing emptiness of their bellies.

Then one day the clouds lifted and they discovered themselves emerging from the vast dark canyon of the Cascades and into a sunlit plain densely foliaged with brush and leafy trees. They paused on a rocky flat to dry out and let the late September sun bake the winter out of their bones. The dogs, hunting together, scared up some geese, which gave Victoria an opportunity she took good advantage of, with her next-to-last arrow. There was just enough meat to feed the mortals sparingly, and the dogs a little better.

Skye had weathered worse, and should have been happy. Instead, he felt taut and irritable, snapping at Nutmeg, glaring at Victoria, and mad at himself. He admitted he was afraid, and that he might be making the most terrible mistake of his life. But there was nothing he could do but go on, his fate not really in his hands.

twenty-two

Skye found himself in an Eden, but it didn't feel at all like paradise. He and Victoria and the redoubtable professor toiled westward through a bountiful land, brimming with wild fruits and nuts, with abundant vegetation and the mildest of climates.

Nutmeg was enthralled and busied himself studying the flora, even though he had no means to preserve or describe or sketch any of it. He was like a bright butterfly, alighting on one bloom after another, drinking of its pollen before rushing off to the next delight.

He got lost one day, wandering afield in his old manner, oblivious of his traveling companions, intent on finding more of a berry bush he had never seen before, and for which he had no name. By dusk he was out of sight of the river and his friends, and hungry. He was also guilty, knowing he had betrayed the trust that the Skyes had placed in him. And yet he could not help it: something as new and exciting as an unknown fruit had raptured his mind until nothing else mattered. This greenish berry was sweet, had lobes, and didn't disturb his digestion, and he wanted various samples, taken from various sites, for closer examination in camp.

He was wandering through some grassed and rocky hills when night fell and he scarcely knew which way to turn. He couldn't help it. He didn't mean to lose track of the Skyes, but his obsessions got the best of him.

That's when the no-name dog found him and Dolly, and moments later Skye loomed out of the dark, the clop of his horse's hooves announcing his approach.

Nutmeg expected rebuke but Skye's voice was gentle. "I'll take you back, Professor," was all he said, but there was a certain tautness in his words.

"Mister Skye, I've strayed and I proffer my sincere apologies," he said.

Skye nodded but said nothing. It took them half the night to reach the camp Victoria had made beside the mighty river. Neither Skye nor Victoria uttered a rebuke, but he knew that the silence itself was reproaching him.

The next morning the sun shone sweetly and all was well. Even Victoria, who had been melancholic this long journey, had been lifted into smiles and joy as she steered her pony through belly-high grasses and exclaimed at the shimmering blue river rolling gently to the sea.

But Skye felt anxious. His muscles were taut. His temper irritable. His humor liverish. He knew himself not to be an anxious person. In the wilds of the Rockies, he had never let dire circumstance worry and abrade him. That had been one of his strengths. For Skye, there was always a way. So the emotion that inhabited his soul surprised him.

He was not comfortable with the constant worry that exhausted him even as the threesome and the two dogs rambled across the benign plains that formed the heart of the empire of Hudson's Bay. Sometimes he turned around and beheld the strange cone of Mount Hood and thought that the very eye of the Royal Navy was upon him, even in this remote corner of the New World. Admiral Hood stood over him, and had him in his clutches.

They were hand-to-mouth now and yet remained fed, for every bush bore fruit: huckleberries, plums, wild grapes, and a dozen more delights Skye couldn't identify. They had passed several fisheries but all on the north side of the mighty river. And he remembered how he had fled along that bank, six years earlier, fled for his life, fled for his liberty, determined to escape or die. By the grace of God he had lived.

They came at last to a broad valley, which shouldered a great pewter river from the south that he could see from the hill where he stood. That, he concluded, was the Willamette, and this was the place. He gazed across the waters, seeing nothing at first, and then just maybe, the hand of man, on the north bank of the Columbia. Was it a stockade? At such a great distance he could not be sure. It sat well back from the Columbia, and well east of the Willamette.

The place wrought powerful feelings in him. On a cold night in 1826 he had slid overboard, leaving a Royal Navy frigate behind him, and worked swiftly inland, never pausing, knowing he would not be safe for a hundred miles. That proved to be a serious underestimate. He had starved his way east for five hundred before he began to breathe easily.

"Here," he said gently, pointing across the enormous river. "That's Fort Vancouver."

"I don't see a thing," Nutmeg said.

Victoria said nothing. She was as taut as he, and he could well imagine what thoughts flooded her mind just then.

Here indeed was an odd thing: he had no means to get across the river. He did not even have a rifle with which to signal the post. The horses and dogs probably could not swim such a vast flood and would drown. Neither he nor Victoria could swim it, nor could Professor Nutmeg.

He studied the hazy fort closely, and discovered another thing: a vessel lay anchored beside it, its masts barely visible and its sails furled. That would be the ship that Peter Skene Ogden had urged him to catch, the ship of passage to England—if he chose to go to England, which he was not sure he would do even if it meant visiting his family, seeing his father, and clearing his name.

He could make out that it was a schooner, a two-master

with fore-and-aft sails rather than square rigging. Had so small a bark traversed the Atlantic, rounded Cape Horn, and then made its way to the Sandwich Islands and across to this misty place? Could that fragile vessel carry the treasure of Hudson's Bay Company, in the form of furs, clear to England?

He didn't know how to cross to the north bank of the Columbia. He hoped to run into a fishing village where he could find a ferry. After that the HBC could come and get the rest, and the horses. But they had passed none as they traversed the last few miles to a point opposite the post. And then it came to him to wait until night and build a signal fire, and that surely would bring a canoe or barge across the waters to investigate.

"All right, mate, we'll camp here," he said to Nutmeg. "Tonight we'll signal. They probably won't start across before dawn."

"Couldn't we try some smoke right now?" Nutmeg asked.

"We could see. But there's a fresh breeze and I think it'll just dissipate."

Even as they talked, Victoria was looking for dry wood, which was scarce in this rain-soaked land. But soon she was pulling driftwood from the shores, and breaking dead branches from trees, and shaving the slimmest imaginable kindling that would form a tiny nest for the embers that would catch under her flint and steel.

Skye helped her. They would need plenty of wood, for only a giant fire would attract attention at such a distance. Then, when all was ready, she crouched over the tiny nest, sheltering it from the breeze, and deftly struck her steel across the flint, raining sparks down on her flammable thimbleful of fuzz. The first strikes seemed futile, but then a tiny ember burned in one spot. She struck more sparks until several burned, and then crouched over the kindling and blew gently.

That always seemed the agonizing moment to Skye, the moment that would spell life or death in the dead of winter, the moment that would tell whether they would eat raw and vile food, or cook a meal and warm their flesh and feel the life of the fire secure their own perilous lives.

The flame flickered, smouldered, and caught, tiny, fragile, but real. She fed hairlike bits of tinder into it until it bloomed into a three-inch-high blaze. He sighed. They were still a half hour from a fire that would boil smoke, generated by moist grasses, into the air high enough to be spotted from that hazy shore so far distant.

The professor perched himself on a boulder and stared across the empty river. It was the end of a failed journey for him, and yet he had somehow risen above the disaster. Here he would await the arrival of Wyeth in a few days or weeks, and then ride home in Wyeth's ship.

Nutmeg was at ease, but Skye wasn't. He could not sit at all, but paced restlessly, waiting for the fire to build. He headed down to the river bank and watched the innocent waters purl by. He felt a terrible temptation to turn the horses east and flee once again. He was still wanted by the Crown, and the Hudson's Bay Company was the long arm of the Crown. And yet he stayed. He was not a man of little faith, but one of hope and courage. He would see what the White Eagle, McLoughlin, was made of, and what would be laid upon the table.

If he fled now they would be helpless. Victoria had but one arrow, and that was the extent of their weaponry. And yet Skye had endured worse times, over and over, drawing from some singular courage and determination to weather the worst that the wilds could throw at him. He would endure now. As he stood gazing across those shimmering waters, his courage stole back into him, and the anxiety faded. He had left the Royal Navy still a boy; now he was a man, and a man among men.

He turned to observe the flame on the slope behind him, and discovered a fine gray plume, wrought by moist grasses. Surely the men at Fort Vancouver would see it. And yet for the better part of an hour, nothing happened. He watched the far shore alertly, watched the distant ship, watched the hazy stockade, and yet saw nothing.

But at last, late in the day when the westering sun was lighting one side of Victoria's plume of smoke, he saw some movement. It took ten minutes before he knew that a canoe was heading across the waters. They had been discovered at last.

He watched its slow progress, knowing that it held his fate on board. When it was still a hundred yards distant and fighting the current, he made out five men in it, two rowing on each side, while one steered. The big canoe, longer and wider than any he had seen, drove straight at him, and finally beached on a strand just below his perch.

A young man peered upward. Four French-Canadian voyageurs rested on their oars.

"Be ye, by any chance, Barnaby Skye?" he asked.

"I am."

"And this is your party. Who have ye with you?"

"My wife Victoria, and Alistair Nutmeg, a naturalist from Leicester. He lectures at Harvard, in Boston, but he's an Englishman and a gentleman, sir. And who are you?"

"Douglas, sir. Hudson's Bay, at your service."

"Well, Mr. Douglas, we need to carry three horses, two dogs, and three mortals, across those waters."

"We'll manage it. Dr. McLoughlin has been hoping you'd arrive in time. She's sailing in two days. Hop in, sir, and we'll carry you over."

Skye paused. "I'd prefer to cross with my wife and colleague, Mr. Douglas. We've come a long way together and we'll finish this trip together."

"The factor will be disappointed."

"Only for an hour or two."

"Very well, sir. We'll likely bring the flatboat over. She's slow, but there's a small sail."

"It can board the horses?"

"From that bench there, sir. The channel runs deep there, and they've a long gangway."

"We'll be ready, then."

A voyageur clambered out, grappled the prow of the canoe, and then hopped aboard as the crew rowed into the blue. Skye reckoned that before dark he would know whether he and Victoria would be going to England.

He stared guiltily at No Name, who sulked beside him, accusation in his eyes.

twenty-three

As the flatboat closed, Skye beheld McLoughlin standing at the bank. It could be no other. This man towered a foot above everyone else, was built on the model of a keg, and his head was crowned with a burst of white hair, which gave him his name: the White Eagle.

Behind him, well back from the Columbia, stood the imperial Fort Vancouver, a large stockaded fortress Skye had seen once before. Everything about it weighed heavy, from its towering stockades to its huge waterfront gate. This western capital of a pounds-and-pence empire struck awe in him. But it was larger now, double what it had been, and a village surrounded it. In every direction he could see agricultural pursuits: orchards, vineyards, hay- and grainfields, a grist mill.

Scores lined the riverbank, but it was McLoughlin who commanded his gaze. The man radiated something regal, as if he were the true royalty here. At his side stood a dark and stocky woman wearing a dress that no doubt would be fashionable in London. That, no doubt, would be the notorious Marguerite, his consort of many years, the widow of the explorer Alexander McKay, but not before she had taken up with McLoughlin.

This was no outpost but a city. The closer the leaky flatboat drew, the higher ran Skye's estimates. Several hundred lived in this self-supporting capital. He eyed, as well, the schooner, a trim white ship better suited to coastal trade than navigating oceans. Did the entire resupply of HBC arrive in that small vessel, and did it take a whole year's gathering of pelts and furs to England in that tiny hold?

But it was McLoughlin who riveted him. The man was lord and emperor here, responsible only to Governor George Simpson half across a continent at York Factory, and thus largely sovereign in his lordship over this northwest quarter. As the flatboat slowed and the voyageurs tossed hempen ropes to shore, a swift fear built in Skye; he knew at once he could not brook the awesome will of that sovereign lord of the wilds.

Then the flatboat bumped land, and voyageurs leapt to drag it up a gravelly beach. Amid a great hue and cry, Victoria slipped close to Skye, unnerved by this white men's world she was seeing for the first time. He plucked her hand and held it tight within his rough one, saying things with his fingers that she would understand.

They were helped over the prow and set foot on the shoreline, and people whirled tight like a sliding noose. Professor Nutmeg stepped out, and the two dogs bounded onto land.

Skye found himself staring upward into a probing gaze.

"McLoughlin here. Welcome to our post, Mister Skye!"

Skye found himself shaking hands with the giant.

"There, you see? I know a bit about you. Have I addressed you as you wish?"

"You have, sir. This is my wife Victoria, of the Crow people, and Professor Nutmeg, a naturalist who started with the Wyeth party but joined us."

McLoughlin's gaze bored into Victoria. "Ah, a most lovely consort, Mister Skye. And may I introduce my Marguerite? You women will have much in common."

Marguerite smiled and clasped Victoria's hand.

Victoria found her voice. "Goddam," she muttered.

"Well said, madam. A woman after my own heart. And Nutmeg? I didn't know about you, sir. Welcome."

"A most amazing post, Doctor."

"Do I detect England in your voice, Professor?"

"Leicester, sir, but now a lecturer at Harvard. A naturalist, a botanist."

"And what are your plans, eh?"

"I'll be returning on Wyeth's ship, the *Sultana*."

"I've not heard of it or Wyeth."

"It's a brig sent round the horn, Doctor. Wyeth plans to set up a salmon fishery on the Columbia and send the proceeds back. It's carrying machinery for making casks and processing fish, and also some trade goods to sell to American trappers."

All that was news to Skye. It had never occurred to him to ask Nutmeg what Wyeth was up to. So Wyeth wasn't going to buck the already fierce competition in the fur and peltry business except as a sideline.

McLoughlin paused suddenly, taking stock of the obvious threat to HBC, and then smiled.

"Come in." He turned to some subordinates. "Put these horses up, and bring in our guests' truck."

Skye led the silent Victoria into the jaws of the post, and found himself cloistered by walls he guessed were twenty feet high. Within, he discovered, to his astonishment, a complete settlement, a gracious headquarters and home for the factor, barracks for the single men, great kitchens, and warehouses for the peltries.

And women, even one or two white women. He had not seen a white woman in more years than he could remember. Marguerite was a half-breed, as were most of the well-dressed ladies present there, but there, indeed, across the yard, stood a fair-fleshed woman.

Victoria sucked breath. She had never seen a white woman.

McLoughlin was looking him over, but making no overt move, and Skye realized that not until the amenities of the evening were behind them would he and the factor have a talk, probably closeted somewhere.

Assorted lackeys settled the guests in two rooms, and Victoria gasped at the interior of the one she shared with Skye. She walked over to the bed and pressed it, marveling. She peered through the glass panes, touched the glass, astonished. She studied the washstand and bowl and pitcher, scarcely believing what lay before her eyes. She studied the smooth, polished plank floor. She sat in a chair, surprised that she didn't need to squat on her heels as she usually did. She explored under the bed and discovered a porcelain thunder-mug, and understood its purpose at once. She pulled back the coverlet and beheld crisp sheets of good English cotton, covered with thick, four-point Hudson's Bay blankets. She poked a pillow and then examined it closely, discovering that it was filled with down, and scowled. Skye wondered whether she would object to sleeping on feathers.

Skye showed her how to pull the shutters tight for privacy, and how to open and close a door by turning the iron knob. He showed her the candles in their holders, and how to light one with a taper sitting near a small iron stove.

He thought she would enjoy these things, but he discovered a fear in her, and understood. All the marvels she had seen in the rendezvous, in the traders' kits, were nothing compared to what she was seeing now.

"Victoria," he said, "don't be afraid of this world. These are all useful things but they are nothing. Dr. McLoughlin's wife is half Cree, and she'll help you with anything you need or wish to learn. I think you'll enjoy these things, but if you don't, say so, and we'll head back to the mountains. If you're unhappy . . ."

"Oh, Skye," she said, pushing tears away with her small brown fists.

He hadn't given much thought to what all this would look

like to a Crow Indian woman who had never seen a white man's city. He hadn't expected anything like this; just another roughhewn fort, which it obviously still was, except for this one corner of it, the factor's own home and guest quarters.

But she was showing a brave face, and next he knew she was pouring water from the white porcelain pitcher into the basin, sampling the ball of scented English soap, whose use she understood intuitively, and was washing away her tears and her fear. She found a towel, marveled, wiped her face and hands, and grinned cockily at him.

He cleaned up and waited, not knowing what to expect.

Victoria spent a while prettying herself. From her small kit she withdrew her prized vermilion and ran a streak down her forehead. She smoothed her soft doeskin dress and cleaned her quilled moccasins. She enjoyed the looking glass.

Skye watched gently, loving her, knowing that his Crow wife would be struggling and perhaps distraught when she faced the dinner table.

"Victoria, just enjoy yourself. You'll see how life is lived in the white men's cities and maybe even how it will be in London."

"Well, dammit, Skye, I don't know nothing."

"Be yourself, and if you have doubts, watch."

They found their way to a dining hall where the factor and his wife and their guests had gathered, a place separate from the great mess hall that fed many of their employees.

This was indeed civilization, though only the veneer of it. The long table and chairs had been crafted locally, but good English china and wine goblets rested on it, and candles in pewter holders lit it, and linen serviettes rested beside silver at each place setting. If the walls were hand-sawn plank, the mirrors and art on them were encased in gilt frames.

The women wore brown, or scarlet, or cream, or muted green cotton dresses, some trimmed in white, elaborately sewn and decorated with myriad buttons. No matter whether they were full-bloods, half-bloods, or white, they were all dressed fashionably in the European manner. The gentlemen were, likewise, dressed in frock coats, shirts, and cravats. John McLoughlin cared less about his dress than the underlings, and wore no cravat.

Skye felt out of place in his calico shirt, buckskin britches, and high moccasins, and he supposed that his bear claw necklace didn't help him any. Victoria clung close to him, not frightened but intensely observant, choosing deep silence as her refuge.

Professor Nutmeg remained casually dressed as well, having lost all his clothing in the Cayuse village. His ancient jacket had been patched repeatedly with leather at the elbows. It was not clean, any more than Skye's hard-used buckskins or shirt were clean.

Still, no one seemed to notice. McLoughlin could scarcely expect company dressed to the nines at such a place.

McLoughlin proved a gracious host. He introduced James Douglas, second in command; then the various women, wives or consorts of the post's administrators. He introduced a white-bearded gentleman in a plain but natty blue uniform as Emilius Simpson, master of the HBC schooner, *Cadboro*, which bobbed on the river a hundred yards distant. Several of his merchant vessel officers were in attendance, also.

Skye, in turn, introduced Victoria, and shook hands with the whole lot of these gentlemen and ladies.

Skye could barely remember such a scene, and dredged his memories for youthful recollections of such things in his family's home. His father and mother had occasionally welcomed guests, but Skye could remember nothing like this glittering banquet, with candles in dizzy numbers illumining the great room, and fashionable guests at every hand.

Such dinners as he remembered had been served by his mother and younger sisters, who were barely visible at table, and Skye wondered if these women would do the same. But when McLoughlin invited the company to be seated, the women sat beside their men, with Marguerite McLoughlin at the opposite end of the great table.

Then Indian women poured in from the kitchen, bearing platters burdened with savory meats and vegetables and fresh bread. Skye marveled. He had not had a slice of fresh bread in a decade. Swiftly the women deposited these massive heaps of food on the table.

McLoughlin rose. His wine goblet was filled only with water, and Skye suspected he didn't touch spirits. But the other glasses on the table glowed with ruby wine.

"Ladies and gentlemen, let us welcome our distinguished guests. Mister Barnaby Skye, his wife Victoria, and Professor Alistair Nutmeg, in case any of you have not met them, Englishmen and friends of the HBC."

They toasted the guests, and Skye arose to toast his hosts and their company. Victoria sat quietly, transfixed by all this.

Skye soon found himself wolfing down food that had only been a memory for many years: beefsteak, potatoes and maize swimming in butter, apples and plums and pears, and breads galore.

Then he noticed Victoria sitting primly, her plate of foods untouched, her hands folded in her lap. She was staring at the rest, and he understood. She had never seen Europeans eat at table, had never seen the uses of silverware, had never seen serviettes across laps, or food enter mouths without the aid of fingers. She had never seen people dab their lips with those cloths, nor had she seen people sip daintily from glass goblets. She had never seen serving women hurry empty platters away and bring fresh ones. She had never listened to polite conversation at table.

He didn't know whether she was afraid or simply observing with those sharp eyes of hers. But he paused, slipped a hand over hers, and squeezed.

"Sonofabitch," she said, and began to eat, flawlessly mimicking her hosts and hostesses.

twenty-four

Skye found himself closeted with the formidable McLoughlin after the dinner. An oil lamp provided the sole illumination, adding a furtive and sinister quality to the interview. They sat in the factor's study, surrounded by ledgers but barren of books. McLoughlin's mind turned more to curios of the wilderness that had been presented him over the years.

McLoughlin motioned Skye to the cut-glass decanter of spirits—brandy, Skye supposed—but Skye declined. This was the interview that would shape his life. He would walk through the fateful portal as a man pursuing something radically new, or he would gather Victoria and ride back to the mountains.

"Well, Mister Skye, I've been following your case for years. I first thought of you as a criminal and lowlife. That's what the blasted navy had to say of you. But then reports filtered in from my men in our trading houses. They have a keen eye and a good ear, you know. And the two Skyes didn't match up. So, you see, I conducted a small inquiry of my own. I gather Ogden told you the rest."

"Yes, some of it."

"Enough to bring you here. That suggests to me that we may have something to offer. Eh?"

"What do you know of me, Doctor?"

"It's John, if you please. I never was much for ceremony. Especially here." A massive hand swept the air, and the gesture evoked a primal lordship.

But it was too much for Skye to call this man John. McLoughlin was the image of Empire, the king's magistrate, the representative of a vast, royally chartered company, and a man of massive size and ability.

The factor continued. "You are a good man. We want you. You can have a distinguished career with us. That sums it up."

"Why do you think I'm a good man?"

"I don't think it, I know it."

"I would like to hear your proposal in your own words, even though Peter Ogden gave it to me, sir."

"We've kept track. You're a resourceful brigade leader. You inspire your men. You don't stoop to the usual Yank trickery or ruthlessness and yet you do the job better. You have dignity and courage. You've pulled out of scrapes that would sink any man I know of in the mountains except Ogden and maybe Bridger and Fitzpatrick. You've revealed an ethical nature, paying off debts that might easily be forgotten. Your word is your bond.

"Ogden may be leaving us in two or three years. I wish to have you replace him. You're an Englishman. We're an English firm. You don't belong with the Yanks. Of course you had to stick with 'em, but I've been busy about that. You can come back to the Union Jack. I have good men here at the post, but none have the field experience you have. I'd put you out there, knowing you'd keep the Yanks from stealing our trappers, and send back peltries and make us a tidy sum."

"You mustn't listen to trappers' tales, sir."

"Would you deny any of it?"

Skye entertained mixed feelings about that. He knew he and Victoria, together, had survived where most men would go under. But she made the other half of it.

"Yes, sir. My consort Victoria . . ."

"Yes, yes, of course. That's understood. I'll confide in you." He glared at Skye, as if daring him to whisper a word of it elsewhere. "I've been looking for a successor. Someone to fill my position in a half dozen years. HBC has damned good men. But the ones in the field would be poor at governing this unruly empire, and the ones around me have no field experience. Then I was thinking about you . . ."

That stunned Skye.

"Show me that you can do it, Mister Skye."

Swiftly, this lord of the wilds answered Skye's questions even before they were asked. Years earlier, when McLoughlin realized that Skye wasn't cut to the Royal Navy's cloth, he became curious. He dispatched letters to London asking for information, and got it. Yes, Skye was a merchant's son who had vanished, deeply grieving the family. They thought him dead. Yes, the family had destined him for a business life. Yes, the press gang had snatched him near the London Dock. Yes, he had been a rebellious and sullen seaman, always on the brink of getting himself tossed into the sea to feed the sharks. Yes, he had become the joke, the byword, of the admiralty; the ultimate bad actor.

And yes, his father lived, but was failing.

Skye choked.

"Why should I go back there, risk my liberty, sir?"

"Because you must. We've friends in the right places. I had an HBC man approach the king's chancellor, Lord Pims, directly about it. We told his lordship that you'd prospered with the Yanks, that you've a stout heart and the destiny of Empire may hinge on fetching you back and jacking you to command. The Oregon country's up for grabs and jointly claimed by the Yanks and ourselves. We made the case, and Lord Pims will see to the royal pardon. Mere form, actually."

Skye listened, amazed that so much whirled around his person. "Who are my adversaries and what might go wrong?"

"Simpson, George Simpson, up in York Factory. He sees

no good in you and he'd clap you in irons the moment he lays eyes on you. He's not only the governor of HBC in America, but he's also the king's man. He rules the territory by leave of King George. If he catches you and sends you off to England, there's not a thing I could do. He's the law. We must obey it. That's why I'm not sending you back via York Factory or Hudson's Bay, but around the Horn."

"Who else?"

"Count on envy to make enemies, Mister Skye. I'm passing over a dozen men."

"Why do you trust me?"

"I don't, entirely. If you go to London, get your pardon, see your family, and fail to return to us, then I'll know the measure of you."

"My circumstance also requires trust. Will I arrive in England and be clapped in irons?"

"The admiralty would like it—if they knew of it. They don't. So far, this is between you, me, my contact on the board of governors of HBC, and Lord Pims. No one else knows."

Skye sighed. This forceful man seemed the soul of honesty, yet a man of cunning and a thousand schemes.

"How will all this happen?" he asked curtly.

"In two days our schooner, under Emilius Simpson, sets sail. You'll be on it. He won't have any idea you're a seaman and you obviously won't reveal it. Your past must remain obscure."

"I have a family here."

"A family, a family?"

"Victoria and our dog."

"Victoria should go with you if you feel she can master it. My women have, easily. Marguerite is, for all intents, a white woman. But the dog, that's up to the master of the *Cadboro*."

"I'll ask him, then."

"By all means. And if he says no, we could subsist the dog here and you'd be reunited in less than two years," the factor added.

Skye didn't like that. Something bad was crawling through his mind.

"We're penniless. I don't even have my rifle. We have nothing for passage."

"Three fine horses, Mister Skye."

Skye nodded.

"Here's what they'll fetch you. A fine suit of clothes and a spare frock coat and boots; two dresses, slippers, shoes, nightgown, and everything else required to outfit a lady for London, including a shawl. A good beaver hat, to replace the, ah, unsuitable one. A few pounds of traveling cash. A mug of soap, brush and razor, and any other toiletries you and Mrs. Skye might require. Good Scottish wool capes to keep you warm around the Horn and in England.

"We'll keep your dog, if need be, and outfit you for work when you return. I'll do an accounting: the value of the saddle horses is considerable here, and we are short and willing to pay a hundred Yank dollars, or twenty pounds, apiece. Sixty pounds will buy you the finest wardrobes this post can supply—and we can do you up, believe me. You'll sail to London and return, debt-free, but with an obligation."

Skye pondered that, half liking it, half itchy and unhappy.

McLoughlin pressed further. "Time's flying, sir. It'll take every hour of tomorrow to fit you out. The women are fine seamstresses, but not even they could outfit Mrs. Skye in less than a day."

Skye hesitated.

McLoughlin pulled a folder close and extracted a letter. "Here, sir."

Skye held it to the lamp so he could read. He needed spectacles but no such thing could be found in the mountains.

It was dated October, the year previous.

"To my son, Barnaby, wherever you might be . . ."

Barnaby Skye's hand trembled. At the base of the brief letter he discerned his father's own signature, crabbed and thick.

Going Home

A kind gentleman from Hudson's Bay Company has sought me out to tell me that you live somewhere in North America, and all the rest. We thought you were dead, the victim of some foul waterfront deed. Your mother and I grieved.

But that is the past. She is gone now, having left us in eighteen and twenty-nine, never knowing that you lived. May she rest with the angels. The rest of us live, though my health is precarious, dropsy and gout afflicting me.

I rejoice in this news, and urge you to come home swiftly, while time remains for me to behold you with my own eyes. The gentlemen have apprised me of your difficulties and assure me that the matter can be remedied in the king's chancery. We yearn to see you, and wish you Godspeed in your long journey. With this news, God has granted me my fondest wish.

With most loving affection,
Your father,
Edward Barnaby Skye.

Skye read it, and again, and let the memories of the man who had sired him flood through him. His sire would be old now, and his slim sisters would be fleshy. Something deep and primal stirred in him. He would go. And he would accept the costs and consequences and risks.

twenty-five

Victoria marveled at the skill of the several women who swiftly sewed her new clothing. That day they hurried her into a room where seven of them had gathered, measured her and set to work.

"These are the latest fashions from London," explained Marguerite McLoughlin.

"What is latest? This I do not understand."

"White women are forever changing their way of dressing. What is good one year is bad the next."

"That is very strange," Victoria said. "They are all mad."

That evoked some smiles and a giggle or two.

They fitted her first for a woolen winter dress of stiff gray fabric, and then for two dresses of cotton. And several of them had dug into their own chests and given her assorted accessories and underthings. One supplied a broad-brimmed straw hat sporting an extravagant feather much larger than any Victoria had ever seen.

"The feather is from Africa," someone told her.

"What is Africa?"

"I don't know."

Victoria discovered that these women sewed clothing in much the way as her Absaroka sisters made it. Two of these women were white, the rest were women of the Peoples, or breeds, such as Marguerite.

"What is England like?" she asked, but they did not know. The two white women were Canadians and had never seen England.

"I would not want to go there," said one Cree woman. "They would look down on me."

Victoria supposed that might be true. Skye had desperately tried to tell her everything he could about London, but she only grew confused. She finally realized she didn't know what he was talking about. He could not explain things she could not imagine. She could not even think about their King George, and what he did, and the people surrounding him. And when he described Parliament, she thought of a council of elders passing the pipe and speaking in turn, and that proved to be mostly wrong.

So she would have to see. And learn. But, she reminded herself, he had to learn the ways of her Kicked-in-the-Belly band of Absarokas, and he had been strange and shocking to her people for many months until he learned the ways, the rituals, and especially what was sacred and deserved uttermost respect.

She knew what she would do: be silent. She would not get into much trouble in this London if she said nothing and was careful to imitate the conduct she saw around her.

But the seamstresses at Fort Vancouver tried anyway to explain matters.

"When you enter a church, you should wear a hat or a veil," one said.

"What's this church?"

"A building where they worship God."

"What is worship?"

This went on through the morning, and by noontime she knew less about Skye's people than before, because everything she thought she knew proved untrue. One thing she knew:

everything white people did was vastly more complicated than her own ways, especially making medicine and talking to the spirits and the winds. When the women finally dressed her in all the proper underthings and the gray woolen dress, she felt constricted and anchored down. Her own durable, supple fringed doeskin dress with its quillwork was stronger, more comfortable, and more beautiful to the eye, and she didn't have to wear layers of little skirts under it.

But the women swarmed over her, fitting the clothing, adding a hat and gloves, and then led her to a looking glass.

Victoria shrank back from the image. She knew this was not herself.

"What the hell do I do when I must go to the bushes?" she asked. "Three of these little skirts and these pants?" She laughed maliciously.

None of them had been to England, so no one knew. They knew of chamber pots and privies, but little else.

Skye would know and she would ask him.

Later that afternoon she found him but barely recognized him. He wore a dove-gray cutaway coat with a double row of black buttons, black vest, a white shirt, blue britches, black leather shoes, and his battered beaver top hat had been exchanged for a glossy new one. He had lost his beard, too, and gazed at her from a smooth and ruddy face.

"Sonofabitch!" she yelled. "You some big medicine man!"

He grinned.

They laughed. She had never seen Skye looking like this. He had never seen her looking like a white woman. Suddenly Skye was a British gentleman; suddenly she was a dusky British lady. She took his arm and they promenaded round about the confines of the fort, following the footsteps of the bagpiper the night before.

That had been a terror. At sundown that first night she had heard the strangest howl, a noise that sent a chill through the marrow of her bones. Skye was closeted with McLoughlin and she didn't know what to do, so she slammed the door of their small apartment and waited. But the howl droned on, never stopping, like the groan of a dying dog, but there was more to it. She heard a whining melody, soft and cruel, like the wailing of mourners when her people lifted a dead person into its scaffold, and this wail sent chills through her. The yellow cur lifted its nose to the sky and howled.

Still, no one seemed alarmed. She heard no shouts, no running, no clamors, no war-cries. She softly opened the door a crack and peered out upon the dusky yard of the post, and there she beheld a man in a skirt, holding some fiendish device, walking in measured paces about the perimeter of the post. Then she had understood: he was a medicine man, chasing away the devils of the night, scaring the wandering spirits away from the post so the people could sleep in peace. Ah! A holy man!

She had watched this strange man, with the strange skirt and strange cap on his head, and this fiendish machine piping away the evils of the underworld, and she knew it was well. Skye had never mentioned this custom to her and she had planned to ask him about it. But she forgot, because when he returned to their apartment, he was filled with his meeting with McLoughlin, and that is what they babbled about.

But now Skye was strolling with her on the very path the medicine man with the fiendish device had paced so slowly that she had wondered if he were ill.

"What was that noise I heard last night?" she asked.

"What noise?"

"Like a hundred dying wolves."

He brightened. "Bagpiper. An old Scots custom."

"A medicine man?"

"You could say that," he said. "I haven't heard one since I was a lad. Call it a warrior's pipe. It's a big flute."

"Ah! It terrifies the enemy."

He explained what he knew of the piper, but she understood little. Maybe she would learn more in this London.

161

"You look very beautiful," he said, with some strange feeling in his voice.

"I do?"

"You . . . remind me of my sisters."

That disappointed her. She wanted him to like her as an Absaroka woman, not someone wrapped in these strange clothes that scratched and tortured her.

"I don't like your stuff," she said.

She saw some sadness in his face. He lifted his top hat and settled it. "We'll be coming back soon. Soon you'll be wearing your beautiful doeskin dresses and I'll be very happy."

"And you?"

"I confess I enjoy these clothes. I am, for the moment, a man of parts."

"Well, goddamit, let's go."

No Name found them and growled his disapproval.

Skye turned silent.

The dog chose a path between them, his pace matching theirs as they hiked around the vast yard.

She knew that silence. Whenever Skye was torn, he turned silent, and now he was terribly torn.

"They will feed him," she said.

But she didn't believe it. This yellow dog was a spirit-animal and such a creature had to go wherever its brothers went. But tomorrow they were going somewhere no dog could go.

They pierced the great gate, strolled down the gentle slope to the riverbank, and stared at the schooner bobbing there at anchor. The dog followed, whining once and then trembling.

The ocean canoe looked mighty to her, another wonder of the white men, but Skye was not impressed.

"This isn't much of a ship," he said. "Big merchant ship would be thirty or forty feet longer and ten or fifteen wider at the beam. This is a little thing for a big ocean. I wonder how the company can store a year's worth of furs in that hold."

She couldn't imagine a larger vessel.

"But she's seaworthy," he continued, talking to himself. "And she'll run. She's rigged to run, fore and aft sails . . ."

The dog was trembling.

She reached to touch its head, and the moment her hand touched the dog, it quieted.

"You must find a way to take him, Skye," she said.

"It will be up to the master."

"If he says no, we shouldn't go."

They stopped their stroll.

"Sometimes a man has to do hard things, Victoria. Give up something to receive something larger. I'm prepared to leave the dog behind if I must."

She didn't reply at first. Then she said, "He will not give you up. If he would give you his name, then he would be an ordinary dog you could give up. Any ordinary dog has a name. That is what names are for. If this dog had a name, you could leave him with McLoughlin. But he has withheld his name and that means he is bound to you for all of his life. He is not just a dog. He is a dog appointed to watch over you. He is more important to you than I am."

"That cannot be, Victoria."

"But it is so," she said, her tone adamant.

The dog was trembling again, and her heart was heavy.

twenty-six

Skye stood on the teak deck of a fine schooner, feeling joy. He was on his way to London to recover his good name. He was an Englishman returning home. He had a future assured in North America, working for a mighty English company. He could return to his homeland in the future. He would see his father and sisters and cousins and return to the bosom of his family. He would see nephews and nieces he had never seen.

He would not lose Victoria or his new life, either. She would go with him and return to her native land with him, and see her own family and tribe a year or so hence. No Name would remain. Skye had tried to win passage for the dog, but the master, Simpson, had flatly refused.

"I've never shipped a dirty dog, suh, and never will," the master had said.

McLoughlin had agreed to keep the animal. No Name would be waiting for Skye here in this massive post.

As he stood at the rail watching the crew smartly prepare to sail, he beheld almost the whole population of this amazing outpost. Several hundred men and women, not least of them the White Eagle, were watching the departure of the ship that linked them to the Mother Country so far distant; the ship that came but once a year and a half, bearing amenities and news of loved ones, as well as the staples of life. Skye waved one last farewell to Nutmeg, who waved back, full of good cheer.

No Name had tried to follow Skye out the short wharf and up the gangway, but two bosuns turned him back and then the dog slinked back to the riverbank and watched quietly. Skye was relieved: this would be all right. The good doctor would look after the strange creature.

Victoria held his hand, resolute in the midst of her fears.

"You have courage," he whispered to her. "We'll be back."

She didn't smile. This trip was for her like sailing over the lip of the world. But it wasn't the trip that held her; it was the dog, watching them mournfully from the shore, its head tucked between its front paws, forgotten by all the excited crowd of Indians, voyageurs, farmhands, clerks, and laborers collected in knots before the fort.

He knew he would not forget this spectacle, this bright October day, this vast panorama.

A breeze freshened even as Emilius Simpson's topmen raised the canvas. The master wore white kid gloves and stood quietly on the quarterdeck watching his hands twist the capstan that raised the anchor, while others looked to the sails.

Skye watched them carefully, knowing his life would be in the hands of this crew, and was satisfied. Simpson's quiet demeanor said much. The man radiated iron command in a curious way, as if some great reserve of force lay behind his gentle direction. He addressed his chief mate and bosuns, or deck officers, softly, but there would be no questioning this master's order. The kid-gloved hands occasionally squeezed shut, only to open again. It was as if Simpson needed the layer of soft leather to separate the duties of his hands from the rest of himself. Such as holding a whip.

But Simpson's was not the face of a martinet, and Skye knew that Hudson's Bay had chosen well, selecting a top man among a seafaring people.

Then, slowly, the schooner slid free of its anchorage and hove into the wind as the shuddering sails caught the breeze.

This trip downriver would rely heavily on the current of the Columbia to take it to sea, but there was nothing like a good two-masted schooner with fore-and-aft sails to employ an adverse wind.

Skye's home would be a cramped cabin on the quarter-deck, behind the master's own. He and Victoria would share a tiny galley with the entire crew, including the master and two mates. There were few amenities. The *Cadboro* was but fifty-six feet from bow to stern, and but seventeen at the beam, and carried a crew of thirty: chief and petty officers, seamen, cooks, navigators and helmsmen, carpenters and sailmakers. It was armed with six brass cannon, good for little other than scaring Indians and saluting passing vessels. But it was a clean ship, well caulked and scraped and enameled, gleaming the pride of its master.

In its eight-foot-high hold rested the entire year's fur catch, the wealth of the HBC borne in a single fragile bark that would sail clear down the Pacific coast of North and South America, round the fearsome Horn, head across the South Atlantic, and then north to England, a journey that would take six or seven months with good winds, longer if beset with troubles. The return, to York Factory on Hudson's Bay and then overland, would fly faster.

Skye felt the ship stir under his feet and heel subtly in the wind as the sails filled and the chattering stopped. The helmsman had measured the wind, checking its direction with a glance at the wooly wind gauge, and quartered north. The river there ran more northerly than west, but eventually would swing west to the sea. That vector made for fast sailing.

Skye said nothing and revealed nothing. His past was a secret known only to Victoria and himself. For the rest of those on board, he was a British gentleman, smartly turned out in serviceable fashion, escorted by a comely Indian maiden he had taken to wife in the fur trade. That suited Skye fine. The less they knew of him, the better.

The shoreline receded and the fort diminished to the rear,

and then there was only the glittering river, shooting sparks off its surface, purling toward the sea, cold and hazy on a bright day. The wooded shores seemed small and distant even as the helmsman caught the swiftest current to carry it along.

They strolled the small deck, where temporary disorder reigned. But Skye knew that no master would allow such disarray upon reaching the sea, where great waves would wash anything not tied down or anchored into the rails.

Then Victoria pointed. There on a promontory, small but unmistakable, was the yellow dog, its head high, staring squarely at Skye and Victoria. The dog rested there, its sides heaving, and then started west again, tracing the shore, never stopping because the ship never stopped.

Skye felt a bitter weight. "It'll turn around and go back," he said, not really believing it.

"It will find a way," Victoria replied. She was sincere; he hadn't been.

"It'll wear out. A ship never stops unless fog or haze forces it to. If the moon's full it can run at night. The pup'll come to a river and quit, and find its way back to wait for us."

"No," she said, and he stared at her.

Most of the next hour they didn't see the dog, but every time Skye thought the dog had quit, it reappeared, ghostly and yellow and staring at the distant ship, sometimes half a mile distant when the helmsman skirted the south bank.

Mr. Simpson appeared at their side. "Here's my glass," he said. "He's a fine loyal dog. The watch up there is talking about nothing else."

Skye lifted the telescoping brass spy glass to his eye and failed to see the dog.

"You're behind it, I think," Simpson said.

Skye swung the lens forward and caught a flash of yellow, and then finally focused on No Name, who was running easily, a few hundred yards at a time before sitting on his haunches to rest a moment.

He gave the glass to Victoria, who found the dog and

muttered bitterly, keeping her thoughts in Absaroka rather than sharing them with the white men. Then she handed the glass back.

"We'll reach the Pacific about nine this evening. Rough water there, some dangerous bars, and often some fog. With a favorable wind, we should be at sea just before full dark. It's the most dangerous point in the entire journey, more so even than Cape Horn. But once we reach the Pacific, we'll head down the coast, riding the Japan current, doing some trading in Mexican California before we abandon the continent."

Skye nodded. His thoughts were on the dog. Even without the glass, he could occasionally see the movement of a bit of yellow.

"Crew's betting when the dog'll quit," Simpson said. "They're taking odds that the pup will quit at the Lewis River."

"No," said Victoria.

"No dog can keep up for long," Simpson said, gently disagreeing. "We are moving at nine or ten knots."

The master returned to his watch, and Skye and Victoria watched the silent world slide by. A chill rose from the river, but neither of them would leave the rail even to fetch a shawl or a cape from the wardrobes hastily assembled for them.

Skye watched the dog struggle along the shore. It was obviously weary now, pausing to rest frequently. Skye could not see his sides heaving, but he knew exactly how that dog would look close at hand, and he sorrowed. He felt helpless and saddened and finally despairing, feeling that the dog would run itself to death rather than do the sensible thing and turn back.

What had Skye done to deserve such loyalty?

They passed the confluence of the Lewis, a large stream out of the St. Helen's wilderness and the crew lined the rail until a sharp word from the mates sent them to their posts again.

Skye did not see the dog. They sailed past the river. The

forest thickened and the shore vaulted upward again. And then, at a rocky point, they saw the yellow dog. The sun caught it until it glowed like gold. It stood proudly in the sun until the *Cadboro* passed, and then ran downstream again.

No one cheered.

twenty-seven

They saw no more of the yellow dog. By the time they passed the Kalama River, Skye knew the dog had given up. He grieved. No creature had ever loved him so much. He was ashamed at how reluctantly he had come to love the dog, how stupid he had been.

He brooded a while, studying the shore, hoping yet not hoping, wanting the dog to turn back to Fort Vancouver but wanting to see it again, a golden streak pacing the schooner as it cut the tide. The confusion of his mind wearied him.

Still, the future beckoned. He turned at last to his cabin, settling himself for a half-year journey home while Victoria still patrolled the deck of the small ship as if to measure her new world. The thought of England stirred feelings so deep he couldn't even name them. Not all of them were pleasant. His father's warehouse stood deep in East End, surrounded by misery and ignorance and depravity. The cruelties he had seen, even as a boy, had made it easier for him to adapt to the New World, where most people had a chance to fashion a life in a fresh, sweet land.

Maybe he would swiftly weary of London. After making his peace with the Crown and embracing his family, he would itch to escape to this vibrant continent where people were carving out a new life for themselves and severing the chains of Europe. He decided not to worry about all that: he was going home for a while, and what else mattered?

He felt increasingly confident about the weathered master, Simpson, who was sailing swiftly but not recklessly down the river, going faster than a square-rigged ship could but never so fast as to endanger his vessel. The *Cadboro* swung easily from one channel to another, responding instantly to the helmsman. Skye studied the men and the ship, seeing in their conduct more than the master suspected.

Victoria had slid into silence, mourning the dog, but later in the day she recovered her spirits.

She questioned him about everything:

"Why does that tree stick out in front?" she asked.

"That's the bowsprit, and it increases the amount of sail for the wind to catch."

"Why do the master and bosun's mates wear blue clothing?"

"Those are merchant marine uniforms, and they express the master's authority over the men."

"Why do the men obey?"

"Many reasons. They are paid to obey. Their life depends on obeying, working in unison. They could be punished if they don't."

"How?"

"Lashes across the back. That's a common punishment. Starvation and thirst. Execution."

"Death?"

"In the worst cases, yes. The sea kills swiftly."

"No war chief would kill one of his people."

"Unless the warrior tried to kill him. On a long voyage, seamen sometimes mutiny."

She wanted to know the names of things and he supplied them: the foremast, mainmast, taffrail, capstan, hold, and crow's nest.

They struck fog suddenly, late in the afternoon, a white blanket that had boiled inland from the Pacific, swallowing the wide river until they could not see twenty yards ahead. Simpson lowered sail, but the current still drew the ship along too swiftly and he finally ordered the anchors dropped, narrowly avoiding a large island dividing the wide river.

The dank mist penetrated Skye's clothing and chilled his face. They were approaching the sea now, and the mood of the weather changed. He smelled the salt sea in the breeze and sensed that they had reached tidal waters.

"I do not like this," Victoria said, and retreated to the cabin. He knew she would not find warmth or solace there. It was sunlight and fresh air that made the cabin comfortable.

Simpson patrolled the deck, making sure the schooner was well secured.

"Well, Mister Skye, what do you make of the *Cadboro* so far?"

"A tight ship, sir."

"You've been at sea. I imagine it holds no terrors for you."

"The sea always holds terrors for me, sir."

"Then you'd make a good seaman. I imagine you arrived at York Factory, Hudson's Bay, eh?"

"No, sir, I set foot on North America at Fort Vancouver."

"Ah! Then this is all familiar. What bark brought you here?"

"It's a long story, sir, for some other time."

"Well, I'd say you know more of sailing than you let on. You are quite at home aboard."

"As you say, sir."

Skye wished to change the subject. He did not wish to lie.

A mate summoned Simpson to deal with a rent in a sail, and Skye stared moodily into the whiteness, the whole world cloaked from his eyes by the soft fog.

It would be a miserable night, with cold sweat gathering on the polished interior wood of the cabin. Only the galley and mess, where a cookfire supplied heat, would offer comfort to those aboard.

The monotonous gray faded into blackness and the ship

bobbed softly in the dark, hour after hour, nothing visible, not shore or stars or even the tops of the masts. Skye felt isolated, caught in a constricting world and aching for the freedom of the open sea.

A bell summoned them to the mess, but Victoria chose not to eat. He realized then how profoundly this was afflicting her, in spite of her fierce loyalty and bravado.

He thought he would at least salvage a few biscuits for her if she hungered in the night. The cabin contained two narrow bunks and was barely six feet wide. A porthole let in dim light. The climate within was so damp that he suddenly feared for her health. How would a woman of the dry interior, the high plains and arid mountains, endure this cloaked and choking sea mist day after day?

But she said nothing, lying in her lower bunk, her gaze watchful of everything he did.

It was two hours after their simple mess, plum duff and raisin pudding, that he heard the shouting from the deck, and left the cabin to see.

The crew hastened up the hatchways and poured out on the slippery deck. The fog had lifted to some extent, forming a low ceiling. They could peer under it to a dark shore a hundred yards distant. But approaching across those inky waters was a big canoe of some sort, bigger than any Skye had ever seen, with some sort of lantern in its prow. It was propelled not by two paddlers, but a dozen.

"Bring the cannon around," Mr. Simpson said. "Load with grape and be quick. Mr. Burgess, prepare to repel boarders."

Several seamen began charging the brass six-pounders while others grabbed belaying pins, pikes, and axes. The mate and his men assembled at the rail, ready for war.

The canoe glided across the glistening water, those aboard making a considerable commotion. They were certainly not sneaking toward the *Cadboro*.

They were Indians of some sort, maybe Clatsop, but Skye didn't know these people. They were nothing more than names he had heard at Fort Vancouver. He found Victoria beside him, wreathed in smiles, and he wondered why.

"Goddam," she said, grinning.

"Who are they?"

"People who listen to the spirits."

That was no help at all. Skye watched the dimly visible canoe heave to, and swing parallel. One old man stood, speaking in a tongue Skye could not fathom.

"Mister Skye, perhaps you or Mrs. Skye could tell us what he wants," said Simpson. "If it's trade, say no."

But Victoria was nudging Skye, pointing at something gold in the darkness of the canoe.

Skye exhaled slowly, refusing to believe.

"Mr. Simpson, they have brought my dog to me."

"Well, send them off. I will not ship a dog all the way to England."

Even as Skye stared, his heart thudding, the dog uncurled, paced forward, and stood high on the very prow of the canoe, arching as if he would jump.

The seamen exclaimed.

"Can you carry him until we reach Monterey?"

The crew waited in utter silence.

"Oh, I suppose. But you'll have to leave him there."

"Then I will pay for his passage."

Simpson paused, weighing matters. "Your passage is paid for by HBC," he said. "Very well. But you'll be responsible for him. I run a tight ship, and if it's fouled, that dog will be donated to the sharks."

An odd throaty cheer arose. Skye sensed that every seaman aboard would see to the cleaning.

"Dog comes," said the old man. "Dog looking for you. Watches water. We see."

"I will take him," said Skye.

The crew lowered a gangway until it hovered just over the canoe. Several strong bronze men lifted the dog to it. The exhausted dog crawled up the cleats and tumbled onto the deck, too tired to move, except for its tail, which wagged once.

Victoria crouched over the half-dead No Name. The crew's silence amazed Skye.

He worked his way down the pitching gangway that rested on the bobbing canoe and clasped the old man's hand.

"You have made me whole again," he said. Maybe he would not be understood, but maybe this Clatsop, or whoever he was, would grasp something of it.

He could think of no way to say thanks except to dig into his money pouch and pull out one of the shillings that McLoughlin had given him, and hand it to the man.

The Indian fingered the coin, smiled, and nodded. Then, with a quiet command, he set his canoe in motion, as oarsmen backed it away from the schooner. Skye found himself scurrying up the gangway and on board just in time.

Victoria was stroking the inert, shivering, half-dead dog, crooning a lullaby in her Absaroka tongue.

He stared at No Name, knowing he would never learn how the dog made it some eighty miles from Fort Vancouver, swimming two large rivers, and then inspired a Clatsop village or hunting party to take it to the schooner.

Victoria was right. It was no ordinary dog.

twenty-eight

Skye scarcely dared talk to the bosuns and able seamen manning the *Cadboro*, knowing that he would swiftly give himself away. Their tongue was his. But little by little he did get to know some of them, including the carpenter's mate and the sailmakers and cooks. They told him of their passages around the Horn, of porpoises and sharks and drifting treasures; of scurvy and thirst and starvation and new sails that fell to pieces.

But always, their queries turned to the dog.

"What's his name?" one bosun asked.

"He has none, sir."

"Then the bloody dog's no pet, eh?"

"No, he's no pet. And I'm not his master. He is here because he wishes to take care of me."

"Now that's a bloody strange mutt. Do ye pet him or train him?"

"No, I barely touch him, sir."

"Then what's the use, eh?"

Skye had no answer to that.

Victoria nursed the dog back to health. For a day it lay motionless in the tiny cabin, more dead than alive, acknowledging their presence with a bare flap of the tail, but always watching. Victoria lifted it to her bunk and crooned softly, ancient Absaroka incantations, but the dog paid no heed.

Then, upon the second evening, it ate and drank heartily, and paraded around the small deck with Victoria, sniffing the endless green sea and measuring the constricted world to which it was now committed.

For Skye, the dog remained an unfinished story. He had resolutely abandoned the dog at Fort Vancouver, torn as he was between the dog and the great promise of England. And now he would have to do it all over again when the *Cadboro* dropped anchor at Monterey Harbor and Mr. Simpson did a trade in sea otter skins and other HBC business.

He wondered if he had cash enough to purchase casks of salt pork or beef to feed the dog clear to London, and knew he didn't. He had five pounds, the residue of his horse sale, supplied by McLoughlin's second in command, James Douglas, in a variety of coin, including pieces of eight, Mexican reales, Yank dollars, and English shillings and pence. That would have to sustain Victoria and him in London.

In any case, he knew Simpson would flatly refuse.

So the dog would find itself among the Mexicans, and for that reason Skye stayed aloof, not welcoming the dog, not wanting his heart to be torn to bits once again in a few days.

They had reached the treacherous tidal waters of the Columbia the morning after they received the yellow dog. The river had broadened to three or four miles there, and seemed wrapped in permanent cold haze. Simpson slowed the schooner, raised the keel, and drifted over the ever-changing sand bars where the river dropped its burden into the sea. Then the master wheeled the schooner south, turned the ship over to the master's mate, and ran the Pacific coast, rarely out of sight of land, whipped along by the Japan current and the westerlies.

Skye found himself loving the sea. He had thought he would hate it after his years of captivity. But here the benign sea sparkled and the salt air refreshed him. Gulls alighted in the booms and watched the world travel by. The cutwater prow sliced cleanly, parting the ocean around the smooth hull, leaving an arrow-straight wake behind them. Clean air swelled the headsail anchored to the bowsprit, and whipped into the two mighty gaff sails hung from the masts until every cord and rope grew taut and the ship hummed.

His own bright spirits affected Victoria's and helped her past her nausea and the strange circumstance of being upon a white man's ship, living according to white men's schedules, eating upon the sound of a bell, sleeping by shift, never pausing night and day so long as the horizons and stars and waters were visible to the men stationed high above. The air was never warm but never cold, and Skye found his frock coat suitable while Victoria usually wrapped a shawl over her shoulders during her endless circumnavigation of the short, slim deck, the ribby No Name at her heels. The dog was devouring every scrap the seamen gave it.

Sometimes when land was in sight he thought about the New World, of which this was the westernmost shore. Across a void lay ancient Asia, and ancient Europe beyond that. Here, in the unknown continent, he had grown into a man. The New World had rescued him from a short brutal life of slavery and had filled him with hope. But he did not reject the civilization from whence he sprang, for in its measured law and charity and protections, most people flowered, and in its sacred beliefs most people found courage and a means to transcend their worst instincts. Maybe some day the old and new would be fashioned into a great nation that protected the peoples it harbored even while granting them the chance to make anything they chose of their lives.

Simpson joined him at the rail.

"That's Mexican California, Mister Skye. A vast land, barely settled. One of the most isolated places on earth. Tomorrow I'll be stopping at Yerba Buena briefly; fresh water and whatever sealskins we can buy. An hour or two, if possible. There's an amazing inland sea there, where several rivers converge. Some day it may be among the world's greatest ports." He paused. "You might see about some salt beef for your dog."

"I'll do that, Mr. Simpson."

"You're partial to that dog; is he a good hunter or bird dog?"

"Truth to tell, sir, he's nothing. Just a tagalong."

"Well, tomorrow's your chance to get rid of him."

Skye stared moodily at the foam-girt swells. "I guess I'll wait until Monterey, sir."

"I've the feeling you're an old salt."

"Why would you think that?"

"Oh, I'd say the practiced eye. The way you examine a sail. Only an old salt looks at sails as you do."

"What do I see, sir?"

"Where the sail is weak; where they've been patched. How they hang wrong, sagging and bulgy, defying the wind. How the ship cuts the water. What sort of wake it leaves. What's in the bilge. How the seamen behave. Whether they respect their master. Whether the deck's holystoned. Whether there's rot in the timbers. Whether the cannon are loose. Whether the crew eats gruel or gets a tasty morsel now and then . . ."

Simpson waited, an eyebrow cocked, but Skye did not oblige him with the opening of his past. Skye liked him. He did not rule the way a naval captain ruled, though Skye didn't doubt that Simpson and his chief mate and bosuns could be just as tough as circumstances required.

The next morning they sailed through an amazing fog-shrouded passage into an inland sea, and hove to at Yerba Buena, a scattered collection of adobes huddled on a chill inland shore. Skye dismissed it at once. Such a mud village had no future.

Simpson launched a jollyboat and was rowed to shore, the Skyes and No Name with him. Skye and Victoria set foot in Mexico for the first time. Yerba Buena was not an impressive village, at least to Skye, but Victoria saw it through other eyes, and exclaimed at the assortment of whitewashed buildings and the brightly clad Mexicans who crowded around the crew and master.

Skye hunted for a butcher, looking for salt beef, and found none. No Name scarcely budged from Skye's shadow.

The negotiations didn't last long. The alcalde, who greeted them on the muddy tidal flat of a small cove, announced that a Yank trader had cleaned out every pelt in town only the day before and had sold numerous trade items, including bolts of calico, at better prices than those of HBC.

Simpson didn't tarry. Within the hour the *Cadboro* set sail, fighting a furious tide as it pushed through the shrouded gate and into the cold Pacific once again.

"I hope things aren't as discouraging in Monterey," he said to Skye once the schooner reached open water. "It's a much larger place and we have consignors and agents there, and those gentlemen have a warehouse and do a regular trade. Did you inquire about salt meat for the dog?"

"I made an effort but without success, sir."

"Well, we can subsist the mutt to Monterey. It's not far down the shore. We'll spend a day there."

The coastal mountains of California erupted high above the Pacific for most of the journey south. Simpson steered far out to sea to avoid hazards, but the coast was usually visible that afternoon. Skye sensed that the weather was moderating a bit; the air seemed more inviting than it had been during the north California passage, where the timbered coast was forbidding and dark.

The second morning found them closing on Monterey Bay.

"What about the dog?" Victoria asked.

"We find a family that'll take him. We've a day to do it."

"He will only die."

Skye sighed. "We will find him a master."

"This dog knows no master. He will run until he dies if we leave without him."

Skye felt bad. "What would you do?" he asked.

She shook her head, not knowing, and he saw the pain in her eyes. He held her, and then supplied the only assurance he could: "I'll see about some preserved meat for a sea voyage. Maybe he'll take the dog if I buy the chow. If Simpson agrees . . ."

She buried her face in his shoulder.

The yellow dog stared, and Skye swore the beast knew every thought crawling through Skye's brain.

They swept into a hook-shaped bay, not a true harbor but enough of a shelter to provide quiet water. Monterey, the rustic capital of the rural province, was indeed a larger place, with whitewashed buildings crawling up steep green slopes, the buildings topped with red-tile roofs.

But that wasn't what caught Skye's eye.

The Royal Navy's Pacific squadron was anchored there.

twenty-nine

Suddenly Skye's world darkened. He spotted a man-o'-war and two frigates. The Union Jacks fluttered lazily from the mainmasts. He could not tell whether one of the frigates was the *H.M.S. Jaguar*, from which he freed himself years earlier by slipping at night into the icy waters of the Columbia.

The Royal Navy had a long memory.

He watched helplessly as the HBC schooner saluted the king's navy and slid toward an anchorage well off shore. The Mexicans had never built a proper wharf. Simpson anchored the *Cadboro* about a hundred yards from the nearest frigate; too far for Skye to make out its name.

But there would be officers on these ships who would know him, or know of him, and delight in throwing him into irons and dragging him to England, or more likely, arranging for Skye's demise at sea.

The chances of his survival were slim if the navy caught him here. And the likelihood was overwhelming that the navy would. There would be courtesy visits. Simpson and any civilians on board would be piped onto the flagship to meet the commodore and his officers and share some rum. In turn, the officers of all three royal warships would be invited for grog by the master of the merchant ship.

Around him, the crew was anchoring the *Cadboro* fore and aft to avoid collision with the fleet. Others were lowering a jollyboat to take Simpson ashore, even as several Mexican craft were launching themselves toward the merchant vessel.

Skye felt that choking feeling that comes of foreknowledge of ruin, but swallowed it back.

Victoria and the dog stood beside him.

"That's the Royal Navy and I'm in trouble," he said. "We've got to get off this ship, leave everything behind, and make for shore and hide."

Fear lit Victoria's eyes. "So big," she breathed. "I thought this boat big, but now . . ."

"That man-o'-war's four times the length of this, and two or three times wider, and it carries forty-eight cannon."

"Skye—"

"We'll try to get off. Before the visits start. We'll be on foreign soil but not safe even there. If one of those frigates is the *Jaguar*, my shipmates are going to be in every grogshop in the city. And some'll be pleased to turn me in."

Simpson materialized beside them.

"We'll, Mister Skye, it's a sight, eh? The royal presence. It always fills me with a certain awe, seeing the fleet. They're flying the welcome ensigns and we'll run up our own, eh?"

Skye smiled crookedly.

"But those pleasures will come in a bit, eh? I'm heading ashore to do business."

"We'd like to join you, sir. Stretch our legs. I need to do some business."

"I have a boatful this time. I've promised some shore leave to the men, and of course I'll need to take my bosuns and master's mate to negotiate."

Skye swallowed back his fear and nodded. "You might employ the other jollyboat, sir," he said softly.

"No, not just now. Later, of course. I'm having my crew clean it out and ready it. We'll take it over to visit the commodore when we're invited. We'll do this by turns."

"Yes, sir," Skye said.

Deckmen lowered the jollyboat from its stanchions and a Jacob's ladder as well, and soon it was bobbing on the azure waters of Monterey Bay. The oarsmen descended, followed by the master and his officers, and the little vessel whirled toward the golden shore, the beach divided by outcrops of dark rock. Skye watched it bitterly, as if watching his sole hope for staying alive grow small. On that very beach, seamen wearing whatever they chose, and officers in blue, watched the progress of the little boat. Most of the seamen were loading water casks into longboats, or storing crates of fruit and vegetables and firewood into other longboats. A lighter carried six bawling Mexican cattle to the man-o'-war. Monterey was alive with the navy, and not just those on the waterfront. Every grogshop in town would be pouring rum into the gullets of the limeys.

He watched Simpson's jollyboat tie up at a crowded jetty on the rocky strand, and watched Simpson shake hands with the Royal Navy. He watched the officers converse, and remembered that he had never disguised his name. He was Barnaby Skye to the master of the *Cadboro*; the navy's most notorious deserter was Barnaby Skye. Sooner or later, when Simpson described his shipboard complement, he would name Barnaby Skye. It was only a matter of time.

It was but early afternoon. Skye thought the mutual visits wouldn't begin until the dinner hour and would stretch through the evening. Darkness was always a friend of fugitives and maybe darkness would preserve him in its gentle hand. Maybe it was pure luck that Simpson declined to take him and Victoria and the dog on the first shore visit.

"Victoria," he said low and soft and out of earshot, "we have to think this through. We're a hundred fifty yards from shore."

"I can swim that."

"Not in that heavy clothing, dress and petticoats and all. And I can't swim in this getup for long."

"The dog can."

She was smiling tautly.

He felt helpless but determined. He lacked a weapon and carried nothing more than an old Green River knife that he had acquired at his first rendezvous. He and his family had to get off this ship, and do it at night, and escape Monterey. If that meant leaving their entire wardrobe behind, he would do it. If it meant abandoning his vision of England, he would do it. The thought wrought pain in him, but the prospect of capture and probable death at the hands of his former officers, feasting on their triumph, was the vision that controlled his every act.

"Victoria, make a small bundle, nothing obvious, of all the clothing you can carry, whatever we'll need. And one for me as well. We'll be going ashore here. We will never reach England."

She glanced sharply at him and wordlessly headed for the cabin.

His mind whirled with ideas but none of them seemed very good. He watched the navy's seamen load cask after cask of water and row out to the warships; he watched Simpson and the *Cadboro* officers dicker with the Mexicans crowding about on the shore. He watched Simpson signal for the second jollyboat, and watched seamen lower and row it to shore, filled with empty casks. He itched to board that boat with Victoria and the yellow dog, but they would step ashore in the midst of ten or twelve midshipmen and petty officers of the navy, very likely some under whom he had suffered. He told himself to be patient; darkness would tenderly cloak them.

An hour ticked by and then one of the bosuns, Abner Gilbert, approached Skye at the rail.

"Mr. Simpson says to catch the next jollyboat in," Gilbert said. "He's mindful you have business ashore. About the dog, you know. He's met a Mexican who'd take it and he'll introduce you. We'll be loading sealskins and water and vegetables until well after dark. Lift anchor at first light."

There it was. Fate hung. Skye could scarcely refuse. But there was advantage. On shore, on foreign soil, he had a chance. On board, he didn't.

"All right, sir," Skye said.

He found Victoria bundling clothes.

"We're going in. Simpson's invited us. Forget this," he said, waving at the wardrobe in their trunks.

Victoria grinned. That grin, famous and huge in his mind, had lifted him past the worst moments of his life. They would leave everything behind if that's what it took. Who needed clothing like that in the mountains?

Victoria did stuff her doeskin dress, and his buckskins, and the two capes into a carpetbag, and they headed for the rail. The jollyboat bobbed on the water below as they descended the jacob's ladder and set foot in the careening little vessel. Minutes later the oarsmen beached the boat on the sand—the Royal Navy had commandeered the little jetty—and Skye helped Victoria jump the last foot from the prow to the sand.

Land! All about them the Royal Navy was at work. The seamen paid no attention to a burly man in a frock coat and top hat, or his dusky wife and ribby mutt. Skye proffered an arm to Victoria, and they paraded amiably past sailors too busy wrestling kegs to study them. Skye pushed the top hat lower on his face to deepen the shadow. His long dark and graying hair, gathered with a string at the nape of his neck, further altered his face.

They ascended a rocky incline that took them above the tidal shore and walked slowly toward the line of small adobe merchant buildings that disgorged or swallowed the burdens of visiting ships.

He began to relax a little: they had passed, in the bright afternoon sunlight, the thickest concentration of tars and officers unscathed.

He spotted Simpson talking earnestly to a Mexican before the yawning doors of a warehouse, and headed that way, as casually as he could manage.

The Mexican delighted the eye: he wore a short black coat, tight britches of fawn-colored cloth, a bright red sash, and a great sombrero. He was much better dressed than the rest of his people, who toiled barefoot in soiled white cottons, loading long, velvety, tan sealskins upon mule-drawn carts.

"Ah! Mister Skye! And Mrs. Skye! May I introduce Don Emilio Baromillo, a fur merchant here, and also Senor Esteban Larocha, Mexican customs, who's making sure we pay our tuppence for every pelt."

They shook hands. "Mr. Baromillo says he might consider the dog—"

But Skye was watching the swift approach of an ensign posted at the next warehouse, a man he suddenly realized he knew.

"Skye!" bellowed the officer, drawing his bright sword. "I'd know that ugly nose anywhere!"

thirty

Skye resisted two impulses. One was to run; the other was to bull straight into the skinny ensign—his name was Plover—and wrest the sword from him.

It was too late, anyway. Plover thundered down on Skye as he stood next to Simpson and the two Mexicans, waving his glittering blade and summoning his work detail to join him with his shrill boatswain's pipe.

A half-dozen tars swarmed out of the next building and swiftly surrounded him.

Victoria was aghast and backed away. She had a way of becoming invisible. The world somehow never paid her much attention, which had saved their lives more than once. No Name joined her.

"Got you, Skye, and don't tell me you're someone else. Oh, what a day this'll be for the Pacific squadron!" He bawled at his seamen, "Hold this bloody devil. Don't let him get away. We've been after him for years, and now he's walked into our parlor."

Skye stood as quietly as he could manage, knowing his chances were slim and growing slimmer by the second as the burly seamen circled him, ready to pounce.

"A damned deserter!" Plover cried to those who were watching.

Don Emilio Baromillo observed all this with a frown. The customs man, Esteban Larocha, grew excited.

"Come along, Skye!"

"I think not," said Skye.

"What? What? Grab him, men."

The seamen, none of whom Skye had seen before, swarmed him and tossed him to the rocky ground. Skye fell hard, hurting himself in the shoulder. Victoria was circling around behind the ensign, though Skye could not fathom why unless to grab his sword.

"Alto!" said Baromillo, in a voice that brooked no resistance. "This is Méjico!"

"I don't care where it is, we're taking this man with us," Plover bellowed.

"Alto," the don snapped. "Do you want to taste my sword, ensign?"

"It's none of your bloody business," Plover retorted.

"It is Méjico's business. When a man is forcibly taken from our country, it is our business. Let him go. I will tell you now, release him."

Larocha sprang into the action. "I will get el gobernador. This makes the war! Madre Dios, what insolence!"

That sobered Plover a moment, but his defiance bloomed again. "Go ahead, get your army for all I care. This man's wanted by the Royal Navy and we'll take him."

Baromillo pressed forward and spoke in that low deadly tone that commands instant attention. "This hombre you want to kidnap is a Hudson's Bay man brought here by Capitan Simpson. I will not allow this to happen, not on our soil. England will not be welcome here if you take him without our consent. Go resupply elsewhere. This is not your country. It is the Republica de Méjico. Tell that to your capitan." He turned to Larocha. "Fetch the guardia, and el gobernador, pronto, pronto."

Skye rubbed his aching shoulder and clambered slowly to his feet, well aware of the sharp blade switching back and forth like a cat's tail and hovering inches from his body. He brushed sand off his frock coat, retrieved his top hat, and stood quietly, his mind awhirl with calculation.

"Thank you, Don Emilio," he said quietly. "I would like to have your governor settle this matter. I am indeed Barnaby Skye, and I am in the fur business and associated with the Hudson's Bay Company. I have been in the fur business six years."

"They call you a criminal, Senor Skye."

"I know of no crime that I've committed."

"Desertion!" Plover yelled.

Skye did not deny it. He ignored Plover and addressed the powerful Mexican directly and quietly. "A man pressed into service against his will does what he must. An unbound English freeman who is made a slave at the age of thirteen, snatched off the streets of London, has every right to free himself. I served seven years, and now am a free man on Mexican soil, engaging in an honorable trade, welcomed here by your officials."

"The Crown wants him," Plover blustered. "If you won't let us have him, the Crown will be displeased, and you'll hear from our envoys."

Plover was not going to surrender his prize lightly.

Baromillo waved a hand impatiently, as if to discourage a pesky fly. "That will be up to the authorities. Perhaps they will release him to you. But you will not drag him away, not on Méjican soil. If you do, you will face my own good Toledo sword, and you will regret your conduct the second your beating heart feels my steel. Do you wish to test me?"

That quieted Ensign Plover and his men.

They waited in the bright Monterey sun. Skye calculated his chances of escape and found them nonexistent. Even if he should escape the navy, Mexican soldiers would track him down fast. He had never seen this country and wouldn't know where to go; it was their home and they would catch him. He stared bleakly at Victoria and the dog, and had no answer for them as they watched him.

Some eternity later a squad of uniformed soldiers from the presidio appeared, the tramp of their boots thudding a cadence through the narrow streets of the province's capital. Along with them came a corpulent, dark, warm-eyed man with a cheerful and imperial air. The soldiers were armed with pikes and muskets. Don Baromillo translated.

"El gobernador is not present, but I am Amarilla, his devoted and loyal lieutenant. What is this I hear? Does the British navy snatch a man off the streets of Monterey, the capital of Alta California?"

Plover made his case in vehement terms, talking furiously while the don translated calmly.

Amarilla considered the case only briefly. "We will hold this man for the gobernador. He is due here within a fortnight, having matters to deal with at his estancia, including the birth of a seventh child, the theft of angora goats, the training of a dozen horses, and a daughter who wishes to marry an unworthy lout from the City of the Angels."

"But we're sailing this evening!"

Amarilla shrugged. "El gobernador will be pleased to entertain your petition, and listen as well to this hombre and his petition, si? There is a small fee involved. Perhaps he will turn this man over to you. He wishes for relations between the English and the province of Alta California, en Méjico, to be warm and fruitful, eh?"

"A reward! I'll return to my ship and we'll supply a bounty for this man. Give me two hours and the bounty will be yours. We want him. Ten pounds for this man! I will get it from the strongbox. The commodore will be pleased."

Amarilla shrugged. "Show us the papers against him, and the amount of the bounty, and perhaps justice will be accomplished in time for your sailing. How could this man be worth so much, eh? He does not look like a criminal, except for that vast and noble nose. Perhaps it is true that evil men are revealed by the size of their noses. That is a theory to look into."

Skye watched his chances diminish to nothing. All this was hard for Victoria to follow, but she signaled to him that she understood. Whatever his chances, everything would be up to her. But to think it was to know that she could do nothing. She was a Crow Indian from the mountains. She had scarcely set foot in such a world as this.

At least he had a better chance among the Mexicans than he did with the navy. The Mexicans might detain him but would not kill him. He was sure of it now: the longstanding resentment at Skye's escape long ago had not diminished, but had become a legend in the admiralty. There would be many a cheerful ensign and lieutenant and captain and commodore toasting Plover this evening. And tomorrow, at sea, they would tie Skye to the webbing under the bowsprit of one of those vessels of war, give him a knife but no water, and let him settle his own fate.

So it had come down to cash. Amarilla was not above a little financial improvement, so long as it could be clothed in bounty and warrants and all the rest of the trappings of international law. Skye knew his life wasn't worth a shilling just then.

They marched him up hill through the dirt streets of Monterey, past lovely whitewashed houses with shuttered windows and red-tile roofs, past staring women and children and old men, all of them dressed in a bright and showy manner, velvet coats and pantaloons, soft slippers, gaudy sashes, thick tortoiseshell combs, and delicate mantillas over jet hair. They were beautiful people, warm-fleshed and handsome, but they eyed him soberly as he passed, surrounded by the stern blue-and-white uniformed soldiers with the pike poles and muskets.

Skye watched Victoria and No Name follow, unnoticed, for they posed no threat nor did reward hang over her head. She wore European clothing and her dusky features could not even be distinguished from those of the Californios. They paid her no heed, and that was good. She would help if she could, but neither he nor she had the slightest plan or any place to escape to. He could not go back to Simpson. The master would probably turn him over to the navy without a second thought.

They arrived at the presidio, a small whitewashed post with commanding views of the blue bay. Skye passed through thick adobe walls into an inner yard, and was led to a small room guarded by a massive wooden door. Victoria paused, and then entered the yard, the dog wandering casually at her side. At least she would know where he was taken, where to find him if she could free him. The soldiers paid her no heed. The last he saw of her, she was hovering just a dozen yards away, her eyes drinking him in.

Amarilla ushered him into a small bare room, lit only by a high barred window, and without any furniture of any sort. "Senor Skye, welcome to Méjico," he said, smiling not at all kindly. "A thousand pardons for this indignity. Perhaps your visit will be brief, or so we both may hope, si?"

thirty-one

The old helplessness visited him once again. He had spent more time than he cared to think about confined in one cage or another. The navy was very good at shackling or confining a man. Now he was snared once again, this time in a mean dirt-floored trap with stained and pocked walls and a tiny grilled window, too small to crawl through, high above.

The place stank. A filthy corner served as the latrine. He paced a circle restlessly, knowing it would do no good, but then willed himself to quiet his spirits. His liberty had vanished and there was little he could do but wait. He slumped against the gummy wall as far from the stinkhole as he could. He could see a few inches of blue sky through that window. For six sweet years he had seen all of the heavens each day.

He remembered his ancient vow: he would die rather than live where he could not see the sky without bars between it and his eyes. He had wrestled his way free by placing his liberty ahead of his life. More than once he had told others that he would die before he would be taken. He had meant it. But now, in a lax moment he had let himself be captured.

But this was only the beginning of the story. He did not know how this would end, but he knew, once again, that he would not board a naval warship alive. If they took him, he would fight them to death. The thought hardened his resolve but didn't console him. His life as a free man had been indescribably sweet, and he had won the respect of the mountaineers, rising to brigade leader. He had come into himself at last.

Time stalled. It always did in confinement. A few minutes seemed like an hour. A day seemed like a month. He had learned that lesson long ago. So he found patience, knowing that all this would come to a head swiftly if what the ensign said was true.

Ten pounds bounty. That puzzled him. He couldn't imagine the pinch-pursed Royal Navy squandering ten pounds to snare a deserter. Ten pounds for a bloody tar who'd slipped overboard six years earlier? For what? To prosecute him as an example to other seamen? Or just because Skye had become a dark legend in the admiralty? He didn't know. He didn't even know why the admiralty had taken such an interest in him. No other seaman in the admiralty's memory had tried longer or harder to escape, and no other sailor had been subjected to such harsh measures to prevent it, and yet Skye had found a way, defeating his lord jailors at last.

Daylight slipped by and no one came. The presidio stayed chill, swept by sea breezes that trumped the mercies of the sun. The coldness and darkness drifted through Skye's body and mind, reducing him to melancholia. He felt raw fear, and hated it.

He wondered where Victoria was. She lacked so much as a shilling to purchase tripe for herself and the dog. She had never bought anything at a market before, never pushed a coin across a counter, but she had seen how white men did things at rendezvous, and again at Fort Vancouver. The warren in which he was confined did not face any street, but stood near the rear of the presidio. He had no way of tossing a coin or two to her. He wondered what she was doing, his lady of miracles. She knew nothing of forts or presidios. They were all fearsome mysteries to her. She had scarcely even seen a permanent building before. But now she knew their uses, including the use put to this bleak closet.

More time drained by, and the light shifted as the sun progressed across the tiny window. He was practiced enough at confinement to know that two, three, maybe four hours had gone by without the arrival of the Royal Navy and its Judas coin.

No one came. No one cracked the door to look in on him. No one delivered water or food. He thirsted, after the morning spent in bright sun. Soon he would hunger, too. He heard nothing without; no soldiers tramping, no shouts, no conversation, no bustle of daily toil, no bugles. Only a mortuary silence, as if the world had forgotten this place or the raging man caged within it.

He began to suffer. His tongue rasped sand. His throat swelled. The light shifted again, darkening to azure by several shades, and he knew the night was stealthily approaching. And still no one came. He rose, paced restlessly to relieve his cramped muscles, round and round his globe, moving nowhere at all, wearing a groove in the earth; a groove already begun by those who had been thrown in here before him. But walking kept him sane.

Darkness fell, and he knew that ten or eleven hours had elapsed since he had been tossed in here and held for ransom, politely described as bounty offered by the king's men for a man who had escaped their control. By dusk, when the light faded and the room plunged into a gloom just shy of blackness, he knew that no bounty was offered for the likes of Skye, and that the commodore of this squadron, whoever that might be, had probably laughed the ensign out of his presence.

Skye hammered on the massive door, thinking perhaps he had been forgotten. But no one responded. By full dark he was desperate for water, his mouth dusty and his throat seared by every breath.

Maybe they would kill him. Maybe this was some sort of local hospitality. Maybe he would die a slow, anguished death from dehydration. He hammered wildly on the door, thumping it with his boots and fists, and heard only the echoing silence.

The cold filtered in and chilled him. He pressed into a corner to conserve what heat he could, and finally slumped into a long bleak quietness as the minutes and hours ticked by.

Dark thoughts visited him. What would poor Victoria do after they let him die? She knew nothing of these people or their tongue. He thought of his father, the man he would not see. The family he would not see. The lanes of London he would not see. The royal pardon, making him a free subject of the Crown, he would never hold in hand.

The HBC ship must have sailed. Simpson planned to pull out while there was yet daylight and make for Cape Horn, with only provisioning stops en route.

He lost track of time. Thirst tortured him and that was all he thought of.

And then, strangely, he fathomed the clack of bars and bolts, and the door opened. A man holding a small candle-lamp appeared. He carried an earthen jug and handed it to Skye, who drank, and again, and again, and then again as fast as his body could accept the sweet water. Skye drank until he had drained the entire earthen jug.

What a miracle was water. Food a man could do without for some while, but not water. Swiftly Skye's body stopped protesting, and he stood.

That was when Amarilla appeared, sidling through the door like some ghost.

"Senor, may your time in Méjico be blessed and prosperous, and may you enjoy Alta California, which is next to God's own paradise in comforts and consolations. May you be a friend to all Californios, and may we welcome you to our province with honors and true and holy affection, as prescribed by the holy fathers."

"It's about time you came."

"Ah, Senor Skye. The English do not waste uno centavo on

197

you. No bounty. It's a pity. The ensign, he said your price was ten pounds. Ah! That is a fortune, senor. That would make a poor official comfortable. The gobernador pays so little, you know. A few pesos a month, and your servant has a large family to support because my esposa is a lusty woman. It is too bad he is not here to take care of this matter."

"Am I free?"

The governor's lieutenant sighed. "How I wish for your sake that it could be, senor."

"What's holding me here? I'm a visitor."

"Ah, amigo, you are here for the crime of being here too long without permission. Have you papers? Did el gobernador approve that you should be here?"

"I was forcibly brought to this prison."

"Ah, amigo Skye, it is a crime nonetheless. The fine is ten English pounds."

"I don't have that."

"It is a pity, si?"

Skye pulled his small leather purse from his frock coat. "This is what I have. It is something less than five pounds. A lot of money."

Amarilla hoisted the purse and poured out the glinting coins in his hands. "Where is the rest? No gentleman travels without much more. I have seen the English and the Yankees."

"Search," said Skye. He handed his frock coat to the bureaucrat, who made diligent search.

"Is that enough?" Skye demanded sharply.

"Ah, senor, it is enough to satisfy one of the charges, but not the other."

"What other charge?"

"Vagrancy. You are now a man without a centavo, without a home, without means of support, a wanderer among us. Therefore a vagrant. We have laws against it. A pity, senor. Such a fine foreign gentleman. So we must detain you here until you acquire means—"

That was too damned much for Skye. He leapt at Amarillo, grabbed him by the throat, and rattled him.

"Aargh!" the man cried.

The old soldier, who had supplied the water, sprang at Skye, who decked him with one massive blow. The man tumbled to the ground, senseless. His lantern smashed and the candle died. Skye peered swiftly about. He had no idea what time it was, but his best guess was somewhere midway between midnight and dawn. The presidio slept. Everything was so black and unfamiliar that he scarcely knew how to let himself out of the presidio.

He lifted the bureaucrat to his feet and grabbed a handful of shirt.

"Take me to the gate," he said. "And if you make a sound, you'll feel my boot."

This wee-hours visit was odd, and Skye sensed that the man did not want to be seen there, cleaning Skye out of every shilling he possessed. Some things were so shameful that only darkness could cloak them.

The man led him past looming buildings to the gate, which was wide open and unguarded. Now at last Skye could see the whole peninsula and the bay far below in the soft moonglow.

"Give me my purse, you pirate," Skye whispered.

Amarilla resisted, whining like a pig that sees the knife approach its throat, so Skye dug around until he found it.

"Go ahead of me. Down to the waterfront."

"Senor, por favor, I wish to depart your pleasant and treasured company. Consider yourself an honored guest of Méjico."

Skye laughed softly. "Go wake up the soldiers and let them chase me if you dare," he said, releasing the official.

He watched the man hasten away, downhill. Then he peered at the moon-glittered bay. It was empty.

thirty-two

Skye watched Amarilla hasten through the night toward a warm bed, no doubt grateful that the distinguished English visitor to Méjico hadn't kicked his ribs in.

The bay caught the moonlight and glittered it back at him, and he studied it. No black hulks bobbed on the waters. No black masts poked the sky. The Royal Navy squadron had sailed. The commodore had better ways to spend the king's purse than purchasing a notorious deserter.

But it was not the sea that caught him, but the dark sky with its pinpricks of light coming from some unimaginably distant place. He could see the whole bowl of heaven; he was free. He possessed himself and his future.

No Name rubbed at his legs. Startled, he beheld the gaunt cur standing guard over him. He knew, intuitively, that if he turned his head just a fraction, he would behold the woman he loved, and suddenly he choked.

"Thank you for waiting for me," he said.

"Goddam, Skye, I thought they take you away. I see these big houses and I think, this is a place of safety. People live behind thick walls and keep the rain and cold away. But now I see that big houses take away a man's freedom, too. Absaroka don't have big houses."

Skye had never thought of that: that white men's structures were both refuges and prisons.

He slipped an arm about her shoulder and drew her to him and then he kissed her, and she kissed back.

"We should leave here," she whispered. "This bad place."

"We will," he said. "I got my money back from that pirate. Maybe we could buy horses. Maybe outfit ourselves. Five pounds isn't much, though. Twenty-five yank dollars."

"How much is a rifle and bullets, Skye?"

He sighed. "I don't know. I can't even speak their tongue."

"They know finger talk?"

"No."

"What you gonna do, Skye? Go to England?"

Skye studied the dark expanse of heaven and knew that something had changed forever: he would never see England. Nothing was the same.

"No, Victoria, we'll go to the mountains. We'll go home."

"You gonna work for Hudson Bay?"

"They can't employ me as a brigade leader unless I have a pardon. I could probably work for them as a trapper in some obscure post, more or less out of sight."

"How we gonna go from here, eh?"

"I don't know. I know there's mighty mountains all around this place, and winter's coming."

He felt dizzy from lack of food, and walked slowly toward the bay. That seemed the safest place until morning, when the markets opened. Victoria followed him down the slope until they stood at the edge of the sea, watching the ebb tide drain across dark sands. England seemed some impossible distance away; a world and lifetime away now. His fate lay here, in this untouched and merciful continent where hope lived. He sorrowed. He had wanted so much to see his father one last time; to be restored to the freedoms of an Englishman. He saw, In his mind's eye, the image of his father soften and fade and then vanish.

"You not feeling good, Skye."

"I was saying goodbye to my father. I'll be all right in the morning."

He settled against a rocky outcrop and listened to the sea as it flooded hope in and out of the lengthy shoreline. Someplace far away lay China.

The dog had vanished again. Who could say what the yellow cur was doing? And then, after a while, it appeared, carrying something large in its jaw. This burden it brought to Skye, who sat slumped into the hard rock, and laid it upon the sand.

One slow slash of the cur's tail informed Skye that this was a gift.

"Sonofabitch," said Victoria.

Skye lifted up a haunch of meat, discovered that it had been well cooked and was fresh. He did not know what sort of meat, but thought it was lamb. The cur eyed him dolefully.

"Where did you steal this, you rascal?" Skye asked.

The dog waited.

Skye dug into his frock coat and found the small skinning knife sheathed at his waist, his sole memento of the mountains.

Tenderly, he sliced a piece of the cold and tender flesh and handed that first piece to the dog. It accepted gently, settled on a grassy spot, and began gnawing at the food.

"Thank you, No Name," Skye said, sudden feeling blooming in him. This dog was not a pet nor a son nor a child; this dog was his New World father, looking after his son and daughter. The dog looked very old and wise, and much smarter than any mere mortal.

Then Skye cut thin slices for Victoria, who ate each one with relish, licking her fingers and clucking with sheer joy. When it came to good meat, no one was more appreciative than an Absaroka Indian.

Finally he himself ate one piece and then another, and then he fed the dog again and Victoria, and they ate thin, sweet slices of lamb until the moon slid down the bowl of the sky and the eastern sky began to lighten. It was very cold, and they had only the clothing they wore. They huddled together, and then the dog crawled across their laps, warming them a little with his body.

They watched the dark bay of Monterey begin to blue as the sun crept over the distant mountains south and east. The bay looked so empty. Had great events occurred on these serene waters just one day before? Had armed might, a hundred and fifty cannon, anchored there? Had the Union Jack flown there, along with the Hudson's Bay standard?

The sun climbed and no one stirred, and Skye suspected that the Californios lived on a leisurely plan and did not rise early if they could help it. Skye ached, and he knew Victoria did, too. They had suffered much in the past hours.

He hadn't the faintest idea what to do. His few pounds might buy an ancient flintlock, but maybe not. The cash would not equip him and his loved ones for a long hard journey to the Stony Mountains, in the middle of winter.

He knew of two men here who spoke English well enough. One was the fur trader, Don Emilio Baromillo, and the other was the customs man, Esteban Larocha. Of these, Skye preferred to deal with Baromillo. He was not keen on seeing an official, with an official's attitude toward foreigners in California without the permission of the governor.

He would try to find Baromillo, if only to obtain some advice. How did one leave California for the interior? And what equipment would the don recommend?

No Name slept the sleep of the innocent. Skye felt less innocent and buried the remains of the haunch deep in sand. Around them now, people stirred. An ancient woman in black combed the shore, eyeing the visitors sharply. A group of fishermen gathered about a beached boat and dragged it into the bay. Then they boarded, loaded some supplies, pushed free of land, and raised a venerable sail.

Children flocked by, and the Skyes found themselves objects of curiosity, but when Skye tried to speak to them, they stared solemnly or giggled, and vanished along the strand.

Skye was weary: he hadn't slept and he had endured one of the most harrowing nights in years. But he didn't want to move, or wander the town, risking attention. So they watched the turquoise bay, watched puffball clouds float over, watched gulls wheel, and watched Monterey brighten into a bold city with red-tiled roofs, rioting flowers, and whitewashed adobe buildings.

Then Skye saw someone stirring at Baromillo's warehouse, the very place where he had been discovered while conversing with Simpson and the Mexicans. He rose stiffly, and Victoria rose as well. But No Name raised one eyebrow, closed it, and dozed on. Skye brushed sand off his begrimed frock coat and britches, repaired to the warehouse, and found a slender young man there.

"Do you speak English?"

The man shook his head.

"Could you direct me to Don Emilio?"

"Don Emilio? Ah ..." the man fought for words. "Una hora?"

"One hour." Skye pointed at himself. "Senor Barnaby Skye. Senora Victoria Skye."

"Skye?" Some knowingness lit the man's face. "Ah, si."

"Una hora," Skye said.

They strolled Monterey, aching in every joint. Skye examined a village tinted with primary colors, cleansed by fresh sea breezes and populated by the most colorfully dressed people he had ever seen. To his eye, the women wore very little; their golden arms were bared to the blessings of the sun, and their bosoms were barely covered. They were mostly jet-haired, and had glowing brown eyes that raked his person as he strolled by.

The caballeros, on the other hand, vied with the ladies to be noticed, wearing short coats, red sashes, and gleaming white shirts festooned with lace. They were, to a man, possessors of proud steeds, which they corvetted and paraded. Victoria could barely contain herself, and gasped at every new sight.

"What a people!" she breathed, after watching a horseman dance his horse past, the equipage jingling and the tassels shivering. "Sonofabitch!"

Skye was glad Victoria was more interested in the horses than the horsemen. And that she had not paid attention to the dazzling beauty of the senoritas, whose glowing smiles had set Skye's heart to tripping.

They passed open-air markets and beheld fruits and vegetables and grains in crockery bowls and baskets, sold by Indians along with rural people. They clambered up narrow and crooked streets, past houses with inner courtyards and tiled or flagstoned patios behind black ironwork, where they could glimpse the domestic life of these handsome people.

Skye was impressed. Everywhere, the Mexicans had created their domestic and commercial life with artistry and beauty in mind. But when he had gauged an hour had passed, he steered Victoria down the long slope to the warehouses on the strand, and found the enterprise belonging to Baromillo.

The trader welcomed them cautiously, and bade them enter a spare cubicle where the clerk huddled over a ledger.

"Senor Skye," he said cautiously. "I do not expect to see you any more ever."

"The navy didn't want me," Skye said without further ado. "And now we need your help."

Baromillo frowned.

thirty-three

The bleakness and impatience in Emilio Baromillo's gaze didn't encourage hope in Skye. Nonetheless, he plunged in.

"I am thankful to find someone who can speak my tongue, sir. My wife and I are stranded here and need your assistance."

Baromillo stared, not a muscle of his face moving, not even a blink of his warm dark eyes.

"We wish to return to our own land."

"You're an Englishman. I think your navy was attempting to do just that."

"My wife's land is in the Stony Mountains, as the Yanks call that country. We haven't the means."

"Then you must wait here. You might earn passage on some Yankee coastal ship."

"How often do they come?"

The man shrugged. "Who knows? Tomorrow? A year from now?"

"Where do they go?"

"Sandwich Islands, usually, and then around the Horn to Boston."

"Is there a route overland?"

"A perilous trail from the village of San Diego, across deserts, to Santa Fe."

"What about northeast?"

"It is late in October, senor. It is already too late, even if you were properly outfitted. The mountains are a great barrier, with no open passes except briefly in the summer."

"What about up the coast?"

"A hard journey, but possible. Hudson's Bay sends trapper brigades south, even into California."

"I led a fur brigade for the Yanks, and Hudson's Bay was planning on employing me. Outfit me and I'll bring you beaver all winter until the passes are clear."

Baromillo smiled thinly. "And what is to insure that I would ever see you again?"

"My word."

"Your past does not suggest that it would be a wise thing for me to do."

Skye fought back his anger. He had always been as good as his word. "There's profit in it."

"I think not. You have nothing—nada. I would even have to clothe you. Horses, traps, saddles, a rifle, camp gear, skinning knives, everything. Beaver bring but little. I buy whatever comes to me, but I get nothing. Not like the sea otter, big beautiful pelts. I could sell every sea otter in California, and for a good price to any trader who sails to our bay."

"I could catch sea otter, then, if you'd advance something."

"Ah, no, senor, that is a vocation much coveted by our own laborers. My company has certain understandings."

"Horses, then. Where can we get those?"

"Ah, horses! We have horses in Méjico. Every estancia has a thousand horses and mules. But good horses are rare and command a price. Bad horses, bad mules, these are given to the Indios for meat. Every rancho has horses and saddles and leather tack. It is what we do best."

"I'll give a shilling for a decent horse, and another for a decent saddle. Three horses and two or three mules."

"Would that remove you from Méjico, where you illegally visit?"

"Yes."

"A shilling is worth about twice our real. You offer too little. Make it three shillings for a horse, four shillings for each saddle and tack, and one shilling for a mule. I will have them here mañana. Do not put much faith in the horses."

"That's sixteen. I will give you four more—make it almost a pound—for good sound stock, good hooves and not unruly, and for your kind service."

Baromillo nodded. "I arrive here with livestock when the bell tolls ten, senor, senora . . ."

Skye left the warehouse, heartened.

Weary as he was, he put the rest of the day to good use. He and No Name visited the mercados. He discovered that prices, in cash-short California, were low for anything locally manufactured. A few reales would buy amazing things. His lack of Spanish was no impediment and fingers served as well as words. The merchants eyed his coins, hard money, and smiled broadly. They were accustomed to barter.

By the time el sol was skimming the Pacific, he had acquired an ancient longrifle of the Kentucky variety, some dubious, locally made gunpowder, powder horn, a pound of precast balls, wads, and two spare flints. He bought a few trade goods, including awls, ribbons, cloth, knives, beads, two worn but thick Mexican blankets, and used canvas ponchos. At that point his few coins were almost gone.

He and Victoria stowed the gear in Baromillo's warehouse. She was absorbing the world of Europeans and kept her thoughts to herself.

His remaining coins, given him by McLoughlin, went for food: flour, dried beans, fresh loaves, coffee, all stored in coarse gunnysacks, as well as one battered tin cook pot that would suffice for them both.

He felt rich. He and Victoria gobbled baker's sweets. She had never tasted such things and smiled. The dog received a one-centavo bone. Then they headed for the shore again, wrapped themselves in their blankets and ponchos, and awaited the dawn.

Late the next morning Baromillo and a pair of vaqueros showed up with the horses, mules, and tack. Baromillo stood dispassionately while Skye and Victoria examined the beasts. Two were bridled and saddled, and these at least had some passing acquaintance with a rider. The others were obviously straight out of the great herds and unfamiliar with anything other than a halter and braided leather rope.

Risking a kick, Skye lifted hooves, discovering one that was seriously cracked. That was on the unbridled horse, and he rejected it. The mules sidled away. He climbed onto the uglier of the two saddlers. The horse humped its back and refused to move. But the other saddler seemed more obedient.

"All right," he said. "I'll take all but the grulla with the cracked hoof. I'll trade that for two packsaddles for the mules."

He ended up with one packsaddle, which the vaqueros strapped to the sullen mule after roping it down.

It was going to take plenty of work to transform this lot of evil-minded rebels into a good saddle-and-pack string, but Skye figured he had plenty of time and trail to do it.

Then, suddenly, it was all over. He and Victoria had an outfit of sorts. He loaded their paltry supplies onto the back of the wild-eyed mule and tied the burlap sacks down with thong. He wasn't happy with that. The first rain would ruin much of his food and damage his tradegoods. There came over him not joy, but an ineffable sadness.

"Senor Baromillo, I have one last thing to do," he said. "I want to write a letter and I want you to post it on the next English vessel. It is to my father. I wish to bid him goodbye. I don't have a centavo left, but I'll trade you a few of these goods I bought."

Something softened in the don's stern visage. "Write your letter, senor. Your story is a hard one."

Skye clasped the man's hand and held it a moment.

The words came hard, and he wrote with difficulty, forming letters and sentences out of his schoolboy learning.

Dear Father,

I had high hopes of returning to England to see you and my sisters. But those hopes were dashed by the Royal Navy here in Mexico, which discovered my presence and made mischief. I am unable to return to England and unable to restore my good name.

It is painful to me that we won't meet again in this lifetime. But I am grateful to Hudson's Bay Company for conveying word of me to you, however late it came. Too late for my beloved mother to know. You had thought me dead when all the while I was the Crown's miserable prisoner, unable to escape, unable to contact you.

So, Father, I am destined to spend my days here in North America, without the solace of your company. I am grateful to you, sir, for bringing me into this world, and for your kindness, and for your nurture during my salad days in England.

I am grateful for your love and for equipping me to face a hard world. If we don't see each other again, be assured for the rest of your days that I honor you above all else, honor my patrimony, treasure your love and proffer my own, and I will devote myself to the good conduct you instilled in me both by instruction and example.

Your loving son,
Barnaby
Monterey, Alta California, Mexico,
October 30, 1832

Skye dipped the nib into an inkwell and addressed an envelope and handed the letter and envelope to Baromillo.

"If you can read English, please read this, sir, so that you might know the kindness you are doing me by letting me send this letter."

The fur trader did, and quietly folded the letter, inserted it, and sealed it with candle wax.

"Now you must leave Méjico," he said.

Skye clambered aboard his unruly horse, which humped and threatened to pitch him off, while Victoria mounted hers and adjusted her voluminous skirts. Then he heeled the sullen horse, which refused at first to go, but No Name intervened, nipping at fetlocks until eventually the train moved, two green horses and two half-wild mules, along the shore of the bay, never far from chaos.

Thus ended a dream. He would never fulfill his desire to live as a free Englishman without stain upon his honor. Nor reunite with his beloved family. He saw no future. His spirits did not lift.

thirty-four

Victoria was too busy wrestling with her rebel horse and the balky mules to notice the glory of the Monterey coast. So was Skye.

Her mare wouldn't turn unless she yanked hard on a rein. It stopped repeatedly, tried to run off, kicked at the mules trailing her, bit at her shoes, waited for the chance to buck her into the ocean, and refused to trot or run. If her horse was bad, the mules on the jerkline were worse. The one carrying the packsaddle, from which their few possessions hung, would stop dead every few yards, jolting her procession to a halt. The other mule occasionally ran forward, threatening to break free. Only the dog, nipping at fetlocks and stifles, managed to keep the horses moving.

Skye, ahead of her, was having his own troubles with a horse that would trot a few yards and stop, try to break for Monterey, pitched on the slightest excuse, and shied at every shadow or bird or for no reason at all.

They came at last to a willow grove, and Skye dismounted.

"Hold this rein while I whittle a couple of switches," he said.

He extracted his Green River knife from its belt sheath and began whittling two stout willow switches. He handed her one and kept the other.

"You lead with the mules. I'm going to walk behind your horse, leading mine," he said. If your horse or the mules cause any more grief, they'll answer for it."

"Sonofabitch," she said. She had heard the trappers use that expression many times, and found it highly satisfying and useful and a valuable addition to the English tongue, especially when dealing with horses. She had the notion that it was vaguely prohibited by some of the white chiefs and that made it all the better.

She attempted to start her mare, without effect until the sharp smack of the switch jolted the mare into a trot. Resounding cracks of the switch behind her let her know the mules were receiving the same discipline, and so the procession north began again, this time with more success. Skye, walking beside her mare or the mules, did not spare the switch, and the three beasts of burden settled into grudging compliance.

Thus they actually made some time that afternoon. Skye eventually mounted and employed the willow on the croup of his own saddler, even when the result was a fit of bucking and rebellion.

The yellow dog bore down, and any foolery by any mule was met with a quick nip. Somehow, No Name evaded the wild kicking that always resulted when he vectored toward the rebel. Victoria marveled. The dog was as good as another herder, maybe better, and the Skyes began to pick up some speed. She squinted at Skye's spirit-dog and thanked the mascot for his great kindness.

Now at last she began to notice the golden panorama before her. At a point well north of Monterey the trail left the bay and headed inland. Skye took it. Trails always led somewhere, and this probably would take them to Yerba Buena. Soon the green ocean vanished and they rode between golden, autumnal hills covered with waxy-leaved green shrubs and junipers.

She had marveled at Monterey. These Mexicans had built their lodges of earth bricks, daubed them white, and covered them with bright red tiles, cleverly designed to drain off the rain. At every hand she discovered marvels: carriages with wheels on them, drawn by burros or mules. Handsome horses, caparisoned with carefully tooled saddles. Women who wore perfumes, amazing scents that invoked envy in her. Great trading buildings heaped with good things: barrels of wine, sacks of grain, shelves of iron-work, and everywhere leather goods. They made leather do for everything, from ropes to vests and riding pants.

But the women fascinated her most. They were honey-fleshed, not as dark as she was, not as fair as Skye, but warm-colored, with glowing eyes and swift, sweet smiles. And they wore mountains of clothing, one skirt over another, as if they did not wish to show the contours of their bodies from waist down. They were mad for jewelry, too, and wore copper and silver and sometimes even gold, or polished stones, and ribbons in their hair, and soft slippers rather like moccasins.

She thirsted to learn everything there was to know about this tribe called Mexicans, and she knew that at the campfires on the trail, she would think up questions to ask him. He seemed to know all about them and she marveled that he knew so much, or could walk into a trading place and come to an agreement with the fat brown clerks without even under-standing their tongue. She marveled at prices. How did any-one know the price of anything? Why were some things so cheap and others so costly? Who set these prices and why?

Skye scanned the heavens, constantly alert for rain. They had little to protect their food and bolts of trade cloth except the ponchos, and that worried him.

"If it's clouding up, look for shelter, Victoria. Anything. Those burlap sacks aren't much use in bad weather."

She marveled at the sacks, having never seen one, hoped she might receive them all from Skye some day.

That evening they camped in a peaceful notch in the hills, watered by a clear, sweet spring that wrought a comet's tail of green vegetation down a gentle grade. The place showed signs of frequent use, and she had to travel a way to find deadwood for their cookfire, but she didn't mind. She liked this Mexico place, and its peace, and the sweetness of the air, and the mildness of the climate.

Skye unloaded the surly horses, put them on improvised pickets where the golden grasses grew thick, and sat down. She studied him closely and knew the sadness had not left him. For many moons he had thought of nothing more than sailing across the big waters to his home and his father and sisters and family. Of repairing the wrong and winning a good name. All this had possessed him, inspired him, driven him from the mountains to Oregon, and then down to this place called Mexico. And now it was gone, destroyed in a few hours by a chance encounter with the Royal Navy, the very ones who had stolen his liberty from him in the first place.

Now he looked weary, and she saw something else in his weathered face: a great sadness. She did not know whether she could comfort him. What could some woman of the People do to console this man, whose family had been ripped from him forever?

What was she to him? Was she still his beloved woman?

After they had eaten some beans she had boiled, and some hard biscuits he had purchased, she knelt beside him while he smoked a pipe of precious tobacco, actually part of the trade goods he had purchased to succor them along the way. He drew deeply and let the fragrant smoke eddy out of his lungs, even as he stared at things invisible to her. He handed her the pipe and she sucked deeply, enjoying the smoke in her throat.

"Skye," she said. "Would you talk?"

He didn't reply at first. "I am a man without a country," he said. "And without a future or a past."

"Without a future?" She was hurt.

"I had always, in the back of my mind, thought of returning to my home; England, some day. I've always wanted to receive my good name back; to be honored among my people. Even if I chose not to stay there, but make my home here with you, I wanted to clear that up. Now I can't. I can never go home, never make the name of Barnaby Skye an honorable one in England.

"A man wants a good name. A man wants to be honored by his own people."

"But you have a good name, Skye. You have a good name among my people, and among the Yankees. You even have a good name with Hudson's Bay, or at least the big man, McLoughlin."

He sighed. "Yes, and that is good. But my heart cries for a good name among my people."

"Ah, it is truly so. I understand this thing. I would not wish to have a bad name among my people. My heart would feel bad even if I had a bad name among your people. This I understand. When you have a bad name, there is no future."

He took the pipe from her and drew long, and exhaled slowly. The smoke was good. The smoke was making him calm, and maybe taking his suffering away. Tobacco was a good thing and the messenger of peace among the tribes.

"You have a very small country," she said. "Your country is me and this dog that lies beside us. We are your country for as long as you will have us."

He smiled and handed the pipe back to her. "That is a very good country," he said.

But there was something in his tone that troubled her and she fathomed what lay behind his words. He yearned for the things she simply didn't understand. He sometimes spoke of books. She had scarcely seen a book, and they were great mysteries to her. How could anyone get something from all those tiny black marks on a thin sheet of paper? He spoke of art and politics and ideas and philosophy and the sciences and applied arts, and she knew she was like a child and knew nothing of these things. What she fathomed, at bottom, was that her life was too small for him, and that he would always be a little sad, even when he was closest to her and they seemed almost happy. She would always give him what she could, and it would never be enough.

thirty-five

The next dawn Skye tried out the old flintlock. He rested the barrel on a boulder, sighted on a knot, and squeezed. The flint snapped sparks into the pan, ignited the charge, and the patched ball whumped the tree trunk, but about two inches lower and to the right of where he had sighted. He tried again, with almost the same result, and knew he must compensate.

The night had been mild, the California slopes peaceful and empty. He saw little evidence of passage along the trail, and concluded that this province of Mexico was lightly inhabited; a sunny wilderness wanting only water to make it a paradise.

He and Victoria had worse trouble with the green horses and mules that morning than the previous; it was as if the beasts had learned nothing from yesterday's discipline. He saddled his balky mount, which reared back and snapped its halter rope and dodged him. His temper heated until No Name herded the horse toward Skye with snapping jaws. Victoria's mount accepted a saddle but threatened to buck. The yawning packmule humped when the packsaddle fell over its back, and lowered its head, ready to buck the burden off. Skye sighed and cut fresh switches from a live oak, and handed one to Victoria.

After some mighty cursing and lashing, they got their unruly transportation moving. The dog helped, nipping at the heels of the stubborn mules. The saddling had cost them an extra hour and slowed their start. But by the time the sun was pouring merry warmth upon the brown slopes, and the hawks were circling the blue sky, the Englishman and his Crow bride were making headway, ever northward, through a land too sweet to permit gloomy thoughts.

This day, at least, the rebel animals settled faster into a routine than the previous day. Skye didn't mind. Where else could he acquire four-footed beasts of burden `for a few shillings? Any horse or mule that had received the benefit of the great equestrian skills of the Californios would have cost fifty times as much.

And so they passed a magnificent November day, pushing ever northward, inland from the coast but never far from a salty sea breeze. The wound up and down great golden hills, and even crossed low coastal mountains, seeing no one but enjoying the abundance of life at every hand: deer, fox, an occasional stray longhorn bearing an elaborate Mexican brand that had been burned into a thigh or shoulder; and always the crows and gulls and songbirds wheeling in flocks as they rode by.

For two days they traveled north, making better time as the livestock settled down. The dog trotted ahead, an outrider alert to danger, and Skye was glad to have him along. The trail crossed few rivers, but offered many springs that emptied down a cleft or rose in a slough. The aching emptiness of this northern Mexican province astonished Skye.

Then, while nooning at a sweet spring purling from a gray cliff, No Name growled quietly and they found themselves in company. Several beaming Mexicans on fancy ponies, dressed in charro clothing, white stitched black pantalones, soft leather boots, splendid embroidered waistcoats, and extravagant high-peaked hats with broad brims, drew up. Among them was a girl dressed entirely differently, in a plain skirt wide enough to permit her to sit astride her horse, and a well-filled but begrimed white blouse.

What struck Skye at once was the weaponry carried by these seven jolly Mexicans: dragoon pistols on each man; rifles in scabbards dangling from each saddle; a sheathed sword on several.

"Hola! Hola!" said one, smiling broadly. This one was barely five feet high and almost as wide, but somehow looked much larger.

"Jesús Santamaría," he said, driving a thumb into his own chest. Then he rattled on in Spanish, and Skye comprehended not one word. "El Grande Santamaría," he concluded, "Santamaría gordo, Santamaría borracho, Santamaría magnifico."

The others dismounted from their groomed steeds and surveyed Skye's animals or washed their faces in the rivulet flowing from the spring. All except the girl. But Santamaría eventually gestured to her, and she silently slid off her horse and walked around a bend and out of sight.

Skye waited warily. Victoria stood, uncertainly, but neither spoke. He thought this might be trouble, but probably was not. Men bearing so many arms might be up to no good, but perhaps this was dangerous country. Skye realized he hadn't been very watchful. So tranquil was this province that he had scarcely kept up his guard.

The visitors seemed to be waiting for something and it was only when the girl reappeared and Santamaría began jabbering, in harsh staccato, that Skye began to fathom what this visit was about. Smoothly, Santamaría pulled his big pistol from its leather nest, and instantly the other six hombres did also, and Skye found himself peering into the huge black bores of seven cannons, the flintlocks cocked back and ready.

Santamaría was obviously shouting directions, but Skye couldn't fathom a word.

"He says put up your hands," the girl said in flawless American English.

Skye did, slowly, seeing his imminent death. Victoria did also.

The weary girl slowly translated Santamaría's next outburst.

"He says he is the great Santamaría, unsurpassed in all of Mexico for robbery, terror, murder, torture, crucifixion, and rape of women, young and old, virgins and whores. He says he is a legend, the scourge of all California, the only man spoken of only in whispers. Men die of fear, of heart failure, when he approaches, and he wants you to know that."

She listened to another outburst, while the fat bandit minced back and forth.

"He says you are being robbed and maltreated by the king of all bandits under the heavens and on earth and upon the seas and under the ground. No pirate has half the reputation as Jesús José Santamaría for murder and torture. That the name of Santamaría will live forever, and be whispered over graves, and put down in history books by those who can write."

Santamaría pointed a finger at Skye and shouted endlessly.

"He says he has killed forty-three men, sixty-one women, eighty children, countless animals, and seventeen priests, but you are a foreigner and wouldn't know these things, so he will have to demonstrate his great prowess to you so that forever more you will know that Santamaría robbed and pillaged you and left you for dead."

That was the first ray of hope. Skye believed until then that he and Victoria would die. Not that being left for dead was much to hope for.

Skye addressed the girl: "Ask him how he came to be a great bandit."

Santamaría listened to her, and smiled, baring gold teeth, and began that staccato again.

"He says that he was the son of a rich man, and got bored because everything came so easily to him. Beautiful senoritas waiting in his bed, fast-blooded horses, heaps of gold, cattle too numerous to count, everything. He lacked for nothing. He got fat from good eating. He says he is a bandit and outlaw because he has everything and is bored, which is far more wicked than being a bandit because he is poor or unhappy or unjustly treated. The only thing that counts is fame. He wants to be the greatest of everything: have more women than any other man in Mexico, more money, but reputation is all that matters. He says he wants to live forever."

"Who are you, miss?"

She looked hesitantly at him.

"I am his woman."

She explained that to Santamaría, who retorted at length.

"He says I should correct that; he has had a thousand women, and he will pitch me to the wolves . . . soon."

She looked frightened.

Skye said, "Tell Santamaría the great bandit that I will have a shooting contest with him. Rifles, pistols, anything. And if I win, we go free, and we take you with us."

Hesitantly she translated, only to meet with wild laughter.

"He says you are loco, crazy. He will not give you a fair contest. He is even now thinking of ways to torment you."

"Ask him for a duel. Any weapon of his choice at ten paces."

Apparently he understood without translating, because he laughed at length, and then fired his pistola at Skye's feet. The ball plowed dirt inches from his boot, just missing the dog. The bandit casually sheathed that weapon and plucked out his second as acrid smoke drifted past Skye.

"He says you are a fool. What do you take him for? Someone who would submit himself to your good aim? Because of this it will go all the harder for you."

Skye laughed, not knowing from what strange corner of his soul the laughter came from. "Tell Santamaría he is nothing, a fraud and a fake, a fool, and no match for any serious pirate and bandit."

Hesitantly the girl translated, this time into a dead silence.

The quietness stretched to forbidding length, and Skye wondered whether the execution squad would dispatch him with a single crash of the pistols.

Instead, the bandit made one small left-handed gesture. His cohorts untied the two horses and mules from their pickets, rummaged through Skye's goods, and told Skye to remove his frock coat.

He did, and they poked through it, as well, and then rudely poked around Victoria's skirts until they were satisfied that no further booty was to be gotten from Skye and Victoria.

Then they gestured Skye and Victoria to a large shag-barked tree and had them stand before it. Skye's heart sank. They formed a ragged line and lifted their huge pistols until seven muzzles pointed at the Skyes.

Skye's pulse soared. The end, then. He saw the dog, the hair of its neck poking up, crouched and waiting to spring at Santamaría.

Victoria turned flinty and silent.

Santamaría stood to one side, sword in hand, arm raised.

He brought the sword down.

A ragged eruption of explosions deafened Skye.

He felt bark slap him, and shattered lead sting him in a dozen places about the neck and shoulders, and the bandits' laughter lacerate his soul. Victoria sagged to the ground and for a terrible moment Skye thought they had murdered her as a joke. The bandits hooted, gathered the Skyes' horses and mules and outfit, mounted, and rode away like a posse of carrion birds.

Victoria wept. Skye comforted her in his arms, but she could not be comforted. Then the dog squirmed close, and began licking them both, the steady scrape of its tongue its way of comforting them. It took an hour for Skye's pulse to settle.

thirty-six

The sun still shone. Skye stared at the heavens, amazed. He led Victoria to the spring and washed her face and his, sluicing drops of blood away from tiny wounds where shattered lead had seared them. They sat in the grass, dumfounded, not wanting anything but to sit stupidly and behold the sunny world.

He saw hurt in Victoria's face and something else: banditry was something new to her, something she scorned. In time, after the mild breezes had restored order to his soul, he began taking stock. Now they had only the clothes on their backs. He stood, recovered his grimy frock coat and dusted it off. She rose also and began shaking dirt off her skirts. He recovered his beaver top hat and discovered a bullet hole in it. He pushed a finger through both holes and wiggled it at her. She smiled at last.

He donned his frock coat and top hat, looking once again the dashing gentleman, and noted that she looked the fashionable lady. They were city-dwellers out on a stroll with their dog. He smiled and she caught his humor and smiled back. It was the best thing to do at a moment when they had nothing. No food, no shelter, no protection, no coin, and no tongue in common with those who lived in this vast province.

"I don't know where we're going or what we'll find, but we may as well head north again," he said.

"I don't know this land," she said, and he understood her meaning. An Indian woman could find foods in the wild if she knew them: roots, berries, nuts, bulbs, stalks. But everything in this Mexican province was new to her, and she would be almost as helpless as he.

They lacked so much as a piece of string. So they were a pair of swells, promenading through the wilds, and somehow that caught their fancy and they started hiking the elusive trail. They would live or die, be rescued or find succor on their own, as Fate would dictate. What else was there but to laugh?

They trudged along the dirt trail, pausing at each of the numerous springs to refresh themselves. The dog was often out of sight, but always scouting. Gentlemen's and ladies' shoes weren't designed for hiking, and their feet felt pinched and blistered. But there was no help for that except to pause frequently. Skye knew that they would soon be lame, and that the lameness could kill them along with all the rest.

So he squeezed her hand and they limped along the trail and hoped for miracles. Maybe the dog would bring them food.

Twilight found them at a comfortable spring, surrounded by choking brush in arid hills, and Skye decided that they had gone far enough and their feet needed respite. He was starved, and knew Victoria was, too.

They pulled off their shoes and bathed their tormented feet in the cool water. The dog had vanished, perhaps hunting.

That's when they heard the snort of horses, and moments later a dozen fierce-looking Mexicans rode in, surrounded them, and stared. Skye rose calmly, hoping that these rough customers might be their succor.

"*Manos arriba!*" bellowed a skinny one with huge mustachios, a cocked eye, and a puckered scar that ran across his jaw to his left ear. He wore a peaked leather sombrero that barely contained an explosion of curly black hair.

Skye didn't quite grasp the Spanish. "Manos arriba," he replied cheerfully. "Nice evening."

"Manos arriba! Arriba!" the skinny man on a ribby bay horse bellowed.

Skye saw the dragoon pistola in his hand, and started laughing. He turned to Victoria. "The man means to rob us."

She started laughing, too.

"Manos arriba!"

This time a shot stopped their laughter cold. One of the horsebacked riders raised his hands, as a demonstration.

Skye and Victoria lifted their arms.

The leader unloosed a furious barrage of Spanish invective that Skye couldn't comprehend, but he got the drift: Where are your horses, where are your goods, where are the others? You couldn't be here alone.

Skye thought a moment. "Jesús Santamaría," he said.

"Santamaría! Santamaría!"

The leader turned sullen. "Santamaría," he snarled.

Two of the bandits dismounted and frisked Skye and Victoria, doing it insolently and rudely.

"Sonofabitch," Victoria said to one.

He laughed.

"Nada," said the other. "Nada."

"Santamaría," said the chief. There followed a furious debate among them, with the name of the other outlaw prominent in it. But Skye could not fathom what they were talking about.

"Comida," Skye said. "Succor, help, food, horses. Get us help." He pressed a hand to his stomach, pointed at his blistered feet, pointed at their horses.

The sinister bandit king paused, stared, and laughed, baring yellow teeth with black gaps between them.

"Succor," he said, and the rest chuckled.

He pointed to himself. "Raul Sacramento del Diablo," he bellowed. "Bandito primo," he announced.

Skye didn't believe him. This cur didn't compare with Santamaría.

"Santamaría, primo," he said. "Numero uno."

Sacramento howled, gesticulated, bawled, and snarled.

Skye pointed north. "Take us to Yerba Buena," he said.

"Yerba Buena!"

"Si."

The bandit snarled something and at length.

"Comida," said Skye, glad he remembered that word.

"Comida! Comida!"

They laughed.

"I will tell everyone that Sacramento del Diablo is the greatest of all Mexican bandits," Skye said.

The bandit squinted malevolently.

The gang stayed, built a fire, and roasted a flyspecked haunch of beef they had loaded on a burro, while Skye and Victoria sat quietly. It took an hour to cook, while Skye sat there, salivating, hungering, itching to put meat between his teeth.

At last they ate, and served Skye and Victoria first, and then the dog, after sawing off tender beef with grimy knives. Skye fingered the hot beef gingerly, and tried to let it cool, but his ravenous appetite overcame his prudence and he wolfed the food. Victoria was downing hers just as enthusiastically.

The food was fine, but the company wasn't. Something bad was in the air, some sort of anticipation that radiated from the swarthy faces of his captors. They eyed him and Victoria with faint amusement and no more compassion than they would feel for a mosquito. A rank odor of dried sweat fouled the air around the cookfire. No breeze blew, not even an eddy of air to cleanse the hollow of the foulness of this bandit outfit. Skye thought he smelled vomit, blood, sweat, and something rank, like a festering wound or two among these watchful birds of prey. Whatever the case, Skye sensed the evening's entertainment was not over and that the next minutes could be dangerous and even fatal.

Victoria sensed it, too, and kept glancing at Skye, sending her silent message of fear and worry.

Then the vulture leading this vicious pack, who styled himself Sacramento del Diablo, Sacrament of the Devil, wiped his lips with the grease-stained sleeve of his leather shirt, and rose. His eyes were on Victoria as he approached, and Skye knew suddenly what was about to happen.

The dog growled low in its throat. Victoria froze. She had no weapon, not even the small and secret hideout knife she normally carried, because the last gang of bandits had stripped it away. She was as helpless as a baby chick.

Skye stood. There were a few things he would die for; a few things in his soul that he regarded as more important than life. His freedom, for one. Avoiding torture, for another. And the sanctity of his woman.

The gaunt, hollow-chested bandit clasped Victoria's arm and lifted her up, his face swimming in anticipation.

Skye slammed into him, sending him reeling backward. They landed on the grass together, Skye on top, and Skye began hammering the chieftain brutally, heedless of the shouts around him, the sudden rush of men determined to pull him off their leader. Berserk rage loosed in him and he fought with the powers of a madman, his great fists smashing everywhere, his thrashing legs booting at any target, his elbows hammering into the chieftain. He felt blows rain on his head and back, turned and booted a man in the groin. He saw the flash of metal and felt a searing pain across a forearm. The snarling dog leapt at the attacker and pulled him down, biting him on the arms and legs and lips.

But now he was beyond subduing, and thrashed about so violently that the bandits could not pin him. Skye traveled to some distant shore where the howls of men and the thud of his fists grew remote, where the taste of his own blood didn't matter.

Vaguely, he heard the savagery of the dog and the shrieks

of clawed and bitten men. But he was losing ground. And then, finally, they pulled him off the chief and pinned him down, eight of them against his writhing strength and the snapping, slavering dog, which was sinking canines into flesh until they were all soaked in blood, and howling great oaths at him.

Skye drifted into a haze, but he could see the bandit chief rise slowly, clasping his crotch where Skye had smashed him, and stand, bent over, his face in agony.

Skye peered about, through puffed eyes, and discovered Victoria standing apart, a flintlock rifle at her shoulder, cocked and ready. Other firearms lay at her feet. The bore of her rifle aimed squarely at the bandit chief, and the man was taking her seriously. Diablo straightened up and let go of his crotch.

Then he muttered a command.

The bandits pinning Skye let him go. He sat up slowly, and then stood, fighting back the dizziness. Victoria's rifle never wavered. Some of the bandits could not stand, and lay in the grass oozing blood from dog bites. The ones that could stand made no effort to rush her.

But strangely, the chief smiled, dripping blood from a corner of his puffy mouth. He bowed, laughed, and issued a stream of orders to his men. The four standing bandits brought two saddled horses to Skye.

"Vaya, Yanqui diablo," the bandit said. "Adios, muchacho."

Skye plucked up one of the pistols and poked it into his waist, another loaded rifle, and helped Victoria mount one horse. Then he managed to pull his tortured body up and into the saddle of the other.

They watched silently. They had defeated him, pinned him down, and yet they had lost, and every one of them was bleeding from dog bites and suffering from the mayhem.

The only happy man among them was the chief, Raul Sacramento del Diablo, whose face was wreathed in joy. Skye did not entirely grasp what had happened, or why the bandit king set them free instead of killing him. Least of all did he understand why the man was smiling with some sort of ethereal joy—unless the bandit simply cherished a good brawl, win or lose.

And Skye and Victoria and No Name fled into the night.

thirty-seven

Guided by a gibbous moon throwing lantern-light over the dim trail, they rode north a mile or so. Then Skye stopped. The dog was limping. Skye dismounted and gathered No Name into his arms. He lifted the weary creature into Victoria's lap.

"Hand him to me when I get into the saddle," he said.

"I'll carry him, Skye. Damn good dog."

"Yes."

"He's like ten warriors."

"He's got war honors, Victoria. Counted coup many times."

"Spirit-dog," she said. "You must never name him."

"You all right?"

"I am all right. You?"

"I don't know."

He surveyed himself. His frock coat was filthy and busted apart at the shoulders. His britches were torn. His body had survived without serious damage except for the knife slash across his forearm. When they reached the next spring he would wash it.

"You are a great warrior, Skye."

"They wrestled me down."

"Dammit, Skye, eight men. It took all of them to do it. And

you humbled the chief. That dog's a great warrior, too. Every one covered with his own blood."

She stroked the head of the recumbent dog, which lay across her skirts. Something about that stirred him.

"You're a great warrior woman, Victoria. Everything changed when the chief saw the bore of your rifle. You were ready to kill him and he knew it."

"You were ready to die to save me." She was peering at him so intently that he felt embarrassed. "I am loved," she said. "You give away your life for me."

"We all risked our lives, including that mutt, for each other. That dog was dodging kicks and dodging a few big knives, too. But he never stopped biting."

This moment was an affirmation, and Skye treasured it.

He found a pair of leather rings, designed to carry a rifle, and slid the weapon into them, freeing an arm at last.

"We got a rifle and pistol out of it, but no powder or balls. Two shots. It'll help."

They started their horses north, and rode another mile until they found a spring. There they watered and washed, and then withdrew into brush to await the dawn. Skye rolled under some manzanita and slept, letting the silence and coolness and darkness of the California night heal body and soul. The dog lay quietly beside him. They were warriors together, bonded by blood.

As he lay hurting through the fretful night, he realized that something had changed. This ordeal was another passage in his life. He had fled from Monterey feeling utter loss, loss of his birth family, loss of a nation, loss of everything familiar. And now, after this ordeal of banditry, and their survival against all odds, he was discovering that he had a new family. He studied Victoria who lay inert a few feet away. Always before, in the recesses of his heart, he had wondered about the future: could he, an Englishman, find bliss with this Crow woman? Would he ever grow restless for another, one of his own kind? Some sweet English-speaking lady, in lilac cologne, who might share everything that had been his inheritance from the Island Kingdom? Would he grow bored with Victoria, who knew nothing of that life? And until now he never had an answer.

But now an answer was forming. Yes, he told his doubtful soul, yes, I can live with her always. I can cease being the Englishman. We can become a new nation, she and I, not English, not Crow, not Yank, but children of the American mountains. And now the dog had joined the family. Strange beast, often out of sight, obscure, unmastered, and alone. But now the yellow dog lay beside him, bonded by war and blood.

Skye stared at the dog, loving him more than ever, feeling at one with the creature. He reached across the weeds to clasp the dog's injured foreleg, and felt its heat rise in his hand. He stroked the foreleg gently. The dog stirred and licked Skye's hand, and sighed.

And Skye knew that he had passed from one realm into another, and that these beloved allies, his Indian woman and his dog, were partnered with him along the long, lonesome road ahead. For the first time in years, he didn't miss his native land.

The next day they starved. Skye rode dizzily, wondering whether he could hang onto his horse long enough to reach a village. Victoria was stoic, and rode in resolute silence, while the dog seemed oblivious of the famine that was tormenting the human beings. Occasionally Victoria dismounted and collected some object or other from the ground. Skye discovered that these were arrowheads, and one old and rusted spearhead, abandoned or lost by the Spanish.

"Go hunt," she said that afternoon. "I can cut meat with these things."

He examined the charge in the flintlock rifle. Some of the powder had slipped out of the pan, but it probably would fire. He would have only one shot, so it had to count. He had the pistol in his belt, but he would need that for other purposes.

He heeled the bandit horse ahead. It responded swiftly.

He had never hunted in an arid, hilly, monotonous land like this, and scarcely knew what sort of game to look for, but he set out, riding ahead, figuring that all game had to water somewhere. The dog did not go with him, which darkened his spirits. But the dog was still limping.

He spotted a spring far up a slope a mile to the left of the trail, a smear of greenery that indicated water, rode cautiously in that direction, and then dismounted. He tied the horse and crept forward until he had a good field of fire overlooking a tiny rivulet that burst from dark rock. Then he settled the rifle barrel over a downed juniper trunk and waited.

But nothing came there. He wondered if his own rank odor had driven game away, or whether this region lacked game entirely. When it grew too dark to make meat he retreated to his horse and rode quietly down to the trail, where Victoria would be waiting for him. He felt faint with hunger and miserable with defeat.

He found her and the dog at a tiny marsh-lined pond well ahead. She had an animal hanging from a limb and was butchering it slowly, with the ancient spearhead, a hard and miserable task, while the dog lay waiting.

Amazed, he unsaddled and picketed the horse beside hers.

"How?" he asked.

She nodded toward the dog. "He brought it. Dragged it. Yearling red deer. I have never seen a red deer."

The deer's windpipe had been mangled.

The dog, again.

He gathered firewood, which lay abundantly about this tiny marsh area, and slowly peeled shreds of dry bark until he had a small pile. Then he gathered small sticks, broke them into fragments that would catch easily. And then he pulled the big pistol from his waist and studied it. He had no worm or other means to disarm it, but he worked powder out of the pan and hoped that would do. Then he nestled a cottony bit of tinder below the frizzen, cocked the flintlock, and squeezed, aiming the weapon away from camp. It didn't fire, but neither did the rain of sparks, as flint struck steel, ignite his tinder. Five attempts later, using various bits of tinder, he was able to transfer a few glowing embers into the little mouse-nest of tinder on the ground, and blew gently upon it. In a few minutes he had a flame. In an hour they had cooked meat.

The yellow dog ate first and best, and settled into a supine languor.

That evening they continued to butcher and cook the meat until they had roasted it all. They ate the whole while against the starvation to come, feeding bits to the dog, which soon surfeited itself and settled into a nap. Skye watched the skies restlessly. This was November, the monsoon season in this Mexican province, and his small family had no shelter at all.

He talked Victoria out of her petticoat, and wrapped the cooked meat in it and hung it high in a limb, fearing bear or wolves.

He did not sleep. Their vulnerability worried him. He had the rifle for protection against predators or mortals, and for food. One shot. And yet he was glad. His mood had slowly risen, like yeasty dough, since fleeing Monterey.

They made good progress the next day, seeing no one. But the following day, when the trail wound close to the great inland bay and away from the coastal mountains, they beheld traffic on the road. They passed coppery peasants with creaking ox-carts laden with hay or melons, and women bearing baskets on their heads, old people in black who were standing and staring at the world. They passed corrals and strings of burros and flower-bedecked graveyards.

They had somehow left a dangerous wild behind and were approaching a more civilized country along the endless shore of a vast and shimmering freshwater sea. Skye traded the pistol for melons and beans and goat meat, and still had enough for an ancient flea-infested blanket.

They exchanged cheerful greetings with all these warm-fleshed people, but beyond that they understood nothing and could not convey their slightest thoughts. They knew they were closely observed, and with great curiosity, especially by women and children. They realized that Skye's stubbled face, torn and stained frock coat, and Victoria's ripped and soiled skirts occasioned much clucking among the Mexicans. The Californios wore clean clothing, much of it snowy white, or black, or dove-colored leather, and numerous gaudy rings, bracelets, and necklaces made to glitter.

The trail occasionally lifted them over majestic hills only to dump them into cloistered valleys verdant with waxy-leaved shrubs. But eventually it led past an ancient mission called Mission San Francisco de Asis, though the people didn't call it that. Skye thought it had been named after some woman.

But it was the first truly formidable building Victoria had ever seen, so he paused there and let her gape at this holy place of the Mexicans, and exclaim at the candles and gold and lovely images. She could not fathom the bleeding Christ, crowned with thorns, or why mortals knelt before him.

"Sonofabitch," she muttered, along with other imprecations. What sort of god was this? She began eyeing Skye suspiciously for signs of adherence to this strange belief.

Late that afternoon, they reached the cold and misty village of Yerba Buena, chilled to the bone, and discovered a settlement of three or four hundred, and a grimy Yank brigantine bobbing lazily in the harbor, riding the ebb tide.

thirty-eight

Yerba Buena sprawled so widely that it gave the illusion of being larger than it was. But Skye swiftly discerned a thriving commercial port perched on the chill peninsula. Burros, dogs, chickens, hogs, and sheep rambled across the village. No Name eyed them carefully but did not contest the neighborhood. Seagulls perched on every roof. The tang of the sea lay in the fresh breeze, a clean scent as old and familiar to Skye as his own name. Old women in black shawls hung on benches, and old men in dark woolen homespuns lounged in the feeble sun.

But it was the brigantine that captured Skye's attention. Where was it headed? The Stars and Stripes stirred lazily from its mainmast. Stain had long since reduced its white hull to a patched tan and brown. The grimy sails had been furled slovenly, bulging loose on every spar. Skye looked in vain for a name. A fine spread eagle, gilded and fierce, decorated its stern. Once it had been a proud ship. Now it probably hauled stinking seal pelts to New England.

He saw no one aboard, but a grubby longboat was moored to a small wharf on the waterfront that extended just far enough to keep a small boat afloat at low tide.

"I want to book passage if it's going north," Skye said to Victoria.

"I don't like that big canoe."

"It's Yank. We'll be safe enough."

"It's a bandit ship. I am tired of bandits."

"No, just a coaster picking up sea otter and selling stuff from the East Coast."

"We have horses. Let's walk on the earth."

"This is where we either catch that brig or get ferried across the water to the north side of the harbor."

"Let's do that. We got horses."

"And nothing to live on."

She didn't respond. He knew she was unhappy, tired of this long ordeal, and above all, homesick. He knew all about that malady. He had been homesick for years in the Royal Navy. The offer from Hudson's Bay had wrought a whole new wave of homesickness. But the navy had cured that in Monterey.

She was plenty homesick now, having seen a large chunk of the world beyond the foothill kingdom of the Absaroka people. The odd thing was, he was beginning to share her yearning, not for England but for her village, and maybe even the company of the Yank fur brigades. And for the great Rocky Mountains, where he had found himself, his manhood, his wife, and his liberty.

"Victoria," he said quietly, "we'll go to the mountains and your people just as fast as we can. I miss them as much as you do."

She eyed him, this time with a certain wonder, and with an infinite trust. He saw that trust form in her face and smiled.

"We'll get there, and maybe in three moons be sitting in your father's lodge."

He stirred his horse and they rode quietly along the waterfront, past obscure adobe buildings that looked abandoned but probably weren't. A taberna near the dock beckoned. That would be the place of food and drink and most dockside transactions in Yerba Buena.

They rode to the taberna and dismounted, hitching their

reins to a rail. The dog settled smack under his horse, as if to prevent it from departing without him.

Skye lacked so much as a shilling. He surveyed his dress ruefully. The sleeves of his frock coat were half-ripped from it, and the rear seam had come undone half up the back. The fabric had been hopelessly stained. His toes bulged through cracks in his boots. The battered beaver top hat now had a bullet hole through it. His shirt was vile. Weeks of stubble decorated his cheeks and his hair hung in strings. His nose had blistered in the California sun and looked like a red mountain between his small blue eyes.

Victoria had managed to do better. Her dress hung limply without its petticoats, but she had somehow kept it relatively clean. The shawl had survived and hung loosely over her shoulders. But the rents in her skirts showed hard use, and her Vancouver-made slippers had virtually fallen apart. She wore her black hair braided, and it shone from the frequent washings she had given it, milking the stalks of yucca for a sort of soap. She was quite the lady, even if he looked the ruffian. Why was it that Indians could endure the wilds and look their best in it, while white men deteriorated the moment they were beyond the reach of civilization?

No matter. He would try to find out about the brig, and about ferries that would take them and their animals across the amazing water gate that almost sliced California in two.

He took her arm and escorted her into the taberna, carrying his rifle with him because he didn't entrust it to the horse outside. The door hung on leather hinges, and the windows lacked glass, though they could be tightly shuttered in squalls.

If anything, the place was colder than the village without.

A Mexican man motioned him to an empty trestle table, but Skye resisted. He couldn't afford a meal or a drink, as much as he pined for both. Instead, he studied the half dozen patrons, settling at last on a bearded Yank in the corner, sitting lazily over a mug of cerveza with a Californio. The master, probably, but there was no way of knowing. This one sported a beard such as Skye had never seen; it bulged outward like a sunburst, reaching his lap and haloing his face with a salt-and-pepper aura. The man's mouth was not visible, and that orifice lay buried beneath a matt of stained hair.

Skye doffed his top hat and approached.

"You the master of that brig?"

The man surveyed him. "Abner Dickens."

"Barnaby Skye, sir, and Victoria. Mr. Dickens, you headed north? I'm looking for passage for my wife and my dog and maybe one horse."

"That was my intent. But if my dickering with this gent here is successful, I'll be heading around the horn."

The Mexican knew English and was following the exchange.

"What would be your price?" Skye asked.

"I don't reckon I'd take your horse. Nuisance and a danger at sea. The rest of ye?" He studied Skye's clothing. "How'll ye pay me? In coin?"

"We have to sell one or two horses here."

"Fat lot of money you'll get. The last thing a Californio needs is another horse. Sit," he said, nodding toward the bench.

Skye and Victoria sat. The scent of cooked meat dizzied him, and the sight of good brandy on the wood table shot hungers through him.

"I'd also sell the rifle if I have to."

"Fat chance of that. No one can afford one. Where do you want to go, exactly?"

"Astoria, mouth of the Columbia."

"You willing to work?"

"We both will work for passage."

"I'm short of men. Ship's company down seven. Two scurvied and died off Chile. One ran into a whore's stiletto. Four deserted, Callao, Diego . . . Can she cook?"

Skye didn't answer. He was having second thoughts. "Where are you bound?"

"Sandwich Islands to get some Kanakas. Good seamen and cheap. But you need to keep a whip handy."

Skye knew that once he boarded that brig he'd not get off it until it reached its home port. He didn't want to go to the Sandwich Islands. "Sorry, mate," he said.

"Mate? I thought so, Skye. You've shipped before. I could use a bosun."

Skye didn't answer. He could not conceal his past even if he tried.

"You're an Englander," the master said.

"London," Skye replied.

"Long way from home," Dickens said. "You hire on and I'll take you and your lady to Boston and see to your passage across the Atlantic."

It stirred him. Passage to England. His dream fulfilled after all, but not on an HBC schooner. Passage to his father and sisters, and kin. That royal pardon, a good name. He sighed, and then felt Victoria stirring unhappily beside him.

"No, thank you," he said. He had already crossed that bridge and would never turn back.

The master's cordiality cooled, and Skye could almost hear the man thinking of ways to shanghai Skye and ditch the woman. He would be on his guard.

"A thousand pardons, senor," said the Mexican. "That fusil—that rifle. I know it. How did you get it?"

Skye weighed an answer and decided to conceal nothing. Half truths and untruths never sat well with him. Silence was sometimes a refuge, but not deception. "It belonged to a bandit in a gang south of here," he said. "Horses did, too."

"Sacramento del Diablo," the man whispered. "How did you get this piece?"

"That was the second bunch robbed us, and I got mad."

"Mad? Loco?"

"Plenty loco."

The Mexican involuntarily made the sign of the cross. "And you live to tell of it. You were coming from Monterey, si, and that is the worst trail in California. Why you are alive I cannot imagine."

"How'd you know this rifle?"

"It was stolen from my son, senor."

"They stole the rifle from him?"

"After they killed him. That trail, it is infested with bandits. No one in his right mind goes by land; always by sea. I begged Andres not to go that way."

Skye sighed. "The rifle's yours. I don't want stolen property."

The man was touched. "A thousand thanks. Ask me any favor, senor. It is Carlos Sepulveda you address."

Skye considered. "We need to go to Fort Vancouver in Oregon. How can we outfit and do that?"

Sepulveda shook his head. "It is too late by land, senor. The mountains to the north are impassible in the winter. Only by sea . . ."

thirty-nine

Skye didn't like that news. This remote province of California was walled by alpine snow much of the year. Not until May could he escape it by land. He sat there, in the taberna, wondering what blow would strike next.

"There is one way, senor, but it is arduous, si?" Carlos Sepulveda continued. "Sail south to San Diego. There one can take a wandering trail across arid wastes to the City of the Holy Faith in Nuevo Méjico, Santa Fe, and from there go north through fierce lands . . ."

Skye nodded. He lacked the means, the patience, and the time. Fort Vancouver lay only a few hundred miles away; not two thousand.

"I'll take ye to Astoria, Skye, for wages," Dickens said.

"It's Mister Skye, sir."

"Mister, is it? How do ye collect a gentleman's title?"

"Because I'm here in the New World, mate. For much of my life I had only a surname and never even a mister. All the officers called themselves mister or sir, but that didn't apply to Barnaby Skye, who was pressed off the streets of Wapping, near the London dock, at the age of thirteen and held prisoner until he escaped here in this free land seven years later. Now I am called a deserter.

"No one will ever take my freedom away again. They may

capture me, but not alive, sir. My freedom is worth my life. Put me on a ship against my will, sir, and I'll fight to death. Take me where I will not go and I'll fight to the death. My freedom is worth my life. I spent all those years with no liberty, mostly a powder monkey and then an able seaman, living only to obey and avoid a flogging and given nothing for it but my gruel. That's no life, sir. It's living death. I was a brute, a beast of burden, to be reined and spurred and whipped, and tossed to the sharks if I did not bend to their will."

Dickens' eyebrows arched.

"So, a warning, sir. I am Mister Skye, not Skye. If you sail for the Sandwich Islands against my will, you'll have a mutineer on your hands. If you're as good as your word, you'll have an able seaman, working hard and true, and an able cook, working hard and true. It's life or death for me, Mr. Dickens, and not all the whips of all your bosuns can subdue that."

Dickens stared. "I'll take you up the coast. I've recruited two boys here, but they're green. We'll train them. I'll do some trading for otter pelts along the way, and sell the last of my trade goods, so it makes sense. We'll deliver you to Astoria and then head for the Sandwich Islands for some Kanakas. You and Mrs. Skye willing?"

Skye studied the man. "Is that your bounden word, and are you good as your word, Mr. Dickens?"

"I'll oath it, Mister Skye. Upon my honor, we'll go directly up the coast to Astoria."

"And release us, Victoria, my dog, and me, there?"

"Upon my honor, sir."

Skye swallowed back the anxiety. "Then we'll sign on. When do you pull anchor?"

"First thing in the morning."

"Time for me to sell the horses and outfit, then. All right, Mr. Dickens, we'll be waiting at that jetty at first light. You'll not be disappointed."

"Far from it, Mister Skye."

They shook on it.

The trader, Sepulveda, helped Skye that afternoon. One of the horses, unmarked, traded easily for ten reales. The other bore a brand no one would touch, and the Mexican finally agreed to drive it out of town and abandon it.

Skye bought worn blankets and two knives with nine of the reales; a supper and shelter on the floor of the taberna with the last. A blanket and knife apiece from Sepulveda. He threw in some cowhide and thong and an awl as well. Victoria smiled. A blanket and a knife was treasure. And she could resole his boots and make herself some moccasins.

The next dawn they waited in the chill while Dickens' crew rowed a longboat to shore. Along side them were two solemn Mexican youths, one of them accompanied by his father. The boys looked frightened and ready to bolt.

Skye and Victoria boarded and settled on the hard bench as the seamen backed the longboat and rowed toward the brig. It was a fateful moment: there he was, a seaman again, though he had vowed he never would be. He eyed the motley sailors, mostly white Yanks, but some half-castes he thought might be Caribbean or drawn from the dives of New Orleans. They looked hung over and surly and he supposed it would be a day or so before they sweated the booze of the sole grogshop in Yerba Buena out of their pores. The ruddy bosun in command eyed the Skyes and the two newcomers closely.

The brig, *Dedham*, looked even worse close at hand than Skye had supposed from shore. Dickens, dressed shabbily in an ancient sweater, nodded them aft, and Skye poked around until he found above-deck quarters that had obviously been vacated by a bosun or master's mate just previously. The two-bunk compartment was little different from the one on the *Cadboro*, except this was filthy.

Victoria grunted. Skye knew that in short order this tiny place would be immaculate, unlike the rest of this creaking two-masted trading ship.

Skye doffed his battered frock coat and reported to work.

The deck hands were reeling the longboat aboard and the seamen were scaling the rigging, heading for the spars on the foremast where the square-rigged sails were furled. Men crawled out on the spars, oblivious of the height, and waited to release the gathered canvas which they would not do until the brigantine had passed through the gate and was at sea, because of adverse winds.

He watched sailors hoist the fore-and-aft mainsail, drawing it up from the boom to the gaff atop the mainmast. That one looked well-used, much-patched, and heavily stained as it caught the air of the great bay.

All this had proceeded in silence, which told Skye that this was a veteran crew needing no direction from the bosuns or master. That was the first good news.

The brigantine heeled in the wind. The helmsman steered it north, and Yerba Buena swiftly vanished behind hills and mist, and the great gate lay ahead, cold and bright and mean. A small ugly thought wormed into Skye's mind. He would know within the hour whether Dickens was a man of his word. Once they reached the sea, there were three directions the brig could go: south, west, or north. They passed the jaws of land, hit choppy waters, and then burst out upon the great Pacific, sparkling green and blue under a cloudless heaven.

The men up on the spars of the foremast dropped the canvas with heavy thumps, and they swelled with the wind. These were as badly mended and worn as the mainsail. Dickens would be lucky to make his home port without losing his sheets. He wondered why the man ran such a ship unless he was very nearly bankrupt.

Dickens approached him. "All right. You've seen the drill. I've good men, veteran seamen, but we're shy right now. Ship's company should be thirty-two; we're at twenty-five not including the new boys and you and Mrs. Skye."

"At your service, sir."

"I'm making you a boatswain. Don't ask me why; I'm just doing it. I'd thought about making Mrs. Skye a cook, but I need a sailmaker worse. That's been part of the trouble. My sailmaker's boy died of scurvy."

"She'll take to it, sir. What do you want of me?"

"You'll do first watch. You can start by putting those boys to work holystoning the deck. After that, I want you to examine the ship stem to stern and report. After that I'll introduce you to the crew."

Skye found the Mexican boys, Armando and Pio, hunted down the equipment and found it in a dock locker, and showed the boys how to scrape the good teak deck of the brig with blocks of soft sandstone. It was high time. The deck was slippery and gummy with the accretions of the sea and the animal cargo. The brig would be a safer place when the deck was immaculate.

Skye inspected the brig, estimating it to be a hundred and five feet from stem to stern, and twenty-eight at the beam. The foremast had been spliced; a sign of sure trouble in times past. He found neglect at every hand, and thought maybe if given his freedom he could bring the ship around before reaching Astoria.

'Tween decks he found a sailmaker's and carpenter's shop, a galley and mess, forecastle berths, storerooms, bosuns' quarters, and abaft these, two cabins, housing the master's mate and helmsmen. Below, in the cargo hold, he found stacked sea otter hides on racks well above the cargo deck, and a small collection of trade goods in crates and barrels. This brig was sailing half empty, which may be why Dickens was cutting every corner.

It would get him and Victoria to Astoria. Whether the decaying bark would take Dickens to Gloucester, Massachusetts, his home port, was a question.

He returned to the spar deck and found Dickens and two bosuns. Wind swelled the sails. The ship laid a course due west. The California coast lay small and dark.

"Mister Skye, meet your watch officers, Lars Pedersen, first mate this watch, and Amos Carter, second mate. The other lads are below. Gents, Mister Skye, here, likes to be addressed as I've addressed him, so that's how we'll proceed. He's been in the Royal Navy and knows the ropes. His wife, Victoria, will work in the sail loft. And the dog will—what will the dog do, Skye, for his keep?"

"He will keep watch over us, Mr. Dickens."

"Ah! I imagine that's worth the salt beef. Very well, gents. There's work to do, and two new boys to bring along."

Skye noticed the shadow of the foremast sliding across the teak deck. The brig was swinging north.

forty

Victoria knew at once what to do. Making a sail was very like making a new lodge. But instead of stitching with other women of her tribe, she was working with a strange little gnome of a man who talked so fast she couldn't understand him. All she knew was that he was very fierce and had a leer that offended her.

She found herself in a large room between decks, the sail loft. Great rolls of heavy fabric the little man called linen, or sailcloth, lay about, along with coils of manila rope, and scissors and knives and needles and thimbles and rolls of thick sail twine.

"This here, she's a new fore top sail. Foremast, top yard, that's how you name them. Now I got her laid out and cut into panels according to pattern, and what you're gonna do is sew them panels up with a real fine double stitch and no wrinkles that let the air through, got that?"

She didn't, but she nodded. "Now this here's how it's done. You take this big needle and thread it with twine like so, and then wax it so the right-hand twist lies true, and then you stitch like so, good straight line, double so she stands in a good gale."

On the floor, the pieces of the new sail were arrayed like the hides going into a new lodge cover, all carefully cut.

"All right, you tackle them seams and I'll sew patches on the corners. We get this sewn up, and we do the hems, the luff first—the forward edge—and then the foot, and then we put in the luff rope and the foot rope. Those help keep the sail from stretching out of shape, you see?"

She didn't, but she nodded.

"Then we sew in the bolt ropes on the luff and foot, and add the grommets, reef points, and the rest."

Maybe, she thought, this wasn't so much like sewing a lodge after all, except that the great pieces were on the floor, and cut according to a pattern.

Two portholes, without glass in them, threw white sea-light over the floor. She could see the benign sea shimmering there, and hear the creak of the ship's timbers as it skimmed the cold waters. She could scarcely imagine how white men had created these giant canoes, big enough to roam the seas and sturdy enough to weather storms. The whole ship had been a wonder to her.

The little man, whose name she learned was Perkins Gouge, never stopped talking and she hadn't the faintest idea what he was saying.

"Them Mohawks was thick with them Redcoats, and the Hurons and Oneida were in the middle of it, too, and we was marching up there near Lake Champlain when we come upon Prevost's column, and next thing was, they formed into a red wall, Brown Betsys poking out at us, bayonets on 'em, and they got on their knees and laid a volley and it sailed clear over us.

"We took cover and begin snipin', but they just march forward in that line, like they is brushing off flies, except now and then a Redcoat topples like a tree, and they cut loose with more volleys, one rank moves up and fires, and then backs off and the next rank moves up and fires, and they're driving us back right into the arms of them miserable Iroquois and that's when hell breaks loose and I'm about to lose my topknot."

Victoria sewed, at least until the little man peered closely at her work and got mad.

"That's not the way, damn ye red hide, it's done like this, see here?"

"Goddam," she said and waited for his instruction.

He made her cut out her stitches, wax the twine again, and start over. The ship creaked, and her mind drifted. She wanted to be up above, on the deck with Skye, free in the morning air, the dog beside them.

He was doing well, he said, training Armando and Pio, putting the rotting ship in shape, scraping away the neglect. He said the repaired sails and new sails were important. Without them Dickens wouldn't make it to his port.

They were following the coast but sometimes it was so far from the ship she couldn't see it, or could see only a thin and mysterious blue line. But then Dickens veered toward shore, reaching a settlement of some sort. He went ashore in a longboat rowed by crewmen, and returned with a stack of sea otter pelts, lifeless, eyeless furs that made her feel cold. She was not allowed on deck, so she knew almost nothing of what transpired, but Skye filled her in.

He said there were settlements along the California and Oregon coast, some Indian, other half-breed, that did business in otter and sealskins, and Yank merchant ships like this one, along with the HBC, bought every pelt they had to offer and paid with trade goods not unlike those her own people acquired in the Rocky Mountains.

She finally rebelled at the little tyrant who worked her until her hands went numb, and took breaks when she felt like it.

"Lazy, worthless redskin," Gouge bawled.

"You sonofabitch," she replied, remembering trapper words with joy. "You ain't worth spit."

She needed the air, and relief from him and his grisly stories of butcheries, massacres of Indians, battles at sea, great fires, roasted flesh, on and on.

Perkins Gouge was asking for a scissors in his belly, she thought. She'd do it, too, and then jump into the sea so as not to shame Skye.

All the while, she was getting an education in sailmaking. They completed the tight-stitched double seams welding the panels of the great sail together, and he actually smiled. Then he showed her how to table the sail: sew hems on its edges, beginning with the luff, or top, and then sewing the rope tightly into the luff. The task was just as intricate and artful as sewing a good buffalohide lodge together, and she began to enjoy making everything tight and strong.

"We finish this, and then we start on a mainsail," he said during a less bloodthirsty moment. "She's got a rip from gaff to boom, and we got to cut out the rotten panel and sew in a new one. That sail, she's too big to stretch in here, so we gotta do it a piece at a time."

But mostly he talked of war and blood and beheadings and amputations, and surgeons with saws, and mortar, and canister, and chain shot. When he was tired of that he talked about swords, dirks, stilettos, and beheading axes. He favored beheadings one whole day. He had seen several, or so he led her to believe.

He was the bloodiest little man she had ever encountered, but she knew she would soon be rid of him. His leering never stopped, but she ignored it. Skye would deal with him if it came to that.

One good thing came of her labor. She discovered that scraps of new and rotten sailcloth were available to any seaman who wanted them, and these leftover pieces were constantly being fashioned into britches and jackets and shirts and even slippers by industrious seamen in the fore castle. She and Skye had nothing, scarcely the clothing on their backs, so she set out to manufacture some. As weary as she was of sewing, she worked hard during their half-day rest, and made him some britches and shirts, a thick blouse for herself, and several sailcloth moccasins for them both.

The sea rose and fell in eternal calm, and she wondered when a storm would come. Whenever they were beyond landfall, she grew taut and upset and cursed these white men for taking her so far from her home. But then the blue rib of the continent would rise out of the mist. It was beyond swimming, but she comforted herself with the notion that she could somehow reach there if she had to.

One twilight the second watch discovered a bonfire on the distant shore just before dusk, and Dickens steered the brigantine shoreward. That was usually a trader's signal. The twilight offered safe passage and they made the coast in a half hour and beheld a great crowd on the distant shore. Black cliffs leapt up behind the settlement.

Skye and Victoria watched as the crew dropped anchor and prepared the longboat for Dickens. But even before the seamen could winch the longboat to the water, a swarm of giant canoes set sail for the brigantine, their high prows brightly painted and the paddling oarsmen stroking the dugout canoes to a great speed.

She thought there were two or three hundred villagers on the beach, and she wondered what people they were. She didn't know the people here on the edge of the world. Behind them was a village consisting of giant longhouses of bark, and racks for drying fish, and carved poles with spirit-figures on them to ward off evil. At least that was how she interpreted them.

These people were barechested even in this cold season, but wore leather skirts or pants, and great necklaces of gleaming things she couldn't make out.

"Good trade, many skins," she said to Skye.

He grunted.

A dozen canoes were closing on the ship, each canoe with twenty or more men in it.

She caught glints of metal things in the bellies of the canoes.

And no furs. No skins, unless it was to dark to see them.

Dickens had pulled the longboat up and lowered the Jacob's ladders so the visitors could clamber aboard and trade.

"Damn, Skye, I don't like this."

"Like what?"

"Them warriors."

"Warriors? They're trading."

No Name's hair bristled.

"Look at the dog, Skye."

"Mr. Dickens," Skye bawled. "Raise those ladders."

The master turned to glance at Skye. "What are you talking about, Mister Skye?"

"War," Skye cried.

But it was too late. The first barrage of arrows from the bows hidden in the dugouts found their mark. Dickens took an arrow through the mouth, tumbled, and fell over the rail.

Another arrow caught the bosun.

A whirling axe struck a seaman who was trying to raise one of the rope ladders. Then, with a ululating howl, the warriors scrambled to the deck, dealing death at every hand.

forty-one

Skye hurried Victoria aft, deep into darkness. The big, stocky tribesmen poured aboard, their faces hideously painted with red ochre, scaling the rope ladder with breathtaking speed. Volleys of arrows from the high-prowed dugouts felled most of the deck hands. Indians clubbed and stabbed others racing from the forecastle up the gangway. Still others raced to the pilot house and butchered the helmsman and master's mate with sickening speed. A howl of red joy bloomed among them, sending chills through Skye.

"Drop the Jacob's ladder off the stern and go," he whispered to Victoria. She slid to the rail, tossed the manila-and-wooden rung ladder over while he grabbed a belaying pin, the seaman's first and last recourse, and braced to fight two of the naked savages who were bearing down on him. He parried the lance of one easily and ducked under the war axe to club him hard. Skye whirled toward the other as a spearhead blurred by him, tearing cloth. The dog leapt, clamped jaws over an arm, and bit furiously. The red-painted warrior howled and tumbled down. Skye caught him across the head, knocking him senseless. The cur let go and leapt at another huge warrior thundering toward Skye.

Too many warriors. Skye whirled his belaying pin at one, the dog bit another, and then it was time to leap or die.

His heart pumped hard. He leapt over the taffrail, fell a sickening distance, hit brutal cold, and rose again to the surface. The sea swelled high about him. He caught his breath, realized he couldn't swim with his boots on and paddled desperately.

"Skye," cried Victoria.

He could scarcely see her in the blackness. She clung to the slippery rudder. He grabbed it too, feeling the icy water numbing him. Neither of them could endure that blast of cold for long.

Above, the dog howled, lonesome and eerie.

"Jump!"

The dog whined.

"Jump!"

The cur gathered itself and leapt, just as dark demons loomed above, and fell in a graceful dive. The dog slid easily into the briny, and Skye grabbed him by the nape of the neck.

The huge swells of the ocean poured over them. The ship had anchored at a roadstead, there being no sheltered water at this place, and the full might of the Pacific beat on her.

"My shoes," Skye growled.

He managed to lift a leg out of the whirling water, and Victoria undid the laces. It fell away. With struggle they got his other shoe off. Skye was still half-snarled by clothing, as was Victoria in her voluminous skirts.

Above them the shrieks and thumps of struggle diminished and Skye believed not a soul of the ship's company remained alive, save for himself and Victoria. It had all taken three or four minutes. The howling of the victors sent chills through him and he wondered what mad celebration was occupying them as they stomped rhythmically upon that newly holystoned teak. Who were they? He did not know. The brig had passed the Klamath River and Dickens thought he would be trading with the Yurok or possibly the Hupa as he dropped anchor. But there were also the Tolowa and Karok thereabouts. Maybe even Clatsop or Chinook.

One by one, butchered bodies of men he had known splashed into the sea. He gasped at the roiling body of the Mexican boy, Armando, who had only just signed on, and at a second-watch bosun he'd smoked with, bobbing lifelessly in the swells.

He took stock. They were protected by darkness and the curve of the hull at the stern, but he knew this ship would be a ball of fire ere long. They were far from shore and could not swim it. Their bodies were weighted by clothing and their arms would eventually give out and they would no longer hang on to the rudder or that life-saving bottom rung of the Jacob's ladder that kept them alive.

Darkness! When the ship started to flame, they would be exposed. No time at all.

He guided Victoria's hand to the dog, released his hand from the rudder and felt a surge of the sea lift him. He needed to swim around the stern. Once he could look down the side of the hull, lit by the huge bonfires ashore, he saw the great red-nosed dugouts poking into the ship like piglets suckling at the sow. They were empty but tied up, and that was the sole chance.

Up above, he heard frenzy and looting. He swam back.

"Got to get a canoe," he gasped. "I might be seen. Enough light there to be the death of me. I'll get it. Hang on here. If I can't paddle it, come to it."

"Sonofabitch," she said.

That was her way of saying everything. He borrowed her knife, let go of the rudder again, and swam through the brutal cold to the nearest canoe, which bobbed violently on the swells of the ocean. He clamped his hand on the gunnel. No one spotted him. He worked toward the prow, staying in shadow from the coastal fires, found a braided leather rope and severed it. The canoe banged into the ship, almost crushing him. He gathered strength, heaved himself mightily, and fell in a heap into the canoe, flat on his back, peering upward, water rivering from him. A warrior stood at the rail straight above him, scarcely ten feet, staring down.

He lay still in the black belly of the dugout. He was lying on some paddles, and slowly extricated one. The man above him turned away. Skye saw the beginning of a blaze up there, pale light. Too late, too late.

He sat, paddled furiously, barely moving the heavy dugout.

No alarm went up. The victors were celebrating. Skye realized they would burn this ship and all its contents, the cargo of pelts as well as the trade goods and everything else that might be useful, in a frenzied celebration of their prowess. What mattered the otter pelts, the hatchets and knives and awls and blankets and flannels and cottons and canvas when measured against victory at war?

He paddled furiously, unable to make headway against the huge swells of the Pacific that lifted and dropped him, and pushed him farther from the brig even though he tried to stay close.

"Skye!"

He spotted Victoria swimming, the mutt beside her, and paddled desperately, unable to turn the dugout toward her. He thought he was losing ground, but she was gaining bit by bit. The swells separated her from sight, and he feared he had lost her, but then suddenly she was there in the faintest of light, and he wrestled her up and into the bottom, where she lay soaked and cold and gasping. He found No Name dog-paddling beside the hull, and got him aboard.

"Victoria, paddle!"

She was weeping and out of breath. She clambered up and took the big paddle he proffered and they stroked hard, even as the sails and ribbing bloomed orange and the crackle of flame raced up the rigging and into the yards, snapping like giant firecrackers.

He thought they were naked there, light upon them, but maybe not. The victors were still whooping, their eyes blinded to the small struggles of two mortals and a dog in the blackness beyond the holocaust. A ship was dying, and these devils were celebrating it.

No Name shivered, shook water off, and padded to the prow, where it set itself a guard over the ocean.

The surf heaved much too powerfully for Skye and Victoria to steer the massive dugout away, so they drifted shoreward against their will. They best they could manage was to paddle the dugout north of the village even as they closed with land. They might be caught instantly when they reached shore. But for the moment they lived.

All their work had brought them only a hundred yards or so north of the village, but at least blackness cloaked them there, and they were somewhat shielded by a rough and rocky shore.

"Save our strength," he muttered.

They let the dugout drift until it struck an obstacle, and began careering violently as the high surf toyed with it, lifting and dropping and finally rolling it over.

They were pitched once again into the sea, but this time there was rock under foot, and even as breakers crashed over them with frightful force, they crawled to land and lay, panting, in the blackness on the stony and hostile continent.

He clamped Victoria's cold hand.

Skye peered into the sea, beholding the murder of a merchant ship. Twenty-seven merchant seamen had perished. Now the warriors were descending the ladders and gathering in their canoes. They would soon discover one was missing.

No time, no time.

Skye stood, pulled off his battered frock coat and wrung it. Victoria stood, undid her skirts, which were weighting her down almost to the point where she couldn't walk, and squeezed water out of them. The mutt shook and shook.

They were barefoot and maybe in worse trouble than ever. Sharp rock stabbed him with every step. They had nothing.

There was little they could do but wait. He led them back from the beach and into a rocky defile where blackness swallowed them. He clambered up the rock, cursing it whenever it lacerated his feet, but eventually he found a perch where he could look down the strand at the shoreside village. It nestled around a creek that tumbled from the inland coastal range into the ocean, providing the village with fresh water.

The warriors had loosed most of the dugouts and were paddling back to the village with easy strokes. There was no sign that they were looking for a lost canoe.

One by one the dugouts beached on a sandy strand where a crowd swiftly dragged them beyond the high-tide line. And there the entire village stood, transfixed by the pyrotechnics on the black waters. The ship's small store of gunpowder blew, shivering the coast with thunder as the whole burning deck lifted upward and fell sizzling into the sea.

Maybe there was a raw, slim chance in this.

He ducked down to Victoria, who huddled miserably.

"We've got the whole village to ourselves," he muttered.

She didn't need encouraging. They were as good as dead the way they were, desperately cold and barefoot, with nothing more than a small knife and no hope of rescue.

They had recovered their breaths and made steady but slow time toward the inland side of the village, suffering the wounds of sharp grasses, driftwood, and rock on their feet. Victoria did far better than Skye, having lived in moccasins all her life.

But at last they made the outskirts, and beheld in the dull orange light a number of cedar-planked longhouses, apparatus for drying fish, some things suspended high above the paws and teeth of animals, and much that they couldn't fathom.

"You ready?" he whispered.

"That first big lodge," she said.

They walked in, plainly visible to anyone on the shore who might bother to turn around. But no one did.

forty-two

Exhaustion beset Skye. The ice water had sucked the heat from his body, and now his muscles barely worked. He stumbled toward the longhouse, helping Victoria, who shivered with every step.

Then he paused, took hold of her and drew her tight to him, cold and wet. He hugged her.

"Worst still to come," he said. "Whatever happens, I just want you to know you are the greatest gift."

She was weeping and clung to him fiercely.

They let go, knowing every moment counted. They found the open entry of the big cedar-planked longhouse, and penetrated fearfully. A fire burned lazily in a central pit, its smoke dissipated through portals in the plank roof. Surely this was the home of several families, or a clan. Raised sleeping areas lined the walls, and a vast array of food and equipment hung from the rafters above.

They were not alone. Skye froze when Victoria pointed. An old man gazed at them from a pallet. An elderly woman stared. Two others, apparently ill or old, lay swathed in blankets or skins.

None of them said anything.

The small warmth of the longhouse revived Skye's spirits and body. He and Victoria needed everything, but most important were moccasins. Tentatively, they moved about, watching the old ones. The dog patrolled the dusky room, sniffing and whining.

Victoria found moccasins, calf-high, lined with sealskin, and richly dyed. She tried them, found them loose, but kept them. She found a cedarbark skirt, and swiftly dropped her own soggy skirts and put it on, sighing.

Skye's search took longer, but he found some good otterskin moccasins that fit, and gratefully pulled them over his bruised feet. The warmth was welcome.

Swiftly they gathered more: sealskin robes, artfully sewn together; a fine bow and quiver filled with arrows; a bone awl and a bone ladle; bags of thick fat, whether whale blubber or something else Skye could not say. And a prize: a broken flintlock, the barrel twisted but the lock intact. Flint and steel made fire.

Cedarbark rope, a fowling net, and that was as much as they could carry. One of the old men was mumbling, whining in anger, and Skye sensed it was time to flee. They had the means to live—if they could escape.

He peered swiftly out the door, beholding the shocking sight of the brigantine burning almost to its waterline, the villagers rapt along the sandy shore. But soon they would weary of the spectacle and Skye intended to be long gone before they did.

He nodded to Victoria, who hoisted her plunder on her shoulders and followed him. He noticed that she wisely took her soaked white-woman skirts with her, leaving little trace of their visit to the longhouse.

He headed straight toward the coastal mountains looming not far back, and plunged into a terrible thicket of brush and vines and fallen deadwood, vaguely lit by the great fire offshore.

Painfully they fought their way uphill into deepening blackness, feeling their way along, scarcely knowing where they were going.

The dog tagged along, then vanished and returned, and then began an odd mewling and whining. Skye's heart was laboring and he paused, exhausted, as the dog trotted off and returned, back and forth. Wearily, he followed the dog on its sideways course, until they burst into the creek bottoms and a clear trail mounting ever upward into the coastal mountains.

The going went easier then, with the dim form of the yellow dog piloting them. A little moonlight cast pale hope across their path, and they continued until neither of them could walk another step.

Skye stopped, his heart pummeling him, his legs quaking. Gratefully Victoria sank beside him.

"We've come a piece," he said. It was all he could do not to fall instantly asleep.

"We can't stay here, dammit," she said. "Daylight, they come."

She was right. But they could rest a while more. No one would come up that steep trail this night.

A misty fog built up, shutting away the view, and Skye feared they would make no more progress and might get soaked all over again. But the moon had vanished, and now there was nothing but Stygian darkness.

No Name whined.

"Can't even see you, old boy," Skye said.

Silently, Victoria found the coil of cedarbark rope she was carrying, and tied a loop into one end. This she slipped over the dog's neck.

"Trust the spirit-dog," she said.

It was all Skye could manage, just to stand and shoulder his load. But in a slow fashion, one small step at a time, they let the dog lead them where it would take them. Skye dreamed of ditching the burden on his back, dreamed of rolling into that scalskin robe, dreamed of being warm. He could hear Victoria before him, her breath laboring, bearing a terrible load of her own.

But then they stepped onto level land, a flat rocky area

devoid of vegetation except for patched grass, and here the fog did not hide the moon. The dog turned away from the trail and took them toward the base of a mist-obscured cliff, to a thin dry recess in the dripping rock. The rear was barely four feet from the overhang but it would do. No mist brushed his cold-numbed face. A small animal whispered away as they ducked in.

"Dog, I owe you my life again," he muttered.

Victoria sank to the rubble-strewn floor of this protected place and lifted the loop of bark rope from the dog's neck, muttering strange Absaroka songs to the mutt.

Wearily, he worked himself out of his soaked clothes, inch by inch, setting the torn frock coat aside, along with a ragged shirt and britches, and then rolled himself into the luxurious coil of the sealskin robe, and felt its gentle heat at once. Victoria had wrapped herself in her sealskin, and was sighing joyous little breaths of happiness. Or maybe she was crying.

In the moonlit gloom, they inventoried their new possessions: the precious moccasins, a coil of cedarbark rope, a fowling net, a horn ladle, the battered musket with a working flint and steel lock, and the smooth, masculine bow, quiver chocked with iron-tipped arrows, and even a spare bowstring of some sort lying coiled in the quiver. One of the leather bags contained several pounds of blubber or seal fat. The other was stuffed with fishmeal, a good coarse flour that could be cooked into something.

Victoria found her sailmaker's knife and whittled some of the blubber and gave it to the cur, who gnawed happily on it.

Skye found himself filled with euphoria. Soon he would drift into sleep. He had never been so exhausted. In the space of two hours they had survived the apocalypse. Death swarming over them in red-ochre masks; terror; the bitter sea that sapped their energies; an exhausting ride to shore; a time of lying numb and helpless on an alien beach; and then succor, taking from this warmaking people enough of the essentials that mortals needed to keep hearts beating in their bosoms.

It rained just beyond their noses, a dripping whisper of discomfort. An occasional gust drove moisture upon them, but nothing could dampen their joy as they lay against the back wall, collapsed into each other, surrounded by velvety and warmth-giving fur, and alive, all three of them, against all odds.

It was a miracle.

Sleep overtook Skye, but a fretful one in which a hundred anxieties tormented him. He woke up frequently, afraid of the red-ochre masks of deadly hunters. But no one came in the night, and when dawn broke gray and cold and dripping, they were alone.

His body ached. No part of him felt good. In spite of the robe, he felt chilled and wondered if he would be fevered here and die, having only escaped the very jaws of death the night before. Within his sealskin moccasins his lacerated soles pumped pain into him, and he knew the going would be hard this day. He dreaded sloshing through muck in those precious moccasins, wearing them out prematurely as the leather weakened.

They would not have a fire. There was not a stick of dry wood or tinder in sight. Victoria stirred, threw off her robe, and stood, which was more than Skye could do.

She eyed her soaked dress and camisole, and then set them down.

"Too damn cold," she muttered.

She looked fetching in her woven bark skirt and nothing else but her moccasins, but Skye was too exhausted to respond to the stirrings of his body.

"I'll not wear anything," she said.

He enjoyed the sight of his half-naked Diana throwing the quiver over her thin bare shoulder and rolling up their few provisions inside her sealskin robe.

It wasn't raining, but the morning would be icy and mean. He forced himself up, discovering more aches than he had muscles, and tried to wrestle himself into his clammy britches, which clung to his hairy legs and wouldn't pull up until he yanked violently at them. He, like Victoria, elected not to wear anything else of their wet duds, and so they started once again up the trail under a glowering heaven, making good progress until their stomachs rebuked them and they grew dizzy for the want of food.

Yesterday's ordeal had sapped today's strength. They rested and trudged forward once more, going as long as they could as the trail slowly vanished and the rivulet beside them diminished into a spring, and then a dry gully. But they were nearing the crest of a mighty ridge, so Skye pulled onward, and Victoria doggedly kept up, until at last they stood at the ridgetop.

Skye's spirits dropped. He had hoped to gaze down upon a mild and grassy land beyond the coastal mountains. Instead, he beheld a jumble of more mountains as far as the horizon, densely forested and impenetrable.

They rested on the ridge, silent and bitter and lost. He hadn't the faintest idea where he was. They needed to escape this dense forest that snared them in its thickets, but he saw no boulevard, no highway, taking them to easier places. The valley below looked impassable, so thick with brush that he knew they could never hack their way through, especially without so much as a hatchet.

But the ridge itself looked better. It trended north and south, and was open in places where rock crowded out life. And north was the direction he was heading. North to Fort Vancouver, the nearest speck of civilization in many hundreds of miles. Walk north. Walk to the Columbia, wherever that was.

The ridge was negotiable. Some spots were easy; some were tough, especially the steep slopes, the defiles, or the thickets of dense brush. A winsome sun improved their mood, driving the moisture out of the air, and they paused to dry their soaked duds on a black, hot, sunbaked slab of rock and rest.

Victoria sliced thin slivers of the seal fat, but she and Skye could barely swallow the stuff. She opened the other leather bag, mixed some of the fishmeal with clear water in a small rocky pool, and made a paste. They managed to down enough of this to keep their hunger at bay, and then fed some of the fat and meal to the dog, who licked every last crumb of it and waited for more with soulful eyes.

"I don't know where Oregon is," Skye said.

"Dammit, I don't care," she said. "You, me, and the dog. What else is there?"

forty-three

They toiled through a trackless wild, the sun often hidden from sight by a dense pine canopy above, or a ceiling of brush lower down. Skye's heart was as shadowed as his body, and he knew Victoria was wrestling with the same darkness that afflicted him. Noble firs rose higher than he had ever seen a tree grow, and water fled downslope from a myriad of springs. But they were lost in a growth so thick they could not even fathom their direction.

They saw no game at all because this tangled forest crowded it out, and their tiny larder diminished alarmingly. Periodically Victoria paused in an open glade to let them escape the heavy weight on their shoulders, and absorb the fleeting sun while they could, and then she whittled fat for each of them, or mixed a mash of fishmeal. Even the dog seemed despondent.

At least it didn't rain, Skye thought. A cold pelting rain just then would have sunk Skye's spirits to the bottom of hell.

But then, as they wrestled across a slope cut by a brook, the dog drew himself up, peered about, and pointed downslope. Skye thought the dog smelled an animal below, and struggled onward. But No Name refused to budge, and stood there quivering and whining and yapping.

"Dammit, Skye, he's telling us to go back," Victoria said.

Skye, in a bad mood, refused, but when Victoria turned back he had no option but to follow along like some pack mule born to obey.

The dog waited until his companions had gathered, and then plunged straight down a terrible slope.

"We'll just be trapped in brush down there," Skye grumbled, but he let himself be led.

Victoria's attitude changed radically. "The spirit-dog will lead us out," she said resolutely.

Skye doubted it.

They skidded down mossy slopes, stumbled on debris, stepped over fallen slippery timber, dodged dense and prickly thickets, and then the land changed subtly and they found themselves on fairly level ground, still surrounded by green hell. Here the dog found a clear game trail, and big animals had obviously used it. Except to duck now and then, Skye had no trouble following it. The dog trotted ahead of them, his tail lifted, barely deigning to see whether his mortal friends were walking behind.

The filtering light brightened, and then the trail veered smack into a riverbank. They beheld a considerable stream glittering over rocks and splashing around a bend hellbent for the ocean. Foliage hugged its banks, but here was light and hope, and a path to somewhere. The dog marched upstream, following multiple game trails that braided the bankside, and they progressed easily that day, covering many miles.

Skye saw big, silvery salmon waggling just under the surface of the crystal water, and ached to catch them. He thought of the fowling net, and supposed its mesh was too large. But maybe not. They paused at a grassy park in an oxbow, and rested for a while in an idyllic and enclosed wild, a terrible distance from other mortals.

He unrolled his sealskin robe and extracted the net tucked in it. Victoria tied a tether to it, using the coil of cedarbark rope. And then he cast the circling net over the busy water. It settled and sank slowly, barely heavier than the water. Skye watched silver shadows vanish and supposed they had failed. But one didn't vanish. It hung in the water with the net over it.

"Don't pull it in," Victoria commanded, as she pulled out of her skirts and moccasins and waded gingerly out on slimed rock. She slowly settled the net over the fish until it was well wrapped in cord, and pulled it out.

Skye swore the salmon was the size of a small shark. He could scarcely guess the weight, but it felt fat and meaty in his big hands.

"Aaiee!" she cried.

The dog sniffed and Skye watched a long canine tongue lick a chop.

While Victoria filleted the big fish, cussing at having to eat such a foul thing, Skye experimented with his broken musket. He pulled some fine inner bark from a dead tree and stuffed it where sparks would shower over it, pulled back the flint, and let it smack the frizzen. Soon he had a smoldering bit of tinder that he nursed along with soft breaths until a tiny flame erupted. Then he added the smallest imaginable sticks to build a lilliputian fire, which burned lazily, yielding no heat. Cooking that salmon would take a while.

They wrestled rock to the fire to make a firepit, and there they roasted the fillets, spread out on the encircling slabs of rock, while the cur munched cheerfully on the fishhead and offal. Dark clouds blotted the sun periodically, and Skye sensed they were in for a drenching, but he resolutely fed the hot little fire.

That's when Victoria glanced up and muttered, "Sonofabitch!"

A silvertipped grizzly was standing on its hind legs, its little eyes staring at them, his nostrils sniffing his dinner and wondering what to eat first.

"Dammit," she cried, and Skye heard terror.

Victoria snatched her bow, and attempted to string it but found it too strong for her. Skye barely managed, and his respect for the coastal warrior who owned it leapt. He handed the strung bow to Victoria, who nocked an arrow. She would not use it except in desperation. Only an arrow straight to the heart, missing the ribs, would stop that humped brown monster from doing whatever it chose.

The grizzly sniffed, studied the scene, lowered himself on all fours and padded swiftly toward Skye and Victoria. The dog snarled. Skye and Victoria eased back, back, into the rocky bank, and then into the cold tugging stream. The bear halted at the firepit, swatted the sizzling fish off the rock with claws as long as human fingers, and sniffed the salmon lying in the grass. It was too hot, so the big bear settled on its haunches and waited, while Skye and Victoria cooled their heels in the ice water of the big river.

No Name watched, crept forward by wiggling along the grass, heading straight for the grizzly, until Skye thought the mutt was daft. One swipe of a claw would shred him and make another meal for the hairy brown giant. The bear sighed, slobbered, and began nipping at the still-hot fillet, tearing it apart with its deadly black claws and feeding small steaming pieces to himself.

That's when the cur nabbed the other fillet, which was lying on the grass a few yards from the bear, and raced away. The grizzly paid no heed, enjoying his feast.

Victoria cursed mightily. Bears scared her. Skye was sweating, in spite of the brutal cold water reaching high up his thighs. The water was poor protection. That bear could splash in, not even feeling the cold under its shaggy pelt, and land on them long before they made the opposite shore.

But it didn't.

The dog dropped the hot fillet, whined, picked it up and carried it to the riverbank, and waited.

The bear ate, poked around, sniffed the Skyes' gear, tore at it with its paws, while Victoria cussed it in English and trapper tongues, invoked her deities, and threatened to puncture the beast with arrows.

271

About the time Skye's feet were losing all sensation, the bear shuffled away.

Skye and Victoria made haste back to their camp, rebuilt the dying fire, dried themselves, and then, at last, shared the fat fillet with No Name.

Skye laughed, a big and hearty thunder rising within him. Bears were good news. This was game country. The menacing beast had left them alone.

Victoria looked at him soberly. "You got bear medicine," she said. "All the rest of your life, you and bears are brothers. I have spoken this."

"Aw, Victoria . . ."

"I have spoken!" she snapped.

Skye had always wondered how she knew these metaphysical things, but she seemed absolutely certain. The beliefs of the Plains tribes had always been a great mystery to him. How did she know that No Name was a spirit-dog destined to look after him and his family?

They devoured the whole fillet. Suddenly the world was a better place. This great ripping river poured out of the continent. It had cut through the coastal range en route to the sea. They would work upstream, find abundant game in this sunnier and grassier country, and at last head for home.

The scattered clouds thickened and joined until a gray ceiling hung low upon them, sawing off mountaintops and shooting cold through them. But the rain held off. Skye began hunting hard for a place to hole up, but this valley offered little to anyone escaping a storm.

They hastened along the river, sometimes along its bank, sometimes distant, and then they rounded a bend and beheld a fishing village: bark houses, an elaborate pole trestle over the rushing water where spearmen could harpoon the salmon, great drying racks, and piles of fish offal. Not a soul stirred. This was a site used seasonally by some tribe or clan, and then abandoned to sleep as it did now.

They reached the first of the bark-clad houses just as fat

cold drops of rain splattered on them. They stepped into a gloomy interior, spared the rain by a deftly shingled bark roof and walls, and welcomed the gloomy refuge as the storm swept over them, rattling rain and hail on their shelter. An icy wind eddied through the building, and Skye knew that it would be none too pleasant within even though mostly dry. The accommodations might be primitive, but the hand of man gladdened him. He had been half mad for other company in that silent, treacherous woods.

"The one I shall not name brought us here," Victoria said.

Skye gazed gently at No Name, who lay contentedly at the door, keeping watch.

forty-four

They stood in the twilight of a winter's day at the end of a year beside the Columbia, staring across a misty sweep of water to a shrouded island. Beyond stood Fort Vancouver, which lay hidden from them even though they knew it was there across the father of western waters.

For weeks they had toiled over the mountains of the Oregon country. One day they reached a divide, and beyond it water trickled east, and after that they descended into a long valley with a river running north.

The Willamette.

Now, near the confluence, they stood gratefully, so gaunt and worn that they scarcely fit the rags they wore. The dog's ribs poked through his yellow hair, and a hollow had formed behind his ribs. Winter had taken its toll even in that mild land. Game had been scarce, and often they had paused to hunt or fish. Victoria's bow and the fowling net were all that stood between them and starvation.

Skye marveled that they had come this far, after so many disasters and so much trouble. He would have died but for Victoria, and the dog. Often it had pointed toward game or frozen before bobbing ducks on water. The salmon had come and gone, and when they left so did their meals.

Silently Victoria gathered dry wood, what little she could find, for a signal fire while Skye peeled back dead bark and scraped the soft fibers within. Once again he would have to build a fire. He doubted that the post would see the bonfire while veiled by the fog, but the fire would warm them.

Fort Vancouver probably lay a little to the east, and it would be quite possible that no one would come when summoned.

The old flintlock was worn, and Skye was having more and more trouble striking flint to steel, but he managed this one last time, after a heart-stopping moment when a piece of the old flint shattered away.

At least there was no wind to thwart his every effort. Wearily he added sticks, and then branches, until the smoky fire rose well into the evening. He saw no lamplight on the far bank as dusk settled.

There was little to do but wait. They had no food. Victoria had turned dour these last weeks, as much because the sun came and vanished swiftly as because they were starving to death. But they had made it here, somewhere around the first of January by Skye's dubious reckoning.

The warmth felt good, and stayed the damp cold. They sat on the bank, huddled together with the dog, and waited. But nothing happened and Skye resolved himself to spending the night there, awaiting the time when the fog would lift. He scratched around for deadwood and debris to keep the fire going, not an easy task without so much as a hatchet, and built up a pile of wood to warm them during a hard night.

Then he and Victoria, worn with cares and exhausted by months of barest survival and threat, dozed lightly in their battered sealskin robes.

"Allo, allo!" came the voice.

Skye awakened with a start, and rolled away from the fire.

"Allo," came the voice again, from the riverbank.

"Here," said Skye.

Moments later two dark figures emerged from the fog.

"We are make come by ze bourgeois, McLoughlin," said one. "It is a signal, oui?"

Voyageurs. "Yes, a signal, and you are welcome, friends," he said. "Can you take us across?"

"We 'ave a petit bateau. You 'ave horse?"

"A man, a woman, and a dog."

"Ah! Bien. Allors. Gaston," he said, pointing at his chest. "This is Honore, oui?"

The pair of them, stocky Canadians, squatted at the fire, examining the Skyes.

"I see you before, le nom est . . ."

"Mister Skye . . ."

"Ah! Mon Dieu!" Gaston, the one addressing the Skyes stared at them as if examining ghosts. And then he stared at the dog and made the sign of the cross.

"We had trouble," Skye said, "but by the grace of God, we're here alive and together."

"Sacre bleu!"

They led the Skyes down to the shore, where a rowboat was beached.

Skye was uneasy. "How are you going to find your way across and not just be swept downriver?"

The voyageurs laughed, which didn't comfort Skye any. But one of them cupped a hand to his ear, and they stood silently for a while. Then, faintly, the sound of a distant gong, muffled by mist, reached them.

Skye nodded. Away from the fire the blackness cloaked them so that he could not even see the faces of his company in that small, wet-bottomed rowboat. But the voyageurs set out upon the river with confidence, and rowed steadily, guided only by the distant gong, which rang every two or three minutes. It seemed a poor device by which to navigate, and Skye wondered whether they would end up far downstream.

The crossing seemed endless, but just when Skye started to despair, the voyageurs reached the opposite bank, and began rowing upstream so close to land that it lay barely beyond the oar. That leg of the journey seemed endless, too, and Skye realized that in spite of the bell, the rowboat had indeed been driven downstream.

But at last the faint lanternlight of the post blurred through the mist, and the voyageurs drove the little boat onto a sandy strand, then leapt out and dragged it with its passengers half out of water.

"Vancouver. The White Eagle awaits," Gaston said.

"What time is it?"

"It makes huit . . ."

Eight. That early. It had darkened at five that time of year.

The dog leapt out easily, but the Skyes were slower gathering up their robes and truck. They plodded wearily through the opened double doors and into the post. Soft light glowed from several windows. The factor's house had real glass windows, not thin-scraped hide or an open window shuttered at night. It amazed Skye to see yellow lamplight pierce through a window, after so many months in the wilds.

Gaston and Honore escorted them into McLoughlin's home.

Warmth and light and comfort smacked Skye palpably, as if he were stepping into a new world.

The White Eagle, towering over them all with his crown of snowy hair and raptor's nose, simply gaped, first at the Skyes and then at No Name, who settled comfortably on the polished plank floor.

"I am seeing ghosts, or am I mad?" he asked.

"We had trouble."

Marguerite McLoughlin rushed into the bright room and gasped. For there were Victoria, wearing the same skirts that had been fashioned by Marguerite's needle, but now in rags; and Skye, wearing a frock coat sewn together in that very post, but now unrecognizable, and the mark of starvation upon their gaunt and shrunken frames.

She clapped a hand to her mouth and cried.

"They are back, Marguerite, and now we shall hear their story," the chief factor said. "But first, my friends, food and drink, eh?"

"That would comfort us, sir."

At once, Marguerite hastened off to pull a meal together.

"The *Cadboro*—is it all right? Has there been a disaster?"

"The schooner's fine, sir. Last we knew, anyway. We sailed as far as Monterey, Mexico, with Mr. Simpson, and there ran into a squadron of the Royal Navy. Why we're not in the schooner, we'll tell you in due course."

"Ah! Already your story comes clear. And I rejoice that the *Cadboro* and Emilius Simpson are preserved. Our whole annual take in furs was aboard. That dog," said McLoughlin. "Start with the dog."

Skye did not dare sit, knowing his filthy clothes would soil the good furniture, and so he stood wearily.

"Do sit down, Mister Skye, and you as well, Mrs. Skye. You'll do this battered furniture no harm, and I fathom you're at your wits' end."

Gratefully, Skye sank into a horsehair sofa, with Victoria beside him. He had not sat upon something soft for months.

"The dog, sir, ran beside the ship, hour upon hour, day upon day, down the river. Mr. Simpson kept assuring us that the mutt would give up at the rivers it had to swim, and go back. But it didn't . . ."

The story of the heroic and indefatigable dog mesmerized McLoughlin. "We did our best to pen him before the *Cadboro* left, sir. But next we knew, he was gone, and I've heard no more since. But I told my people the dog and his master would be parted nonetheless, for what dog can walk on water? I seem to have been in error."

Skye described the miraculous dog, and how its heroic chase finally persuaded the master, Emilius Simpson, to permit the creature to board at least as far as California.

Then Skye turned to the desperate events in Monterey, his discovery, the chase, the headlong flight, the difficulties in provisioning, the weary trek north, the two sets of bandits, the reception in Yerba Buena, the discovery of the Yank merchant trader heading north, and their signing on . . .

"Dickens. I know of him. He's never brought that brig in here, but my people on the coast compete with him."

"He suffered a lack of hands, sir. Lost some to scurvy and others deserted, so he was glad to take me on, if only for a way. He had two new Mexican boys aboard, and after delivering us to Astoria, he was headed for the Sandwich Islands to find some Kanakas. But we never made it."

Marguerite rushed in, bearing hot tea and some scones.

"Here you are, and there's more. And plenty of jams and jellies."

Skye marveled, and was reminded again that this post operated farms and orchards and diaries. He ate greedily, scarcely believing the goodness of the scones. Victoria tasted them tentatively, and smiled.

Then, at last, he turned to the attack on the Yank brigantine, describing the swift assault and desperate defense that lasted but a few minutes, and the ultimate destruction of the entire ship and its contents, with a loss of twenty-seven men, including the two Mexican boys recruited in Monterey.

"Terrible, terrible," McLoughlin muttered. "This must be dealt with. Do you know the tribe?"

"No, I don't. Dickens showed us the Klamath River when we passed it, and we had sailed another day and into the evening when we spotted the bonfires and Dickens decided someone wanted to trade."

"We'll look into this! We'll deal with it! HBC and the Yanks always stand together on matters like this! We have men in that country, trading along the coast just as the Yanks do, and we'll find out! By God, this is insolence!"

And then, to the amazement of both Skye and Victoria, McLoughlin told them that Professor Nutmeg and Nat Wyeth and his men were there, at Fort Vancouver.

forty-five

S kye and Victoria listened incredulously to McLoughlin's news. Nat Wyeth's brig, the *Sultana*, had been lost at sea. The news reached Fort Vancouver shortly after the Skyes had sailed on the *Cadboro*, brought to the post by another Hudson's Bay ship in from the Sandwich Islands.

Because of the disaster, Nutmeg had not returned to Boston, and Wyeth's enterprise had foundered. All the equipment to preserve and pack salmon and send the casks east had perished. What's more, most of Wyeth's men had abandoned him, discovering choice farmland up the broad Willamette Valley. Skye and Victoria had unwittingly passed several rude farms operated by the Americans, and also a few run by Creoles retired from HBC service.

"And what are the professor's plans?" Skye asked.

"He's looking for a way east."

"And what are Wyeth's plans?"

McLoughlin smiled. "He's a man of great enterprise. A setback merely spawns a dozen new ideas, so he runs hither and thither here, getting ideas. He talks now of visiting some of our fur posts, no doubt to master the business and compete with us. But withal, he is good company and I admire the man."

Skye marveled. Here was a man who had lost everything,

was a continent away from Boston, and yet brimmed with
schemes to make his fortune some new way.

"I should like to see them both, if the hour is not too late.
I scarcely know Wyeth, but Nutmeg, that's quite another
matter."

"He'll be pleased to see you, Mister Skye. He is worried
about returning to his university."

Skye sighed. "Perhaps he should sail out on the next brig."

McLoughlin laughed. "That, sir, would deprive him of
the chance to pluck up more plants and roots and butter-
flies."

"That's what I was afraid of."

"And what of your plans, Mister Skye?"

Skye stared disconsolately into the fireplace, watching
orange flame lick a log.

"Dr. McLoughlin, we will return to the mountains."

McLoughlin pondered that. "HBC can employ you as a
trapper, but not as a brigade leader. We've several men in our
ranks who've eluded British justice, but they're invisible and
not even Simpson knows of them. I've quietly put them to
work with traps at small posts. But we can't put you in a visible position in HBC. You understand, of course. Simpson not
only runs the company; he's the king's man." He paused. "I
still want you. You've rare skills and courage. This escape . . .
this resourcefulness. We've few men of your caliber, Ogden,
Ermatinger, one or two others. I say, Mister Skye, let me give
some thought to this."

"Things have changed, Doctor. Victoria and I and this yellow dog who's been our companion and our help in time of
need . . ."

Those great eyebrows frowned, and Skye felt the piercing
stare of a powerful man.

"Mister Skye, a man's name is of little account here. It's of
little account at the Yank rendezvous. I hear there's men
among the Yanks whose real name will never be known.

There's a career in Hudson's Bay for, say, a man who bears any name other than Skye . . ."

The great factor waited expectantly, filling his parlor, so formidable that Skye quailed slightly before him. But Skye knew what he must answer.

"I have a good name in the mountains, no matter how matters rest in England and at the admiralty. That, Doctor, is worth my life. Beyond that, it wouldn't take long for my true name to be revealed to Governor Simpson's ears. I am not unknown, after six years in the wilderness."

Simpson sighed. "You know, Mister Skye, the very nature of your response only adds to my esteem. I'm afraid your honor is Hudson's Bay's loss, but there is something in it: it is my gain, for I have found a man among men, a man I admire. And I wish to emphasize the esteem I hold for you, my dear Victoria, intrepid woman and able hunter and loyal consort."

She smiled.

"You'll be going to the Yanks, then, I suppose."

"We plan to go back to the Americans, sir. The next rendezvous. Where is it, do you know?"

"At the head of the Green River, I hear. The Yank Captain Bonneville's building a post there."

Skye nodded. Once he got to the Seedskedee, as he preferred to call the Green, he'd find it.

Marguerite summoned them to her table. In the space of a few minutes she had loaded her table with cold beef, bread, potatoes, and beans.

"Please eat," she said. "You look like you might need a bite."

"Madam McLoughlin, that is an understatement," Skye said.

He settled into a real chair at a real table, and Victoria joined him. This was no campfire meal, hastily swallowed while resting on their own heels, but a meal served on china.

Skye sighed, and dug in, pleasuring himself with real salt

on his meat, and real butter and jam on the biscuits set before him. Victoria watched, swiftly copying his manners, and managed to feast with barely controlled haste.

He dosed the rib roast with salt and sliced off juicy pieces, and then slathered butter over a biscuit and felt it crumble under his touch. He sliced some boiled red potatoes in two, inundated them with butter and a little salt, and felt his teeth clamp the delicate red skin. He returned to the beef, sawing slice after slice, feeling them leak juices into his mouth. He spooned huckleberry jam over a muffin, and let the concoction settle on his tongue. It was too good to swallow. He beheld, before him, a goblet of ruby port, as clear as stained glass, and sipped delicately, and then quaffed mightily. Ah, the things that food and wine did to a man's spirit!

Victoria smiled at him. When had they feasted like this? And rested in a safe, warm place like this?

He turned to the chief factor. "This is too good to be true," he said. "Our diet has largely been whatever the dog dragged in."

The thought galvanized him.

"Would it be possible to feed the pup?"

Marguerite smiled and pointed toward the door of the kitchen.

"He has a bone with lots of beef on it," she said.

Skye could not remember the last time his belly felt comforted. They had eaten raw mallard, a goat, various seeds and nuts and roots Victoria had scrounged, a marmot, assorted fish, often raw and barely edible because they often could not start a fire.

McLoughlin sipped tea and waited for the Skyes to finish, but Skye knew he had much more to discuss.

"How are you going to the Rockies?" the doctor asked at last

"I should like to work for you, sir, and earn enough for an outfit."

"We're always short of men. There's plenty to do, especially for someone who knows about peltries. They need to be sorted and graded and baled. You up to it?"

"Yes, sir."

"What about me? I work," said Victoria.

"There is work to be done, Mrs. Skye. Consider yourself employed by HBC." He turned to Skye. "Now, the matter of Professor Nutmeg is much on our minds here. You see, Nat Wyeth absolutely refuses to take the man east. He says he lost days trying to find the wayward botanist, and sent search parties out in all directions, and finally supposed the man was dead until he stumbled on one of your messages. That suffices, in his mind, to refuse the naturalist. Nutmeg, of course, is most desirous of returning by any means. You willing to take him to rendezvous?"

Skye didn't really want to, but nodded.

"There's more, you know. He's not, ah, welcome. What we hear is that the Yanks won't take him back to St. Louis when their supply train leaves rendezvous. What'll the professor do then, eh?"

"Maybe he should wait here for the next Yank trader, and go by sea."

McLoughlin stared into space. "I like Professor Nutmeg and admire his great enterprise. Come, Mister Skye, let us find some way of getting the man safely back to Boston, eh? He has no funds here but eventually he'll pay you, no doubt sending a credit out with the next supply train from Missouri."

"If you're thinking I should escort the professor clear back there, sir, I must respectfully decline. Mr. Nutmeg has means by sea."

"And by river, Mister Skye. What I have in mind is taking him to that new American Fur post, Fort Union, at the confluence of the Yellowstone and Missouri. From there, if you reach the post in time, the professor can go downriver on the fur company's river packet, eh? Safe aboard, unless they let him loose and he wanders out of sight while they're cutting wood, in which case it's their own fault."

"Have you proposed this to him, Dr. McLoughlin?"

"No, because there's been no one to take him to Fort Union, and Nat Wyeth wants nothing to do with the man."

Skye thought about that and liked it. He could drop the professor and then accompany the American Fur Company men to the rendezvous. And better still, he could talk to the factor there, and see about employment.

"The flower collector is a good man," Victoria said. "I will keep an eye on him."

Skye knew she was urging him to say yes. He grinned. A trip to Fort Union would take them right past her Kicked-in-the-Belly people, and there would be a joyous reunion.

"I like the idea," he said. "But we'll have to see if Professor Nutmeg likes it, too."

forty-six

John McLoughlin liked to warm himself in the bright winter sunlight streaming into his office through small glass windows. Those windows were the only glass he knew of in the western half of the North American continent, and he considered them a luxury beyond price. What other room, in a thousand miles in any direction, possessed glass windows?

He spent some of that morning wrestling with the problem of guests. The post, an isolated island in a vast wild, offered succor to any passing white man. Nat Wyeth and his men, for instance. He arrived there only to discover that disaster attended his plans, and suddenly the Hudson's Bay Company became his only refuge.

McLoughlin did not turn him—or any other Yank or Canadian or Englishman—away, no matter that the directors in London strictly forbade him to succor or cooperate with any of the company's rivals, especially the Yanks. The Oregon question had not been settled and the company did not wish to act in any fashion that would deprive England of territory, or deprive itself of a secure and permanent monopoly of trade.

But what seemed logical in London was not feasible in the midst of a vast wild. Dr. McLoughlin had no intent of turning stray and desperate people away in their moment of need. So he had permitted Nat Wyeth to make himself at home, even though Wyeth's plans for a salmon fishery and some trade in peltries ran against HBC's own interests. Who could turn away a man who had lost a ship, and a dream, at sea?

So the post was burdened with several people who consumed its meat and produce and grains, burned its firewood, ate its fish, lived within its shelter, and earned HBC not a shilling. He liked Wyeth, and didn't quite know why. The New Englander bubbled with enthusiasm and enterprise, throwing one or another wild idea into the air, striking sparks to McLoughlin's imagination and setting the tinder aflame.

Skye was another sort. From the moment he arrived the previous evening, gaunt and worn and destitute, Skye had assumed that he had obligations. No sooner had he told his tale and eaten Marguerite's swiftly wrought meal, than he offered to work for his living. And so did his lovely Victoria. He was not a man to accept endless hospitality and return nothing. Even now, as weary as he was, Skye was employed in the warehouse grading pelts with an expert eye, and helping with the pressing and baling. Victoria had given herself over to the women of the establishment, to mend and sew and make the rags they all wore about the post endure a while more.

Thus it was that Skye, from the day of his arrival, was contributing to the company, along with his good wife. There seemed to be not a thought in his keen mind that he should enjoy the hospitality of the company and return nothing.

To be sure, he and his lady needed an outfit, but McLoughlin would have provided one whether or not he worked for it. The factor had given numerous men, defeated by wilderness, an outfit sufficient to take them wherever they were headed. The outfits he gave away at a dead loss at least had the virtue of lessening the number of people dependent on the enterprises of Fort Vancouver.

But not Skye. That man, no matter that he was half sick from starvation, was earning his way in the world, and McLoughlin set him apart in his mind as a sterling Englishman who had been dealt one cruel blow after another by the nation he still called his own.

The Skyes would leave Fort Vancouver better off for their presence. Hudson's Bay could use men like that, and it grieved the factor that Skye would not have a chance to contribute to the company. But Skye was doing the right thing. He would have a better chance among the Yanks than within the company, doomed to be an obscure trapper beyond the Cyclopean eye of George Simpson.

The doctor finished his eggs and breakfast kippers, and now it was time to invite Professor Alistair Nutmeg to a small but vital meeting of the minds.

The man was not lazy, but neither had he contributed to the company that succored him. He had drifted out upon the fields and forests day by day, plucking up his botanical specimens and beginning a new collection after losing the old, pressing his plants between precious papers he had begged. That was, indeed, a good thing for science and knowledge. It might even have the practical result of giving the world new herbs and medicines.

There had been several alarms when the good man had vanished for days at a time and was feared lost. But just about when McLoughlin was readying a search, the half-starved savant would drift in, utterly unaware of the mounting concern about him. A pleasant man he might be, and civilized, and a fine companion over dinner wine, but not a man to be let out of the academy, except with a warder. No wonder Wyeth, and every other son of the mountains, would have nothing to do with him.

McLoughlin summoned the man, and the professor duly appeared in the chambers, looking as gentle and distracted as always.

"Please sit down, Professor. We've a little something to discuss," he said.

Nutmeg perched like a butterfly upon the edge of a

wingchair, alighting for just as long as necessary before fluttering off.

"The Skyes are here," he said.

"No! How could that be?"

"A long story, and you'll learn it. I've taken the liberty of discussing your plans with them. I think we've found a means to restore you to Harvard College."

"Oh, indeed, capital, capital."

"Overland travel is pretty much confined to seasonable climates, but in the spring, at the appropriate time, they will take you east to the confluence of the Yellowstone and Missouri rivers. And from there, you'll travel by river packet to St. Louis and civilization. After that, it will be up to you to arrange river passage up the Ohio and to New England."

"Why, sir, that's most kind, but I must resist. How am I to collect specimens and put this continent in botanical order from the confines of a riverboat?"

McLoughlin ignored that. "You have two choices, Professor. Leave here by sea, on the next coastal ship of any flag, or go with Mister Skye and Victoria."

The professor blinked, not liking it. "All for nothing," he muttered. "I can't complete my work on a wooden deck."

McLoughlin stared into the fireplace, where a thick log burned lazily. He decided not to respond, for anything he might say would seem a rebuke to the professor. He had never met a man so devoid of practical sense, and even the ordinary courtesy by which one makes commerce with others. There could be no arguing with a man oblivious to the strains he created upon all those who suddenly were forced to look after him.

"The Skyes have volunteered to take you," McLoughlin said. "They'll leave in early April, or maybe late March if the weather's good. They need to make Fort Union, the new American Fur Company post there, before the riverboat turns around and heads for St. Louis in June or early July."

"Is there no other choice, sir?"

"Mr. Wyeth has his own difficulties, and lacks the time or men to look after you when he heads for the Yanks' rendezvous."

"I see. Well, then, I shall go, and count it a loss, this wretched trip."

"I think it's really a great advance in your work, sir. You have in your head, and in the notes you've written here, a major start to a North American botany."

But the professor was lost in his own world, so McLoughlin led him out of the study.

"Really, Professor, you ought to say hello to your companions. They're about the post now, Skye in the warehouse, Victoria with the women, and the yellow dog somewhere. He and your mutt are friends, I take it."

"Oh, the dog, too? Yes, rather. I shall welcome them. Thank you for reminding me. I admire the rough chap and his squaw."

McLoughlin bit back a retort, and saw the man off.

The Skyes would have a burden once again, but McLoughlin intended to make it up to them with a good outfit; a better outfit than their labors could purchase.

Later, McLoughlin found Nat Wyeth out in the shops, surrounded by cordage, weights, floats, pulley devices, and sketches tacked over a workbench. He was attempting to make a new sort of gill net with floats on top and weights at the bottom that would harvest salmon by the boatload and earn him several fortunes.

"See here, John, I've got this vee-shaped net, you see. It folds in on itself with a tug of the rope, and the salmon won't be able to duck out. Oh, what a fortune, what an improvement in the ways we fish!"

"Nat, the Skyes are here. Returned last evening, worn out."

"The Skyes? Did the *Cadboro* go down?"

"No, it's a long and bloody mean story, and I'll tell it in time. But they're here, and they've agreed to take Professor

Nutmeg with them to Fort Union in time to catch the AFC riverboat. So you're free from that matter."

"I always have been free. I absolutely refuse to shepherd a half mad fool through dangerous country again. I simply thought you'd pop him on the next brig to sail up the river."

McLoughlin nodded. Nat Wyeth entertained his own grand vision of the world and its glowing opportunities, and would not, given his tinkering and enterprising nature, be inclined to help an innocent and somewhat daft professor from his home city if that meant slowing things up. Not that he didn't like Wyeth, whose Promethean enthusiasms struck sparks and lit fires in every mortal who came into contact with him.

It had been a profitable morning, and he had resolved the matter of the fort loafers. He would mention it all in his regular reports to Governor Simpson, of course, but he would be a little vague about certain aspects of it. Such as the names of those who would take the professor to the Missouri River.

forty-seven

Barnaby Skye found pleasure in his daily toil. He graded pelts, and then pressed and baled them for shipment, a task that required muscle and patience.

After that he split cedar shakes from thick logs hauled and floated great distances by the post's woodsmen. Like most seamen, he understood wood and how to shape it. With axe and wedges and maul, he snapped shingle after shingle free, and day by day built a great pile of them for Dr. McLoughlin's perpetual building projects.

Once in a while the factor paused in the yard outside the post, watched him at work, and wandered silently away, making Skye wonder whether his work was adequate.

The skilled work heartened Skye, but even more pleasant was the knowledge that he was earning his keep, and maybe collecting some credit for an outfit. He saw little of the illustrious visitors. Professor Nutmeg had visited with Skye briefly but obviously was restless, preferring the company of better educated men, or at least idle men. Nutmeg and the post's second in command, James Douglas, had become fast friends, each of them starved for the company of literate men.

Victoria had been working hard, too. A community of two hundred consumed clothing, and there were too few women at hand to mend the heaps of torn shirts and britches, and to transform all those bolts of English wool and linen and cotton into shirts and skirts and britches and gloves and underwear.

When the women weren't sewing they were knitting, an art that totally eluded Victoria, and which fascinated her. First they ran sheep's wool through a spinning wheel, and then knitted the yarn with a great clatter of needles, so fast that Victoria marveled. Out of all this effort rose a pile of stockings and some sweaters.

Skye watched the winter elide into spring, which came early in that mild land. Then, as March dwindled, he knew it was time to settle accounts with Dr. McLoughlin and go.

He found the factor out in a sunny field watching a Canadian plowman scratch the earth behind big mules.

"I'd like a word, sir. It's nigh the time for us to leave and settle our accounts."

"Of course, Mister Skye. I've been meaning to ask you about it."

Skye followed the factor through the great gate of the post and into his study.

He opened a ledger book and examined it through oval wire-rimmed spectacles.

"You and Mrs. Skye have a credit of fifty pounds and a few pence," he said.

"And what is the cost of our board, sir?"

"We haven't charged Wyeth or Professor Nutmeg board, sir, so why should we charge you? There is ample."

Skye twisted his hat around in his hands, scarcely knowing what to say.

"You'll need some sort of outfit, I imagine."

"Yes, sir. And something for the professor."

"He's made his arrangements with us. We'll outfit him and he'll send a draft to our secretary in London."

That was good news. Skye didn't know how he could afford to outfit the botanist.

"The horses we bought from you are fat and sound, and

you may have them again," McLoughlin said. "We'll add a greenbroke pack animal and you can break him on the trail."

That pleased Skye.

"Come along, now. We'll go to the store."

Skye always relished the sights and smells of that place. He drank in the pungent scent of leather, the scents of bolts of woolen cloth, the scents of blankets and dried fruits and the iron scent of traps and axes, and the scent of a well-oiled rifle.

The factor found the clerk at a desk.

"Mr. Rutgers, I'll want you to outfit the Skyes. They'll be wanting saddles and tack, including a packsaddle; two pairs of four-point blankets, flint and steel, an axe, a good rifle, powder, powder flask, bullet mold, lead, and spare flints; a cookpot and a few kitchen utensils, some cord suitable for picketing horses, and whatever else . . ."

Skye objected. "I can't afford all that, sir. I have no means to repay."

McLoughlin stared down upon Skye from his Olympian height.

"Your sole obligation is to treat our HBC men fairly out in the trapping country. Ogden despises the Yanks who tricked him and failed to keep their word. You're an Englishman. That's all I require."

Skye was so gladdened that he fairly danced. "You have that promise, sir."

"Very well, then. Get everything together, and I'll get the professor started. When do you wish to leave?"

"As soon as possible."

"Tomorrow, then. We'll miss you, Skye. It will be my regret that we couldn't employ you. I've never seen a better man to help us along."

Skye marveled at the compliment.

That fine fat afternoon Skye selected his equipment, testing each item piece by piece. He decided on a good English military rifle converted to mountain use with a shorter barrel. He selected a pound of precast balls, wadding, powder, a flint and steel in a leather pouch, two pairs of thick, heavy, well-carded Hudson's Bay blankets, gray with black stripes so as not to advertise their presence.

He chose two used English saddles, a sawbuck packframe, three saddle blankets made of unmarketable pelts, three halters, fish hooks and line, two bridles and bits, picket ropes, a light copper cookpot, two metal ladles, two bowls, a fine-edged steel axe made in Manchester, an awl, patch leather for boots and moccasins, sugar, coffee, beans, flour, tea, a ball of real soap, a big belt knife and two smaller knives, some metal arrow points for Victoria, two used blanket capotes for rough weather, and an oilcloth cover for emergencies.

That was a fine outfit, and its price ran twenty pounds higher than the credit. He owed McLoughlin all that the man had asked: proper treatment of HBC brigades in the wilds.

He had learned, over the long visit, something about wilderness war from McLoughlin and Douglas. Bridger and his men had played a deadly trick on the newer American Fur Company men by leading them into Blackfoot country and setting the rivals up for an Indian ambush. In fact, the Blackfeet did attack the American Fur brigade, killing its partisan, William Vanderburgh, a West Point man who had made a fine name for himself in the fur trade.

It was true, McLoughlin added, that the American Fur brigade dogged the steps of the Bridger outfit, horning in on the beaver grounds. But the result was very close to being murder and certainly was an act of putting the rivals in harm's way.

The news shocked Skye. Would the fur brigades resort to extremes in the course of their rivalry? His opinion of the men in the Rocky Mountain Fur Company diminished sharply on that news, and that was a very good reason to find his employment elsewhere. No commerce was worth such a price and he vowed then and there that he would never, for as long as he lived, work for any firm that behaved in such a fashion.

That meant saying goodbye to old friends: Jim Bridger,

Tom Fitzpatrick, Milt Sublette, Henry Fraeb, and Baptiste Gervais. As individuals, he treasured them all. But as a company, they had crossed the borders of honor. He knew they would try to justify themselves to him; tell him that American Fur's Vanderburgh and Drips were horning in and following them. Argue that in the wilds, a savage law prevailed and had to be heeded or the company would go under. But none of those arguments sufficed to justify what Bridger and his colleagues had done. They had sullied their souls. A man had to draw a line somewhere, and Skye drew it right there.

So, maybe this time he would not go to rendezvous. It was something to think about.

The next morning he and Victoria said their goodbyes to Dr. McLoughlin, collected their ward—for that was what he seemed to be—and began the long trek up the Columbia River. They crossed new-plowed fields, splashed along a muddy trail, and soon left the brooding Hudson's Bay imperial city behind them, slumbering in a tender sun.

The season at Fort Vancouver had repaired their bodies, allowed them to live in comfort, and restored their outfit, and thus their chances of surviving and earning a living. Skye knew that the wilds would shock his body and mind, but he also knew Victoria would slide easily into living in nature and probably be happier away from the great post than within it.

He let Professor Nutmeg catch up and ride beside him.

"Well, Professor, we'll get you to Fort Union safely—if you wish to get there and you wish to be safe."

"How do you mean that, Mister Skye?"

"If your passion for collecting samples overcomes your common sense, you are likely to lose not only your samples and notes, but also your life. This time, it will be up to you. That is a decision that you, as an adult man, must come to."

"Why, forgive my wanderings, my dear Mister Skye. I never really saw the harm in them."

Skye didn't reply, for there was nothing more to say.

forty-eight

hey pierced inland without trouble, following the right bank of the Columbia. Professor Nutmeg was never so happy as when he could capture new-minted leaves and twigs, or sketch an odd plant. Skye didn't mind so long as the naturalist stayed in sight and used ordinary cautions. There were so many ways to get into trouble.

Maybe the professor was going to do better.

They passed occasional fishing villages and from these the Skyes obtained dried salmon for the larder, with a few treats for No Name. They were in no rush: it would not be until May that they could negotiate the snowbound continental divide and enter the Missouri watershed.

Within two weeks they had reached Fort Walla Walla, and enjoyed the hospitality of its factor, Pierre Pambrun. Skye remembered the post all too well; he had come within an inch of losing his life there during his desperate flight from the Royal Navy. But that was another factor and another time.

At a hearty salmon feast that night, Pambrun questioned the naturalist closely.

"Monsieur, does your lovely wife suffer from your long absences?"

"No, no really," Nutmeg replied. "The old dear's used to it, and anyway she considers me a nuisance about the house."

"But surely you're eager to resume lecturing at Harvard."

"No, I can barely stand those musty amphitheaters and bottles of formaldehyde and alcohol. No, my good man, what makes my heart sing is simply wandering, free as a meadowlark, plucking up whatever strikes my fancy."

"But where will it all lead, monsieur?"

"To a cataloguing of all that grows in North America."

"And what good is that? Will it earn anyone a living?"

Nutmeg gazed at the factor as if he were a freshman. "My dear man, it's for the sake of knowledge. There may be some slight practical advantage in it—a new medicinal herb, or a decorative new bloom for a garden, or maybe even a new tuber or nut for food. But that's not it. It's the glory of getting the natural world straightened out and understandable."

"Ah, food. Yes, we've sampled every berry here. I look for purgatives, you know. The banks of the Walla Walla River lack digestive aids, which is a great lack for me. But maybe you'll find one. Do you know of any?"

"I can't say that I do, Mr. Pambrun. My task is to advance science."

The factor was not quite satisfied with all that and regarded Professor Nutmeg as an odd gent, but Nutmeg didn't seem to mind. His thoughts were always elsewhere, as if mere mortals didn't much matter in the natural world he was cataloguing.

They proceeded up the Walla Walla River in a tumult of spring, with flowers rioting at every hand. Now Skye found himself being slowed by the professor, who abandoned all thought of catching the riverboat that would carry him home. He took to ignoring his horse, leaving its management to Victoria while he dashed here and there, up slopes, down to the river, examining everything from thistles to cattails, and never forgetting a tree, many of which the dog had already marked.

"Professor, we'll need to move fast now. I'll want you on your horse and keeping up. We've an appointment in early June, and we're slipping behind."

"Yes, of course, my dear Skye. We'll carry on, eh? March, march, march."

But it did little good. Skye realized that he could really not influence the trajectories of his naturalist friend any more than he could command the dog to heel. Not any more now than on the trail going west. This man's vision was not focused on anything but the leaf or root in hand. He was in his own Eden: gentians, buck beans, marsh felwort, milfoil, mares-tail, mulberry, four-o'clock, white water lilies, evening primrose, juneberry, silverweed, blue-eyed Mary, Queen Anne's lace, oxeye daisy . . . each day a dozen new treasures for the naturalist.

Increasingly, Nutmeg vanished from sight, over the brow of a hill or around a bend, often with No Name watching over him. (Nutmeg had left his dog Dolly at Fort Vancouver.) Sometimes he vanished for hours on end, leaving Skye and Victoria uneasy. Even in that warm valley dangers lurked at every hand.

At dinner one evening, as they were penetrating the Blue Mountains, Skye decided enough was enough.

"Professor, tomorrow I'll want you on your horse, and from now on Victoria will lead it."

Nutmeg was aghast. "But that would keep me from my work!"

Skye didn't respond. They had been through all this a dozen times.

The next morning, after rolling up their blankets and saddling the horses, Skye silently led Nutmeg's nag to him and waited. Nutmeg sighed, put a foot in a stirrup, and hoisted himself upward.

They made good progress that morning, but Nutmeg sank into reproachful silence. At one point he did cry out, so Victoria let him dismount, dig up a reed growing alongside the Grande Ronde River, and scribble some notes. Sullenly he mounted again after discovering that the Skyes would not permit him to walk.

Skye worried plenty now. He figured they had six weeks

to reach Fort Union, and that wasn't time enough unless they could persuade the professor to abandon his researches altogether.

"Mr. Nutmeg," he said, as they sat under a makeshift shelter that turned away a drizzle, "beginning in the morning, we're going to make a dash. We've got to make thirty or more miles a day up the Snake, over the divide to the Three Forks. We're stopping for nothing."

"But—"

"Next time, Professor. Do it next time. Consider traveling with the army's mapping parties. They send out topographical outfits all over the American West, and you'd be safe and at your leisure. Part of Captain Bonneville's business is reconnoitering the West."

The professor nodded curtly and turned to his blankets.

The silence that followed stretched into the next day and the next. But at least the professor was obediently getting aboard his horse and letting himself be drawn up the Snake River with all the speed Skye could muster. By the beginning of May Skye was working up Henry's Fork toward the Missouri headwaters, and he was thinking that, with luck, he could make it. The professor had fallen into perpetual anguish, and began complaining constantly.

They crossed a snow-patched divide into the Missouri drainage, followed the Gallatin River and plunged into the vast, rolling intermontane basin where the Gallatin, Jefferson, and Madison rivers formed into the great Missouri. But this verdant grassland was prized Blackfoot country, and Skye knew he would need to be cautious. Puffball clouds scraped shadows across the hills making it difficult to spot the ancient enemies of the trappers, and even hard to spot game because the whole world seethed.

Skye kept his party low, reconnoitered from ridgetops, and raced ever eastward to Jim Bridger's pass to the Yellowstone. They made few fires, shot no game, rode apart from visible trails, and never moved without examining their flanks, rear, and what lay ahead. The dog stood guard, roaming out on the flanks to detect trouble, and watching the shadows of the night with such acuity that Skye came to feel safe in the dog's custody.

They reached some steaming hot springs, the banks white-rimmed with minerals, the odorous water draining through pools into a small marsh alive with cattails and sedges and lilies. Stately cottonwoods, in new leaf, guarded the oasis. The dog sniffed suspiciously, detecting the faint spoor of ancient enemies. Skye watched the dog, every sense alert.

"I should like to stop here for a while," the professor said. "Unique, you know. There'll be a dozen variants or new species here, and I've never had a chance—"

"Sorry, mate, but this is Blackfoot country, and they come here. It's a favorite spot. This is not safe."

Nutmeg looked so bitter that Skye almost relented. But the thought of a party of Blackfeet drifting this way to enjoy the hot waters, hastened Skye away. They proceeded another two miles before dusk caught them, and settled under a low cut-bank carved eons earlier by a creek now a quarter of a mile away. The surrounding brush would conceal them and their horses well. The dog sniffed out the territory and settled just outside of the camp.

They were depending entirely on Victoria's powerful yew wood bow. That afternoon, she had driven an arrow through the neck of an antelope and they had hastily butchered it, taking only the hindquarters and leaving the rest to the wolves and the dog, who stayed behind for a feast.

They were in a good spot, invisible, out of the wind, far removed from the creek, and shielded by brush and trees that would dissipate the smoke from Victoria's hot fire. Victoria cleaned the ground for their bedrolls, taking care to remove the smallest rocks and twigs, and then laid a mat of sedge over the cold earth while Skye climbed a nearby slope to reconnoiter. Early night was always an excellent moment to spot distant campfires. He waited for his eyes to adjust to the blackness, found the North Star, and began a quiet study of the country. Spring breezes steadily raked the area, and he drew the air through his nostrils, seeking the slightest scent of smoke: sour smoke if it came from cottonwood, sweet smoke if from pine.

He could not tell. His skills weren't the half of Victoria's who had been born to this life and whose instincts were often intuitive. He saw, smelled, and heard nothing, and then retreated to his own camp, satisfied, the dog a shadow behind him.

He always slept lightly, in part because hard ground didn't foster deep sleep, and partly because his ears were attuned to subtle changes in the rhythm of the night. He and Victoria always slept close, but the professor usually unrolled his blankets at a distance, out of a certain delicacy.

Skye awakened in the gray half-light before dawn, sensing something was amiss. He glanced about fearfully. The horses stood quietly. The camp gear was undisturbed. He padded over to Nutmeg's blankets and found them neatly rolled beside his gear. But he was not present. Skye waited a moment. The man might merely be in the bushes. But the professor did not return and Skye knew at once that the naturalist was heading back to the hot springs and the unique flora that grew there.

Annoyance built in him.

"What?" said Victoria in a voice that carried only a few feet.

"The professor."

She rolled out of her blankets, stretched, and padded over to the professor's ground.

"At the springs," Skye said. "He wanted to go back there, collect and sketch, and return before we broke camp."

"We gonna wait?"

"I suppose. Country's empty, far as I could tell."

"This is no damn good," she said.

Skye wasn't so sure. "He'll be back soon," he volunteered. The dog will find him."

"And if he don't?"

Skye had no answer to that.

forty-nine

No one was at the hot springs. Skye and Victoria and the dog searched the area and found nothing. The only hoofprints were those of their own horses. Eerie silence greeted their calls.

"Well, dammit, let's circle around," Victoria said.

She and Skye had broken camp, packed the professor's kit and loaded it on his horse, and searched the campground area thoroughly before returning to the hot springs. Plainly, the professor had dressed—his clothing and boots were gone—and gathered his collection bag and sketch paper and drifted away just before first light.

But he wasn't at the springs or in the marshes below it or along the creek racing to the Gallatin River a few miles distant.

Victoria studied the moist earth, looking for the professor's bootprints, but saw nothing she was certain were his.

"I'll go down one side, you the other," Skye said. "If we're separated, meet at the campsite, and if we're in trouble, head for Bridger's Pass."

She nodded, wove her pony in and out of thickets, her eye keen and focused, her senses tingling with all the sights and smells and sounds reaching them. The dog came with her, sniffing, pausing, growling now and then.

"Nutmeg," she cried, her low voice reaching just as far as she wanted it to. "Professor Nutmeg."

But all she managed to do was stir up the magpies and startle two crows. The dog paused, sniffed, whined, and then trotted on. Victoria studied the spot where the dog had paused, finding nothing.

She turned the pony out of the river brush and rode to a nearby hill to reconnoiter, squinting hard at distant horizons, trying to separate the fleeting shadows of clouds from the movement of armed men or drifting herds of buffalo. The May morning was benign, a copy of the previous day.

From her vantage point she spotted Skye now and then, working down the creek, until at last he turned toward the springs. She met him there, and the dog burst out of the bush, panting.

"Vanished," he said.

"Not Siksika," she said. There were no moccasin prints in the soft spring soil. No Blackfeet or other People had wandered by.

"No prints of his boots, either," he said, awakening to something. "He never came here."

The realization startled them both.

They rode cautiously back to their abandoned campsite. But only silence greeted them when they reached the cutbank.

This ground was higher and harder than the ground around the hot springs, and less likely to reveal Nutmeg's tracks, so they dismounted and began their search on foot.

Victoria wondered once again what sort of man would drift away, scarcely aware of those who were shepherding him, obsessed with his work. Beyond the creek lay the grassy slopes of the first foothills of the Spanish Peaks, and she scanned them for the familiar image of the man.

One could not know what interested him: one day he would be hiking ridges, the next day studying river bottoms, the day after that wending through rock at timberline, yet another day studying the life in a still pond. He had no favorite haunts; he sought to open the whole natural world to his understanding.

She climbed a ridge and cautiously peered over it, always alert, and saw only the magpies.

Magpie. Her spirit-helper.

She lifted her arms, a thin young Crow woman sitting in the white man's saddle, reaching upward and outward with a prayer:

"Fly over the man. Lead me to the man," she asked.

But the magpies did not fly.

She slumped in her saddle and closed her eyes and beseeched the Old Ones of the earth and sky and under the earth.

"Old and Wise Ones, have pity on your poor daughter; bring this man who collects all the growing things of Mother Earth to put in his books, bring him safely to us, and keep him safe, and answer the mystery," she whispered.

She opened her eyes and beheld a land warmed by a gentle spring sun, empty and peaceful. The dog lay beside her, questions in his eyes. She watched a soaring hawk far distant, and crows talking in shrill alarms, and the eternal breezes whispering the leaves and rustling the verdant grasses. And not a sign of the professor.

If he did not go to the hot springs, then where?

She circled the campsite again, hoping to cut his path, but saw nothing but a fresh track of a young grizzly bear. She turned to follow the tracks as they drifted toward the foothills along a rivulet that would soon dry up in the summer's inferno. The bear would be cross and hungry after the winter's sleep, and ready to kill. She would be wary. It could run faster than her pony, at least for a short stretch.

The bear had descended into brush, so she followed it there, reaching a larger stream where it had fished, or eaten a rotten carcass and left. She smelled death, and hunted the ground carefully. The dog sniffed and whined and poked his nose into the brush.

But the professor wasn't there, nor could she find the remains of any creature. Relieved, she backed out of the brushy cul-de-sac and headed back to the campsite, where she found Skye, his face like a thunderclap.

"We've left enough hoofprints here to bring the whole Blackfoot nation down on us," he said.

"But the prints go every direction, back and forth, here and there."

"That'll make them all the more curious. We've got to move."

She wondered if he was about to abandon the professor.

He led them up the middle of the creek to a long slope leading toward a spring high in a grassy notch, and then settled their horses, along with the professor's, in the notch and out of sight, and waited. The dog had vanished again, and returned.

He had chosen well. Her man always chose well. From this high point they could see much of the surrounding country. They could see the sky, and read the weather, and prepare for distant storms. From this vantage point they could peer straight down upon their campsite, a tiny spot in the distant emptiness, but close enough to reveal the movement of the professor should he return there.

They picketed the horses and let them graze, watched clouds build over the peaks to the south and east, and waited. All that day they waited, often misled by scudding shadows racing across the great basin of the Three Forks. The dog lay beside them, not interested in the hunt.

That day passed. In the evening they descended. On foot, they searched the slopes and creeks, pawed through brush, sniffed the air for the iron smell of blood and decay. They padded by moonlight toward the hot springs again and probed the area, smelling the rank sulfur of the mineral water, studying earth and brush and secret places, and even trees.

The dog whined and shivered.

Nothing.

Skye grew morose. Victoria watched him sink into bad humor. He was hating this vigil now, and itching to leave, but she knew he wouldn't. These white men stuck together, and that was often their salvation. He had told her about the time Jim Bridger had abandoned the wounded and feverish Hugh Glass to his death, and how Glass had miraculously survived and heroically dragged himself hundreds of miles to succor. He would not be a Jim Bridger. He would not abandon a man, or lead rivals into the deadly arms of the Blackfeet, as Bridger had done just last winter.

They retreated to their small aerie at the top of a slash in the foothills, and slept uncomfortably, with Nutmeg's ghost haunting them. The dog was gone all night.

The next day passed slowly and silently, and the next. Each day they scoured a broad area, riding quietly through meadows and groves of aspen or cottonwood, poking around brush, studying streambanks, only to return mystified to their high lookout. Their food was running out along with their patience. But still Skye stayed put, studying their campsite far below for any sign of the missing naturalist.

Four days had passed. Skye's temper was not far behind his eyes now, and she could say nothing to temper it.

"He's either dead or faint with hunger and wandering wherever his collector's eye leads him," he said. "The way he did to Wyeth after the rendezvous."

"He is a good man, but a child," she said.

"He's an irresponsible fool."

"Making bad words about him does no good."

Skye subsided. The anger in his face slipped into desolation. He had lost a man in his charge. He had lost a friend. He had lost a man who was attempting to bring new knowledge to the world. Only the intervention of the Above Ones would ever bring Professor Nutmeg back to them.

She knew that in the morning Skye would leave and she

knew that if he gave up and headed over Bridger's Pass, this would haunt him all of his days. He would blame himself, feel the sting of failure. But she knew that none of this was his failure. Nutmeg had made his own choices. He had been severely warned over and over.

She brimmed with curiosity that itched and scratched at her. Where did that man go? What was his fate? Did he live? Skye was half-crazy for knowledge, too. They both knew that this was the worst of all endings because it didn't end. He was alive or dead or wounded and immobile. He was a captive or slave or not. He was sick or not. He was wondering across meadows, looking for specimens, unaware of time—or not. They would never know, and that was a burden that could scarcely be borne.

In the night the weather changed, and Skye and Victoria awakened to overcast and the iron scent of rain in the air. Their unprotected ridge-top aerie was no place to weather an icy spring storm. Birds no longer tarried in the sun, but flew with purpose. The breeze no longer toyed with their clothing, but stabbed icy fingers into their flesh.

Darkly, Skye saddled his pony, and then the professor's, and loaded the gear onto the horses while Victoria made ready to leave. They had not eaten, and were out of food. The dog was spending more and more time rummaging a living. But they would make for Bridger's Pass this day and leave Professor Alistair Nutmeg, lecturer at Harvard on the natural world, to the fate he had carved for himself.

Darkly, they rode away.

fifty

arnaby Skye was enjoying a hard-won peace. The disappearance of Professor Nutmeg still haunted him, but he believed that the man himself caused his misfortune, and the Skyes had done everything within their power to look after him.

Still, they missed the man, missed his innocent cheer, missed his boyish enthusiasms and the ecstacy in him whenever he added a new plant to the catalog. No one could know whether he was dead. They found no body, nor any place where carrion-eaters congregated. They had scoured the whole country, finding not a trace of the man. If he had been taken captive, it was by men on foot because they found no hoofprints marking the passage of any large party.

And when they left, at last, they put a message into a cairn at the campsite, telling Nutmeg to head east over the pass and into Crow country where Victoria's people would be alerted and ready to care for him.

That was all anyone could do.

He and Victoria and No Name arrived at the Green River rendezvous on June tenth, and found that many of the free trappers, along with Wyeth's party, Bonneville's group, and the rival outfits, American Fur and Rocky Mountain Fur, had set up shop. There was even an English noble named Stuart, along with his entourage, camped in colorful tents with coats of arms flapping in the wilderness winds.

Victoria discovered that several lodges of Crows were present along with many Snakes, and she discovered friends among her people, which gladdened her heart. But Skye roamed the gathering restlessly. His mood was not helped by a heavy overcast that carried occasional cold showers and hid the tops of the distant mountains, turned the world gray, and made dry firewood a scarce item. There were times when he pondered the stupidity of living out of doors year-round; times when a hearth, a roof, a soft bed, an easy chair, and a good kitchen seemed more inviting than this wild life.

He lacked so much as a cent and hadn't a single pelt to trade, and often roamed hungrily through the two trading posts, or even through Captain Bonneville's crude fort where other goods might be purchased. But a penniless man could only yearn and study, and sometimes scheme of ways to squeeze some small item out of these ruthlessly commercial enterprises.

He passed knots of his old friends, talking and smoking their pipes, enjoying the luxury of tobacco after most of a year's privation. Sometimes he joined them, and they always welcomed him, and once he even sucked some smoke into his lungs when they passed a pipe around. But he was famished in a dozen ways, and sat irritably as they spun yarns, bragged about the pelts they had gathered, the bears they had subdued, the icy rivers they had crossed, the Blackfeet that had chased them, the rattlesnakes they had captured by hand, the Indian maidens they had conquered, the tribes that had adopted them, the buffalo they had eaten, and the jugs of trade whiskey they had demolished . . .

He could not bear any of it and retreated, a solitary misfit, as itchy and angry as he had ever been. What had the year brought him? It had started so high, a chance to recover his good name, word from his father, a trip across the sea followed by a high position in a company spawned by the nation of his birth. Then it had sunk so low, so dangerous, so desperate, so impoverished, so devoid of succor. Only the kindness of John McLoughlin had rescued him and Victoria and enabled them to reach the mountains again. And then the final blow, losing a great naturalist and friend, as if he had stepped off the edge of the earth.

His old comrades at Rocky Mountain Fur greeted him amiably but not with the whoops they reserved for their old brethren. His departure for the Hudson's Bay Company had changed everything, even though he had ended up not joining the British concern. So he and the mutt drifted through the vast grassy flat along the icy river, choked with snowmelt out of the mountains, poking into Bonneville's fort and trading post, visiting the tented stores of the rival companies, and studying the vast herds of Indian ponies and white men's mounts.

He felt again like a man without a country, especially when he spent time with Sir William Drummond Stuart, a Scotsman, actually, and captain in the Royal Army. In the presence of the Empire's military, Skye was wary and did little to promote a friendship with Stuart and his men. But that only left him all the more bereft of comrades.

Then one morning Andrew Drips approached him, and invited him for a little stroll along the purling river. Drips was somewhat older than the run of the mountain men, a veteran of the fur trade, the head of American Fur Company's mountain operations, and backed by the powerful Chouteau family of St. Louis, which had the means to muscle into the Rocky Mountain fur trade.

"I hear you're a free agent," Drips said. "Tell me what happened. Last I knew, you were accepting a tender from McLoughlin."

Skye told him the story as they hiked past Snake lodges, and the dog shuttled back and forth ahead of them.

"Ah! That naturalist was a man who could not help himself, Mister Skye. He went under. You bear no blame. You never abandoned him."

"But I feel bad, and I've lost a friend."

Drips stopped, peered into the crystal river as if to discern the future in its waters.

"Mister Skye, you are well known as a veteran, resourceful, and gifted mountaineer. I've been watching for years, but never more so than this rendezvous. You've survived circumstances that would put other men under. You're a natural leader. We need you. We've lost our best brigade leader, Vanderburgh, and I've settled on you to replace him. Would you consider an offer?"

"I would, sir."

"You would be our brigade leader, second only to me. I'm in charge of all the mountain operations. We'll pay you five hundred a year, deposited in St. Louis, plus your outfit. You'll avoid trouble as much as possible, gather peltries, and see to getting them either to McKenzie at Fort Union, or here, where we can pack them back. I'll be with you much of the time but at the post in the winter."

"We accept, sir."

"We?"

"Victoria, this dog of mine, and me."

"Good, good. We've good relations with the Crows. We even have good relations with dogs."

He laughed. Skye knew he was going to like this graying man. He knew that Drips had been born in Pennsylvania in 1789, worked in the fur trade since 1820, and was much admired. At age forty-four, he was a decade older than most of the three hundred white men gathered across the bleak prairie cut by the Green River.

Five hundred was good money.

They drifted back to the American Fur Company store, where mountaineers traded peltries for jugs of whiskey, if that is what pure grain spirits, mixed with water and flavored with a plug of tobacco and a little pepper could be called. Here, spread over the grass or on makeshift tables, were bright bolts of flannel, iron traps, bits and bridles, packframes, thick blankets bearing two to four stripes that indicated their weight; here were shining mountain rifles, powder, awls, knives, canvas, gaudy calicos, powder horns, spare flintlocks, percussion caps, vermillion, beads, bells, mirrors, and all the foofaraw with which to trade with the tribes.

"Mister Skye, let me introduce you around—Pete Fontenelle especially, my right-hand man—and then you just take what you need on account. Outfitting items we'll provide; drink and other items, such as gifts for your wife, we'll post against your earnings. Later, we'll make some plans for the next campaign, and you'll let us know what you have in mind. We've forty trappers, more or less, plus more men at Fort Union."

Just like that. It was as if all this had been destined by some hand of Fate. As if Andrew Drips had decided on Skye long before Skye arrived at rendezvous. As if a man without a country had been given a home once again, and esteemed not for his connections or ties, but solely for his abilities in the mountains and among men.

Skye accepted the trust and esteem accorded to him.

Drips left him there. Skye ducked under the canvas shelter of the store, watching rain slide off the edges of the canvas. What riches lay at hand! All this meant warmth, dry feet, sugar for his sweet tooth, coffee and tea to hearten a man in icy weather, a caplock rifle to replace his flintlock, which usually didn't fire in rain; powder, lead pigs and balls, woolen long underwear, skeins of beads for Victoria and anything else to delight her heart. Oh, good times were coming!

The rain lifted and he beheld a sinking sun gilding the grassy flats, poking under the pancake clouds and silvering their edges. To the west the clear blue sky promised a great day, a sky warm and transparent and infinite. A sky as wild as the land, without ceilings or the cramping of clouds.

He patrolled the Crow lodges where smiling Absaroka

people nodded to him, watched fresh-killed elk roast over fires. An evening breeze swept away the moisture. He found Victoria with some Crow women sitting in a circle and gossiping.

She rose at once, and he led her back to the American Fur Company store.

"I'm a brigade leader with AMC," he said. "Quite a talk with Drips. We'll have everything we could ever want. Tomorrow, I'll get a good caplock rifle, and you'll get my flint-lock."

She eyed him, a faint expectant smile twisting up the corners of her mouth. "And tonight, Mister Skye?"

"Well, I was getting to that," he said.

He stopped at the rude bench, a plank atop two stumps, where a clerk was doling out trade whiskey.

"One gallon, Mr. Privet," he said. "Put it on account. Also, two tin cups and a jug if you have one."

"No jugs, sir, too heavy, but I could lend you a kettle."

"That would be just fine, Mr. Privet. One measured gallon, one kettle, and two tin cups. Put the gallon on my account and we'll return the kettle and cups."

"Very well, Skye."

"It's Mister Skye, mate."

"Sonofabitch," said Victoria. "Tonight, the rendezvous begins."

No Name laid back on its haunches and howled.

Author's Note

Most of the fur trade characters in this story were real people. All the Californios are fictional. Dr. John McLoughlin was a formidable force in the Hudson's Bay Company at the time of this story, and he and his wife and James Douglas are portrayed accurately.

Nat Wyeth, the inventive Boston ice merchant, met defeat time after time, and yet remains a major figure of the era, and perhaps the most important reason that the Oregon country is now under the American flag.

Peter Skene Ogden was the most formidable of the HBC men, and I have portrayed him as he was. He did not, however, attend the rendezvous where I have placed him. He was at that time far to the north, dealing with the Russians.

Professor Nutmeg is loosely based on the British naturalist Thomas Nuttall, whose trips west, one of them with Wyeth, contributed greatly to North American botany. He was as careless about his safety as his fictional counterpart, but survived.

—Richard S. Wheeler